ACTIVATED

A Genesis Novel

CHASELYN RODERICK

Activated

Summary: In the quiet town of Joshua, a secret community exists that 18 year old Tess James knows nothing about- until the day a painful sensation erupts in her chest. The first of many signs that her life is changing forever. She is plunged into the secret world of the Munera, a race of power-wielding super-humans, and is instantly faced with enemies she didn't know she had and a war she never knew existed. The dangers of the Munera Society and their leader, the Salvator, suddenly become a deadly threat to her. An unexpected ally offers to hide her, but his protection is short-lived as she discovers he isn't at all who he portrays himself to be.

As Tess works to unravel the mysteries of her past, her friends and family become snared in the chaos. How much of herself is she willing to lose in her search for answers? And how many people will she be forced to sacrifice before she accepts that some secrets are best left undiscovered.

Clear Fork Publishing

P.O. Box 870 102 S. Swenson Stamford, Texas 79553 (325)773-5550
www.clearforkpublishing.com

Printed in the United States of America

Print ISBN: 978-1-950169-46-7

Ebook ISBN: 978-1-950169-50-4

*To my mom, who has been
with me the whole way through.*

PROLOGUE

Run.

Tears streaming down her face, she sprinted through the streets. Weakened from the experience she'd endured less than an hour ago, and devastated by the emotions and terror that filled her soul.

Her daughter was gone.

And now, she was alone. Hunted.

Run.

Every shadow and sound made her heart thunder, her pulse pound in her ears.

They could be anywhere— waiting.

She whimpered.

They would kill her.

And not simply *kill* her. They would make her beg for death.

After they tried to force her to give information about the baby.

My baby.

She pushed herself to run faster, thoughts of torture allowing her to exceed her physical limits.

As she raced down an empty alley, memories accosted her.

Koden Mason, the newly-elected Salvator of the Society of the Munera, standing at his podium. Giving his speech about the invisible war being waged on their people.

"Munera are being wiped out!" he demanded, his words angry, persuasive.

He was a strikingly handsome man. Dark-haired, dark-eyed, and charismatic.

Psychotic.

The youngest Salvator in Munera history.

Munera, an ancient race of people. In fact, Munera history taught that they were the *first* people. People born with a gift. A Genesis. An innate trait that allowed children to be born with abilities only written in myths and folklore.

The law of the Munera formally called for elections, but the control exerted by the Mason family during the political and electoral process had ensured a hereditary succession for three generations.

Meaning the whole thing was rigged. The Mason family would *continue* ruling the Munera until the people finally united for change, or someone even more corrupt managed to depose the tyrants.

Enzo Mason III, Koden's father, had ruled for decades. As his health began to deteriorate, Koden, his eldest son, began slowly taking over various state tasks. When Enzo had died, Koden was announced as his successor.

His voice was a deep, smooth baritone that comforted you. Convinced you. Deceived you.

He'd transformed the entire Munera world in the few short months since the election.

Koden was an expert manipulator. A modern day Hitler, stirring up ancient prejudices and nursing the unease and fear amongst the people.

"Every day we see the evidence. There is an unprecedented decrease in births of *the people*! The tolerance of the Lusus Naturae is a *disease*. It is destroying us! Weakening our people with their toxic genes. Those who oppose the new mandates are terrorists. They are levying war against the Society and will therefore be considered our enemy. Treason against the Society cannot be tolerated. These blood traitors, these *Proditors*, will be shown *no* mercy."

In other words, he was ordering the death of the Caines—

The death of *her* and her family.

And her baby.

Run.

A deep pothole sent her sprawling, forcing her to refocus on the world around her.

She cursed as she moved to stand, shaking from exhaustion. Immediately, she felt *it* and froze.

The Trace.

A drumbeat exploding in her chest, almost in rhythm with her heart. Letting her know without a doubt, that she wasn't alone. The Trace grew stronger, faster.

Whoever it was, they were getting closer.

One final explosion rocked her insides, and then, hands grabbed her, roughly covering her mouth, dragging her backwards into the shadowed alley.

She fought against her captor, kicking and screaming, but she was still weak from the recent birth. His hands muffled her screams. In the darkness, he shoved her against a building, pressing an elbow into her throat.

"Where's the child?"

She forced herself to slow her breathing.

Calm.

This man was larger than her, but certainly not stronger.

"Koden. He sent you, didn't he?" she gasped, prolonging her escape in an attempt to get as much information out of the man as possible. "You're wasting... your time."

He laughed, an ugly harsh sound, then leaned into the arm at her throat until she began to choke.

"Where's the child?" he repeated.

Her daughter. *Her* newborn baby girl that she'd given up just an hour earlier.

The decision had nearly broken her. The thought of her beautiful angel growing up without her mother. The idea of another family watching her take her first steps, say her first words.

Nearly broken her.

But the decision had strengthened her as well. Her daughter would be safe. For the first eighteen years of her life, her daughter would live in the normal world. The world where the Lusus Naturae— the ungifted —were all that existed.

Where myths and legends were just that: A fairytale.

"Where's the baby?"

His words reawakened her anger. She gritted her teeth. "She's gone. You will *never* touch my daughter."

The man shifted, moving his face into the orange glow of a street lamp and revealing his features. He had eyes like steel — gray, hard, and cold. Dangerous.

Ares Torray. An assassin?

One of Koden's Ambassadors, who lacked any extraordinary abnormal powers, but was extremely loyal to the Society.

"You're a traitor," he hissed. "That child could *save* our people."

Fireworks danced behind her eyes as the man increased the pressure at her throat.

Enough.

"You aren't trying to save our people. You want to *control* our people. You would use her as a pawn," she snarled. "A *Caine* on the side of the Society."

He had given her the proof she needed. Koden wasn't just after her. He wanted her baby.

It was time.

She exploded towards him, her inhuman strength sending him flying across the alley. Sucking in a deep breath, she paused, watching him. Waiting.

He cursed, curling his lip in agitation. Then, Ares spread his palms, and the ground under her feet shuddered. Cracks spreading and widening, threatening to grow and swallow her whole. She ducked low, rushing away from the shifting earth, tackling him to the ground. His focus on his abilities was destroyed, and the shaking, rumbling of the cracking pavement ceased.

Instead, he fought back, struggling against her grip, but he knew.

Even in her weakened state, he was no match for her.

She was a Caine.

Leaning in, she breathed into his ear. "I pray you're still alive when Koden finds you."

His eyes widened as he met her blue stare.

She smiled. "No mercy, right?"

Drawing in a calming breath, she closed her eyes and released a trickle of power.

The shadows around them began to shimmer, flowing in inky rivers and waves towards them. A familiar ache localized in her head as the darkness engulfed them, shadows funneling into her hand, materializing until she had a blade in her palm.

Solid and cold. Black. Razor sharp.

Deadly.

She hated this man.

Hated everything he stood for.

Yet, she still paused.

I'm not a murderer.

She closed her eyes, drawing strength from the memory

of her baby girl's beautiful face. Her tiny turned-up nose and delicate eyelashes, laying dark across her soft cheek.

I'll see you again, baby girl, she promised, abruptly slashing the blade across the Ambassador's stomach.

I'll see you again.

She wiped Ares's blood from her hands, looking into his face a final time as he struggled to breathe. She should end it now. No one deserved to suffer like this. And no one deserved the fate awaiting him if Koden found him before he passed.

She raised the knife, holding it above his throat.

She would show him mercy.

His eyes stayed on her face.

"Filthy blood traitor," he whispered. His voice came out soft, but full of loathing. He puckered his mouth, spitting in her face.

She jerked back, shocked, then wiped away the saliva dripping from her chin. Leaning down, she kissed his forehead, smiling, before murmuring, "Say hello to Koden for me."

Then she stood, moving away swiftly as she checked the scene for evidence.

Now, she had to stay alive long enough to keep her promise.

I will *see you again.*

CHAPTER 1

18 Years Later...
Tess

Tess James closed her eyes. She had failed. Again.

Senior year, just days past her eighteenth birthday, and she was *still* a champion procrastinator.

Every single New Years, she resolved to do better. Every single year, her mom bought her a planner, hoping she would master the art of organization.

And every single year, she failed miserably.

Today's current failure was an English essay. Due tomorrow.

It was several pages of watered down Cliff notes, and it was *full* of mistakes. And even still, she knew she wasn't going to put much effort into editing it.

Her best friend, Chloe Hale, was sprawled out next to her, ignoring her paper entirely. She was playing a game on her phone, and the tinny, repetitive music was grating on Tess's nerves.

"Okay, how does this sound?" Tess asked, scrolling to the top of her screen to read out loud.

"*Most of all I longed for death. I know that now. I invited it, a release from the pain of living. My invitation was open to anyone. Sailors, thieves, whores and—*"

Chloe yawned dramatically, interrupting her. "Oh my God, Tess. That's amazing. So good that I don't even *need* to hear the rest of it."

Tess glared at her, indignant. "Mrs. Harper said it had to start with a quote from the book. It's not *that* bad."

Chloe frowned, tipping her head to the side. "What book is it again? I stopped paying attention once we opened it."

Tess rolled her eyes, shutting her laptop. "*Interview With The Vampire*."

She stuffed the computer back into her bag at the foot of the bed, and reached for the TV remote.

Chloe shrugged, turning back to her phone and muttering. "First it was *Lord of the Flies*, now it's generic *Twilight*."

"It's nothing like— nevermind. You're hopeless."

The small flatscreen came on with the harsh, loud music of a news report intro. Chloe jumped at the sound, glancing at the screen.

"Ew. Fox News," Tess muttered, annoyed. "My dad watches this *all* the time."

She started to change the channel, but Chloe reached out, putting a hand on Tess's arm.

"Wait. Look. Why is *Joshua* on a National news channel?"

Tess rolled her eyes, turning her attention to the TV.

Not expecting much from the political drivel she was forced to listen to every day.

Until she saw the blood.

On the screen, there were pixelated images of a kitchen, barricaded with bright yellow crime scene tape. The walls were splattered in dried blood, and the room was a disaster.

Debris and glass was strewn across the room, littering the floor.

"—reporting nine confirmed deaths at this time. The following images may be disturbing to some viewers. Viewer discretion is advised," said the voice of the host. She sounded grave, and it made the hairs on Tess's neck stand up straight. "Three different homes were involved, two of which had children living in the residence. The homicides are believed to be connected, but no further information can be released until next of kin can be notified."

Tess covered her mouth, her eyes wide.

The images on the screen were horrifying, but Chloe was right.

The caption running along the bottom affirmed her words.

The scene was happening here, in the sleepy town of Joshua.

She had grown up hearing stories about the last murder to happen here— almost twenty years ago.

The victim had been stabbed. Sliced across his stomach and left to bleed out. But the police never found a weapon or footprints or DNA... *no* evidence leading to the killer. Just a body that no one ever came forward to claim. Even twenty years ago, there should have been *some* evidence.

The newscaster kept talking, pulling her out of her grim thoughts and back to an even more grim reality.

"Now, to our on-scene reporter, Noah Berkley. Noah, what, if anything, are the local law enforcement saying about this investigation?"

The man on the screen sighed, his dark eyes grim.

"Yes, Jessica. Not much has been released at this point, though we know police received a noise complaint from one of the neighbors around four o'clock this afternoon. When the responding officers arrived to follow up on the complaint, they were met with this horrific scene. It's absolutely terrible, Jessica. Very disturbing. There are suspicions this *may* be cartel related, but details about the victims are not available to be released to the public quite yet. Also—"

Chloe spoke up, drawing Tess's attention away from the screen. She had pulled Tess's computer from her bag, and was furiously scanning the screen.

"Turn that filtered crap off. I found an article."

Tess wasn't sure she *wanted* to read the article. She hated hearing about people being hurt. It made her sick to her stomach. And even worse, *kids* had been killed...

But despite her reluctance, she was also curious.

A cartel hit? In *Joshua*?

Other than the murder twenty years ago, their town had one of the *lowest* crime rates in the state.

It didn't make sense.

Tess reluctantly scooted towards Chloe, reading over her friend's shoulder.

The article was poorly written, and displayed *very* graphic images with no warning posted to prepare you. It was obvious that this information had been leaked straight from the scene.

"The injuries of the nine victims vary, which is unusual in itself. Usually, murderers kill all of their targets the same way. Instead, three of the victims' throats were slit. The blood-stains shown here are probably blood splatter from spurting arteries. But the wounds on the victims couldn't possibly have been done with blades or bullets. They're too clean and precise."

As Chloe read the article's print, she pointed to a grainy picture of the blood on the walls at the home. Tess's stomach heaved.

She wanted to tell Chloe to stop, but she knew it was no use. Chloe was already *involved*. Tess would be hearing about this incident for the next few weeks, even after it had become 'old news'.

She needed a distraction. She tried to busy herself, looking around the room.

Studying her reflection in the mirror across from the bed. Her long legs pulled up to her chest, and hazel eyes staring back at her in the mirror. She ran her dark hair through her fingers, which were shaking slightly. And not *just* from the murder article that Chloe was still reading aloud. She didn't feel right.

She rarely came to Chloe's house to study, and she had *never* come to a sleepover here. Even if she wanted to, Chloe had never invited her, insisting that she'd rather stay at Tess's. And that was absolutely fine— Chloe's parents, Reese and Charlotte Hale, seemed to wear a perpetual scowl on their faces. Charlotte in particular, tended to glare at Tess, curling her lip in disgust when Tess was near.

"Four of the victims were burned," Chloe continued reading. "But there are no scorch marks or smoke residue in sight, other than those on the bodies themselves, leaving one to wonder why the fire didn't spread through the home and burn it down. The last three victims... and... no evidence... "

Tess blinked, confused. Chloe's voice was fading out. Like a radio with static drowning out the words. Her ears were ringing, and her eyes moved out of focus.

A cold sweat broke out on her forehead and ran down her neck.

What was happening?

"Tess?" Chloe's voice sounded far away, even though she could feel her breath on her ear. "Tess, what's wrong?"

Chloe shook her, jostling her, returning her vision to normal.

Tess looked around, panicked.

The vanity and mirror against the wall, the oak dresser,

the bed with a turquoise and black comforter. Everything was fine. Nothing had changed.

She exhaled, relaxing as the room around her swam back into focus.

Everything was the same despite the weird—

Her chest exploded in pain.

It felt like a heartbeat. But it wasn't. She could feel her heart. Pounding against her ribcage. This was different. Too hard, too fast. Painful. And there were *two* of them. *Two* of those God awful beats, slamming relentlessly into her chest like they were trying to escape.

She doubled over, gasping for air. Clutching a hand to her chest, trying to make it stop.

"Tess!" Chloe was shaking her, her voice urgent.

Make it stop!

"Tess!"

Stop!

The hammering in her chest vanished, and she was left bent over, gasping.

"I'm... I'm fine," she rasped, trying to draw a full breath

Chloe looked worried, and continued to stare at her. Doubtful.

"Really, I'm fine," Tess gave a weak smile. "It was just my chest. It felt like my heart was—"

She stopped, whimpering, burying her face in her hands, as the sensation in her chest was replaced with a sharp pain at her temples. She tried to muffle her cries, willing the pain to fade. The initial shock began to slowly morph into a headache that rivaled any she'd ever had.

"What the hell, Tess?" Chloe put a hand on Tess's back, her golden eyes terrified. "Hey, what's wrong with you? Do I need to call your mom?"

Before she could answer, to tell her friend that she had *no* idea what was happening, the door to Chloe's room was thrown open.

Chloe's mother stood there, arms crossed, her expression *livid*.

Through a haze of pain, Tess heard her best friend make a tiny sound in her throat, a small strangled cry.

"M- Mom?" she whispered, shrinking back. Then, her eyes landed on Tess, and she straightened. "Sorry if we were being too loud... Tess just—"

"Tess needs to leave," Charlotte snapped.

The woman's mouth twisted when she said Tess's name. Momentarily, Tess's pain gave way to indignation. What had she ever done to this woman?

"Go on," Charlotte demanded, placing her hands on her hips. "I'll see you out."

Slowly, Tess staggered to her feet. She glanced at Chloe, worried. During the few times Tess had been here, the Hales had never burst into Chloe's room, demanding that she leave.

Her friend's usually bright and bubbly grin was gone. Her dark-olive face had gone pale, and her golden eyes flitted nervously between her mother and Tess. Curly strands of her dark hair stuck to her forehead, covered in a sheen of sweat.

Chloe noticed Tess's staring and gave a forced smile. "I'll see you at school tomorrow. Get ready for the track meet— I'm gonna run your relay times into the ground."

Still confused, her head throbbing, Tess gave her friend a small grin. "We'll see."

Her father, John James, was the school's head track coach, and Tess and Chloe both competed for him. Rival schools envied him due to his teams' consistent record breaking times. They almost always took home the gold.

After a final glance at Charlotte, Tess grabbed her computer, closing it— and the disturbing article about the murders —and edged out of the room. Charlotte practically jumped away from her, like she was repulsed by the thought of Tess touching her.

She wanted to be offended, but her head was pounding so hard that she was struggling to keep her eyes open.

She moved forward, Chloe's mother a silent shadow behind her.

As she stepped onto the front porch, Charlotte Hale slammed the front door. It shut with a loud bang.

Tess glared at the door briefly, though the woman had already disappeared back into the house.

Glancing into the driveway, Tess cursed, dismayed.

She had gotten a ride from her dad to Chloe's after school, so she didn't have her car.

To make matters worse, the street around her was dark, lit only by street lamps that cast ghostly shadows across the pavement. It wasn't a bad neighborhood. In fact, just one block away, there were literally *mansions* that looked like they belonged in Hollywood. Certainly not in Joshua.

Chloe's family didn't live in a mansion. Her street was full of elegant brownstones and pretty cookie-cutter houses. Chloe's home was one of the latter.

Still, she couldn't get the image of the burned and mutilated people from the article out of her mind. Or the reawakened memory of the unsolved murder case from years ago.

The thought of walking home alone terrified her. She debated calling her parents to pick her up, but she doubted the Hales would let her wait inside if she did.

Taking a breath, Tess started to walk, using the flashlight on her phone. She shined it on the road in front of her as she jogged.

Her head was still pounding, but the comfortable rhythm of her feet hitting the pavement gave her a small amount of courage. While she was nervous about being alone, late at night, in a town that had just witnessed a small massacre, she could probably outrun anyone trying to catch her.

As she raced past closed shops and restaurants, her courage disappeared. Tess was approaching a bus stop, and she had realized that she wasn't alone. Someone was sitting on the bench, hunched over a phone screen with their hood pulled up over their head.

Instantly, the painful sensation was back. Her chest erupted with the same pulsing beat. Though, now she only detected one. She faltered as she felt it, nearly tripping over her own feet.

The man's head snapped up, his face illuminated by his phone.

The beating stopped.

Tess's breath caught in her throat.

What the hell *was* that? Why did it keep happening?

Angry tears stung her eyes, and she blinked them away.

She glanced behind her, seeing the man as she passed by the bench. Still staring at her, his eyes narrowed. His hand pressed to his chest.

She half-expected him to lunge for her as the murders flashed through her mind again. Her thoughts were jumbled. She felt confused. The beat in her chest and the pain in her head were colliding in an uncomfortable duet.

She pushed her jog into a sprint.

Would he follow her?

Nerves twisted in her stomach. A riot of emotion.

But the stranger disappeared behind her without incident. She resisted the urge to turn and see if the man's eyes were watching her.

When she finally reached the end of the street, she turned, allowing herself to look back.

The man was nowhere in sight.

She sighed, relieved, but quickened her pace as her home came into view.

She didn't slow until she reached her porch, and then she stopped. Panting. Raising her hands above her head as she worked to catch her breath. Already, her muscles ached, and the pounding in her head had returned with a vengeance.

She hoped it would go away once she laid down. She wouldn't be able to sleep with a headache like this. She felt like her head might explode.

She straightened, took a deep breath, and pushed open the front door. Her mom was curled on the couch, waiting and anxiously watching the same news story that had been on Chloe's TV.

She leapt from the couch, rushing to Tess and wrapping her in a hug.

"Jesus Christ, Tess!" she murmured, her fingers squeezing into Tess's back. "I was so nervous! You didn't tell me you'd be staying so late at Chloe's. Why didn't you answer your phone? The *one* day you don't answer my call, there's a murderer on the loose! And—God, Tess! Don't do that to me!"

Tess began to apologize, but her mom started to ramble again. "You're almost an adult, so I know you feel like I should treat you like one. But being an adult means being responsible. If you're going to stay out late with Chloe, at *least* let me know in advance. I can't go to bed until I know you're home safe, *especially* after I've seen this!"

Her mom gestured frantically towards the television.

Tess gently pulled away, offering a small smile through the pain of her headache— now worsened by her run and her mom's panicked barrage of worries.

"I'm sorry Mom," she said, massaging her temples. "We got distracted with homework and then with the stuff on the news... I know that doesn't make being late okay."

"No, it doesn't," her mom agreed, still fuming, but obviously relieved.

"But Mom, I got this really bad headache. Like, *really* bad. Then the Hales basically kicked me out. You know how they are... Anyway, it's just been a long night. I'm so sorry I made you worry."

Her mom reached out to hug her. "Are you feeling better now? Do you need anything?"

Tess smiled, squeezing back tightly. Her mom could *never* stay angry with her.

"It still hurts, but I'll take some medicine. I'll be fine. I just need to go to bed, okay, Mom?"

Her mom gave her a soft kiss on her forehead, then reached to turn the television off. "Sounds like a plan, honey. Goodnight."

Laying in bed that night, her headache got worse, keeping her awake for hours. And when she did finally manage to sleep, she slept restlessly, repeatedly waking to the memory of the man's eyes following her.

Too soon, her alarm for school went off.

5:00 AM already and *no* sleep. God, this meet was *not* going to go well.

CHAPTER 2

Chloe

Chloe exhaled as the door to her room shut behind Tess.

Tess.

Her best friend.

Her lifeline.

The only joy she had most days and her escape from the reality she was trapped in.

Without the noise of Tess talking or her own voice reading the article, she was left to contemplate the silence. Silence was not a peaceful sound in her home. Silence was the unknown.

A heavy stillness. Like the emptiness that filled the air around you right before a storm erupted. Unleashing its hell on earth.

Her home was the earth. Her parents were the hell.

Why had her mother wanted Tess to leave?

As soon as the question crossed her mind, she shook her

head, dismissing it. Her parents didn't *need* reasons for what they did.

She walked to her door, pushing it open silently, knowing that if she closed it, she was breaking one of her dad's many rules.

She wasn't even allowed to lock the bathroom door, though at least she could close herself in there.

Her dad liked open doors.

What are you trying to hide? Honest people don't need *to close the door!*

And open doors gave him the freedom to barge in whenever he wanted. Screaming. Drunk. Angry.

At least an open door let her avoid waking up to the heart-stopping *bang* as it slammed into the sheetrock wall.

She stood at her door, listening. Trying to read the feel of the silence.

It might sound crazy, but not all silence sounded the same. Not all silence carried the same weight.

She waited.

Waiting.

It was torture.

Her mother had announced they needed to 'talk' to her.

And by 'talk', they meant 'punish'.

Honestly, maybe she *should* shut her door. Get it over with. A closed door would *definitely* be a trigger, setting her dad off, sending the night into a downhill spiral that when finished, would give her the peace she needed.

There was a time when she had longed for her parents to love her. To cuddle her at night, or comfort her when she woke up from a nightmare. But she'd learned early on that her mom was missing the gene for affection. And her dad...

She sighed as a vague memory of her father pushing her on a swing surfaced.

She *thought* he might have loved her at one time.

Not anymore.

Over the years, she had discovered the best way to survive her home was to be invisible. Stay out of the way. Because no matter how hard she tried, nothing was ever good enough.

A 90 on a test should have been a 100. A third place in her track event should have been first. What was the point of doing *anything* if her mom was always quick to point out that her friends were better than her?

And every mistake she made, her parents believed was made intentionally.

When she was six, she'd seen Shawn Mason, a boy that lived several blocks away, riding his bike without the training wheels. She didn't know how to ride, but she was convinced it couldn't be too difficult.

She had never even got to try. She had sliced her finger to the bone just trying to remove the training wheels. She had run to her mother— who was doing laundry —blood streaming from her hand. Her mother hadn't even paused in her sheet folding, her eyes flickering to her young daughter, and back to the sheet.

"Rinse it off Chloe," she had said. "We can go to the doctor if we need to once your father gets home."

They hadn't gone to the doctor. She had doctored it herself. Biting down on her toothbrush to keep from screaming as she poured alcohol on the wound.

When her dad came home from work, her mother let him know what she had done.

Cut herself as she participated in *vandalizing* a bicycle.

He had hit her. Six lashes for each year. She had tried to explain. She had just wanted to ride like a big girl.

But her explanation fell on deaf ears, only serving to infuriate her mother further.

Eventually, she had simply stopped trying to win her parents' approval. And since over the years, her dad's evening toddy had slowly grown to an evening *bottle*, being invisible meant being safe.

Now that Tess was gone, Chloe cautiously pulled off her sweater, wincing as the rough black material brushed an open welt on her arm. She clamped her teeth tight, grinding them and willing herself not to cry out. Instead, she bit down on her lip as the sweater finally came off.

She sighed in relief at the job done, then began to roll her sweats down her legs carefully. She threw both into a heap of dirty laundry on her floor, and sat down gingerly on the edge of the bed.

She stared at the bruises on her legs. The vivid, red welts from her father's belt. Crusted over or oozing in various stages of healing. Even as she told herself not to, her gaze panned up from her legs, towards her mirror, and then at the hunched girl reflected there.

She studied her own image, hating the angry, raised lacerations in her skin. They criss-crossed her back, crept up her shoulders and neck, and decorated the backs of her thighs.

Each one was a vivid reminder that she was alone.

And she was unworthy.

Worthless.

Tears clogged her throat, pooling in the corners of her amber-gold eyes and blurring the room.

Most of the bruises were easy to cover. She kept her hair long, hanging in her face, and wore copious amounts of extravagant makeup. Tess's dad, their school's track coach, let her race in her sweats, and she always wore Dri fit under her tank. She never wore anything that would reveal the marks. Her faults. Her mistakes.

No one could know.

Not even Tess.

Beautiful, happy Chloe Hale. With unusual golden eyes,

curly dark hair, and olive, freckled skin. A radiant smile that never left her face.

Until she got home.

She tried to hold them back, but silent sobs shook her, along with the ever-present thoughts.

I wish I could tell Tess. I wish I could tell Coach James.

I wish I could tell someone.

But she couldn't. Couldn't say a word about it, because she had no one to go to.

Her parents had always made sure she understood that.

Her grandparents weren't in the equation, she didn't have aunts or uncles, and she would never ask Tess's parents to help her.

She knew they cared about her. But she also knew they didn't *really* know her. She was a burden.

Unloveable.

Her parents had made sure she knew that as well.

No.

She couldn't tell anyone.

She flinched as she stood, pulling a blanket off of her bed and throwing it over the mirror. She hated herself.

"CHLOE!"

Her breath caught in her throat at the sound of her father's voice, filling her with fear. She ripped the blanket off of the mirror and tossed it over her bed. Snatching her clothes off the floor, she slipped back into them, the fabric scraping across each of her wounds.

Meekly, she stepped out of her room, keeping her eyes down. Sweat began beading on the back of her neck, terror crawling like a spider up her spine.

"Yes sir?" Her voice came out tiny and terrified.

Her parents were sitting at the dining room table. A whiskey glass sat half empty beside her father, and he himself was slouched in his chair.

Her mother's eyes followed her as she entered the room, but her lips formed a small, malicious smile.

"What the hell are you hiding?" her dad demanded.

His eyes were red and his voice slurred.

Chloe's gaze instinctively traveled to her father's leather belt, thankfully still threaded through the loops.

"I- I'm not—"

"Seventeen years old, and she *still* can't stop lying," her mother hissed into her father's ear. Quiet. Cold. Calculating. "*What* did you do?"

Her stomach dropped to her feet, all the blood rushing from her head in a second.

What *did* she do? Was it about her grades? Was it Tess? Having company over?

But she had asked for permission!

"I... I really don't know..." she whispered, her eyes still fixed on that damn belt. "I'm so sorry, but I don't know what I did—"

Her father slammed his fist down on the table, the sound ringing through the house. An involuntary cry escaped her throat, and she covered her mouth, trying to force the growing sobs down.

Her parents believed crying was a weakness.

Her mother murmured something to him under her breath, just barely audible.

"It had to have come from her. She's hiding it."

The tears blurred her vision until the dining room was just smudges of color.

"Dad, please—"

"Entitled little shit," her father grumbled, moving unsteadily to his feet.

His hands moved for his belt. Chloe stepped backwards, her skin beginning to tingle and burn in anticipation.

"I'm sorry!" she tried to say, but the words stuck in her throat. She didn't even know what she was apologizing for.

She whimpered as her father advanced on her, turning quickly to look at her mom.

Her mother's eyes were fixed on Chloe's face. A smile turning up her lips.

She made no move to stop him.

Run.

Every instinct *begged* her to *move*.

But where would she go?

Before she could react, before she could run or hide or cry, he was there, belt in hand.

Despite how close the neighbors were, she knew that no one would help her.

Her dad spoke. She heard her mom laugh, then murmur goodnight, clearing the glass from the table as she walked into the kitchen.

And then she heard herself scream. Felt pain slash across her body.

No one but her parents would hear her.

She was alone.

And now she longed for the silence.

CHAPTER 3

TESS

"What *was* that out there?" her dad demanded after the track meet that evening as they drove home. "You looked dead on your feet!"

Tess said nothing, leaning her head back against the headrest and letting her eyes slide shut. She was exhausted and humiliated by her performance. She'd placed 3rd in two of her events, and hadn't even medaled in her last race. She groaned, already anticipating how many extra laps her dad would assign her at their next practice.

Not to mention, there could have been college scouts at that meet! And she'd blown it.

She had *never* raced that badly.

"If you hadn't stayed out so late with Chloe," her dad was ranting, "maybe you wouldn't have been so tired. And Chloe wasn't even *there* today! I had to put in Michelle! *Michelle*!"

She had been calling Chloe all day, and hadn't received a response until the end of the day. A text that said simply:

I overslept.

She was worried. It wasn't like Chloe to let down her team. And after Charlotte Hale's strange behavior last night, Tess had an uneasy feeling that something was wrong with her best friend.

She sighed, frustrated.

Her dad was upset, but he wasn't really *mad* at her.

He was obviously annoyed, but mostly, concerned and confused.

Truthfully, Tess was concerned, too.

Not just about her best friend, but about herself.

She hadn't felt that odd sensation in her chest again.

Thank God.

But she'd been in a *terrible* mood all day. The slightest thing today seemed to set her off. She had spent the entire day alternating between feeling furious at the world and wanting to dissolve into tears. The subject of the *massacre* had come up in third period, and Tess had unexpectedly started to cry.

So freaking embarrassing.

"It wasn't because I was with Chloe, Dad," she muttered, putting down the sun visor.

And it really wasn't.

She *hadn't* gotten much sleep the night before after being out late at her friend's, but she'd slept through all of first and second period, then halfway through third. She'd woken up feeling great, but by the afternoon, she was back in a complete fog. Her legs felt like jello, and her arms ached like she'd spent the whole day in the weight room. And her *head*!

Maybe I'm getting sick. She reached up to touch her forehead, but she felt cool. Cold even.

"Tess?" Her dad gave her a sidelong glance as he drove.

"I'm fine, Dad. I just had an off day," she muttered.

The headache had grown almost unbearable, and involuntary tears sprang into her eyes. None of this was her dad's fault. She knew that.

But she felt snappy and irritable and just wanted him to back off.

Maybe it was just a lack of sleep. The headache had kept her up, preventing her from falling asleep. And the fear that when she closed her eyes, she would see the murdered children from the news report.

Her dad didn't respond, leaving her instead to sit in silence and contemplate her pitiful performance.

She kept her eyes closed, breathing deeply and willing the pain to fade.

"We're home."

He spoke the words softly, not wanting to startle her. She felt an irrational urge to cry at his thoughtfulness as she opened the door and began trudging up the driveway.

"Tess," he called after her.

His voice was serious. She stopped and turned to stare at him.

"Yeah?"

"You sure you're feeling okay, Porkchop?"

She scowled, not wanting to discuss or even *think* about her lousy performance at the meet.

"I'm fine, Dad!" she said again, more forceful this time. "I told you, I just had a bad day. Can you please just *back off?*"

She stormed into the house, slamming the door behind her, leaving her dad outside, open-mouthed and staring in disbelief.

She was being unreasonable. She *knew* she was being unreasonable. But she couldn't summon the energy to feel guilty. She ran her fingers through her hair, before taking a deep breath, and heading towards the kitchen where her mom was making dinner. Honestly, Tess didn't want to eat anything. All she wanted was sleep, and lots of it.

She stopped a few feet from the kitchen, hovering near the dining room table.

"Hey Mom."

Her mom looked up, smiling at Tess as she worked to open a glass jar.

Her smile. Fake. Guarded.

Great.

Dad had *obviously* already warned Mom how bad she had sucked tonight.

She groaned inwardly as her mom grunted, trying to turn the lid on a jar of pasta sauce.

"Mom, let me help you," she offered, starting towards her.

Her mom waved her off, then gripped the jar tightly in the crook of her elbow.

"No. Sit. Relax. You've had a rough day." She frowned, "Um... I mean... anyways..."

The room fell awkwardly silent again.

Her mom blushed, turned her attention back to the jar and avoided eye contact with Tess.

Tess stared at her mom, wanting to break the silence and say that everything was fine— it was just one bad day.

But the words she prepared didn't come out, because suddenly, the room felt strange.

Not because her mom was being all weird, but she felt the weighted feeling of anticipation. The thick, heavy atmosphere before a storm.

She watched her mom, squeezing the jar with her right arm and trying to turn the lid with her left. But her body moved like a slow motion video. Tess watched every move, confused. Why was her mother acting this way? And suddenly, the jar slipped, sliding towards the edge of the counter.

It was going to fall. Right onto the tiled floor. Tess watched it, inching across the counter.

Why isn't Mom stopping it?

It tipped off the edge, turning slowly in the air as it fell.

Catch it.

The thought crossed Tess's mind, even while she told herself how absurd that was. How could she make it across the room to stop a jar *already* falling off the counter?

But I could.

The tiny voice in her head argued against the logical outcome of gravity.

Her feet stayed rooted in the spot.

Finally, the jar hit the ground, exploding into hundreds of tiny shards of glass.

The sound on impact was ear-splitting. Her mom's mouth moved, but her words were lost to the amplified sound of the shattering, like a gunshot beside Tess's ear.

Tess fell to the ground, covering her ears as the sharp headache returned violently.

Through her pain, she watched the jar come apart, transfixed as cracks snaked through the glass like spiderwebs. Broken bits of the jar erupted in all directions, bouncing off the floor only for the fragments to burst into even smaller pieces. She could see the distinct shape of every piece. She watched them fly up towards her mom, then begin their downward spiral.

Each shard glittered like diamonds, beautiful but dangerous. Razor sharp. The red sauce moved up and out in a slow crimson splash, pooling on the floor and splattering the white cabinets.

Her ears were ringing.

Her head was spinning.

She felt like she would implode. Like her entire world was crashing down on her.

The rich aroma of tomato sauce filled the room, assaulting her senses. Suffocating her with the mix of spices.

Stop! Whatever the hell is happening, make it stop!

The sound. The *pain*. It *hurt*.

She curled into a ball on the floor, screaming as bits of glass embedded in her skin and the sounds continued to echo in her ears.

"Tess!" A strong hand clamped down on her shoulder.

Silence slammed into her, filling her mind and ringing louder than the cacophony of dripping sauce and breaking glass had been. Her head pulsed with a growing pain as the headache returned behind her eyes. But the sound, the haze, was gone.

She forced herself to look up and found herself looking into her dad's horrified stare. She turned quickly, and met her mother's frightened gaze.

"What the hell is going on in here?" Her dad's voice thundered in the silence, making her wince. "Lily, are you okay?"

"I'm fine," her mom snapped, moving around the glass to hover over Tess.

"Honey, what happened? What's wrong?" Tess stared at her mom, wanting to explain, wanting to tell them what she'd seen and heard and felt but she knew it sounded crazy.

I am *going crazy*.

Unable to speak, Tess struggled to her feet, glass clinging to her forearm. Her dad tried to grab her, but she pulled away, leaving her parents and the unexplainable insanity behind.

CHAPTER 4

SHAWN

S hawn Mason laid across his bed, absently typing an essay for his Economics and Government class. His pale blue eyes skimmed the screen, reading over his work. Black strands of hair fell into one of his eyes every time he moved, and he growled in annoyance, brushing them away. He needed a haircut.

Just as he began to type again, the front door opened downstairs. He froze. Cautiously, he focused on the sound, waiting for the feeling to hit him.

There it was. A few strange Traces pounding in his chest like a new heartbeat. He counted, trying to decide how many Munera had come.

Three, he decided, narrowing his eyes. Something serious was happening if *three* people were here this late.

He sighed unhappily, closing his laptop and sliding off his bed to shut his door.

He had no interest in dealing with Society politicians

right now. All they ever did was backstab and kiss ass. Trading information, forming alliances, and developing ways to carry out whatever chaos Koden organized.

Just the thought of Koden sent his spine straight, thoughts of agony and screaming bombarding his mind.

Memories of that bloody night.

Don't think about it.

He exhaled slowly, trying to force a better image into his head.

Long legs, thick hair, shy smile.

Of course. It was always her that appeared, thankfully replacing the violent images that played on repeat in his mind's eye. Her dark chocolate hair and hazel eyes that gleamed like amber when the light hit them just right. Her tan skin and the splash of freckles across her nose...

A soft smile took over his grimace.

Shawn couldn't remember a time when he *hadn't* had a thing for her. She'd only spoken to him a handful of times. He treasured those moments, but he could *never* do the same.

For one, he didn't talk to *anyone*, much less her.

But more importantly, she wasn't like him.

She was a Lusus Naturae. A subspecies that Koden Mason had been trying to eliminate from Munera culture for the last twenty years. Was *actively* trying to eliminate now.

He sneered as he contemplated the words. Munera. *Gifts*.

A word as pretentious and stuck-up as the people downstairs. Used by people that believed being born with supernatural abilities made them God's gifts to the world.

Shawn didn't believe being born with Munera abilities was a gift. He believed it was a curse that he was unfortunate enough to bear.

He preferred the seldom used slang term, 'Abnormals'.

And while the Society higher-ups used the traditional and degrading name, Lusus Naturae, Shawn tended to refer to the powerless as 'Basics'. It was a kinder expression than the Latin word— literally translating to *freak* —that frequented Koden's speeches.

Regardless of what they were called, Abnormals and Basics didn't mix well, and the Society had done everything possible for centuries to ensure the two species remained segregated. In fact, after hundreds of years coexisting, the large majority of Basics were completely ignorant of the existence of the Munera. Only a handful of Basics had ever discovered the difference in their Abnormal neighbors, coworkers, and superiors. And even then, it tended to be a weakness within an Abnormal that allowed discovery rather than intellectual insight from a Basic.

Truthfully, Koden had a valid reason for creating the laws he had. For trying to wipe out those who stood with the *freaks*. Mainly, the Caines and their supporters.

For years, Shawn had believed in the Salvator's cause.

But no longer.

The way Koden went about enforcing his laws made Shawn physically ill.

When Koden Mason had been appointed as Salvator, he had immediately enforced mandates, *forbidding* their kind to procreate with the Basics. The mandates made it an offense punishable by death. This created a major problem for those Abnormals *already* married to Basics. For those Abnormals who already *had* half-Basic children. Hybrids who didn't belong in either world.

His stomach churned as he thought about the final fates of those children. The experiments they'd endured in Society hospitals and research labs. The cruel race that Munera doctors and scientists across the world competed in, all desperate to discover a way to reverse the toxic, powerless genes produced when a Basic and Abnormal reproduced. Their inevitable failure.

Don't think about it. Not your problem.

Worrying about justice and rights for Basics had only ever brought him trouble.

He focused again on the Traces downstairs.

Not your problem, Shawn. Stay out of it.

Stay out of it!

Growling in frustration, he stood, moving across the dense Persian rug towards his door and reaching for the handle.

He never had learned to mind his own business. A tiny bolt of electricity escaped, crackling around his fingertips, and the lights in his room flickered.

Calm down.

If he blew a fuse or something, he'd have to explain why.

He took in a slow breath, and the lights stopped flickering. The bolt of lightning still danced across his palm, only now, he used his mind to mold it into a tiny ball that he rolled between his fingers. The ball of electricity glowed a blinding blue and gold, shrinking until he finally closed his fist, extinguishing the light. One of his mentors had introduced the method to him when he was six, and still learning to control his abilities. Now, it calmed him. Helped him to find his center.

He had to relax or he'd give himself away.

Shawn silently opened the door of his room, slipping out into the upstairs hallway.

He leaned over the mahogany banister, trying to see the late night visitors.

The Mason's home was stunning, meant to impress. Sprawling across a five acre lot, complete with tennis courts, two swimming pools, and an unobstructed view of the city from it's rooftop deck. It was luxurious enough for a king.

Or the brother of the psychotic sociopath Salvator.

Three strangers stood in the grandiose marble entryway, conversing with his parents.

Officials. He didn't recognize them, but they were low-ranking based upon the insignia embroidered across their chests.

One was a tall brunette woman with fiery dark eyes. She stood straight, exuding a commanding aura. Still, it was obvious that she was intimidated being in the presence of his parents.

Alyssa and Konrad Mason.

As Orator of the Munera, his mother ranked highly among the Society officials, answering only to her husband, and the Salvator himself. And Shawn's father, well— he was next in line.

Shawn smirked, imagining his father ascending to Salvator.

What a joke.

While he *was* powerful, he'd become weak at the same time. He'd allowed his wife to supersede his authority, both at home *and* in the political realm.

Koden rarely called on him for advice these days, increasingly relying on his sister-in-law, who occasionally spent weeks at a time away with the Salvator.

On '*business*' trips.

The brunette's partners, a lanky blonde man and another with reddish hair, appeared even more nervous, shifting from foot to foot as they spoke and avoided eye contact.

Shawn was able to catch snatches of the conversation, and the words startled him.

"Turncoat location... sympathizer..."

The Turncoats?

Hearing the name shook him, though it shouldn't have come as a surprise that officials would be bringing news of them. But it made him uncomfortable, stirring up memories that he'd been working to suppress for three years.

Even before Koden's rise to power within the Society, during Shawn's grandfather's term, groups of rebels had started to appear. They would raid Society archives, hold huge anti-Society rallies that threatened to expose the Abnormal world, and stage boycotts of Abnormal-owned businesses, instead throwing support to their Basic competitors. Then, as Koden's threats morphed into action, and mixed families of Abnormal and Basic descent started to vanish, the rebels began attacking Koden's followers and officials, eventually even killing several Senators.

The Turncoats were legendary. By *far* the most notorious rebels, spanning several continents and harboring some of the most powerful Munera to ever *live*.

Rumor had it that the *Caines* led them.

The Caines. One of the Tribus Viribus families.

The oldest of the three wealthiest, most influential, and powerful Munera families, tracing their roots back as far as history had been recorded.

Shawn, in his naive, idealistic adolescence, had *revered* the Turncoats, studying every written document about the organization and memorizing even the most minute details about them. All under the guise of childhood curiosity. His parents and mentors would *never* have tolerated his fascination if they had ever suspected his true feelings.

He had *worshiped* the Turncoats, especially the famed Caine family.

And then, he had made the mistake of trying to find them. To join them.

Memories of his punishment came to him again. Koden's mocking smile and the pleasure he seemed to take from Shawn's suffering.

And his parents. Turning away from him even as he begged them to intervene.

The memories were so real, so poignantly powerful that he cringed, and his stomach heaved at the remembered agony.

"That will be all."

His mother's icy tone brought him back from his thoughts.

Clearly dismissing the three officials.

They nodded and turned, eager to leave.

He was tempted to play with them. To give them a taste of his abilities. They deserved it. *All* the Society did.

Closing the door, his mother turned suddenly, glancing up and seeing him leaning against the banister. Her icy eyes fixed on him. He met her gaze.

She knew what he'd been planning. She always seemed to be able to read his mind, even though that wasn't within her abilities.

She smiled. A threat. A reminder that while he might be a Munera prodigy, *she* still had control.

He held her gaze for another moment, then finally, looked down in defeat.

Shawn was third in line for the position of Salvator, but it only made him more vulnerable. Growing up, Koden had been like a second father to him. Shawn had *adored* him, unaware of the insanity lying just below the surface of his favorite uncle.

But as Shawn grew older and more powerful, Koden became distant, often berating Shawn for his *softness* and forcing him into situations where failure was guaranteed.

And then Shawn had disobeyed him. He had been angry at his uncle for using him. For *lying* to him.

For destroying him.

And *no* one disobeyed the Salvator.

Ultimately, Koden no longer saw him as his nephew, his godson— but instead, his competition.

And Koden would kill him if he stepped too far out of line.

His mother crossed the room silently, staring up at him. The air around him felt thick and suffocating, but he didn't know if it was his mother's work or just the natural effects of her presence.

"It's so good to see you out of your room for once."

She studied him, wrinkling her nose as she took in his disheveled appearance. "Clean yourself up. I'd like you to be presentable and downstairs in five minutes."

A lump formed in his throat. He was sure she wouldn't answer, but he asked anyway. "Where are we going?"

She ignored him as she descended the stairs.

He backed into his room, slamming his fist into the heavy door as it closed behind him.

Intense pain radiated down his arm.

That was stupid.

Now he had to spend his night moonlighting as a Society flunky *and* he'd probably broken his hand.

He turned to look in the mirror at the long dark hair falling in his face and the grungy clothes he'd been wearing all day.

He halfheartedly brushed his hair back with his fingers, and it immediately fell back into his eyes.

No reason to dress up for what I'll be doing anyway,

He left his room, meeting his father in the foyer.

Silently, they walked out the door to the Aston Martin where his mother was waiting, and drove the short distance to the location the officials had provided.

A man opened the door, grinning.

Obviously expecting visitors.

CHAPTER 5

SHAWN

For a moment, his enthusiasm faltered as recognition flared in his eyes.

They were *obviously* not the visitors he had been hoping to see.

He quickly replaced it with a jovial smile.

"Konrad! Alyssa! Welcome!" he exclaimed. "And you've brought Shawn. How can I help you?"

His wariness was blatantly obvious, but his parents' pleasant expressions remained in place.

Shawn vaguely recognized the man as an Ambassador in the Society Court, a branch of government under the Senate.

"Jonas, how lovely to see you. May we come in?"

His mother asked the question, but it was clear that the man wasn't being given a choice. Even if the Ambassador *wanted* to refuse, he couldn't. That would raise suspicions. *No one* denied his parents anything.

Jonas nodded, opening the door wide and ushering them in.

Once they were inside and the door closed behind them, his father turned to Jonas, his tone friendly, conciliatory.

"We recently received some information, Jonas. About you... and your wife."

The man was a good actor. Not even a hint of concern crossed his face.

"I'm sorry?" he asked, chuckling as he looked at Shawn's father. "I think whoever gave you this information is mistaken. You know I've never been married, sir." He grinned, patting the belly that protruded unattractively over his waistband. "I think it's my figure."

Shawn snorted appreciatively, hoping his parents would back off. He really wasn't in the mood to participate in an interrogation.

Alyssa glanced at her son, raising her eyebrows, then faced Jonas again.

For a moment, no one spoke. The silence in the room was heavy, thick, electric.

Shawn's stomach tightened.

His mother laughed lightly. She reminded him of a snake.

"Jonas." She wagged her finger at the Ambassador play-fully. "You're too hard on yourself."

She spread her hands out, gesturing around the room. "You don't mind if we spend a few minutes visiting with the help you have employed here, do you? In particular, your kitchen help. Corina, right?" A knowing smile spread across her serene face. "She's of Lusus Naturae descent, isn't she?"

The corner of Jonas's mouth twitched, hardly noticeable, as he shook his head slightly. "She's visiting family out of town, right now."

His words came out measured. Cautious.

Shawn watched the man carefully, waiting on a vision.

Waiting to see the man's fears.

Shawn took in a breath as an onset of information assaulted him, then exhaled, looking down, disappointed. Unable to school his expression into something that wouldn't confirm his parents' information.

Seeing his father's eyes on him, he nodded slightly, affirming their suspicions.

Why bother helping this man? Why should his life hold more value than my own?

The officials had been correct. Jonas Vandenburg had many fears, but one trumped them all: being discovered as a traitor to the Society.

His parents didn't need any more justification.

Shawn had given them all the information they needed to begin the *real* interrogation.

He closed his eyes, the horror of what he'd done washing over him.

Coward.

Blood roared in his ears, loud. Too loud.

I've already killed him.

He heard a dull *thump* as the man's body hit the floor.

But Jonas wasn't dead. Yet. Though he would soon wish he was.

He opened his eyes.

Shawn's father held the man paralyzed, his piercing gaze focused on Jonas.

The man had no control over his muscles, but he could still think, see, hear.

More importantly, he could still *feel*.

And that was all the Mason family needed to terrify this man into giving up whatever information he held.

Shawn watched numbly as his father forced the man to his knees, the movements jerky like a puppet.

His mother stepped in front of Jonas.

"Jonas, you've committed a crime. Treason against the Munera people. You have entered into a relationship with a woman of Lusus Naturae descent. That is unforgivable. By order of Society law, you should be executed, as well as should your wife."

She knelt down, cupping his chin in her hand and smiling sweetly.

"I don't want to do that Jonas. I want to help you. I know you have secrets. Your wife, her pregnancy, your plans to leave the Court and start a family together." Her voice was melodious, even beautiful— a siren song.

"I don't *care* about that. I'll even turn a blind eye to your treason. But I'm going to ask you a question. I only want to ask once."

She tightened her hand on his jaw.

"Where are the Turncoats hiding?"

A moan escaped the man's mouth. His father had released the muscles around his mouth and throat.

He kept his lips pressed together, resisting the temptation he would be feeling from Alyssa's coercing. Her gift of persuasion was discreet, but effective.

His mother sighed angrily, shifting the air, restricting the flow around the man. Patience was *not* Alyssa Mason's strong suit.

He gagged. His eyes widened as an invisible force blocked his airway, making it impossible to breathe.

Then she turned on her son.

"Shawn."

Reluctantly, he moved to her side— an obedient dog.

I'm just trying to stay alive. I don't have a choice.

"Should I start off slow?" he asked quietly.

She crossed her arms, finally releasing her hold on the man.

He gasped loudly, coughing and desperate for air.

42

"Just make him talk."

Shawn nodded, locking eyes with the Ambassador.

Unfortunately for Jonas, Shawn was a *very* gifted Abnormal. A prodigy. His Genesis, the very *being* of a Munera, had begun to develop at four years old.

Torture presented no challenge for Shawn, and Jonas Vandenburg's mind provided very little resistance.

Instantly, images of water filled his mind.

The Ambassador had a fear of drowning.

Jonas began to gasp, choking on nothing, yet in his mind, in the vision Shawn created, he was drowning.

He was dying.

His mother spoke, breaking through his concentration, and Shawn fought to stay focused.

"*Where* are the Turncoats hiding?" she asked again.

Jonas's eyes were bulging, his face turning blue as he struggled to breathe.

"U-Un..."

Shawn's focus snapped as the man began to speak.

Shawn himself has spent years seeking out this information.

The illusion lifted, the water disappearing from Jonas's reality. He began to weep.

Shawn's mother turned to glare at him, annoyed at his retreat.

"Shawn!"

"Sorry, he... I got distracted." His voice faltered as he met his mother's furious stare.

"Underground," Jonas gasped, tears streaming down his face. "They're underground."

"*Where* underground?" his father demanded.

Jonas's gaze hardened, though he continued to gasp in shallow breaths. He closed his eyes briefly before he spoke.

"You disgust me."

Idiot.

Shawn's mother raised her eyebrow.

"Continue, Shawn."

Shawn hesitated, then he moved closer, concentrating this time on the man's worst fear.

I just want this over with.

An image swam into his thoughts. A woman with light hair, a warm smile, and an infectious laugh. His wife, her belly swollen with Jonas's baby.

Jonas adored his wife, living and breathing solely for her. And the baby. It was going to be a boy.

He was *terrified* of anything happening to them.

This would be his breaking point.

Behind the pregnant woman, Shawn placed an image that even terrified *him.*

The Salvator.

Koden watched the woman, his dark eyes running over her bare skin.

Tiny slits appeared in her flesh, flecks of crimson oozing from each one.

It made bile rise in Shawn's throat, sickening him.

I am a terrible person.

The illusion of the woman began to cry. Begging for mercy for her unborn child. A line of red appeared at her throat, dripping blood down her chest like a ruby necklace.

"*No!*" Jonas begged, watching as his wife's face contorted in agony. "Please! I'll do anything! *Please!*"

"Shawn."

It was his cue to stop. The man was broken, ready to talk.

"*Shawn!* Enough!"

He snapped his gaze away from Jonas. The vision dissolved, the woman and Koden fading from Jonas's sight.

Shawn's father stood over Jonas, finally allowing the man to collapse.

"All we're asking for, is a location," his father said, as Jonas curled into a fetal position, shaking and wrapping his arms around his knees.

His eyes were wide, bloodshot, traumatized, his breath ragged.

"Please," he whimpered, "Please don't—"

"For God's sake, Jonas. You're crying over a *freak*. And a *mutt*." His father rolled his eyes, annoyed at the other man's weakness.

He stepped forward, grabbing the man by his throat and yanking him up.

"Do you want to watch her die?"

At that, the man's eyes flicked to Shawn, his gaze full of terror. Anguish. Hate.

Aimed at him. Because the visions were his fault.

And if something happened to Corina Vandenburg, that would also be Shawn's fault.

He was the murderer here.

His stomach roiled, threatening to bring up his dinner. He turned around, rushing out of the kitchen.

"Shawn! Where are you going?" his mother demanded. "We're not done."

"*I'm* done!" he retorted. "I have enough blood on my hands because of you."

His parents glared at him, but he refused to relent.

"Fine." His mother threw up her hands, sending a wall of air rushing towards Jonas. It hit him in the chest, knocking him back to the ground.

"We're almost finished here anyway."

Shawn continued moving away, seeking out the furthest corner of the house, but the screams still followed him.

In the end, Jonas proved to be weak, giving up the names of several dissenters and sympathizers in the Society.

But he didn't give up his wife. He refused to give up her location or any more information about the Turncoats.

Exhausted, the man lay across the floor in a pool of blood, vomit, and urine. The smell was overpowering.

Both of his parents were breathing in ragged gasps. Neither of them typically used their abilities for an extended period of time, preferring to supervise.

"Well?" his father asked, as they sat down heavily in the leather loveseat. He rubbed his eyes wearily. "What do you think?"

Alyssa cocked an eyebrow. "About?"

Konrad motioned towards the Ambassador, laying limp and lifeless on the kitchen floor.

Alyssa's lips pulled upwards, her fist clenching on the armrest.

In response, Jonas began to gasp, grabbing his throat in desperation. He looked towards Alyssa in wild panic.

She frowned in mock concern. "Jonas. Hasn't anyone discussed your weight with you?"

She stood, walking over to him, and observing him with cold eyes. "I think you might be having a heart attack. You should probably see a doctor."

As if on cue, the man stopped breathing.

His mother shrugged, smiling at her husband. "Too late."

His father sighed, rubbing the bridge of his nose, "Alyssa, are you sure that was prudent? He still had more information to give."

"I'm tired, Konrad," his mother hissed. "It's late."

His father stood, raising his hands in defeat. Deferring, as always, to his wife.

"What do you want to do with the information?

His mother turned, raising a manicured eyebrow. "We could turn it over to your brother, but..." she paused, a slow smile on her face. "It could be worth more to us if he doesn't know. Until we have determined the value of the information."

No surprise there.

His parents had been skimming from the Society and betraying his uncle for years, though Shawn suspected his mother would betray his father just as quickly.

His mother looked up, noticing he'd returned.

"Clean up."

Her eyes flicked to the bloody mess surrounding the Ambassador.

"And Shawn?"

He raised his eyes to meet her penetrating stare.

Waiting on his orders.

"Do a better job this time. We don't need to draw more attention."

He sighed, idly wondering where Corina *really* was, then he raised his hands, sparks flying and lights flickering as he began to cover up his parents' crimes once again.

Shawn didn't listen as his parents continued to talk.

Instead, he focused on Jonas. On the death of a good man. A foolish man, but still good. A man who had wanted a better world. Justice and fairness for the Basics, and *all* Munera.

CHAPTER 6

TESS

"Tess! *Tess, wake up!*"

Her mom was leaning over her, shaking her shoulders. "*Tess!* You're going to be late for school. *Again.*"

Tess opened her eyes and peered blearily at her mom.

Confused.

She had set her alarm, but obviously...

She glared at the offending clock on her nightstand, then winced.

Her head throbbed, but now, the headache had been going on for over a week, and the pain had grown *almost* tolerable.

The house was in its usual state of morning chaos. Her mom was still speaking, and Tess stared at her, struggling to focus on her words as the alarm clock blared from the nightstand. Her dad was shouting questions from the kitchen, where the oven timer was beeping incessantly, and Fox News was broadcasting on two different TVs, causing an echo that instantly grated on her nerves. Tess rubbed her eyes, struggling to shake off the sleep that still seemed to hold her captive.

"Alright, Mom. Sorry, I'm up," she muttered, moving to sit up.

"Third day this week you've overslept Tess," her mom said, frowning at her in frustrated concern as she moved towards the door.

Her parents had been looking at her like that a lot lately. Especially after the tomato sauce fiasco in the kitchen last Friday.

"I said, *I'm sorry*. I'm up now," Tess snapped, massaging her temples and instantly regretting her tone as her mom cast a hurt expression her way.

She groaned, frustrated, whispering, "Sorry, Mom," as her mother disappeared out the door.

She could *not* seem to control her emotions lately.

"Tess!" Her dad's voice boomed from the hallway, getting louder as he moved towards her room. "Porkchop?"

He peeked his head into her room, smiling at her. "It's a meet day! Your uniform! Don't forget it!"

She glanced at the clock as she snatched her uniform and stuffed it into her bag.

"Okay, Dad!" she called out.

Annoyed with herself for oversleeping again, she quickly pulled her hair into a messy ponytail and yanked on a pair of jeans and an old tee.

The headaches were still keeping her up at night, but she didn't dare bring it up to her parents. Her mom was the *queen* of overreacting, and her dad wasn't much better. Fortunately, she hadn't had any more chest issues. She knew if she did, she would probably have to let her dad know. As a coach, he insisted all his athletes bring their health concerns to him.

Driving to school, she replayed the confusing scene from

last Friday in the kitchen. No matter how many times she tried, she had no explanation for it.

The way time had seemed to slow. The instinctive knowledge that she could catch the jar of sauce before it hit the ground, even though she was all the way across the room. The echo of the shattering glass and the splash as the tomato sauce exploded against the tiles.

And she hadn't just *heard* the splash, the breaking glass. It had been a *deafening* crash of noise, overwhelming her.

And no one else heard it like I did.

And the smell! How was it possible that a small jar of tomato sauce had infiltrated her senses to that degree?

A horn honked beside her, and Tess's gaze refocused on the road, startled. She was drifting out of her lane, inching too closely to a man in a sleek black car that was trying to pass her.

He honked again, staring at her through his dark tinted windows.

Aggravated, she flipped him off, then quickly corrected the wheel.

"Rich prick," she mumbled, then mentally apologized.

Tess, chill out. And focus.

She forced her mind to go blank. Today, she had to do her best, especially after her crappy performance at the previous track meet. She'd been staying late after practice, trying to make up for last week's failure. She had cut a full second off her time, and was determined to break her personal best time.

She reached the school, and hopped out of her red Volkswagen Jetta, fighting her way through the packed crowd of teenagers to the cafeteria.

Chloe was waiting for her at the door, arms crossed over her chest. Her curly brown hair blew in the wind as she stood, tapping her foot impatiently

With her black winged eyeliner and outrageous lashes, her eyes looked enormous and luminous. Of course, her makeup was done perfectly, and her outfit belonged on a runway.

She still hadn't given Tess a *real* explanation for missing their last meet. And when Tess had asked her about Charlotte Hale's strange and unfriendly behavior, Chloe had averted her eyes, avoiding the question.

"Where have you been?" she snapped, annoyed when Tess walked up to her.

"Slept in," she mumbled, rubbing the sleep from her grainy eyes.

"Again? What is that, the third time this week? You should go to bed earlier."

Tess smirked. "Alright *Mom*."

Chloe stuck her tongue out, then reached into her purse, pulling out some lipgloss and mascara. She cupped Tess's chin tightly and began applying the makeup.

Tess swatted her and groaned, "Seriously Chloe? I'm gonna sweat it off at the meet anyway!"

Chloe sighed dramatically. "The meet isn't until this afternoon. You could at least *try* to look like you care until then."

Chloe aspired to be a fashion designer, and it drove her crazy that her best friend was *completely* fashion impaired.

Tess raised her eyebrows and wiped her lips defiantly, grinning.

Chloe rolled her golden eyes, reluctantly putting the makeup away and grumbling, but perking up as a bout of raucous male laughter broke out nearby.

A sly smile turned up the corners of Chloe's lips, and she turned to Tess. A mischievous twinkle in her eye.

"Well... Are you ready for the track meet? You will probably get to see *Logan*," she teased as she reached out to straighten Tess's messy ponytail.

"Shhh! *Shut up*!" Tess said, lurching to cover her best friend's mouth. "He's *right* there!"

She glanced over to the group of guys— Logan among them —who were laughing and wrestling a few feet away.

The *recently-single* Logan Tucker was one of the best distance runners their school had ever seen. His times were incredible— not to mention, he looked great while doing it.

And even when he wasn't running, he was *perfect*. His eyes were a soft, warm brown with an emerald ring around his pupil and tiny flecks of gold scattered throughout his iris. He was tall, with lean muscles from years of football and track. And his hair... gorgeous and golden-blonde, and he had a smile that just—

Okay. Maybe, she had a *tiny* crush on him. And maybe, *maybe* she had been in love with him since the second grade, but he was the most popular guy in school. He'd never shown interest in her— in *that way*, at least —and even if he did, he was *way* out of her league.

They had been friends since kindergarten.

But definitely *not* the kind of friend she wished they could be.

Maybe it had something to do with growing up in such a small school, but Logan had always seemed to view her as just 'one of the guys'.

Probably because he remembers when I used to take my shirt off and play in the sandbox with him and Dalton.

She groaned inwardly, hoping he didn't think her chest was still *that* flat. Not that he ever looked at her long enough to notice that she had finally filled out.

She had gotten lucky enough to get paired with him as lab partners in forensics, but lately, she got so nervous that she ended up blabbering like an idiot anytime she tried to talk to him.

"Of course I'm going to see him," Tess hissed, tearing her eyes away from him.

"He races right after our relay."

Chloe studied him, tilting her head in thought. "I wouldn't know anything about his races," she said, giving Tess a smirk. "I don't *stalk* him."

Tess crossed her arms indignantly. "I do *not* stalk him! My dad is the track *coach* remember? I know when everyone races, not just Logan!"

She paused, taking a breath "And stop staring at him!"

Chloe rolled her eyes, mimicking Tess.

"*I don't stalk him! I just stare at him all the time and follow every account on social media he has! And sometimes I sneak to his window and watch him sleep. I love his Ninja Turtle pajamas.*"

Tess scowled, trying to maintain her irritation.

Chloe frowned slightly. "What? Are they Power Ranger PJs, instead?"

Tess's resolve broke and she giggled, shoving Chloe.

"You're a brat."

Chloe smiled widely, holding up her hands.

Tess peeked out of the corner of her eye, looking in Logan's direction.

Unfortunately, he looked up at that exact moment, catching her eye. He smiled at her, giving her a small wave.

"Oh my God," she looked away quickly. Embarrassed.

"Forget Logan," Tess announced. "I need breakfast. I'm starving!"

CHAPTER 7

SHAWN

"Hey, nice blinker dumbass!" Shawn snapped, slamming on the brakes of his Mercedes Maybach as the old Chevy in front of him suddenly braked to turn right.

If something happened to his car, his parents would kill him. Literally.

Not because they couldn't afford to scrap this one and purchase another, but simply because the Masons were always searching for a reason to punish him.

He pulled into the school parking lot, sighing as he glanced around, considering skipping class for the day. He wasn't in the mood for forced socialization, and it wasn't like he *needed* to sit through these lessons. It had been years since he had found a Basic teacher that could teach him anything.

Actually, it had been years since he had found *any* teacher that could teach him anything.

He looked around, watching students pour out of their vehicles.

He wasn't a fan of Joshua High, but at least it gave him a break from his family. A temporary illusion of safety.

Last night had been a typical night at the Mason home. After his mother had dismissed the kitchen help, conversation had revolved around all the Society drama and the recent '*disappearance*' of an entire Lusus Naturae family. Then the bickering had begun between his parents when Alyssa had mentioned an impending business trip with his uncle.

To Paris.

Followed by his father's petulant silence.

Truthfully, Shawn thought the love triangle between his parents and his uncle was amusing. It kept things interesting at least.

They had spent the whole meal ignoring him, which was fine with Shawn. Until Alyssa had made an announcement.

The Salvator was coming to Joshua.

Shawn cringed, his mind instinctively shying from the thought.

His psycho uncle was flying here for a visit.

Not likely.

The leader of the American Muneras, didn't just fly in for a *visit*. His mother went to the Salvator often, but it had been years since Shawn had been forced to endure his uncle's presence.

Everything Koden Mason did was done with a purpose. He was the most goal-driven person Shawn had ever met, or even heard of. He was planning something, and whatever it was, it involved Shawn's family.

Just the thought of Koden coming *near* him made every nerve in his body come alive, electrified.

The smell of melting plastic assaulted his nostrils, and he glanced down in alarm. His hands were locked around the heated steering wheel, tight and desperate.

Blue and yellow sparks danced around his hands, turning the rubber under his hands to a fast-forming black puddle.

Cursing, he released the wheel and closed his fists to extinguish the bolts.

He groaned, eyeing the melted areas.

"Well, shit."

He opened the door, stretching his long legs out the car, then flipping his hood over his sleek black hair that shadowed his icy eyes.

I hate this day already.

Slamming the door, he moved rapidly through the parking lot. Most people here didn't pay attention to him.

Actually, most of the students didn't even know his *name*, and he liked it that way. Needed it that way.

Invisible.

As he maneuvered through the crowd, he scanned the grounds for *her*. A daily habit. One that would get him killed if he wasn't careful.

There.

He finally spotted her.

God, she was gorgeous. Just seeing her lifted his spirits. But he could see from her tight smile and tired eyes that she was still in pain. She had been for at least a week now.

Several times, Shawn had considered asking her if she was okay, and several times, he talked himself out of it.

She would probably think he was a creepy stalker. He wasn't even sure if she knew his name.

Yeah. Definitely creepy. Quit staring dude. She's a Basic, remember?

Any kind of relationship with Tess James was something that neither his parents *nor* Koden would tolerate.

And ultimately, though he didn't approve of the *methods* the Salvator used to eliminate Basic and Abnormal interbreeding, he agreed with the science behind the mandate.

Even if he *did* manage to grow a pair and ask her out, they could never be together. It was just *wrong*.

Still... no one said he couldn't look.

And he *definitely* looked. As often as he could.

She was breathtaking. Her long hair was pulled back, displaying her beautiful face, and her long legs were squeezed into a pair of dark denim jeans.

Tight denim jeans.

She was different from other girls. Genuine. Kind. Perfect.

He wrinkled his nose in distaste.

Almost perfect.

Her taste in men lacked something to be desired.

Today, her gaze was focused on a crowd of rowdy jocks a few yards in front of her. Specifically, on Logan Tucker.

Just the *sight* of that one incited Shawn's anger, making his fists clench at his sides.

Of course, she was looking at Logan. Every girl in the school did.

Rolling his eyes, Shawn made his way into the school building. Logan Tucker was *definitely* a Lusus Naturae.

One Basic that he wouldn't mind going '*missing*'.

He grimaced, quickly trying to dispel the thought.

He didn't really mean it. While he didn't *like* Logan Tucker, the Basic didn't deserve that fate.

If he was being completely honest with himself, he didn't like Tucker because he was jealous.

His first period classroom door was open, and he slipped inside. Mrs. Thompson, his calculus teacher, was gone. Thankful for the quiet isolation of the empty room, he slid into his desk, and laid his head down.

He was dreading his uncle's visit. He hadn't seen him since—

No. No reason to dwell on it.

Whatever the Salvator had planned for him, he would accept it. He *deserved* whatever horrible fate was coming his way.

The bell rang, startling him, and he sat up as more people streamed into the classroom, invading his few precious moments of silence. A hand clapped down on his shoulder and shook him roughly.

Hunter Garcia, the school stoner. One of them, anyway.

"Shawn," Hunter dragged his name out. "My favorite asshole!"

"Piss off," Shawn muttered, swatting Hunter's hand away from him. "Not in the mood."

Hunter was pretty much the only person at Joshua High that Shawn interacted with.

Freshman year, Shawn had rescued the guy from getting pummeled by half the football team in the boys' bathroom. It had been an accident, really. The quarterback was angry that Hunter had shorted him on a bag of weed, and Shawn had walked in, interrupting Hunter's demise.

Since then, Hunter thought they were *buds,* and *insisted* on following him around.

Shawn wasn't sure he really liked him, but he was the closest thing he had to a friend. And it was nice not to be *totally* invisible.

But with Koden and his parents in the equation, he couldn't afford to get close to anyone. Shawn didn't know why Hunter still bothered to talk to him. He wasn't exactly *friendly* to the guy. But he didn't question it.

"Fine, fine."

Hunter raised his hands over his head in mock surrender, then grinned, smacking him across his forehead as the teacher came in. "What's got your panties in a wad?"

I indirectly killed someone last week, Shawn imagined saying.

Instead, he muttered, "What part of 'piss off' didn't you understand?"

The last few students walked through the classroom door.

Mrs. Thompson closed the door, and in that moment, Shawn's chest came to life. A beat marking time with his heart.

Strong. *Extremely* powerful. And then it was gone.

He gasped, doubling forward over his desk, clutching his chest with one hand. It wasn't painful, just unexpected. The shock of it was powerful enough to take his breath away.

Hunter stepped back, staring at him suspiciously. "What the hell is wrong with you? Did you get some bad shit?"

"I'm fine," Shawn managed, forcing himself to sit up and scan the room.

Calculus was a senior level class, and *no one* in the senior class was like him. There were several activated lower-classmen that he occasionally ran across. They mostly ignored him, uncomfortable by his presence. But he was the only Munera in his grade with an activated Genesis— he had been for the last four years. Or so he'd thought. But he was wrong. There was *undoubtedly* another active Abnormal here.

"Hunter, back off," he snarled, trying to feel where the Trace had come from.

Annoyed, Hunter smacked Shawn's head again, then slunk away, leaving Shawn with a clear view of who the Trace belonged to.

Tess James.

CHAPTER 8

TESS

Tess felt restless, uneasy, and so tense she thought she might explode.

Par for the course lately.

She stretched, rolling her neck from side to side. She was ready for the meet to start.

Her forensics teacher was lecturing about DNA and fingerprints, but Tess wasn't paying attention to her. While she was worried about the meet, she now had a bigger, more immediate concern.

Her heart. Or more accurately, her chest.

It had happened again. Just for a moment in Calculus. But it had scared her. She wondered if she should try and talk to her dad before the meet.

Logan sat beside her, peering down at the phone in his lap and ignoring the lessons just like she was.

A tiny smile curved the corner of his lip as he scrolled past post after post. His hair was falling over his forehead, almost in his eyes, and Tess watched each strand catch the light of the overhead LEDs in the lab ceiling.

Suddenly, he glanced up, his eyes alert as their teacher called on him. She pointed to the answer choices on the board.

He barely skipped a beat, scanning the answers before saying, "D."

His response was effortless and smooth, and he kept that radiant smile as he said it. He sounded so confident that even if the answer was wrong, Tess would have believed him.

God, he's hot...

Their teacher smiled, indicating that he'd gotten the answer right, then turned back to the board.

Logan looked to Tess then, his eyes bright with amusement as he let out a slow breath.

"I guessed," he murmured, still smiling and raising an eyebrow.

Thankfully, her brain didn't implode at the sheer fact that he was looking at her and talking *directly* to her. Even her headache temporarily faded into the back of her mind.

"I couldn't tell," she whispered back, and he grinned mischievously.

"You ready for the meet?" he asked her quietly, shutting off his phone and sliding it into his pocket.

She tried to breathe normally, forcing down a maniacal smile.

"Coach put me in sprints this week," Logan continued, oblivious to her screaming thoughts. "Said that Donovan sprained an ankle and can't run it."

Tess nodded eagerly, glad that he clearly intended to keep the conversation going. "I heard about that. Dad was pissed."

As they spoke, Tess felt a chill travel down her spine, making her shudder. Someone was watching her.

"Hey, Shawn Mason is looking at you."

Logan's voice had dipped lower, and at some point in the conversation, he'd leaned close enough that she could feel his breath as he murmured in her ear. How had she *not* noticed how close he was?

"He is?" she asked, unconcerned now that she knew who it was.

Shawn Mason.

She sometimes caught him staring at her during class, but today it'd been even more often than usual. His vibrant blue eyes had hardly left her all day, his brows drawn together, his mouth set in a tight line, and his raven-black hair falling across his face.

He didn't even seem to care that she *knew* he was staring.

Shawn was an enigma. He was a loner. He was in the National Honor Society like her, which meant he had good grades and a spotless behavior record, but he never seemed to be paying attention in class. When he was *in* class. He tended to miss a *lot* of school.

Tess sometimes thought that if he cut his hair, gained a few pounds, and hung out in the gym, he might actually be popular. Underneath that curtain of hair, he was actually cute.

She had thought about trying to talk to him. He *obviously* wanted to talk to her. But every time she caught him staring, it freaked her out.

Talk about a stalker.

"He's kinda creeping me out," Logan whispered, glancing over Tess's shoulder to peer at Shawn.

My thoughts exactly.

"It's really not a big deal,"she lied, shrugging nonchalantly.

Logan's eyes narrowed. "Still... I'll walk with you when they call us out."

She didn't even get time to say, "That'd be *great,*" before the final bell chimed.

"Freedom!" one of the boys in the back sang, earning a scowl from their teacher.

The ancient intercom came on with a crackle of static.

"All track students report to the football field immediately," the secretary droned. "All track students."

"Finally!" Tess breathed.

"Come on," Logan said, grinning her way.

Feeling Shawn's gaze following her, she got up and walked out the door.

As Tess stepped outside, Chloe immediately appeared at her side, stopping short when she saw Logan walking beside her.

"He-ll-ooo," she drawled out hesitantly, looking from Tess to Logan with raised eyebrows.

Logan tossed out another of his ridiculously mesmerizing smiles.

"Hey, Chloe."

Chloe glanced at Tess, lifting her lips in a grin, then wiggled her eyebrows comically.

Tess looked away, trying to keep her cool, but with Logan beside her, his hair gleaming gold, his eyes like melted chocolate... it was *really* hard.

"So, Shawn Mason..." Logan started, glancing over his shoulder. "Is something going on between you two?"

Chloe reached out, grabbing Tess's shoulder and stopping her.

"Wait, *Shawn*? The creepy one who's always watching you? What did he do? Do I need to kick his ass?"

Tess rolled her eyes. "It's not a big deal Chloe. He *always* stares at me. It was just a little more noticeable today... "

Logan's eyes widened. "*Always*? So he's stalking you?"

He'd clearly meant it as a joke, but the words made her stomach crawl and she laughed uncomfortably.

"Whatever."

The three of them moved to sit underneath the canopy in the middle of the football field, navy and red among all the other schools' colored tents.

Monroe, Marble Springs, Mesquite Ridge, Eagleheights, and a few other schools. Other athletes milled around, mingling with each other.

Or trash talking.

"Twenty bucks that that guy from Monroe starts a fight," Logan said, smirking.

"You're on!" a boy responded, joining their conversation.

Dalton Smith, a guy with dark hair, even darker skin, and an infectious grin sat beside Chloe, grinning at Logan.

He stuck out his hand, like he was actually placing a bet.

Logan snorted, slapping Dalton's hand away. "No way. You'll go *start* that fight, dude. I'm not losing twenty bucks so that you can get suspended again."

They laughed as Dalton stuck out his lip pouting playfully.

More of Logan's friends jogged up to join their group, staring for a moment at Tess in surprise.

She could practically read the question on their faces.

Since when did Logan hang out with Tess James?

No one questioned Chloe being there. Everyone liked Chloe. But most people tended to overlook Tess. It wasn't that people didn't *like* her. She just didn't quite fit in.

I'm just Chloe's awkward friend.

And yet, here she was, sitting under the tent with Logan. And she couldn't help but notice that his attention seemed to be focused on *her*. Her heart raced, and she found herself relaxing. Laughing at Dalton's jokes. Watching Logan's friends pick on each other. She felt practically giddy.

Geez Tess. Get a grip.

"Second call for the mile relay," the announcer's voice boomed.

Chloe glanced at Tess, then shot a regretful look at Dalton. Clearly, she'd been enjoying their conversation, too.

"We gotta go," she said, standing.

Tess followed her, her heart sinking.

Her time with Logan was over. Sighing, she started to make her way to the start line, then realized she'd been so distracted talking with Logan, that she hadn't stretched.

Great, I'm gonna blow another *meet.*

Furious with herself, she stepped out from the shade.

Just as she and Chloe stepped away from the tent, a hand snatched hers.

She turned, stunned to find Logan holding her hand.

"Good luck," he said, giving her a smile that left her breathless. "You've got this."

She smiled at him, a wave of renewed excitement running through her.

"Thanks."

She turned away, hurrying to her position. She was excited. Relaxed.

Not nervous at all.

This was where she felt at home. Where she felt confident and comfortable.

And she planned on taking home the gold today.

The other runners were already lined up when Tess arrived, the first and fastest leg in their team. The announcer was making the last call for the race.

She bent over, adjusting her start block, and gasped.

The sensation had returned. It was brief, and not as overwhelming as the previous times. But it left her feeling a little anxious.

I should've talked to dad.

She took her place in the third lane next to a dark-skinned girl with beaded dreads.

Tess smiled reassuringly in her direction.

The girl scowled at Tess. A look of confused frustration on her face. Her hand moved to her chest like she was saying the pledge. Tess frowned, unsure of why the girl appeared so unfriendly.

"On your mark!" the announcer yelled.

Tess shook her head.

"Focus," she mumbled to herself. "Eyes on the prize."

She glanced into the stands and froze. Shawn was sitting in the bleachers, his black hair blowing out like a dark flag.

Since when does he come to track meets?

She could feel his eyes on her, and she quickly looked away.

"Get set!"

"GO!"

Tess took off at a sprint, looking ahead. She heard approaching feet, so she pumped her arms faster. Within seconds, she was running so fast, she felt like she was flying. She'd loved that feeling, loved getting lost in the run. The throbbing of her head was gone, her aching legs suddenly numb to the pain of not having stretched. The wind blew in her face and howled in her ears, whipping her dark ponytail around madly.

Tess rounded the last curve and was approaching the second leg of the relay.

She slapped the baton into Chloe's hand, pressing her hand into her friend's back as they made the transition. Chloe stumbled several yards forward from the impact. For a brief second, her friend's face contorted, and she glanced back at Tess in surprise. Chloe shook her head, and started to sprint.

The fans roared, screaming as she finished her lap and handed the baton off to the third leg, Marissa Martinez. Tess's team had an impossible lead by the time Marissa shot down the track and tagged Janie Greenfield, the last leg.

Tess's incredible speed, not to mention the inexplicable

shove that had boosted Chloe's run, had put them almost a lap ahead of the competition.

Janie took off running, not slowing her pace until she had long passed the finish line, claiming first place for the team.

Tess stood perfectly still, the noise of the crowd amplified in her ears. Everyone around her was smiling. Ecstatic. This was an important meet and the relay team had *surely* just bumped Joshua to the lead.

But Tess didn't feel excited. She felt *wrong*.

She wasn't out of breath. Her legs didn't ache. In fact, she wasn't tired at all.

Her dad raced up to her, shoving a stopwatch in her face.

"*40.06!*" he breathed in disbelief. "That's almost three seconds faster than the world record!"

Under different circumstances, it would have been amazing! Tess had beat her personal record by ten seconds. And a *world record?* If there had been college scouts there, she'd *surely* get a scholarship now.

But, she felt no happiness.

Something is wrong.

She couldn't pinpoint it, but she felt it.

Her dad was still rambling, and a few of her teammates rushed up to her, asking questions she couldn't answer.

How'd you run so fast?

I've never seen you sprint like that!

What the hell are you on? Can I get some?

She felt like she *was* on drugs. Everything around her seemed too bright, vivid, and slow. And loud.

Her heart was hammering in her chest. She could feel the chambers working. Pumping the blood through her body.

She needed them to leave her alone. To give her some space.

"Hey, Tess!" Logan hollered as he dashed up to the group surrounding her.

His voice made her jump.

She turned quickly, trying to force her way through the crowd around her, leaving her team, her dad, and Logan behind.

Her breathing came fast, hard, and scared.

I'm going crazy. I'm literally going crazy.

She felt the beads of sweat slowly rolling down her arm. Felt it as it touched each individual tiny hair. Felt the moment the sun began to evaporate it in minuscule increments as it traveled between follicles.

She quickly ran her hands down her arms, eliminating all possibilities of 'magical sweat thoughts'.

Thankfully, no one followed her. She planted herself on a bench under an oak tree in the parking lot, trying not to panic.

Just breathe.

Just—

"Tess!"

So much for not being followed.

She glanced up, dismayed to see Logan jogging towards her.

After her race, with confusion clouding her feelings, the magic of *'Logan Tucker'* had lost its effect. She felt inexplicably angry.

"You're not gonna celebrate with everyone else?" he asked, gesturing to Tess's teammates who were laughing and high-fiving.

"I'm not in the mood," she muttered.

Logan's gaze turned serious with concern.

"Are you okay?"

No. No I'm not. I think I'm losing my mind!

"I'm fine."

Logan sat beside her, leaning towards her and gently bumping her shoulder.

"If something's wrong, you can tell me," he offered.

Why do you care? The words sprang to her mind, almost escaping from her mouth.

She felt furious, resentful. But he hadn't done anything to her— she had no reason to be mad. Especially not at him.

He was only trying to help.

"Really, Logan, I'm okay. I promise."

He was silent for a moment, watching her curiously. But his gaze was soft. Inquisitive. Sweet. Not prying like Shawn's or the girl on the track.

"Alright, well, *you're* the champion." He reached out, unexpectedly poking her nose.

"Whatever happened, I'm impressed. Forty seconds? That's gotta be a world record." He puffed out his chest in mock bravado. "I mean, you're still not as fast as me, but..." He shrugged. "You'll catch me someday."

His silliness had the desired effect, breaking through her shell of confusion and anger.

She giggled. "My dad said the same thing."

He smiled sweetly, and Tess acutely noticed a little red creeping up into Logan's cheeks. She blinked to make sure the heat wasn't making her hallucinate.

Suddenly, they heard the announcer call for the boys' sprint races, and Logan grinned.

"I gotta get to my event, but I'll see you later."

Tess still stared at him, trying to decide whether the red in his face was from the sun or something else.

"Y- Yeah...okay."

With that, he started off to the track.

Halfway there, he paused glancing back at her, then at the track, then back at her.

Shaking his head, he jogged back to her side.

"Hey, can I get your number?"

Yep. I've definitely gone crazy.

Her mouth moved, trying to form the word *'yes'* but she couldn't make any sound come out. She resorted to nodding eagerly and slipping her phone out of her athletic bag.

By the time Logan walked away— Tess's number in *his* phone —she was lightheaded.

He'd asked for her number!

I have to tell Chloe!

She glanced toward her teammates again, spotting Chloe getting ready for her second race. A thought suddenly occurred to her, and she let her gaze drift into the stands again, searching.

But there was no splash of black hair or icy eyes watching her every move.

Shawn Mason was gone.

CHAPTER 9

Tess

That evening, Tess lay across her bed, hanging up from blabbering to Chloe for an hour about Logan.

"*You're gonna scare him off if you don't chill,*" Chloe had laughed.

"*How can I* chill*? He asked for* my *number!*"

Her mind was still reeling, and even though it was unlikely, she was hoping that he would text her.

"Tess! Dinner!"

Her mother's voice, not to mention the scent wafting into her room, pulled her away from her thoughts.

Tess could smell steak straight off the grill, mashed potatoes, and fresh yeasty rolls with butter.

Her good mood was instantly eliminated.

Moments ago, she'd been ecstatic about the victory dinner being prepared by her father, but something was wrong.

Her room was about as far from the kitchen as you could

get. And while it was normal to get an occasional whiff of delicious flavor, it was *not* normal to be able to differentiate each seasoning her dad had used. She could pick out the strong smell of garlic, the dash of pepper, and a hint of Worchershire that he'd used to marinate the steak. She could distinctly smell the drop of honey her mom liked to add to the butter before baking the rolls. She could even pinpoint the lemon they'd drizzled on the lettuce, before mixing the salad; something she *hated*, but didn't have the heart to tell her parents.

She should *not* be able to isolate every single item used to cook their dinner. She should not have an extra beat pounding in her chest. She should *not* have been able to watch a jar fall in slow motion, or cut her racing times by a full ten seconds overnight.

And she *definitely* should *not* be able to clearly hear her parents discussing her new 400 time when they were half a house away!

Her brain was screaming at her.

Something is wrong. Something is really *wrong!*

"Tess!"

She stood quickly, grateful for the distraction. "Okay! Just let me wash my hands real quick!"

She sprinted down the hall.

Not anticipating how fast she would reach the bathroom, and still distracted by her thoughts, she ran right into the door, slamming her head into the wood with a loud *thunk*.

"Jesus..." she moaned, massaging her forehead, then opening the bathroom door.

She leaned over the sink and turned on the cold tap. It was a relief to cool her sweaty hands. Her skin felt too hot. And too sensitive. Tingly.

She reached to open the medicine cabinet, then paused,

realizing for the first time in forever, she didn't actually *need* Tylenol.

Her mind raced as she tried to remember the last time her head had been pain free.

My headache is gone. That's a good thing.

But the scale of good things versus weird things happening to her lately was ridiculously tipping towards the latter.

She looked up into the mirror and groaned in horror. The week of stressing over her headaches and abnormal senses had given her bags and dark circles under her eyes. Her ponytail was messy from the meet, strands sticking out in every direction, and a bright red pimple had planted itself right in the crease in her chin.

I had a face-to-face conversation with Logan *like* this? she thought, horrified and fighting to keep her composure.

She felt her throat tighten, and closed her eyes, willing herself not to cry as she rested her hands on the faucet knobs.

Think Tess. There's got to be an obvious explanation.

She was probably just overreacting? She thought back, trying to recall what strange things had *actually* happened during these past couple weeks..

Her headache.

It had been a never ending headache. Torturing her until she thought she'd go crazy. Until today, when she'd suddenly become faster than the fastest person on earth. *Now* her headache had decided to vacate the premises.

And that person at the bus stop when she'd left Chloe's that night. It wasn't unusual for someone to be out at night, waiting on the bus. But the feeling she'd gotten.

Tess shuddered, remembering those eyes, glowing from underneath a hood, watching her. Which brought to mind Shawn's icy eyes. Following her every move. And the girl's reaction at the meet?

All weird.

Now, her senses had gone berserk, and she apparently had the nose of a bloodhound!

What the hell?

It was like someone had flipped an *on* switch inside her and she'd suddenly powered-up!

"Tess? Are you coming? Your steak's getting cold."

Her father's voice startled her, and her hands instinctively tightened around the bronze knobs.

The metal bent under her grip like play dough.

She yanked her hands back, staring in horror at the crushed knobs.

What the actual *hell?*

This wasn't real. This *couldn't* be real.

"Yeah, Dad!" she yelled back. "I just... got distracted. I'm coming."

Glancing one more time at the bent faucet handle, she forced herself to relax, and walked to the kitchen, dazed. Fixed herself a plate of steak and mashed potatoes. Sitting at the table, she tried to ignore the growing panic in her chest and the overwhelming smells assaulting her nose, and she listened instead, to the normal conversation of her parents.

The steak was done medium-rare just how her family liked it, the mashed potatoes whipped to perfection and topped with a dollop of sour cream. Her mother, who had recently abandoned her low-carb "*lifestyle*", had made her famous yeast rolls to go with the meal.

The best meal in the world.

She needed to relax and enjoy it.

"Oh! I forgot to get the mail. Tess, could you go grab it real quick?" her mom asked.

Nodding, Tess hopped out of her chair, opening the front door and snatching several envelopes from the tin box attached to the side of her home.

The envelope on top was colored with blue and gold. A mascot of a griffin was printed on the surface.

On the label was her name, stamped in small black letters.

She set the other letters on the table and ripped open her envelope, reading its contents.

Her heart pounded in her chest as she read.

"Mom... Mom! Dad! Look!"

She sat back in her chair, thrusting the letter towards them.

"A coach at Canisius College wants me to go to a tryout! And this came *before* today's meet! They haven't even seen my new times yet, and they already want me to—"

"Tess, honey, wait," her mom interrupted.

Tess froze, eyeing her mom's dubious expression. "Mom, this is huge for me!"

Her mother bit her lip. "Maybe, Tess, but *New York?* That's so far away. I won't be able to look after you."

Tess couldn't believe what she was hearing.

"I'm eighteen! You don't *need* to look after me."

She turned to her father, glaring, an irrational fury building in her chest.

"*Dad?* You can't seriously agree with her! What about my new times? With those, I could probably get into Canisius *without* the tryout!"

"Tess—" he started, but Tess cut him off.

"I've been working towards this for years! I've been running track since sixth grade! Now I have this opportunity and you're *both* gonna say no?"

Her mom rolled her eyes. "Really, Tess? There will be a ton of other *in-state* colleges you'll get accepted to. But I'm not sending my eighteen-year-old daughter a thousand miles away."

She spread her hands wide, exasperated.

"Seriously honey, what difference does it make if you *know* there will be other offers?"

Tess tore her fingers through her hair, ignoring the sting as several strands came loose.

"It makes *all* the difference in the world!" she snapped. She stood up, shoving her dinner chair back. "It's *my* future, and *I* should be able to decide what I want to do with it!"

With that, she turned on her heels and stormed out the front door, slamming it behind her.

How could her mom expect her to pass up this chance? She buried her hands in her hair, growling in frustration. No way she was going to let her mom win this fight.

Canisius was a *once* in a lifetime opportunity!

And now, she was quite *literally* the fastest person on earth! She could easily get into that college! Probably get a scholarship too.

But her mother was worried about sending her out of state because Tess couldn't take *care* of herself? Seriously? She'd be fine!

Tess threw herself into a lawn chair, taking in a deep breath, then exhaling slowly.

Maybe it was a bit stupid to make this into a big deal when she *could* get opportunities in her own state. Honestly, she wasn't even sure she *wanted* to be half a country away from her parents.

But this was the first college that had shown interest in her! And right away, her mom had refused— didn't even think about it. Didn't even say she was proud of Tess!

Feeling restless, and not ready to deal with her parents, she stood up and broke into a sprint across the yard. The wind howled in her ears and pulled at her ponytail. Her legs felt completely weightless. Like she could run forever.

Everything felt completely surreal.

She was very possibly going crazy. Either that, or somehow, something in her had changed and she was suddenly able to do the impossible.

She ran into town, headed no particular direction. She just ran. It was a trip that usually left her winded and dreading the run back, but she didn't feel tired at all.

Passing closed stores, darkened homes, parked cars, and bus stops. Nothing seemed different or out of the ordinary. Except her. Overnight, she'd become a freak.

With superhero speed, superpower senses, and apparently, super strength.

She brought her pace to a trot, trying to calm her thoughts.

And super villain emotions.

She slowed to a walk, glancing around, then turning onto a side street. Everything about it was unkempt. It had a strangely vacant feeling. Almost abandoned.

The road was riddled with potholes, the grass around her unmowed, and some of the windows of the surrounding buildings were broken in, leaving black holes like mouths in the side of the buildings.

She stopped, standing in front of a house, wedged between two larger abandoned office buildings.

It was a tiny, decrepit white house with faded green trim around the windows and several shingles missing from its black roof.

A sign posted in the front yard proclaimed in bright orange letters, FOR RENT.

Jesus who would even think *about wanting this place?*

Still, curiosity got the best of her, and since she had no desire to head home, she found herself glancing around, inspecting.

No one was there, and she sighed in relief. The last thing she needed was to have the cops called on her.

She made her way up the steps and turned the handle.

The door opened, creaking loudly as it moved on its hinges.

The place reeked. A mixture of mildew and death. No doubt there were dead rats in the walls or something.

The door was so swollen that it was hard to shut, and the window nearest her was shattered, glass laying in huge shards around the sill.

Her feet stirred up dust on the floor of the house, and she coughed. Her eyes darted wildly about the room as she tried to adjust to the dark.

Tess held her breath, trying not to gag from the rotten stench of the place.

What am I doing here?

Tess had *never* been the adventurous type, always preferring to play it safe. She didn't speed. She didn't cut class. She didn't even eat a grape before buying it at the grocery store, and when she *did* eat grapes, she cut them lengthwise to avoid choking. So what the hell was she doing, trespassing in some disgusting, 'Nightmare on Elm Street' house?

Probably another sign that she was losing her mind.

The room she had stepped into was mostly empty, save for a moldy couch, a side table with rotten wood, and a lamp with no shade.

"No wonder no one wants this place," she grumbled, fighting a sneeze as dust floated through the room.

Her voice echoed in the empty space, disrupting the silence.

A soft rustling noise came from a dining room. Tess immediately focused on the sound.

Something small, moving across the floor. A tiny breath.

She stiffened, glaring through the darkness around the room.

Snake, she thought, shuddering as she spotted the long, thick shape curving and slithering its way towards her.

As the snake closed the distance between them, her breath caught.

But not in fear.

In fury.

Something about the sound of the snake's breath, it's slinky body sliding across the floor, *irritated* her. Grating on her nerves and reawakening the pent-up confusion and frustration that had been building for weeks. Since that night she'd left Chloe's, fighting the beginning of a monster headache.

She heard a soft puff as the snake exhaled.

Normal people can't hear a snake's breath.

Normal people.

Tess's hand shot backwards, an almost unconscious movement. Her fingers closed around a shard of glass from the shattered window. The edges dug into her fingers, but she didn't hesitate.

She flung it at the reptile, hoping to make it leave. She wanted it gone. She needed it to disappear.

The glass *should* have skittered across the floor, startling the snake into leaving the room.

Instead, there was a soft *thunk* and a furious hiss. Something dark and wet leaked onto the floor, glistening in the moonlight.

Tess froze, her chest heaving, her hands clenched into trembling fists. At last, the anger drained out of her.

Taking a slow breath, she moved to kneel by the snake's twitching body.

The shard Tess had thrown was embedded in the floor. Pinning the snake down under it.

She realized she couldn't hear it breathing anymore.

Silence.

"Shit..." she muttered, poking at the dead snake with a hesitant finger.

Then she winced, glancing down at her hand. Blood welled from a tiny, but deep wound on her finger where the glass had cut her.

She rolled her eyes, pressing her other hand to the cut.

Great, now I'll have to come up with an excuse for this too, she thought, biting her lip.

But she didn't *want* to make up an excuse. She wanted to talk to *someone*.

Suddenly, a loud *ding* came from her phone, interrupting the quiet and making her jump. It was probably just her mom, texting her, furious and worried.

Tess ignored it, knowing she would have to deal with her parents eventually. But not now. She stood, making her way back through the house, ready to explore the place. More as an excuse to avoid going home and admitting that she was acting absurd than actual curiosity.

The musty scent of mold and mildew was almost too much to bear. She lifted her shirt over her nose to cover the scent.

And she froze.

The blood on her finger was still there. But it was dried, and the cut had closed.

With skin. Not scabs.

Panicked, she licked her finger, then scrubbed the blood away, waiting for the sting of touching the open wound to hit her.

When it didn't, she flexed her fingers experimentally, even holding her hand up to the moonlight in confusion, hoping it would begin to bleed.

She inspected it carefully. Pale new skin covered the area. The wound appeared weeks old rather than minutes.

She groaned, mashing her thumbs into her eyes, then trudging to a corner and sliding to the ground.

"Okay, Tess,"

She forced herself to take a deep measured breath and calm down before she *really* lost it.

"Focus on the solution, not the problem."

She focused on her breathing. Focused on *not* freaking out. She could do this. She just needed to relax.

Was there *really* anything wrong?

The new speed, the strength, the healing. *That*, she could live with. Kinda cool. Like Peter Parker.

But she still wanted an explanation. The unknown was the issue here.

A loud crunch from the back of the house drew her attention. The sound of a foot stepping cautiously onto broken glass.

She hauled herself up and backed out of the house, not interested in dealing with a vagrant.

She took off at a sprint, and her home came into view much faster than she was hoping.

Her mom was sitting on the couch in the living room waiting for her, arms crossed and TV on mute.

Tess looked at her silently, then stalked through the room and closed her bedroom door. She sat on her bed, and again, tried to remind herself to be calm. It didn't work as well this time.

"What is happening to me?" she muttered.

She threw herself back on her bed and finally allowed herself to cry.

She didn't even know *why* exactly she was crying.

Crazy. She *had* to be going crazy.

She cried until her head began to pound. Cried until there were no tears left to cry out. Cried until she fell asleep.

Her dreams were full of eyes.

Logan's brown eyes, staring at her in concern. Shawn's icy gaze watching her from a distance. The invasive eyes she'd seen under the stranger's hood the night she left Chloe's.

The night everything changed.

CHAPTER 10

LOGAN

L ogan was really starting to hate today. He considered himself a pretty laid back and positive guy. As a general rule, he didn't let much get to him.

Typically.

His ex-girlfriend, Lauren, and her tantrum in the middle of the Mesquite Ridge mall were an exception.

His best friend, Dalton, had invited him to the mall with a group of friends this morning. Logan went, hoping Tess might be there.

She'd been on his mind a lot lately, and that made him nervous.

No. *Tess* made him nervous.

His stomach fluttered as he imagined the shy smiles she gave him when they passed in the hallways.

As long as he could remember, she'd always had that effect on him. It'd taken him over an hour to build up the confidence to ask for her number yesterday, and he'd *still* almost messed it up, just about to back out at the last second.

Unlike his ex, and most of the 'clones' in his school, Tess was so sweet. Funny and adorable and shy.

He wished he had the courage to ask her out.

Despite his hopes that Dalton might have invited her to the mall as well, his only connection with Tess was a warning from her best friend.

Chloe Hale. Overprotective, and slightly scary.

He glanced at the passenger seat of his old Bronco, where Chloe sat and stared morosely out the window. Weird how her mood had shifted like that. At the mall, she'd seemed full of fire. Almost angry.

She had pulled him away from the group, cornering him by the James Avery store.

"So, I'll be quick," Chloe had said, glancing at a display of silver charms. A piano, a paintbrush, even a pig.

He'd spotted one shaped like a heart, engraved with a winged track cleat.

I wonder if Tess would like that... he'd thought.

"Tess has been crazy stressed lately," she'd said, running her fingers over one of the charms. "I don't know why. She hasn't told me anything."

Suddenly, she whirled around, her golden eyes intense.

"She doesn't need you making her even more stressed."

He stared at her, confused. "I'm stressing her out?" he asked.

What had he done? Was it something he'd said?

Chloe's gaze softened, a tiny smile lifting her lips.

"No. She's actually ecstatic. You should text her today."

She said it so easily, like texting Tess should be simple for him.

"Alright," he'd said, his mind starting to analyze everything he could say to her.

"What I'm saying is, I don't want you to give her all these signals, put all this hope in her head, or any of that if you don't mean it. Tess is like my sister, and she deserves to be happy."

She smiled. "I don't know if you're just *that* oblivious, or if you ignored it on purpose, but Tess has been crazy about you since second grade. And she's *not* been too subtle about it." Her eyes narrowed. "So treat her right. If you start something with my best friend, you'd better see it through. Okay?"

He wasn't sure if he should be annoyed or amused. He wasn't used to being threatened. Either way, it was sweet. She obviously loved Tess. Then again, who wouldn't?

"Got it," he'd said softly, reaching around her to grab the heart charm.

Chloe had smiled when she'd seen it. Lauren, had not.

Dalton had immediately started heckling him when he saw Logan leaving a *jewelry* store. He'd snatched the bag from him, and the heart and bracelet had dumped out, on display for the entire group.

Lauren had taken one look at the charm and immediately started crying.

It turned into an ugly scene. His *'friends'* immediately dispersed, leaving him to deal with her hysterics.

He'd broken things off with Lauren Byrd *well* over a month ago. At first she was fine— sweet, hot, fun to hang out with... And then she had turned toxic.

Lauren made it clear that she didn't approve of his friends, thought it was weird that he spent so much time with his little sister, and thought his parents were old-fashioned. She hated track, his car, the music he listened to, and pretty much everything that made him happy.

To be honest, he couldn't even remember why he'd wanted to date her in the first place. When he broke things off with her, she had proven to be the kind of crazy ex that you hear about in horror stories.

"Who's that for?" she had demanded, gesturing to the bag.

Logan hadn't answered, instead, turning to leave. She moved quickly, blocking his path.

He rolled his eyes, crossing his arms as he had resigned himself to the confrontation.

She glared at him. "I saw you walking with that freak yesterday. Looking for a little rebound action, huh?"

Tess.

Logan clenched his jaw, but had remained silent. If he engaged in an argument with her, she'd flip out even more. The only way to deal with Lauren, was complete passivity.

When she'd screamed enough that she had drawn the attention of the mall security, she'd finally stormed off. Logan had exited quickly, hoping to avoid a second round. Chloe had been outside, and he'd decided to offer her a ride. He'd been eager to hear more about Tess, but she was clearly not in the mood to talk.

He glanced over again at Chloe. He thought she'd be on her phone.

Instead, she sat silently, jaw tight and biting her lip as she stared out the window. As her fists clenched and unclenched, her long acrylic nails left deep marks in her palms. Her shoulders were tense as she watched each house that passed, and her eyes were stretched wide.

She looked terrified.

How had he not noticed?

He tapped her shoulder. "What's wrong?"

Chloe flinched. "What? Oh! Nothing. I'm fine."

No you're not. You are absolutely not *fine.*

"Are you sure? You just seem—"

"I'm *fine*," she snapped. "What, are you my freaking therapist now?"

He winced at her tone, and went silent, giving her space. He didn't want to push her, but there was obviously something on her mind.

He signaled, turning into what he was sure was the entrance to her neighborhood. He noticed how nice and spread out most of the homes here were. One was absolutely massive, with a grandiose wrap-around porch and— was that a tennis court in the backyard?

Rich people, he thought, a little jealous.

Spoiled rich people.

As he drove, the houses gradually became more modest. Tennis courts and pools and elaborate mansions, replaced with slightly smaller cookie-cutter homes. As he passed a large, yet plain brownstone, he noticed her terrified gaze focus on the home, her shoulders tense and braced for impact. He slowed down, assuming she would let him know when to stop. Instead, she remained wordless, snapping her head to face forward as a woman walked out the front door.

The home disappeared behind them.

Chloe let out an involuntary sigh. Her shoulders relaxed and she leaned her head back on the headrest, closing her eyes.

That was her house. It had to be.

So why didn't she correct him?

"Chloe," he said, trying to keep his tone gentle and not accusatory. "You don't want to go home, do you?"

She stiffened, her eyes snapping open. The seat rustled as she sat straight up.

"Why would you say that?" she demanded, back on the defensive.

He took in a breath, avoiding her eyes and trying to choose his words carefully.

For a moment, the only sound was the rumble of his Bronco's engine.

"You didn't correct me when I missed your house," he muttered, finally breaking the quiet. "And you just look uneasy... I guess..."

Chloe glanced out the window, feigning surprise. "You missed my house? I didn't even see it. Sorry."

Logan bit his lip, making a decision as he saw a house with a For Sale sign. He pulled over abruptly, and parked his car in the driveway of the empty house.

She glared at him. "What are you doing?"

He stared at her, observing her more closely. Her denim jacket was loose, gaping at the back and exposing her low-necklined sweater.

And the bruises on the back of her neck. Her shoulders. More disappeared underneath her sweater.

It looked like someone had grabbed her by the neck like a cat. With enough force to bruise her. Like someone had held her down.

He reached out, moving her jacket to the side. She didn't stop him, sitting stiffly as he looked at each bruise.

Sickness turned his stomach as the pieces clicked together.

She finally winced and pulled away. She scrambled to fix her jacket, yanking it tightly around her. But it was too late. Logan had seen the marks, and he couldn't *unsee* them.

"Who did this to you?" he breathed.

Her mouth moved silently, but no words came out. Her eyes grew wet, filling with tears, then overflowing to run down her cheeks.

The silence felt heavy.

What was he supposed to say?

Someone was hurting her. Probably someone in her home. What was *he* supposed to do? He couldn't just leave her there! But at the same time, he didn't really have a choice.

"What can I do?" he whispered.

Chloe didn't answer. She just sat there, in silence, the tears leaving black trails as they streamed down her cheeks.

"Is there anyone else you can stay with?"

Finally, she shook her head, then buried her face in her hands. Her shoulders shook violently as she sobbed.

He reached out, softly touching her head.

"Chloe, let me help you."

He let her cry, hoping she would open up to him. Maybe he could take her to his parents. They'd know how to handle this.

Gradually, her tears subsided, until finally, silence overtook the Bronco again.

"Chloe?" he whispered.

She finally sat up, wiping her eyes carefully with her sleeve.

"Please just... take me back to the mall or something. I'm fine."

God, no you're not!

"Please let me help you."

She crossed her arms, glaring at him resolutely. "I said, I'm fine. I'd like to go to the mall."

He nodded mutely, turning back down the highway in defeat.

Minutes later, he turned into the mall. He idled in the parking lot, watching her, searching for the right words.

"Chloe... Does Tess know? Does *anyone* know?"

"No!" she hissed, her hands shaking as she snatched her purse out of the floorboards and slung it over her shoulder. "And you aren't going to say a word."

Logan frowned. "But— But you're— someone could help! Tess could help you. Or Coach James? He'd do something."

Chloe snorted, wiping her eyes. "Do what?" she asked. "What could they possibly do? I'll be fine. I don't need help. Just drop it."

When he didn't say anything, she turned away from him, starting to leave the car.

"Wait!"

She paused, glancing over her shoulder angrily.

"I can be here for you. You can come to me, you know? Like, if you need to talk, or whatever."

She sighed, moving slowly as she climbed out of the car. Their conversation seemed to have drained her.

"Logan."

The word came out patronizing, her tone making it clear that she wouldn't come to him. That she wouldn't take him up on his offer.

"Just promise me you won't say anything. Especially not to Tess."

No. I can't promise you that.

Her expression hardened when he didn't respond. "*Promise me*. I'm begging you."

So he did.

But moments later, after waiting for Chloe to walk into the mall, he sped off.

Looking for Tess. Fully intending to break his promise.

CHAPTER 11

TESS

Tess ran, turning onto the side street that led to the less attractive part of town. It didn't appear as rundown as it had last night— probably because it was the middle of the day and the sun was bright and high in the afternoon sky.

After yet another blow up with her mom that left Tess running out the back door, she needed somewhere to go. The empty house was as good a place as any.

Chloe was at the mall and had begged Tess to come, but she had bluntly refused. She had no interest in hanging out with girls who whispered snide comments about her behind her back.

Tears pricked her eyes, and she wrapped her arms around herself, walking faster.

Gravel crunched behind her and a loud rumbling filled the air. She leapt onto the sidewalk to avoid being hit. An old Bronco shuddered past her, slow enough that she knew the driver was looking at her. The window started to roll down, and in a panic, she bolted.

The rumors about the town's legendary murder were rooted in this neighborhood, and she wasn't about to be the next victim.

She sprinted, not turning around until she'd rounded the corner, out of sight. The old rental house loomed just a few yards ahead of her and she quickly ducked through the doorway, listening to the sound of the Bronco rumbling off.

Sliding down to the dusty floor, Tess hugged her knees to her chest, trying to quell her gasps as her rationality finally overrode her paranoia.

Her eyes followed the sunbeams streaming through the shattered window and the illuminated dust floating through them. She squinted, trying to focus on one particle. Trying to hear the dust as it fell.

Instead of hearing each piece scrape against each other, or seeing every particle individually, she saw...

Dust. Plain old dust floating through the air.

She felt strangely disappointed. She was terrified of a repeat of the heightened senses, but she also wanted to understand what was happening to her. To know if it was even real. Or if she was just going crazy.

But the only thing her senses picked up was the strong, acrid smell of dried blood from the dead snake.

A reminder that she had managed to impale a snake, from ten feet away, with perfect accuracy. Not to mention, her finger had *healed itself* after the glass cut her.

A reminder that she was a freak.

She covered her nose, trying to concentrate on taking in shallow breaths.

At least the condition of the house allowed her some privacy. No one was likely to bother her here.

She let out a wail, angry and confused, tears erupting from her eyes. Hot tears.

Burning hot tears that she could feel individually, sinking particle by particle into her pores.

She growled in frustration, wiping the back of her arm across her face as she stood.

Her shoes left prints in the dust as she made her way to one of the two bedrooms in the house.

A stained mattress lay in one corner of the room, next to a wicker chair with no cushion.

She needed to tell someone about what was happening to her. She needed help.

Chloe.

They'd been friends their entire lives. Chloe wouldn't think she was crazy. She'd probably laugh and tell her it was a side effect of her hormones, or that it was all in her head.

In fact, she'd probably be angry that Tess hadn't come to her earlier.

Maybe it *was* all in her head.

Before her resolve could break, she pulled out her phone, ready to call Chloe and beg her to come back early from the mall.

Her finger landed on the contact just as a rumbling approached the house.

The Bronco. Why was it circling back?

The engine shut off, and a door slammed shut.

"I swear she went this way…"

Her breathing was too loud, and her knees suddenly refused to stop shaking. She knew that voice.

No no no no!

The ancient front door reluctantly opened, and she heard a yelp.

He's in the house. He must have seen the snake. I have to get out of here before he sees me.

93

But the only way out was through the front door, and *he* was there!

"Tess? Are you in here?" Logan called, hesitant as he stepped into the empty house.

Her heart pounded urgently.

Why is he here?

She needed to get out, but her feet were stuck, immortalized on the spot. She could only wait helplessly as his steps grew closer, and then he stepped into the room.

He froze when he saw her. She realized how disheveled she must look. Ripped jeans, a white tank top with an embarrassing ketchup stain, messy hair, and bloodshot eyes.

"Tess?"

His voice was a soft question, but in the silence, it echoed loudly through the room.

She flinched, her cheeks burning and her eyes threatening another round of tears.

Of *all* the people to see her like this.

"Why are you here?" she blurted rudely.

Stupid, stupid, stupid!

She clamped her mouth shut to stop herself from talking.

Logan's soft gaze slid across her face, taking in her damp eyes and trembling lip.

"I was driving Chloe home from the mall and I saw you walking," he muttered, "I wanted to—" he shook his head, dismissing his words.

"Nevermind," he said. "Are you okay?"

He moved over to her, reaching hesitantly for her arm.

"Chloe said you've been stressed out."

"Chronic migraines!" she said loudly, forcing a smile. "From my mom's side."

He raised an eyebrow, skeptical.

"Are you sure? I mean..." He counted off on his fingers.

"You've obviously been crying, you look exhausted, and *why* are you *here?*"

Logan glanced around, his eyes taking notice of the decrepit state of the room.

"Whatever is wrong, just let me help."

No, you can't. Just go!

She wanted to tell him to leave. That she was fine and didn't *need* help.

And that she was still *normal*!

But she couldn't make herself form the words.

The weight of her worry was too much to bear, pressing down on her until she felt like she couldn't breathe.

And here he was, ready to listen.

More tears welled in her eyes, heating her cheeks and blurring her vision.

"Tess?" Logan asked again, worried now.

She tried to breathe past the lump in her throat.

"If I tell you, you won't believe me," she whispered, willing the tears back.

Maybe he was the kind of guy that couldn't deal with crying. Then he'd make an excuse and leave before she could further embarrass herself.

He didn't leave.

He came forward, wrapping his arms around her in a tight hug.

She stiffened, then relaxed as she breathed in his scent. She buried her face in his shoulder, shuddering.

"I feel like I'm losing my mind," she whispered. "All these weird things have been happening lately and I really, *really* need someone to talk to."

He pulled away, gently lifting her face and resting his hands on her shoulders.

"What do you mean?"

Tess took in a breath, trying to piece together her thoughts.

"I went to Chloe's a couple weeks ago and— and I got this horrible headache and it just wouldn't go away. And my heart feels like it's beating all wrong. And I feel so angry all the time. For no reason. Then I knocked all that time off my races, and everyone is giving me this weird look! And I—"

Logan's hands tightened on her shoulders, his firm voice cutting her off. "*Tess*."

She froze, breathless from her rant. She breathed deep, trying to relax.

"I'm sorry, Logan— I just—"

"Don't be sorry," he said, tipping his head. "Just don't pass out."

He smiled, and the effect was contagious. She giggled, despite the tears rolling down her face.

"I *do* feel lightheaded," she laughed, wiping the tears away.

Relief swept through her, like a tidal wave washing away some of the weight. Logan winked, his chocolate eyes full of understanding. He held out a hand.

"Would you like to get out of this place?" he asked, then jerked a thumb over his shoulder. "Maybe go get something to eat?"

His words were hesitant, and his eyes flicked around the room to her face and back to the front door.

He was nervous. About her little tantrum or something else, she wasn't sure.

"Um...I'm a little hungry," she said, smiling.

"So you got a headache, and suddenly... what? You see things in slow motion and break a world record overnight?"

Tess frowned. "When you put it that way, I guess it doesn't sound like a huge deal."

They sat at a table in Hazel's Bakery, a tiny shop near the old rental house. Behind the counter, the owner of the store, Hazel Dawson, dropped four sopapillas into a basket.

She dropped the honey-sugar treats on their table, collecting the empty basket.

Logan plucked another sopapilla from the new basket, thanking Hazel as she left.

Tess nibbled on the corner of a square, even though she didn't like honey. As they ate, she explained everything, with Logan stopping her occasionally to clarify a point.

She told him about the things she felt and saw and smelled, going into detail about the broken jar and the explosion of sound that followed. She spoke about the beating in her chest. She explained how some people had started giving her odd looks, like Shawn, the girl at the track meet, and several people she'd passed on the street. Against her better judgement, she even told him about the snake and how her finger had seemed to heal.

He struggled to find an appropriate response. "I don't— That's—" Logan made a wild gesture as he searched for the word.

"Crazy?" she offered, anticipating the worst.

He was going to leave. He'd never talk to her again. He probably thought she was a freak, and a *lunatic*.

"Definitely," he said, massaging his temples. "But no. It's just... unreal. And weird."

"I *know*!" she sighed unhappily. "But I don't know why it's happening. I'm just confused."

He looked skeptical, leaning forward on his elbows with narrowed eyes.

He doesn't believe me.

She tried to ignore the hurt settling in her stomach. Really, she couldn't blame him.

"Have you told anyone? Do your parents know?"

Tess shook her head. "Before you came, I was planning to call Chloe."

His shoulders stiffened and he looked away, biting his lip.

Tess's stomach twisted.

Chloe? Did he dislike Chloe?

Or worse, did he *like* her?

"What? What's wrong?" she asked him, She wasn't sure if she wanted to know the answer.

He cleared his throat, glancing up to meet her eye.

"It's nothing," he smiled, waving away the question. "So, moment of decision. What are you going to do?"

Tess forced a grin, trying to lighten the mood. "I guess I could go to the Olympics," she teased.

Logan grinned back. "Yeah?"

"Mhm."

They laughed, and Logan seemed to relax, his smile less forced, more genuine, as Hazel came over to offer them refills.

"I'm just glad you don't care that I'm losing my mind," she shrugged, only half joking.

His smile vanished and he looked away, his cheeks turning red.

"You aren't losing your mind," he said, shaking his head.

Tess rolled her eyes. "You're just saying that. I know you don't believe me. *I* wouldn't believe me."

She tried her best not to sound accusatory, but she couldn't keep the hurt out of her voice. His gaze softened.

"You're *not* crazy, Tess," he insisted. "There has to be an explanation. I mean... there's like seven billion people on the planet. You can't be the first one to experience this, right?"

She crossed her arms, as she considered his words. Maybe he was right. But she doubted it.

"I think you're even more delusional than I am," Tess replied, shaking her head at Logan.

He laughed, eyes sparkling. "Maybe."

As he spoke, he glanced down, looking at something in his lap. The corner of his lip twitched into a smile. Tess raised an eyebrow, peering around the table to see what he was looking at.

"So..." he said, shifting his gaze back to hers. "This has been... nice," he finished lamely. He looked down again, and his face flushed bright red.

She leaned forward, more curious than ever. At least he was smiling. Kind of.

Should I say something? Should I ask if he wants to hang out again? Why am I overthinking this?

She suddenly felt shy, which was ridiculous after everything she'd just shared with him.

Logan cleared his throat again, then lifted a bag from his lap. He sat it on the table.

She heard the distinct sound of metal as he rearranged the bag awkwardly on the table. She could smell it too. The scent reminded her of her dad's change jar.

"I didn't get to wrap it," he mumbled, pushing it towards her.

Her tongue stuck to the roof of her mouth as she wordlessly took the bag and poured the contents into her palm.

Her eyes widened as she saw the expensive silver bracelet glittering in her hand. The heart-shaped charm shone, engraved with a track cleat.

"It's beautiful," she murmured. "Thank you."

The words didn't feel right, but she couldn't summon anything else to say.

"It's not much," Logan said, rubbing the back of his neck.

" I hope you don't think it's weird for me to get you jewelry, but I just wanted to say congratulations about your race yesterday." He laughed. "I'm guessing this is just one more 'weird' thing for you to deal with."

He made air quotes with his fingers around the word 'weird'.

She grinned, fastening the bracelet on her wrist, and holding it up to sparkle in the light.

"So you don't think I'm crazy?" she prompted.

He shook his head, in mock seriousness. "Oh, you're *definitely* crazy."

He reached out, squeezing her hand. "We'll figure it out, okay Tess?"

Her stomach fluttered at the word 'we', and a ridiculous grin stretched across her mouth.

"Yeah. We'll figure it out."

CHAPTER 12

Shawn

Tess James.

She was supposed to be a Basic. With two Basic parents. Living one of the most Basic high school lives he'd ever seen.

He had to talk to her. He had waited all weekend for this moment. The chance to figure out how it was possible that she had a Trace.

You're making a mistake.

Don't do it.

You're going to humiliate yourself.

Several Traces pounded in his chest. There were three other detectable Traces in the lower grades. And now, there was hers. He wasn't sure *why* he couldn't feel her Trace all the time. He had never heard of anything like it.

But now, even from twenty feet across the hall, he could pick out her unique beat.

The Trace was a fascinating part of being a Munera

adolescent. Learning how to differentiate between Traces. How to detect the number of Abnormals in a room. It was like a game.

Shawn still recalled the wonder he'd felt when his Genesis had activated at four years old. Most Munera activated at eighteen. While it wasn't uncommon to activate a few years early, it was *unheard* of to activate prior to puberty.

His parents had been elated. He was the youngest Munera in history to go through Genesis. His mom has taken him for ice cream. Just the two of them.

He blinked, forcing the memory of his mother's proud smile to disappear. Instead, he stared at Tess, memorizing the rhythm of her Trace.

She was happy today. A constant smile lifting her lips, and reaching to brighten her eyes.

She seemed oblivious to his Trace, which also should have been impossible.

Munera with a newly activated Genesis typically felt Traces stronger than those like Shawn, who'd been active for years.

He watched her fumble with the combination on her locker.

He had to know if she was at *all* aware of what she was. And how it was possible that he *hadn't* been aware of her until now. That *no one* was aware of her.

Today, she wore her red letterman and tight-fitting jeans with fringe in the knees. It was hard to focus on his objective without getting distracted by the way her hair fell over her shoulder. The crimson in her jacket bringing out the coppery flecks in her eyes.

He blushed, hoping she hadn't seen him staring. Again.

Get a hold of yourself.

She finally undid the lock, opening the locker door. He moved, pushing through the people streaming towards their classes. Only when he was a few feet away did he realize he had no idea what he was going to say.

I can feel the beat of your chest. Can you feel mine?

He'd sound like a psychopath.

Forget it.

He was about to turn around and leave, but before he could, she closed the locker and spotted him waiting.

Staring at her like a freak.

"Uhh... I was... I'm..."

Tess stared at him, hugging her trig textbook against her chest. Her eyes were even more beautiful up close. And she had freckles!

Which showed plainly now that all the color was quickly draining from her face.

She shifted uncomfortably.

"Hi...?" she asked hesitantly.

Shawn swallowed, then spit out the first thing he thought of.

"I'm glad your headache is gone. "

Her eyes widened, and he had the sudden urge to throw himself in front of a bus.

"I mean," he amended quickly, "you've— Last week, you— you looked like you had a headache or something."

Tess still hesitated, biting her lip.

"Yeah," she said softly. "It's gone, thank God. What a nightmare."

A smile broke out across her face, and slowly, as his embarrassment faded with her smile, he managed a shaky grin of his own.

"Can I... Can I ask you something that might sound a little... *weird?*"

She immediately stiffened. Her hazel eyes darted around, as though just realizing she was talking publicly with the school outcast.

His heart fell, disappointed. He'd thought she was better than that. Less shallow than the rest of the senior class.

"Depends on your definition of 'weird'," she answered cautiously.

He winced, trying his best to hide his nervousness.

Just do it.

"How'd you run like that at the meet last week?" he asked. "I heard people talking about your time, and it just didn't seem possible."

She shifted from foot to foot. "I don't know what you mean," she whispered.

She's lying.

"Okay, yeah, that's a hard question, I guess. I mean, how do you know how you suddenly run like the wind," he joked, forcing out an awkward chuckle. "It's just... You haven't noticed anything... off? Or felt anything different?"

She frowned, her gaze unfriendly. "No."

Her tone had changed. She felt threatened.

Shawn paused, balling his hands in his pockets, debating the ethics of the decision he was about to make.

He met her gaze, then slid into her mind, searching out her fears.

Her chest hurt. It confused her.

A jar, falling off a kitchen counter. In slow motion. Shattering with an ear-splitting crash, and a scream. Her scream.

Forensics class. The day he'd first felt her Trace. She'd felt his eyes on her. He saw himself, watching her intensely.

A pang of remorse hit him as he realized that she was frightened of *him*.

With good reason.

A snake lay on the floor, a shard of glass impaling it. He saw a flash of blood dripping from her fingers where the glass had cut her, and then, the wound was closed, replaced with new skin.

It was daytime. Someone came to her.

Irrational anger pushed into his thoughts, constricting his breath, when he realized who it was. Logan Tucker.

He pulled her into a tight embrace, and she murmured into his shoulder.

"I feel like I'm losing my mind."

Shawn blinked, forcing away the images.

He understood. Tess thought she was some random freak of nature, but she was *so* much more. He blinked again, staring into her eyes.

Eyes filled with fear. Looking through her thoughts had caused her to relive them, forcing an onslaught of worry.

"I'm fine," she muttered. "Thank you for checking on me, but I have to go."

God, you're a moron!

He'd crossed a line. He'd sworn to never use his abilities on someone he cared about.

But I've never cared about anyone until her. Except...

"Wait, Tess!" he tried as she hurried passed him. "Please, I'm sorry. I can—"

She didn't stop, but she glanced over her shoulder.

"I'm fine," she repeated, before she disappeared around the corner.

He sighed, staring around the empty hallway. No point going to class now.

He pushed away from the lockers, heading for the main doors to slip out of the building.

The electricity from the security cameras buzzed through his veins like an insect, and he waved an irritated hand, absently disabling them. The last thing he needed was to get stopped by the vice principal.

He crossed the street to a convenience store, frequented by the high school crowd during lunch and after school, but largely vacant during the rest of the day.

He slid around the back of the building, and sat, thumping his head against the wall.

He couldn't believe he'd done that to Tess.

And for what purpose? She was probably more confused now than ever. And so was he.

As he'd picked through her fears, he'd detected more than two abilities. No Munera in the *world* had more than two—one from each parent's side.

Yet Tess displayed speed, strength, and enhanced senses. And healing. An *extremely* rare gift.

He had so many questions.

She was clearly an undocumented Abnormal, which could land her in life-threatening trouble if she was discovered.

He was fascinated by the secrets Tess James held. And he was terrified.

If anyone found out... if his *parents* found out....

The last time he hid a secret from his parents, he'd been punished.

A shiver ran across his skin, and he fisted his hands tightly to stop the trembling.

His skin prickled with the phantom pain of a thousand scars.

Scars inflicted by his uncle as his parents had stood by. Watching. They'd abandoned him.

It won't happen again.

It won't happen again.

Grinding his teeth, Shawn buried his face in his hands.

Lies.

He only saw two options.

He could tell his parents about Tess. Since she genuinely had no idea what she was, it was unlikely they would have her killed.

More likely, they'd *'educate'* her. Teach her about the *goodness* of the Society, and the weakness of the Lusus Naturae.

And if he revealed an undocumented Abnormal, he wouldn't be punished. In fact, he might even be rewarded. Particularly with the gifts Tess seemed to possess.

Or he could approach her privately. He could reveal himself to her. Reveal what she was.

He could help her. Together, they could figure out why Tess seemed to have more than two abilities and where she'd come from, *without* any help from the experts.

But he'd be risking his life. He was out of second chances.

Could I live with myself if I turned her in?

He imagined his parents talking to her. Educating her. Indoctrinating her.

Whispering Society's lies until they were too ingrained in her head for him to save her. She'd believe them.

She'd become his enemy.

Then I can't *let that happen.*

His phone vibrated, startling him.

"Yes?" he sighed wearily, massaging his temples.

"Home. Now."

His mother hung up.

Shawn blew a strand of hair out of his face.

"Yes, master," he muttered sarcastically, standing and quickly moving across the street. "Love you, too."

The bell rang, and people began streaming out of the building as Shawn crossed into the parking lot.

Hunter stopped him before he could slip into his car.

"Hey, asshole, help me out," he said, glancing around.

"Yeah, not happening," Shawn retorted.

Hunter groaned. "Dude, Isen screwed me over on a dimebag. I don't have enough to cover it."

Shawn glared at him. "I'm not giving you drug money. You should know better than to buy from Isen anyway."

Hunter grinned, unwilling to give up. "Dude, come on. I'll owe you. Just this once. Whatever you want!"

Shawn rolled his eyes, ready to get into his car and leave Hunter to beg someone else for money.

Then he paused. "Anything I want?"

Hunter's gaze turned suspicious. "Yeah, why? What do you need?"

"A favor," Shawn replied. "The next time I need one. No questions asked."

"Done!"

Hunter grinned, holding out a hand. Shawn sighed, slipping a small wad of cash into his friend's palm.

Hunter laughed, turning away to find Isen, but Shawn gripped his wrist tightly, stopping him.

"*No* questions asked."

"Yeah, yeah. I got it." Hunter jerked his arm from Shawn's grip and backed away.

Shawn sped out of the parking lot, trying to interpret his mother's call.

She'd sounded urgent. What did it mean?

He parked in the driveway, taking a breath and counting Traces before he even got out.

One for his mother, one for his father.

And a third.

The hair on his neck rose, his skin prickling.

He could picture the dark-haired man lounging at his dining room table, conspiring with his parents. Waiting on him.

No.

No, please... For the love of God, not today.

Not after what he'd just discovered about Tess. Not after he'd allowed himself to consider hiding her. To consider betraying his family.

Thoughts of betrayal were dangerous. In the Society, *all* thoughts could be dangerous if twisted the wrong way.

They might kill Tess, considering her a rogue Abnormal. Undocumented, uneducated, and unpredictable.

Or worse, they wouldn't kill her. They would use her.

Taking a breath, Shawn moved his hair out of his face and kept his eyes forward.

He couldn't stay out here all night. If Shawn could feel the Salvator's Trace, then he could feel Shawn's.

That realization gave him a sense of finality.

He forced himself to breathe slowly and empty his mind.

If he appeared too confident, it would come off as defiance. On the other hand, if he was too submissive, he'd look suspicious. And weak. He couldn't show weakness.

The Society did *not* tolerate weakness.

There was nothing else he could do. He had to face the man in his home.

He turned the handle and stepped through the door.

And Koden Mason looked up, meeting his nephew's gaze.

CHAPTER 13

KODEN

The chair squeaked as Koden Mason leaned back, staring at the boy waiting in front of him. This was the child he'd once loved as his own, who he had believed for years would be his successor. His own blood.

A *disgrace*. A *Proditor*.

His nephew stared back at him, his stormy blue eyes flashing with barely-veiled emotion. The boy hated him, and with good reason. One of the scars Koden had given him peeked out from Shawn's collar.

The sight of it made him smile.

"Shawn," he said, spreading his arms as he stood. "It's been ages since I last saw you. How long has it been? A year?"

His nephew flinched, clenching his jaw momentarily before he spoke.

"Three years, Salvator," he corrected politely, bowing slightly at the waist.

Konrad and Alyssa seemed to sag in their seats, in relief

or annoyance, he wasn't really sure. The child was mocking him. *Always* mocking him. With his promising abilities, his intelligence, and his *beliefs*.

"Please, there's no reason to be so formal," Koden offered, masking his irritation.

Shawn nodded in deference. "Of course, sir."

Konrad spoke up from his seat. "Shawn, sit down. We have something to discuss."

Koden stifled an annoyed groan.

His brother.

Such a disappointment.

It was disheartening to think that should something happen to him, Konrad would inherit the position of Salvator.

He loved his brother. How could he not? He was family. But he was weak. Koden's lip curled in disgust.

He'd almost rather his disgraced nephew lead the Society than Konrad.

He let the thought linger for a moment. Shawn was no doubt stronger than Konrad, almost the equal of the Salvator himself. But where Konrad lacked the backbone and power to rule, Shawn lacked the correct mindset. He didn't support many of the Society's beliefs. More importantly, he didn't support the topic at hand.

The Lusus Naturae experiments.

Perhaps one day, his nephew could be made to see reason. And if so, arrangements could be made to ensure Shawn would be his successor. Konrad *had* always been accident prone.

But if not....

He sighed, running his hands through his dark hair.

The Lusus Naturae experiments.

He had flown down specifically to check on the research labs in this state, in the vain hope that they had made progress.

Almost two decades ago, Koden had ordered the detention of all hybrid children in the Americas— the mutts with their ruined DNA. It was common knowledge that interbreeding Munera with the powerless Lusus Naturae destroyed the Genesis, leaving the offspring powerless. But it was vastly unknown that the gift was still *there* in these children. Like a broken limb. Useless, but it still *existed* in the child's DNA. Koden himself had been unaware of the phenomenon.

Until recently.

He had dedicated his life to discovering a cure. Spending his youth studying the genetics of both Munera and the Lusus Naturae, and later, providing researchers with the funds, facilities, and subjects to continue the trials. He'd even gone as far to induce selective breeding, creating stronger and stronger Munera with each generation, until he felt almost certain they'd be able to withstand the filthy Basic genes. But the breeding took time. And he didn't *have* time. His people were dying.

He was *sure* there had to be a suppressor gene that would repress the Lusus Naturae DNA.

And after almost twenty years of waiting, they might have found a breakthrough.

"Alyssa," he began, blatantly ignoring Konrad, addressing his sister-in-law instead. Despite her lower rank, she was much more capable than her husband.

Incidentally, she had all the characteristics needed to fulfill the role of Domina— the wife of the Salvator.

Ruthless. Powerful. Intelligent.

She licked her full lips, breathlessly anticipating his announcement.

Attractive.

Unfortunately, Konrad had met her first. And married her

at 17 before Koden had made a decision how he wanted to proceed.

Divorce was not tolerated among the Munera elite.

He reached out, squeezing her hand gently, then trailing a finger up her arm.

It had been too long.

He glanced towards his brother. Konrad grimaced, but looked down quickly, unwilling to meet his eye.

Koden smiled in cruel satisfaction, removing his hand.

"The researchers at the facility have made a discovery. Likely the most revolutionary discovery of the *century*."

His sister-in-law's blue eyes glowed. "They've done it?"

The hope in her melodious voice was so strong that he was loath to disappoint her.

Alyssa shared his beliefs. She always had. He studied her angelic face, testing the atmosphere for traces of her gift.

"Not yet," he said, tapping a finger on the polished mahogany table. "But they believe they have a lead. And so convinced are they in their theory, they are willing to test my patience by requesting my presence here."

He could only hope their fear of his disappointment would push them to a swift solution.

"What lead?" Konrad asked eagerly, leaning forward.

"It's so unsettling. I can hardly believe it myself," Koden muttered, splaying his palms on the table, "but they believe the answer lies with the Caines."

Across the table, Shawn made a choking sound.

"Do you have something to contribute to the conversation, Shawn?" Alyssa asked sharply, her fierce gaze settling on her son.

He shook his head, eyes wide in fear as he quickly broke eye contact with his uncle.

"No ma'am."

He admired her swift response to the boy's impertinence.

A fond memory rose to the front of Koden's mind as he observed the fear in his nephew. The day he'd finally put Shawn in his place, after discovering the damage he'd inflicted on several Society families throughout the city.

The fires he'd started. The graffiti tags.

The official he'd almost killed.

Of course, those crimes could have been forgiven and brushed aside as common teenage mischief, if not for the betrayal at the root of them. The fact that his nephew, the *future* of the Society, had desired to go rogue. Attempted to join the blood traitors.

Thankfully, Alyssa had discovered his treachery before further damage had been done to the family's honor.

And when Konrad had failed to appropriately remedy the situation, Koden had taken the liberty of teaching Shawn the flaws in his beliefs.

"No, nothing," Shawn answered quietly. "I didn't mean to interrupt."

Alyssa glared at her son for a moment longer, then turned back to Koden. "My apologies, Salvator. You were saying?"

Koden grimaced. "I hate to admit such a despicable lot of people could be essential to our cause. However, the Caines *are* the oldest, most powerful Munera family in Tribus Viribus. Maybe in *existence*.

Unfortunately, they are... estranged at the moment."

Shawn smirked, gazing quickly down at the table in an effort to appear neutral.

"In any case, has any of this been proven? Tested?" Konrad demanded, his tone annoyed and petulant.

Alyssa sighed, narrowing her eyes at her husband in irritation.

"Not yet," Koden responded, managing to smile through gritted teeth at his brother. "But we finally have a clear direction. We just need to discover where the *Proditors* are hiding."

Again, Koden noticed Shawn's features shift. He was growing weary of the boy's underhanded disrespect.

"Well," he began, clasping his hands on the table and meeting Alyssa's strong blue gaze. "That is my news. But I do recall you asked me to stop by for another reason entirely."

Both Konrad and Alyssa glanced at their son. He looked up at them, confused. Then, understanding dawned on his face, and he clenched his fists.

"Shawn has been demonstrating... unorthodox behavior lately," Alyssa started, making no effort to mask her satisfaction at the horror in Shawn's eyes.

"Unbelievable," he muttered, his fury overriding his fear.

Alyssa continued to speak. "I think he would do well with a simple reminder that *orders* are not requests. And they are to be obeyed without question."

Koden nodded solemnly, maintaining a professional composure. "Anything for the good of my family."

He gestured towards the front door, indicating a dismissal. Konrad stood immediately, avoiding Shawn's gaze. Alyssa stood more slowly, her eyes lingering on Koden. He smiled, acknowledging her admiration, then nodded towards the exit. The door shut with a final click behind Alyssa and Konrad, leaving Koden alone with his nephew.

He expected Shawn to beg. To insist he had nothing to hide, as he had done three years ago.

Instead, the boy rose from his seat, moving around the table to stand in front of Koden. He dropped to one knee.

"'Anything for the good of my family'," he announced, his blue eyes mocking. Full of venom.

Disrespectful.

His hatred was fully unmasked.

As was his terror.

Koden stared at Shawn, searching for obvious signs of deception.

Silence fell over the room as he waited, watching.

Finally, Koden slammed himself roughly into Shawn's thoughts. His ability, *Amino*, could have been used without causing the boy pain.

Koden could have easily searched Shawn's current thoughts, for quite an extended time, in fact, and his nephew wouldn't have ever known.

But what fun would that be?

The images he saw were different. Unnatural. These were forced, concealing his true thoughts. Still, he focused on them, interested to learn what the boy was hiding.

Koden saw himself.

Running a hand up Alyssa's arm. Smiling as she spoke. Watching her sway as she made her way out the door. His groin tightened as he watched her leave.

Fury tore through him, and he ripped himself out of his nephew's mind. Shawn appeared to be in pain. He was clutching his head in his hands, his back shuddering.

No. The boy is laughing.

"What?" Shawn croaked, looking up through a pained expression. "It's not like you need his permission to have her."

The back of Koden's hand cracked against Shawn's cheek, rocking him sideways.

"You will *not* address me with such disrespect!"

Shawn gasped from the blow, his pale skin red from the strike.

"You realize," Koden hissed, leaning down to meet his nephew's burning gaze, "that you've given yourself away. I know you're hiding something from me."

Shawn didn't answer, trying to push himself back to his knees.

"And you *will* tell me what it is."

As the boy settled back on his knees, he raised a hand, wiping blood from his lips.

"Of course, Salvator," he wheezed.

This time, when Koden dove into his nephew's thoughts, the entrance wasn't gentle. Even through the haze *Amino* created, he could hear his nephew crying in agony.

Flickering images flashed in front of him.

Alyssa. Her wide mouth curved in a wicked smile.

And then a girl. A girl he'd never seen before. Shy smile. Dark hair.

Then she vanished, replaced with Alyssa's alluring voice, breathless as she spoke to him.

He tried to focus, ignoring Shawn's screams and the seductive image of his sister-in-law, but the girl was impossible to make out.

In frustration, he released Shawn.

The boy had collapsed, curled on his side, his hands pressed tightly to his temples to ease his suffering. Tears ran down his face, dripping into the plush, white carpet.

The girl was important to him.

Koden knelt next to him, a smirk on his face. "What's her name?" he murmured, voice soft and dripping with contempt.

Shawn stayed quiet, his shaking breath and quiet sobs his only response. Koden reached out, gripping his nephew's chin and forcing him to meet his eye. The boy was in pain, but his eyes blazed with a determined blue fire.

"What's her name, Shawn?"

His eyes sparked defiantly.

"She's... nothing... A Lusus Naturae," he managed through labored breaths.

Intrigue grew in Koden by the feeling he perceived in the way Shawn spoke about her. Reverently. Protective.

So the little boy thinks he's a man...

He narrowed his eyes at Shawn, tightening his grip on his nephew's chin.

"I will have Alyssa keep an eye on this," he warned.

Shawn groaned, still struggling as he gasped for air.

The boy was done. His mind had nothing left to offer tonight.

He allowed himself a moment to entertain an image of his sister-in-law. Her parting smile as she left the room.

An invitation.

He smiled down at his nephew.

"I believe your mother and I have business to discuss tonight. See that we aren't disturbed."

CHAPTER 14

TESS

Tess sighed, burying a hand in her hair and trying in vain to focus on her trig test.

A difficult task when her mind kept drifting to Shawn Mason. She wanted to believe he didn't know anything. That he was just being "Stalker Shawn" and had no idea what she'd been experiencing.

But he clearly knew *something* weird was happening to her.

And if he knew something was happening, did he know *why*?

She frowned, dismissing the thought.

Shawn was virtually a stranger. He knew *nothing* about her. He couldn't just magically know about her problem if she'd never told him.

A buzz from her lap made her jump, and she glanced to the front of the room quickly. Thankfully, Mr. Perry was half asleep, his hand resting on the enormous pile of homework he was supposed to be grading.

She smiled down at her phone, heat rising to her cheeks as images of Logan eliminated all thoughts of Shawn Mason.

Chloe, sitting in the desk next to her, raised a questioning eyebrow.

Logan! Tess mouthed.

Chloe frowned momentarily, before catching Tess's gaze on her. She smiled, flashing Tess a thumbs up.

"What?" Tess whispered, narrowing her eyes, remembering Logan's expression at the bakery when she'd mentioned Chloe.

Had something happened between them?

Her friend waved her hand dismissively, pointing to the test, and rolling her eyes.

Tess stared, trying to read Chloe's body language, then opened her phone to read the message.

Would you like to go to a movie later?

Oh my God!

She tapped Chloe, showing her the text, and her friend grinned widely, nodding frantically.

She had no idea what she wrote down on her test, but when the bell rang, she handed it in to her teacher and rushed into the hall.

"Do you have a problem with Logan?" she asked Chloe when they met up at the door.

Chloe smirked. "Yeah. He's a Democrat."

She rolled her eyes, then playfully punched Tess in the arm. "Don't be a moron, Tess. There's nothing wrong."

Tess sighed. "Okay. Call me later?"

Her friend gave her a thumbs up, disappearing into her next class.

After forensics, Logan walked with her outside, glancing down at her wrist where her charm sparkled in the sunlight. He grinned.

"You're wearing the bracelet!" he exclaimed.

Tess laughed, playfully bumping into his shoulder. "Duh."

When did I get so comfortable with him?

As they walked to his car, she found herself staring at his eyes.

Dark brown with emerald green flecks in the irises. Tiny spots of gold and copper floated through the kaleidoscope of color around his pupil. Everything in perfect detail like a close up picture.

She gasped, looking away quickly.

Logan's grin wavered. "What is it?"

She shook her head, blinking. "Nothing," she said, returning his smile. "What movie are you taking me to see?"

T hree days later, they stood at opposite ends of an air hockey table, knocking the puck back and forth.

Logan hadn't kissed her at the movies. He hadn't even held her hand. A fact Tess was *sure* meant she had fallen into the friend zone, though Chloe insisted she was being ridiculous.

"You may have beaten me at bowling, Tess," Logan boasted, struggling to return the puck each time she hit it. "But air hockey is *my* game!"

Tess glanced at the scoreboard: 7-6. Logan had the lead.

Grinning, she hit the puck back as hard as she could. There was a resounding *crack,* as the little plastic puck bounced against the walls at incredible speed before slamming into the goal.

"You were saying?" she taunted, smiling.

She flexed her hand, reminding herself to relax. Lately, she had a habit of crushing things when she got excited. She restrained herself, making a conscious effort to hold the paddle lightly. It was getting easier every day.

"That's not fair!" Logan pouted, taking the puck from the

hole, and tossing it back on the table. "Using your 'super-human strength' is cheating."

He winked when he said it, and she wondered what it would take to make him believe her.

He hit the puck her way and she returned it, leaning over the table in concentration.

"Don't cry. *You* know you love me!" she sang.

At her words, he hesitated, cheeks turning red.

Oh no.

Her face was on fire.

Did I really just say that?

She looked away, hitting the puck in an effort to hide her embarrassment. The white disc slid into his goal, making the game buzz, but Logan didn't seem to notice. He blushed, smiling at her shyly for what seemed to last an eternity.

At the back of the arcade, a bowler screamed out, "A damn gutter ball *again*! I quit!"

They both laughed, grateful for the interruption. She cocked her head, pursing her lips as she observed him.

"Now, *who's* game did you say this was?"

C hloe screamed.

Heads in the cafeteria turned in their direction at her raised voice.

"He wants to ask you to prom! I know he does!" Chloe squealed.

She had obviously gotten over whatever issue she had with Logan, though Tess didn't like that she hadn't disclosed what that issue was.

Chloe was *obsessed* with prom, convinced it was the most important event in a girl's life. She hadn't shut up about it since the committee had announced the date— one month from today.

"We need to go dress shopping soon. Not here, obviously. There's no cute shops here. Well, maybe at Mesquite Ridge. And we'll have to get your nails done and, oh my God, Tess! This is going to be great!"

Tess's mouth twisted. "I always trip in dresses."

"We'll find you a short one," her friend declared, winking.

"I can't wear high heels either," Tess protested. "And I look weird in makeup. And I don't even have a *date*!"

Chloe glanced over her shoulder, studying the group of boys at the table behind them. "You will," Chloe assured her. "You are *perfect* Tess. It's obvious Logan sees that, too." Then she smiled slightly. "Okay, so when he *does* ask you, you have to be prepared. I think you look good in red, so that's probably what color dress you'll need to buy. And then we—"

"Tess?"

Both girls jumped, turning around quickly to stare.

Shawn Mason. Standing awkwardly behind them, his hands fidgeting with the drawstring of his hoodie.

Tess froze. She hadn't spoken to him since their first, and last, conversation by her locker. Instantly, the fear she'd been repressing resurfaced. She didn't understand why, but he made her nervous.

She smiled, attempting to hide how uncomfortable she felt.

"Hey Shawn. What's up?"

His gaze flicked between the girls, then back down at his hands.

His eyes were stormy and dark, and there were black circles under them. On his cheek was a bruise.

"Can we talk? In private?" he added.

Chloe rolled her eyes, but moved to stand up. Tess reached out, touching her friend lightly on the arm. Stopping her.

"I really don't—"

"It's kind of important," he insisted, his voice low.

He sounded scared.

Reluctantly, she let go of Chloe's arm, motioning for Shawn to sit.

He stared at the spot next to her, hesitating.

Then suddenly, Logan was there. He hovered behind Shawn, staring at him with a menacing expression.

"Hey Shane. Do we have a problem here?"

"*Shawn*. Not Shane. And no. No problem," he quickly sat, returning Logan's scathing glare. "I'm just talking to my friend Tess here. Didn't realize I needed your permission."

Tess gaped at him, surprised by his description of their relationship.

Shawn turned towards her, ignoring Logan and examining her face. "You need help, Tess. Let me help you."

Logan's eyes widened at what Shawn was implying, and a hurt expression settled on his face.

Chloe saved her from having to respond.

"Here's an idea. Leave. *Both* of you. If Tess wants to talk to you, she'll find you—" She paused, raising an eyebrow, "*later*. Got it?"

The air felt thick as Shawn's eyes continued to search hers, his gaze imploring.

Then he stood, abruptly tossing his black hair out of his eyes. "Later, Tess."

Logan stayed a moment longer. "Tess, I didn't mean to—"

"It's okay," she whispered, keeping her gaze on the table. "*I'm* okay."

She was going to start crying if he kept pushing.

Shawn *knew*. There was no other explanation. She didn't understand how, but somehow, he knew.

"I just know he makes you uncomfortable and—"

"Logan," Chloe snapped, cutting off his words. "Take a hint. She said she's fine."

He reached out, gently touching her shoulder, then turned and walked away.

She leaned against Chloe, relieved.

"What would I do without you?" she questioned, as her best friend wrapped an arm around her.

"I don't know, but I think you can stop worrying about finding a date."

Chloe stuck out her hand, fanning herself with exaggerated motions. "Hubba hubba! Mamacita! Got herself *two* hotties."

Tess breathed a laugh. "Yeah right."

Chloe chuckled, plucking a soggy fry from her tray. "What was Shawn talking about, anyway?"

"I have absolutely no idea," Tess lied, as a new concern crossed her mind.

Logan thinks I told Shawn about my problem.

"I think I'm going to talk to him," she announced, ducking out of Chloe's embrace.

Chloe smirked at her. "Seriously? Why? Trying to make Logan jealous?"

Tess frowned, declining to answer as she glanced around, searching the cafeteria. Shawn was nowhere to be seen. She groaned, agitated by his absence.

Eighth period. They had eighth period together. She would have to wait until then.

Impatiently, she moved through the rest of the day. Relieved as eighth period came. She was the second student to walk into forensics. She sat, sighing heavily and resting her forehead on the desk.

Logan was the only other person in the room. He sat beside her, and she could feel his eyes burning into the back of her neck.

"You can stop staring now. It's weird," she muttered, glancing up and attempting to smile.

He grinned back at her softly. "I'm worried about you." Then he raised an eyebrow, smirking. "Wait. How come *you* get to stare at me, but not the other way around?" he teased, nudging her shoulder.

"I don't stare at you," she insisted half heartedly, putting her head back down. "Really, Logan, I'm okay."

He was quiet for a long time before asking, "Did you tell Shawn?"

Tess avoided his stare, keeping her voice neutral. "No. He just knows. I don't know how. I think you're right about me not being the only one. But I can't be sure until I talk to him."

Something hit the corner of the desk, and her head snapped up.

Shawn.

He blatantly ignored Logan sitting next to her, glancing pointedly at the paper he'd dropped on the desk.

"In case you need me," he declared, meeting her eyes.

She stared at him. Unease coiled in her stomach. He looked bad. His face was paler than normal, and the faded purple bruise covered the majority of the left side of his face. She instinctively wanted to ask if he was alright, but he didn't give her the chance.

Without another word, he turned, slipping out of the classroom, unnoticed by the sub.

She reached out, grabbing the paper, aware of Logan's eyes on her. She leaned close, reading the neat handwriting scrawled across the page.

Here's my number. I know you need me.

His phone number was written in large numbers at the bottom, along with one final message.

You don't have to do this alone.

CHAPTER 15

CHLOE

"You sure you don't mind practicing in the rain?" Tess asked, glancing up at the gray sky, heavy with a pending storm.

"Nope." Chloe grinned, glancing at her friend. "I'm hoping to pick up some tips from watching you."

Tess smiled, her hazel eyes dancing with excitement.

Does she know something's up?

Logan had called her last night, enlisting her help. After explaining his plan, the last of her annoyance with him had disappeared.

Whatever makes Tess happy.

She held out her hand towards Tess, who took it immediately, hooking her pinky around Chloe's.

The closer they got to the football field, the harder it was to contain her excitement, but Logan had made her *swear* to secrecy.

Across the track, six male figures stood silhouetted against the stands, standing in a line.

"What are they doing here?" Tess asked.

Chloe shrugged, hiding a smile. "Race you there!"

They took off, and Tess immediately pulled ahead.

That girl has definitely *gotten faster*.

By the time they reached the boys, Chloe was out of breath and aching from her newest bruises. She tried her best to ignore the pain as Tess stopped quickly, mouth hanging open as she stared at the vision in front of her. Five half-naked boys from the track team stood on the 50 yard line, all displaying a black letter painted on their bare chests.

Dalton winked at her, wiggling his eyebrows suggestively, making her blush. Hands on his hips, he thrust out his chest, proudly displaying the **P** painted there. The others boys followed suit, showing off the letters, **R- O- M- ?**

Logan stood in front of them, his face a deep red. A nervous grin spread across his face as he held up a poster board with the dorkiest, yet sweetest message, written in sharpie.

'I've been dis**TRACK**ted with Prom running through my mind. I'd re**LAY** like to go with you'.

Tess stared at him, her face flushed.

"You want to go to prom with *me*?" she squeaked.

Logan frowned, feigning annoyance. "Well, duh!"

Tess began to giggle uncontrollably, burying her face in her hands.

"Give the guy an answer!" Dalton prompted, laughing. "The suspense is killing me!"

Tess didn't answer, instead rushing forward and crushing Logan in a hug.

Chloe watched quietly, happiness for her friend swelling in her chest.

"Aaaawww," Dalton cooed dramatically, pretending to wipe away tears. "Aren't they adorable?"

He smirked at Chloe, then held up a finger, pointing it sternly at her. "Wait."

He ran to the bleachers, disappearing under them.

When he came back—

"Oh. My. God!"

Chloe stared in absolute shock as Dalton reappeared from under the bleachers, leading a donkey on a rope.

Around the animal's neck was another sign.

'Let me take YO ASS to prom?'

All of them exploded into laughter, and the donkey brayed loudly.

"You brought a *donkey*?" Chloe giggled.

Dalton grinned widely, scratching the donkey's neck. "Well, I caught you looking at my ass the other day, so ... what do you think?"

Chloe laughed again, nodding frantically. "Yes!"

Dalton whooped, handing the reins to Logan and scooping her into his arms. He squeezed her tightly, making her yelp, then dipped her into a low bow.

Eyes sparking, he kissed her on the forehead before letting her stand.

"Now. I have to get Roscoe back to my neighbors before they notice he's gone. Call me later?"

The tears in her eyes blurred her vision, and she blinked, willing them to disappear.

This was *not* the time for tears.

She nodded happily, and with a parting smile, he grabbed the donkey and began leading it across the field.

Tess tackled her in a hug, squealing with infectious exhilaration. Before she knew it, Chloe was laughing too.

She knew it was wrong, but she had been jealous of Tess when Logan had announced his proposal idea.

Of course she was happy for her best friend— she'd be a horrible person if she wasn't.

But life seemed to come so easy for Tess. Her parents adored her, teachers praised her, and Logan thought she hung the moon. Tess was *loved,* and she knew it. She'd been told her entire life that she was wanted.

Chloe had *not*.

Her parents reminded her daily that she was worth nothing. A stupid, useless, disappointment.

But they were wrong.

She wasn't worthless.

She felt elated. Buoyant.

The lightness in her chest expanded until she felt like she could walk on air.

Her parents didn't exist right now. The bliss of the moment was all that mattered, because today, she *didn't* feel worthless. Today, she was wanted.

T hat night, her mother came into her room. Chloe looked up, immediately on guard.

Her mother stood silent in the doorway, staring at her with an unreadable expression. Chloe waited expectantly. When the silence dragged on, she finally spoke.

"Yes ma'am?"

Her mother frowned, obviously agitated with her impertinence.

"Chloe, your 18th birthday is coming up in a few months. Your father and I have made plans for that weekend. We will be having *very* important company over for a visit. I don't want to hear a single complaint from you. And you will be on your *very* best behavior. Do you understand me?"

She nodded automatically. "Yes ma'am."

"And I expect you to be *polite*. I won't have you telling *lies* while our company is here. You are not to discuss our home life. With anyone. Is that clear?"

"Yes ma'am."

Her mother turned, starting out the door.

"Mom?"

She regretted it as soon as the word left her mouth.

Her mother stuck her head back into the room, eyebrows raised.

"I- I was wondering if the 24th of next month is available?"

Chloe shuddered as her mother's cold eyes narrowed, appraising her with calculated interest.

"As far as I know, nothing is scheduled. Why?"

She rubbed her arm nervously, drawing courage from the memory of Dalton's sweet smile.

"Prom is on the 24th, and I'd really like to go. I'll wear something I already have and I can find a ride. I'll even stay the night with Tess so I won't bother you coming in late, if you want me to. I just... I'd like to go."

Her mother's gaze was suspicious.

Please, God, she thought, trying to maintain eye contact. *Please just let her say yes*.

Finally, her mother sighed, sounding annoyed.

"Fine."

Chloe sat up straighter. "Really?" she asked, excited. "Thank you!"

Her mother grunted, studying her face, before continuing.

"You haven't been an easy child to raise."

Chloe looked down, anticipating the worst.

"You have always been disrespectful, rude, and selfish. The first words out of your mouth were lies and there hasn't been a single day of your life you haven't *continued* to lie. Your father and I have done the best job we could with what we were given, but you simply have refused to learn. You are lazy and you are a liar. I don't know what will become of you, but regardless, it is not our fault. We have done everything possible to teach you. To remove the taint from within you. I suppose some children are inherently bad. It would do you well to remember that, and strive to overcome your nature."

"Yes ma'am," she whispered.

Her mother gave her a curt nod, then retreated from the room quickly.

That was fine with Chloe. The words had stung, but they weren't unexpected. Chloe couldn't remember a single kind word her mother had ever spoken about her.

Two more months.

Two more months, and she'd be free.

Her parents would never have to worry about her '*inherent nature*' again.

She tried not to feel disappointed about her birthday. Truthfully, she supposed she should be excited. It was the first time in *years* her mother had mentioned her birthday. Tess had already started to make plans for the day, but her friend would understand. Maybe they could celebrate on a different day.

Pulling out her phone, she began googling dress shops in the area.

She felt hopeful.

She wasn't used to that feeling. Hope.

But it was undoubtedly there.

CHAPTER 16

TESS

Tess sat in her room, trying to stop fidgeting. She'd already messed up one of her crimson-painted nails.

Closing her eyes, she tried to imagine what Logan would see when he looked at her. She had felt like a princess while the stylist and Chloe had worked on her, but now, she had to wonder. Did she look stupid? Were her eyebrows *supposed* to be this dark? Would Logan take one look at her and laugh?

Stop it. What matters is how I feel. And I think I look pretty. Even though the slit in this dress goes up pretty high...

She looked at her phone. He was supposed to be here at 6 o'clock. It was 5:50. What if he wasn't coming? What if he changed his mind and didn't want to go to prom with her at all?

She growled, annoyed with herself, and experimentally moved her foot in the torture devices that Chloe had insisted were high heels.

They'd spent all day together. Picking up her dress from

the cleaners, getting their hair and nails done, and doing Tess's makeup.

She grinned, remembering Chloe fussing over the red and gold eyeshadow, trying desperately to blend everything just right and panicking when Tess's eyes had started to water.

Chloe had left an hour ago to finish getting ready at her own house, even though Tess had begged her to stay for moral support.

Chloe insisted that three was a crowd, and that she *definitely* shouldn't be there when Logan showed up. Dalton was picking her up at 6:00 as well, and they were all meeting up at the school.

She heard Logan arrive at her house at precisely 6:00. Relief flooded through her. At least she hadn't been stood up.

She sat upstairs for a few moments, leaving her parents to make conversation. She was nervous. She was *terrified*.

What had she been thinking?

She should just change into jeans. She should take off all the makeup and cancel and—

"Do you remember this one, Logan?" she heard her mother say. "This was the 3rd grade talent show."

Tess sprang off her bed as she realized what picture her mom was about to show Logan. She almost face-planted as she stumbled over her heels, screaming, "I'm coming down!"

Panicked, she snatched the photo from her mom's hand, just managing to hide the little girl in cowgirl boots and pigtails, then tucking it back in it's album.

Her parents laughed, and she glared at them, eyebrows raised. "Don't make me take out *your* embarrassing pictures!"

She glanced at Logan, smiling and breathless. She'd expected him to look natural and confident, with his black tux and styled hair. Instead, he looked awkward and uncomfortable. He was fidgeting with the edge of his sleeve, and tugging on his red tie like it was too tight. He looked even more nervous than she was.

His gaze focused on her, and his eyes widened as he took in the plunging neckline of her crimson dress. The open back with criss-crossing bands. The long slit that ran from the glittering, ruby-colored skirt to the top of her thigh.

"Woah..."

He smiled, his eyes lingering on her brightly painted lips.

"Pictures!" her mom begged, pulling out her phone. "Just a few, I promise!"

Tess returned his smile. He wrapped his arms gently around her waist, and her dad cleared his throat from across the room. She laughed, pressing her cheek against his shoulder.

After her mother was satisfied, her dad reached over and squeezed Logan's arm, giving him a look. "Have her back by midnight. No later."

"Yes sir, Coach," he answered, shrinking a little under her Dad's gaze.

L ogan gently held her arm as he led her across the parking lot.

"Careful," he warned as her gold heels sank into a deep pothole.

She heard muffled music coming from the football field, where prom was being held.

Holding her hand, he twirled her around, before dipping her into a low bow. He smiled down at her. "Are you ready for this?"

She giggled, tugging at his tux for leverage.

"Not really," she pouted. "I can't dance. Chloe gave up trying to teach me, like four years ago."

He swung her up in one quick movement, his lips brushing her ear. "I guess I'll have to teach you."

She shivered, leaning against him as he pushed open the gate.

She was looking into a sea of faces. All staring back at her. Some with neutral expressions or welcoming smiles, but many more with surprised sneers and whispers. Tess felt her smile start to slide from her face.

A sudden voice rose above the rest.

"Freak."

Lauren Byrd stood a few yards away, gossiping with a group of girls. She examined Tess from head to toe, a slow, mean smile transforming her face. She raised her eyebrows, meeting Tess's eye.

Tess burned with embarrassment. And anger. She hadn't done anything to these girls. There was no reason for them to hate her.

A glance at Logan confirmed that he hadn't heard Lauren. He smiled sweetly at her, but faltered when he saw her expression. He looked around quickly to find the cause of her mood change, stiffening when he saw the girls. He glared at his ex, then turned back to Tess in concern.

With her crazy range of emotions lately, he was probably terrified she was going to cause a scene.

Under ordinary circumstances, she might have cried. Or screamed. Or ran away in embarrassment. Her self-esteem was low enough without this. But today was different. She felt strong. Confident.

She gripped Logan's hand tighter, narrowing her eyes at Lauren.

She *was* a freak.

And honestly, what this girl thought of her was the least of her concerns.

She turned to Logan, pulling him away from the gate and into the prom.

"Maybe," she murmured, smiling into his face, "*you* can teach me to dance?"

He beamed at her, relieved. "With pleasure."

She glanced over her shoulder, and in a moment of uncharacteristic confidence, winked at Lauren.

They made their way to the dance floor, where Chloe stood with Dalton.

Her friend's gold dress glittered in the lights, the fitted bodice and decorative back perfectly accenting her figure. Her dark skin and honey eyes contrasted beautifully with the gown. As Tess opened her mouth to tell Chloe how beautiful she looked, Chloe turned, catching sight of Tess and Logan. She shrieked, and began fawning over every detail of Tess and Logan's matching ensemble.

"You guys look *perfect*."

Tess laughed, and Logan squeezed her hand softly.

"I'll be right back," he said, moving to get drinks.

She nodded as Chloe began pulling and tugging at her hair, fixing every stray strand.

"So you and Logan." She sighed dramatically. "When's the wedding?"

Dalton laughed. "*Wedding*? Please. He *hates* that tux. You'll never get the guy in a suit again, Tess, so enjoy it now."

Tess rolled her eyes, grinning.

Logan arrived, passing around cups of punch.

The D.J. started another song, and Logan grinned, hearing the slow rhythm. He took her cup, setting it on the grass.

He arched an eyebrow. "Ready to learn?"

She took his arm, and he took her straight to the middle of the plywood dance floor. He pulled her towards him, and she wrapped her arms around his neck. Relaxing, she leaned against his chest.

His lips brushed close to her ear as he murmured instructions and guided her feet. "Two steps back. Two left. Two forward. Two right."

They completed a small box and he spun her, smiling as she got the hang of the dance. She twirled back into his arms, and her dress fanned out in a bright red swirl of fabric.

"You're a liar," he said, and she stopped moving, staring at him in confusion.

He laughed at her expression, explaining quickly. "You are a *good* dancer. Chloe just gave up too quickly."

"Maybe I just needed a different teacher."

Logan's grin widened as he glanced over her shoulder.

"Heads up," he warned, spinning her away from him.

Dalton caught her, laughing at her surprise.

"May I have this dance?" he asked, bowing dramatically.

She nodded, beaming at him.

"Thank you, by the way," she whispered. "Chloe seems so happy."

He raised a dark brow, tilting his head. "You don't have to thank me. Chloe's awesome! I've wanted to ask her out forever." He leaned in, whispering conspiratorially in her ear. "I'm just glad Roscoe is so handsome. I'm not sure she likes my 'ass' quite as much.."

Tess laughed, then looked at him seriously. "You better treat her right."

Dalton held up his hands in surrender, smirking. "Obviously. Now, if you'll excuse me..."

They spun again, and Tess stumbled back into Logan's embrace. He dipped her as the song ended.

Over already?

It felt like they'd just begun.

He swung her back up, and she waited for him to let her go. Instead, he held onto her, keeping her pressed against him. He ran a finger down her cheek, across her lip, then lifted her chin to meet his eyes.

He leaned in, pressing a chaste kiss to her forehead.

Her breath hitched as Logan pulled away.

"I'd really like to kiss you," he whispered, eyes searching hers for permission.

She froze, nervous and hopeful. And hot.

Why is it so hot?

She smiled shyly, pulling him towards her. Their lips met in an explosion of senses. Her mouth felt hot. In fact, her entire body was on fire, electric shivers traveling down her spine.

It was perfect. Everything disappeared. The staring eyes. Lauren. Dalton hooting behind them. She was oblivious to everything but him.

A hand clamped down firmly on her shoulder.

"Alright Romeo," Mr. Perry scolded. "Why don't you two go cool off with some punch?"

Logan smiled against her lips, pulling back enough to peek at their teacher.

"Yes sir," he chirped, saluting cheerfully.

Tess avoided Mr. Perry's gaze, uncomfortable that everyone around could clearly read what was on her mind.

Logan guided her to the refreshment table, ignoring the looks people were giving them. Lauren sat near the edge of the dance floor, shooting daggers at Tess, and virtually ignoring her date.

As Tess sat down, the euphoria of the moment began to fade, replaced with an awkward silence. What was she supposed to say?

Kiss me again?

Logan finally spoke, leaning back in his chair and puffing his chest out comically. "Well, I hate to toot my own horn, but I'm pretty sure that was the best kiss you've ever had. Am I right?"

She stared at him in silence for a moment.

He frowned in mock seriousness. "Am I wrong?"

She bit her lip, pretending to think, before dissolving into hysterics as Chloe and Dalton joined them. She sat back, relaxed. Listening to the conversation and casually observing the tables around her.

Until her eyes fell upon a striking boy three tables over.

Shawn Mason.

She hardly recognized him.

And he was *not* watching her.

She'd been ignoring him since he passed her his number, suppressing all thoughts of her 'issue' for a month now.

She stared at him. He didn't look like himself. In fact, he looked gorgeous. Like a European model.

And he was *smiling*. The guy actually looked happy.

It occurred to her that she'd never seen him *truly* appear happy. His smile was radiant, changing his face into something else *entirely*.

He'd gotten a haircut, showing off his brilliant blue eyes, and his tux was clearly not of the same quality as the rest of the boys at the prom. It looked tailored specifically for his body type. His body type that until now, she'd considered unhealthy. Too skinny.

She observed him quizzically. He was laughing at something his friend said. Bright white teeth. Long legs. Strong arms. Broad chest.

Her cheeks flushed.

Logan tapped her shoulder, smiling broadly. "Are you getting hungry?"

Suddenly, an idea came to her, and she faced Logan, trying to sound nonchalant.

"Hey, I think I'm going to talk to Shawn."

He glanced over, frowning in Shawn's direction. His entire demeanor changed.

She gave his shoulder an affectionate bump. "Don't worry. I'm just going to *talk* to him. Not kiss him."

He sighed, finally nodding. "I don't like it. I just don't trust the guy. But I get it."

He leaned forward, brushing a few strands of hair from her face. Closing the distance between their lips.

The kiss only lasted a second before he pulled back.

"Go talk to him."

She took a breath, steadying herself, and stood, making her way to his table. Shawn looked up, glancing her way, and paused, mid laugh.

For a moment, his expression changed. He looked nervous. Apprehensive.

Then, the look disappeared. He listed his head to the side, waiting for her to make the first move.

Here goes nothing.

"I'd like to talk to you."

Shawn's icy-blue eyes flashed in amusement. "That's a first."

Guilt pricked at her conscience, and it must've shown on her face, because he laughed, standing. "I'm kidding, Tess. But here probably isn't the best place."

Shawn looked pointedly towards his table mates, Hunter Garcia and his date, Jeanette Brown.

Tess nodded.

The fewer people that knew about her, the better.

He smiled, his eyes flicking arrogantly towards Logan, before offering her a hand.

"Dance with me?"

CHAPTER 17

SHAWN

Shawn's heart was pounding in his chest, right alongside Tess's Trace. Unlike the last few times he'd felt it, the beating was now constant, and he memorized the unique rhythm.

He smiled brightly, hoping to conceal his anxiety.

He had spent the last month waiting on a call or a text. *Some* kind of communication from her. *Refusing* to creep her out even more by attempting to speak up first.

He had been worried about her.

The awakening of a Genesis came bearing pain and confusion. Adolescent Munera were typically assigned a mentor to make the transition easier. In his case, he'd been assigned *three* mentors. A toddler's temper tantrum was hard to handle when that toddler could manipulate electricity.

As a newly-active Munera, Tess should have been going *crazy* without guidance.

Then again, he'd only ever known of one other *undocu-*

mented Abnormal— a young boy who'd been hiding out with one of the rebels that his parents had...

He shook his head to extinguish the thought before it could fully form.

Not right now. *Not* here. Tonight was *not* the night to be focusing on the atrocities his family had committed.

Tess walked with him to the dance floor, unbothered by the incredulous stares they got.

She hadn't exactly been *ecstatic* to accept his offer. She'd stared at his hand for a second, like his outstretched palm was a trap. But then, she'd met his eye and placed her hand lightly in his.

"Sure."

He could hear the whispers following their progress.

Is that Shawn Mason?

I thought Tess was here with Logan?

Why is she dancing with him*?*

His lip curled in agitation. Was it really *that* unbelievable that he would have a beautiful girl on his arm? He closed his eyes briefly, trying to ignore their audience.

Tess's hand, loosely wrapped in his, was soft and warm. And *tiny*. How could she do anything with hands that small?

He chuckled, and she studied him, intrigued. "What?"

He smiled, shaking his head slightly.

A warning went off in his brain.

Watch what you say.

Koden may have left to go back to his duties weeks ago, but the danger with his parents remained. *Always* remained.

Shawn pushed away the warning as a new song began to play. Tess swayed loosely in his arms, maintaining a safe distance between them.

He took in a breath, drinking in her presence. It was unlikely he'd ever get this opportunity again. She looked incredibly sexy in her gown. Long and crimson, pooling around her in a bright red swirl like a rose. Accenting her figure and complimenting every curve.

The equal to *any* Society debutant.

Actually, that was incorrect.

No one at the annual Salvator's Ball had ever compared to Tess James.

Shawn let his eyes run the length of her body, trying to determine what made her so unique. Other than her beauty, of course. That much was obvious.

He took in the smudged paint on her ring finger and the wisps of hair escaping from its pins. And it hit him.

At the Salvator's Ball and the Society weddings that he was forced to attend, every guest looked perfect.

There was no smudged makeup or messy hair, and it was the flaws in her that made her even more appealing. Even more stunning.

She was different. Wholesome and *good*.

He didn't deserve that.

"You look incredible," he said simply, his words a mere whisper of what he wished he could say.

You're everything. You're real.

She pursed her lips as she studied him. "Thank you. You look..."

She frowned slightly. A delicate crease forming between her eyes. "Different."

He laughed loudly, twirling her out, then spinning her in quickly. She let out a squeak as she landed against his chest.

He leaned in close, inhaling her sweet scent. Honeysuckle and vanilla.

"If the word you're looking for is '*happy*'," he murmured, "then thank you."

And he *was* happy. Ecstatic even.

His visit with Koden had been unpleasant, and his home had become a hostile environment since his departure.

Tensions had grown between his parents over his mother's *indiscretions*, until his father had exploded.

Konrad had called Alyssa every vile name he could think of, while she attacked him violently for being a weaker, less impressive version of his older brother.

And yet, Shawn felt happy. He'd accomplished a feat he hadn't thought possible. He had buried Tess in his thoughts. Making her so obscure that Koden was unable to detect his intentions.

He'd *won*.

A sheepish smile settled on Tess's face as she touched his arm, running a finger absently over his Brioni Vanquish suit.

The touch sent a shiver down his spine, and he forced himself to remember that this moment meant nothing to her. It was just a dance.

"Okay. Fine." Her small grin broadened. "You look *happy*."

He laughed again, holding her closer now as they moved to the music. He wished they could stay like this forever. It was the first time she had been in his company without looking so uncomfortable.

But she had asked him here for a reason.

"So, you wanted to talk?" he asked.

Surprisingly, Tess's smile stayed on her face as she leaned into his embrace.

"Are you like me?"

"Yes."

Her feet came to an abrupt stop at his direct response.

He gave her a soft smile, then pressed his hand gently into her back, reminding her to keep moving.

"But you already knew that."

He turned her quickly, moving her out of earshot of the other dancers on the floor.

She stared at him, eyes wide with relief, and blurted, "How do you know what I am? What *am* I? What are *you*?"

"That's…" he sighed, searching for the right words. "That's complicated. I can't explain it."

The spark of hope in her eyes dimmed, and he immediately amended his words.

"I can't explain it right *now*."

He searched her face, hoping to prolong their dance.

"You still have my number?"

She nodded, obviously disappointed.

"Then call me. When you're *alone*. Then, I can explain everything."

She looked like she wanted to press him for more information, but she gave in, her shoulders relaxing.

"This is crazy," she breathed, releasing a quiet laugh.

This is dangerous.

"Maybe," he teased, spinning her around, then pulling her back in time with the music. "Or maybe, it's your *destiny*."

It was cheesy, but Tess giggled anyway.

The moment was nice. He'd never seen her so calm. So tranquil. Especially not in *his* presence.

Suddenly, her fingers tightened on him, digging into his shoulders. She gasped, and her knees buckled.

He caught her before she fell, glancing around to see if anyone had noticed.

Thankfully, no one had. Except Logan Tucker, who looked ready to charge the dance floor and make a scene.

Shawn stared back at him for a moment, an open invitation. Logan glared, but didn't move.

Shawn turned back to Tess.

"Are you okay?" He fought to keep his voice calm as he guided her towards the edge of the dance floor. "Tess, what happened?"

Her labored breathing slowly evened out, though she still clutched a hand to her chest.

"I'm— I'm fine," she whispered. "I just felt something. It's been happening a lot... My heart. But, it *isn't* my heart. It's just there and then it goes away."

He sighed in relief, easing her hand away from her chest and back to his shoulders. They couldn't cause a scene in front of all these Basics. His parents would kill him.

"That was a Trace."

He spoke in a soothing voice, hoping to keep her calm. "Can you still feel it?"

Her hazel eyes were wide and confused. Frustrated. She waited a moment, concentrating, before shaking her head.

"It's gone. What's a Trace?"

He frowned.

But I'm still here.

He squinted, trying to recall if he'd ever heard his parents refer to an abnormality like this. Traces were constant once an Abnormal activated, assuming they were around other Munera.

He squeezed her arm, trying to reassure her. "A Trace tells you when others.. others *like* you, are nearby. It's like a sixth sense. You should have felt it when the headaches started."

Tess nodded, looking up at him. "I did."

Her hazel eyes bored into him intently, making it hard to focus. He swallowed, trying to keep eye contact.

"You should feel it now. I'm not sure why it disappeared, but I'm pretty sure there's an explanation."

"*Pretty sure?*" she cried, on the verge of panicking again.

He snickered, trying to guide her when she failed to move back into step. She looked so adorable when she was angry.

Tess glared at him.

"Stop laughing at me!"

He forced his features into a serious expression. "I'm sorry," he apologized diplomatically. "I *promise* you, Tess. There's an explanation."

I just don't know what it is.

She still scowled at him, visibly shaken by the Trace, but the alarm in her eyes had faded.

"Tess?" he asked quietly as the song slowed, about to end.

She looked up, waiting.

"I want to apologize. I know I've been a little... um..."

"Creepy?" she offered.

He grimaced. "Well, I was going to say *'persistent'*, but I guess *'creepy'* is justified. I've just never met someone like you. I wanted to help."

Shawn lowered her into a final dip as the song ended. "Just remember that, okay? I'm here for you."

She nodded, taking a step back as the music stopped. "Thank you, Shawn."

He bowed, a formal, habitual act that was common courtesy to him.

Tess's brow furrowed giving him a confused frown. Rather than explaining, he led her by the hand off the dance floor.

"One more thing?" he added, nodding towards Logan. "Can you *try* to explain to your boyfriend that I'm not out to steal his girl?"

The word 'boyfriend' tasted bitter on his tongue, and he hoped the lie wasn't as obvious to her as it was to him. He forced away the painful image of Tess and Logan kissing on the dance floor.

He didn't care one bit about Logan Tucker, and Tess's love life wasn't his business.

Unfortunately.

If she was happy with Logan, that was fine. But he refused to ruin her night by arguing with that idiot Lusus Naturae.

Tess rolled her eyes playfully. "Whatever, Shawn."

He grinned, letting her hand drop from his and walking quickly back to his table before he had to witness her return to Logan. Or hear his inevitable lecture about how 'he didn't trust Shawn' and 'to be careful'.

There was no reason for him to worry. He would *never* hurt Tess.

Hunter was gone when he reached his table again, no doubt smoking a joint with Jeanette in the bathroom.

He sighed, savoring the moment. And the memory of dancing with the girl he could never have.

CHAPTER 18

DR. MIRANDA NANDEZ

The fluorescent lights beamed overhead, illuminating the doctor's bronzed skin as she strode down the hall. Her glossy black hair was pulled into a tight bun at the nape of her neck, a standard blue mask covering the satisfied smile on her lips.

The Salvator had visited her facility recently, praising her for her progress. Her discovery.

She was *convinced* that the Caine family held the key to their survival.

Her research was going to save the people.

As would her test subject.

"Dr. Nandez."

The words, coming from the armed guard by the door, were spoken in a deep, monotone voice. He was young and attractive, with cold gray eyes and brown hair, shorn neatly on the sides.

Ace Lane. His Trace was quick and erratic. Unusual, but

she'd grown accustomed to his unique rhythm after the last year of working with him.

She nodded to him curtly. "Open the door."

The young guard pressed his hand to the scanner, and a green light flashed. The door swung open, revealing a large white room.

To her left, were computers and scanners, printers, and stacks of neat files. On the opposite wall, racks of syringes, small vials, and test tubes sat along the counter. The center of the room was taken up with two large chairs, similar to those in a dentist's office, with several reinforced straps attached.

They were primitive, but necessary. Even a powerful Munera struggled to hold her subjects conscious and immobile for hours on end. Binding them in a chair was the simplest solution.

In the very back of the room, were two small, identical chambers. A shower head, latrine, and curtain in the back. A small mattress, and a food drop box in the front. The rooms were separated from the rest of the lab with reinforced glass, several layers thick, though there was no door.

The only difference between the cages was the inhabitants.

Her assistant stood quickly, closing his laptop. He gave her a respectful nod. His straw-colored hair stuck out in all directions, and his lopsided glasses gave him a boyish look, making him appear years younger than he was.

"It'll work, ma'am," he insisted, gesturing to the rack of vials. "I'd bet my life on it."

"Bold words," she murmured, but smiled as she gazed to the back of the room. "Ahh, they're awake."

Two girls looked up when Dr. Nandez spoke.

One, a fourteen-year-old mutt with light eyes and dirty brown hair, had been detained four months ago. They'd found her living in the city with a couple of *Proditors*. Elizabeth Bell.

The other was a seventeen-year-old girl. Her hair, previously a curtain of shiny black silk, over time had become dull and coarse. Her once full cheeks were sunken, and her dark skin was sallow and sickly. Unfortunately, loss of bone marrow presented repercussions. Unfortunate, but necessary. The girl's cerulean eyes, however, never lost their fiery glow. She'd been detained several months ago, living in *deplorable* conditions with her older brother and sister. Maintaining an existence hidden from the Society's eye was difficult, and came with a cost. Her siblings had escaped detention, a fact that perturbed the doctor.

It would have been preferable to obtain them all.

However, she was resourceful. They really only needed one.

Sapphire Caine.

The girl's strong Trace pounded relentlessly, beating in time with her own. It was almost painful.

And it *excited* her. The power contained within her prisoner was incredible. Unlike anything she'd imagined.

"Bitch," the girl hissed, narrowing her eyes. "Come to put me out of my misery?"

Dr. Nandez frowned, irritated. "Language Sapphire. It's really so unbecoming of a lady."

The girl's attitude was terribly difficult to deal with.

She smiled, trying to regain her earlier good mood.

"Ladies, very exciting news today. We have something *very* important to test. Hands on the wall, please."

Sapphire stood, leaning on the glass for support. She pressed her hands to the wall as Nandez had instructed, then stuck up her middle finger.

Devil child.

Ignoring Sapphire, Nandez nodded to Ace. "Bind her."

In an instant, Ace vanished, reappearing inside Sapphire's

cage. The girl whipped around, slamming her fist into the guard's mouth. He grunted in pain, evading her next punch.

Her assistant gasped, moving towards the button to signal for assistance, but she held up a hand.

In the early months, Nandez would have reacted the same, calling in extra guards to restrain Sapphire.

Now, she knew better. She simply had to wait for the girl to tire herself out.

And she did, finally pinned to the mattress beneath Ace's iron grip.

Sapphire broke into laughter, that edged towards insanity.

"One day, I'm going to slit your throat, Doc," she whispered.

"Sapph!"

The mutt, curled in the corner of her cage, called out softly. "Sapphire, please. They're going to—"

"Kill me?" Sapphire shrieked, struggling again as Ace pressed a knee into her back. "Really, Liza?"

Nandez rolled her eyes, tapping her foot impatiently. "Ace. Come out."

The guard sat stiffly, silent as Sapphire began to giggle. He sighed, nodding at the girl beneath him.

"I can't."

As annoying as she found the girl, her ability was absolutely fascinating. The girl could deactivate anyone's Genesis with a single thought, rendering them powerless.

It was what made her so *valuable* to the cause.

If she could *deactivate* the Genesis, surely, that effect could be reversed. And if Nandez was right, it could possibly reverse— or even *cure* —the damage done to Munera DNA when mixed with Lusus Naturae DNA.

Still, now wasn't the time for a demonstration of her gift.

Dr. Nandez carefully constructed a shield, watching the

air waver in front of her. Once protected, she turned to the mutt.

The child began to gasp, clutching her throat.

The doctor grinned as she constricted the oxygen in the girl's lungs.

Suffocating her.

Her eyes were wide and panicked. Pleading for release.

Sapphire's blue eyes darted to Nandez, filling with frustration as she sensed the shield.

"Let her go," she demanded, thrashing wildly. "Let her go!"

The doctor tsked beneath her mask, tilting her head. "Elizabeth doesn't have much time, *Sapph*. Oxygen deprivation can leave some nasty brain damage, and we don't want that, do we?"

Sapphire let out a wail, bucking furiously under Ace's grip. "I reactivated it! I did it! Please! Let her go!"

Nandez glanced at Ace for confirmation, and he nodded quickly.

"Let her go!" Sapphire begged. "*Please!*"

The mutt gasped, coughing as air rushed to her lungs.

Nandez clicked her tongue in disappointment. "So much wasted potential," she muttered as Ace reappeared outside the cell, Sapphire in his grip.

She slumped, defeated, reluctantly waiting as Ace bound her to the chair, then moved to retrieve the second girl from her cell. He worked quickly, and within a few moments, he had both girls restrained. Though, unlike with Sapphire, he was gentle with the mutt. Nandez noticed that he even gave the girl's hand a reassuring squeeze before moving to stand dutifully by the door.

She would have to talk with his superiors about that— he'd clearly become too close with the subjects.

She motioned to her assistant, anticipation growing. "Set up the materials. *Now.*"

He rushed past her, moving silently to the mutt, attaching electrodes to her skin, then taking her vitals.

She watched him for a moment, then moved to Sapphire, putting a finger under the girl's chin, forcing her to meet her gaze.

"You are going to change the world," she murmured.

The girl snarled, wrenching her face away. "It won't work. You'll fail again, like all the other times."

Nandez smiled softly as her assistant placed a syringe in her hand. The glass tube sloshed with dark liquid, almost black. The consistency of fresh blood.

She tapped the needle experimentally, glancing towards the mutt. "Not this time."

The mutt stiffened, shying away from her.

Sapphire froze, her blue eyes intent on the syringe in Nandez's hand.

"Wait..." she whispered. Then, louder, screaming as the needle sank into the mutt's arm. "*Wait!* What are you doing to her?"

She strained against her bonds, kicking and yanking at the straps.

Dr. Nandez watched as wisps of black spread through the girl's veins. She cried out, gasping.

"So dramatic," she muttered, looking over at Sapphire. "It won't harm her. It should chemically stimulate her Genesis into activation."

"And if you're wrong?" Sapphire hissed, her chest heaving. "She's a *child!*"

A loud *slap* echoed through the room as the back of her hand connected with Sapphire's face.

Nandez shook out her wrist, wincing, before straightening her coat.

"She's an abomination," she whispered, leaning close to the Caine's face. "As are you. You're on the wrong side of this war, child."

Drawing back, she studied the girl.

One of the legendary Caines. With incredible abilities.

Reduced to crying over a *freak*.

"It's genocide!" Sapphire insisted. "He won't stop with a cure. He'll kill all the rebels! He will destroy *half our population*! And then, he'll kill the Basics! Don't you get it? You aren't solv—"

She stopped abruptly as a new beat joined the others.

It was quite possibly the weakest Trace Dr. Nandez had ever felt, but it was a Trace nonetheless.

The mutt gasped, startled. She glanced down at her own chest, then around at the room.

"What— what is that?" she asked, panicked.

No one answered. It was too incredible.

Fourteen *years* without a Trace, and now...

"It worked..." the doctor whispered. "It worked!"

She'd done it! She'd *saved* their people!

She rushed to the girl, pressing a hand to her forehead.

"No fever? No shortness of breath?"

The mutt shook her head, turning to look at Sapphire, who was sagging, relieved, in her chair. "The Trace? But I thought— I thought I couldn't have one?"

Nandez ignored the girl, murmuring for her to move her fingers, to look left and right and up and down.

"I feel fine," the girl said, smiling at Sapphire. "That really strong one... is that you?"

Tears welled in Sapphire's eyes as she nodded silently.

Dr. Nandez glanced at Ace. "Take her back to her cell," she said, waving at Sapphire. "I'll need to run some tests."

The guard nodded, releasing the bonds around Sapphire's wrists and ankles.

He clasped her arm, ready to move her back to her cell. She ripped her hand away from him, sliding from the chair and rushing to the mutt's side. Ace moved to restrain her, but Nandez held up a finger, watching with disinterest.

"Let them have a moment."

Ace backed away, slow to relinquish control.

The girls laughed, both in relieved tears.

"You scared me, kid," she murmured, pressing her forehead to the mutt's.

Nandez sighed. "Touching. Now if you will—"

A gasp cut her off. The mutt eyes grew wide, and Sapphire lurched forward.

"Liza? What's wrong?"

The girl didn't answer. Something dripped from the corner of her mouth.

Blood.

Nandez stiffened, scanning the girl for information.

"What is happening to her?" Sapphire demanded, grabbing the doctor and shaking her roughly. "*Help* her!"

"Ace! Now!"

The guard grabbed Sapphire around the waist, hauling her backwards. The girl's hands released Nandez's jacket, and she rubbed her neck where Sapphire's fingers had dug in.

"Put her back in her cell!" she demanded, racing to stabilize the mutt.

You can't die! I'm too close!

"We're losing her!" her assistant called frantically.

Ace yelped, then screamed out. "She deactivated my—"

"LIZA!"

Too many voices. The mutt began to heave in her restraints, coughing up blood.

All of Nandez's hopes hinged on the erratic beeping of the heart rate on the monitor. It slowed.

And then stopped.

Flatlined.

Sapphire screamed, lunging towards the chair, and holding the mutt's lifeless face.

Nandez *seethed*.

For *years* she'd researched this project. She'd found a solution. She'd waited *months* for a Caine. Then, methodically drained the blood and marrow from her, praying for the solution.

Now it was over. The most compatible mutt was dead.

She'd have to start from square one.

She whirled around to look at her assistant, who cowered beneath her glare.

"*You* prepared the solution. This is *your* fault! Guards!"

His eyes widened in horror. "Wait— please! I didn't—"

His voice cut off as she restricted his airflow.

Several guards streamed into the room, waiting for her command.

"Take him," she ordered, pointing to the man. "I want him dead. And detain her!"

Sapphire screamed and kicked, sobbing and fighting as the guards pried her away from the mutt's lifeless body. The man wailed in protest as her soldiers secured his hands.

Ace followed them out, silently carrying the body of the mutt against his chest.

Nandez leaned over the counter, panting, furious tears stinging her eyes.

So close... *so* close.

She needed another Caine as soon as possible. Sapphire would die if Nandez resumed work with her so quickly, and she had to continue testing. It was *imperative* she find a cure.

She closed her eyes briefly, a tinge of regret at the loss of a fine assistant, then sighed, rubbing a hand across her stomach. Feeling for the small bump.

Her daughter.

The mutt that she'd brought upon herself for the sake of her research.

The mutt she'd already fallen in love with.

She *had* to find a cure.

Otherwise, her daughter would meet the same fate as Elizabeth Bell— an abomination, expendable. A tool to further their efforts in saving their people.

CHAPTER 19

SHAWN

The exhilaration from his progress with Koden and his dance with Tess had only lasted about a week before it was destroyed.

Three additional Traces lingered in his home. The officials must have discovered another traitor.

Shawn sighed when he heard the front door close, counting down the seconds until he would be summoned.

3.. 2.. 1..

"Shawn, let's go!" his mother demanded, and he complied immediately. Without resistance.

What was the point?

There was nothing he could do.

On the drive, he tried to find an optimistic approach. He had no idea what his mother needed him for. There was no guarantee this trip would end in another death.

There was a chance that the information given to his

parents was actually wrong. That his newest victim would be found innocent.

"Shawn, we're here."

His father's clipped words drew him out of his thoughts, and he glanced around. Alyssa had already slipped out of the car, heading towards the front door of a run-down townhome.

"Who lives here?"

"His name is Ace Lane."

Shawn raised an eyebrow when he heard his father answer instead of his mother. Lately, Konrad had been *attempting* to regain his authority over Alyssa.

I guess when your brother is banging your wife, it's probably rough on your self esteem.

"What is he accused of?" he pressed, crossing his arms as he walked.

His father glanced at him, pursing his lips. "He's grown too close with some detainees from the research facilities."

His mother glared in his direction. Clearly, his father had given too much away. It wasn't the first time Konrad had revealed classified information. He often forgot his son's criminal record against the Society meant that Shawn couldn't be trusted.

He sighed, shuffling forward slowly.

He would do whatever his parents wanted.

As long as they didn't find out about his newest crime.

As long as Tess stayed safe.

His mother knocked, and the door was opened immediately.

A guard. Young. His uniform half unbuttoned. Staring out from wary, tired gray eyes. The man straightened when he recognized who stood on his front steps.

"Generalis. Madam Orator." He addressed Shawn's

parents formally, rather than by name. A clear sign of his low rank.

"Please come in."

The guard stepped aside, and his mother reluctantly stepped over the threshold, wrinkling her nose as she entered the foyer.

Why are we here?

This man was a mere guard. His parents could have easily sent an official to check up on the situation.

What made him important enough to warrant a *personal* visit from the Generalis and Orator, *and* an interrogation from Shawn?

"Are you Ace Lane?" Alyssa asked, her blue eyes narrowed.

He inclined his head humbly, confused. "To what do I owe the honor of this visit?"

His mother opened her mouth to speak, but Konrad interrupted, cutting her off, quickly listing the offense he had been accused of. A small smirk played across Shawn's lips. He admired his father's attempt to keep his composure while under Alyssa's seething glare.

The guard looked down, chagrined, and began fastening the buttons of his uniform up to his collar.

"If I'm being entirely honest," he said, lifting his eyes to meet Konrad's stare. "It's not always easy working under the circumstances that I do, though I'm grateful for the opportunity to serve the Society."

He was surprisingly well-spoken. Most Society soldiers and guards never went to college, often jumping straight into their work at the onset of their Genesis, sometimes without earning even a high school degree.

Ace did not match that description, and that alone intrigued Shawn.

"I spend many hours with the subjects, and it's hard not

to grow somewhat fond of them. Though I assure you, I never allow my feelings to interfere with my work."

He lifted a shoulder, shrugging slightly. "It's similar to feeding a stray cat, I suppose. You tell yourself not to get attached, but…"

His mother watched her son expectantly, completely uninterested in listening to Ace Lane. He sighed, waiting for the guard to face him.

He saw exactly what he'd been dreading.

Ace, like so many others, was horrified, that one day, he'd be discovered for his crimes against the Society.

And there was something else.

An image of a teenage girl, pressed against a wall of glass.

An uneasy feeling settled in Shawn's stomach.

Why was this guard, a fully grown Munera man, afraid of a *child?*

Ace spoke to the girl from the other side of the glass. "You're a Caine. You've repeatedly tried to kill me. How can I trust you?"

The girl was a *Caine?*

Koden had said the answer to a cure might lay within the ancient family, but Shawn never imagined he held one captive.

It was incredible.

It was inhumane.

"I don't choose to be a killer. None of the rebels do," the girl— the Caine —whispered, her blue eyes flashing desperately. "We've been given no choice."

"I know." Ace's eyes filled with tears. "My husband. He's a healer. He would never hurt anyone. I don't even know if he's alive."

Another vision.

A man, angry tears running down his face.

"I had to, Morgan," Ace pleaded. "It was the only way to ensure you'd be safe."

The other man, Morgan, jerked his hand away, furiously

twisting his wedding band. "You've sentenced our friends to death! And now you're joining them?"

Shawn blinked, trying to process the visions. He felt sick.

Ace had been one of them. A Turncoat.

He'd given up fellow rebels, all to protect Morgan, then joined the guard.

Shawn could *feel* the pain and guilt that overwhelmed Ace, leaving him a hollow shell of the man he'd been before. It had almost killed him to betray his loved ones. But he'd done it out of love. To save the man who was his entire world.

If Shawn did his job, that sacrifice would mean nothing

"He has nothing to hide," Shawn announced glumly, turning to look at his parents. "Your reports were wrong."

They both visibly deflated. His father, no doubt disappointed at losing the opportunity to stockpile more black market knowledge. And his mother— honestly, he wasn't sure what his mother's agenda was anymore.

"Are you positive, Shawn?" Konrad asked skeptically. "Surely you missed something."

Shawn glared at his father, knowing he had to be convincing. If he was caught now, Ace and he would *both* die.

"What more do you want from me?" he demanded petulantly. "You've forced me to condemn more people to death than I can count for being traitors to the Society. But don't ask me to condemn an innocent man." He crossed his arms defiantly across his chest. "I won't do it. Kill him if you see fit, but you're wasting your time here."

Ace's features didn't change at the mention of his impending death, but Shawn could sense the man's heightened fear carefully hidden beneath his ambivalent mask.

Thankfully, his parents couldn't.

His mother stared at Shawn for a long time, and he met her gaze. Her blue eyes softened as she looked at him.

Finally, she spoke, and her voice was soft and melodic.

A sweet siren song.

"Thank you for your help Shawn. But are you absolutely sure?" she murmured. "The man has *nothing* to hide?"

The words washed over him, soothing and sweet. Like honey. He felt a warm lethargy spreading throughout his limbs, and he suddenly *desired* to tell his mother the truth about what he saw. He *needed* to tell her.

It would be so easy.

He swallowed hard, shaking his head slightly. "He has nothing to hide," he repeated stubbornly.

His mother glared, and an icy chill rippled through his body as his mother withdrew her gift, releasing him abruptly. He fought the urge to gasp in relief as his parents moved towards the door.

"I apologize for the misunderstanding, Officer Lane," Alyssa said, giving the house a final glance, curling her lip in disgust.

The guard bowed his head, acknowledging her respectfully.

As they moved towards the car, Ace's eyes followed Shawn anxiously. Confusion and relief both evident in their gray depths.

Shawn didn't need his gift to clearly assess what the man was thinking.

Why hadn't Shawn Mason, the Salvator's nephew turned him in?

Shawn nodded to him before climbing into the backseat. His good deed towards the man didn't come from entirely pure intentions. When the time arose, he would collect interest for the act. He had an interrogation of his own to do.

CHAPTER 20

TESS

For the first time in her life, Shawn Mason crossed her mind, and she drew comfort at the thought of him. Gripping her phone, she anxiously pressed the numbers. Anticipating his voice and hoping for answers.

Her finger hovered over the final button.

Call me. When you're alone. Then I can explain everything.

His words replayed in her head.

He'd seemed so confident when he spoke about her...Trace?

She pressed *'call'*.

One, two, three rings before a deep, familiar voice answered.

"Hello?"

She suddenly found herself tongue tied.

"Hello?" He repeated, sounding weary.

She forced herself to answer.

"Um, hey Shawn. It's Tess."

Her voice came out in a small squeak. Heat immediately rose to her cheeks.

"Aww, Tess! You flatter me. I'm not even *trying* to be creepy and you're already scared?"

He laughed a little, but it sounded forced. A little off.

She hesitated, wanting to ask if he was okay, but something told her he wouldn't be honest if she did.

"Can we talk now?"

"Are you alone?"

She scanned the room around her, empty and quiet.

Her parents were out of town shopping for new kitchen appliances, and Logan had left an hour ago. The memory of his lips along her neck sent prickles down her spine.

Her parents didn't know he'd been there, of course. Her dad would probably murder him if he did.

She forced her thoughts back to Shawn. "Yes."

"Then yes. We can talk."

A million questions.

How is this possible? What's going to happen to me? Am I going to get worse?

She took a breath, trying to think rationally.

One thing at a time.

"What am I?" she whispered.

Shawn responded immediately.

"The technical term is Munera. It's Latin for *'gift'*. But occasionally, people say *'Abnormal'*."

What the hell was Munera? She'd never even heard that word before.

Shawn took her silence as an invitation to keep talking. "On the other end of the spectrum are the Lusus Naturae—Basics... uh... humans. God, this is difficult over the phone."

Tess raised an eyebrow incredulously and reminded him, "*You* told me we couldn't talk about it in person!"

He laughed again, and this time, it sounded genuine.

"Yeah, I guess I did. Honestly, this will take weeks to explain, regardless of how I do it."

Weeks?

"Just start from the beginning."

"The beginning..." Shawn chuckled, like she had made a joke.

Tess tightened her grip on her phone. "Well obviously there *has* to be a beginning. Like did a nuclear power plant explode? Did aliens invade and we're their half-breed children?"

She felt her voice rising, but she needed *something* to make sense. She could handle aliens or radiation.

Shawn's explanation involved none of that. No aliens. No nuclear radiation.

Instead, he brought it back to Adam and Eve.

"Not *exactly* Adam and Eve," Shawn admitted. "But the Munera were the first people, Tess. There was no mutation that *caused* the abilities, we just... *are*. Our abilities came from the Genesis, which is biologically, part of who you are."

Tess tried to wrap her head around it while he kept talking.

"This is just a theory, but a lot of historians believe the first people possessed the ability to *create* more abilities. *Omnem Potestatum*— all power. It's such a widespread belief that most Munera treat it as fact."

He paused, politely giving her an opportunity to question him. Or stop him. Either way, she remained silent.

"Think of the Genesis like a seed, lying dormant in every Abnormal until it activates."

Her hands were shaking. She wasn't sure if she was relieved or terrified. Probably both.

"So... So that's what caused my headaches and... and everything?" she asked.

"Activation," Shawn agreed. "The headache is normal.

Powers going out of control." He let out a snort. "Like hormones and going through puberty. Usually, you'd have a mentor hired, or assigned to you if you're a Charge. And—"

"And?" she asked quietly.

"And humans. Lusus Naturae. We don't know *why* some Munera lost their abilities. Inbreeding in powerful families? An outbreak? Truthfully, no one actually knows, but—"

He cut off, sensing he'd lost her.

He sighed, and she could picture him, brow furrowed and rubbing the bridge of his nose.

"I think I've heard enough for now," she whispered.

Her head pounded as she tried to process everything.

A Genesis? *Munera?*

Shawn was crazy.

No, he isn't.

In a way, it all made sense.

No, it doesn't.

Tears stung her eyes. Relieved tears. Scared tears. Confused tears.

Really, *really* confused tears.

"Tess?" Shawn asked.

His voice held the same protective edge Logan had started to use when she got too emotional. She hated it. She hated feeling *so* weak, when everyone around her seemed so strong.

Stop it.

She'd been searching for answers for months now. She couldn't just wuss out when she heard something she didn't like.

"I'm fine," Tess answered, struggling to sound stronger than she felt. "I don't want to talk about this over the phone. Can I come over? To your house?"

"No!"

She winced, pulling the phone away from her ear when his voice came out in a loud, panicked bark.

"No," he repeated, quickly amending his tone into something more friendly. "My house isn't an option. What about the park on Yale Street? Or the school?"

An uneasy feeling settled in her stomach.

Why didn't Shawn want her at his home? Was he embarrassed of her?

"The park is fine," she said. "I can meet you there?"

"Sure. I'll—"

He stopped, cursing under his breath.

"Nevermind Tess. I have to go. My parents are back earlier than I expected, and I'm sorry, but it'll have to wait. I'll call you back when I can."

The phone went dead.

It took all her effort not to throw her phone at the wall in frustration. She had more questions now than she'd started with.

W aiting was not Tess's strong suit. Thankfully, she didn't have to wait long. Shawn called the next afternoon, saying he could meet her at the park. She sat on a swing, waiting for him.

A sleek black Mercedes Maybach pulled up, and she watched curiously, interested to see who was in it. She blinked in surprise as Shawn opened the door.

His eyes darted around quickly, scanning the area.

"Nice car," she commented, pushing her feet against the ground to stop her swing from moving.

"Thanks." He sounded sullen, even a little angry, and he glared at the car like it had insulted him.

Then, as he turned to look at her, his expression softened. "You look really pretty today."

She glanced down at her worn tank and baggy sweats. "Um, thanks? I guess?"

She laughed quietly, wondering why she hadn't ever noticed how attractive he really was.

"I'm glad you came. I'm sorry I couldn't explain more yesterday. My home life is... complicated, I guess you could say. But I brought something to show you. It will probably help explain things better than I can. I wasn't really the best student when it came to learning Munera history." He gave her a mischievous smile. When he smiled, his whole face lit up.

He held a paper out towards her.

The edge was torn, like it had been ripped from a book.

"I know it is going to seem confusing at first. But, there *is* an explanation for everything." He gestured towards the paper. "Here it is. Yesterday, I mentioned *Omnem Potestatum*. Do you remember?"

She frowned slightly. "Yes. The myth that some Munera actually *created* powers."

He nodded, a small smile lifting his lips. "You're a good listener. If *Omnem Potestatum* ever existed at all, it was diluted through the bloodlines over time. A lost gift as more abilities were created and passed down. You've probably guessed that the Genesis is a genetic trait?"

She had. She'd also realized that her parents didn't have one.

Shawn kept talking, oblivious to her thoughts that were demanding answers

"It's hereditary, as are the abilities that Abnormals are born with. All Abnormals have two abilities— one each from the maternal and paternal side of the family, but they can be very unpredictable. They can skip generations, occasionally causing an Abnormal family to go years without seeing a gift reoccur. It's rare for low-class Abnormals to have multiple children, while those of higher standing *mostly* try to branch out and keep their bloodlines strong." He grimaced and paused, looking uncomfortable. Like he'd exposed something he hadn't meant to say.

"However, when there *are* multiple children in a family, the abilities aren't always the same. They might be stronger in one child than another, or occasionally, they are entirely identical. Does that make sense?"

She nodded again, determined to memorize every word he said.

"Geneses tend to activate around eighteen, though that's not *always* the case. In certain circumstances, a Genesis may activate at a much younger age, but I've never heard of one activating *after* eighteen. Pretty simple really."

Tess stared at him, incredulous. *Nothing* about her life felt simple right now.

She scanned the paper. It looked like a page torn from a biology book, with diagrams and scientific terms and phrases, all written in a different language.

Latin?

She didn't understand a word of it.

At the bottom was an endless list of Latin phrases, divided into sections.

G-3, G-4, and G-5.

"What are these?" Tess asked, pointing to the list.

There were so many that half of the last section was cut off, probably on the next page of whatever book Shawn had taken it from.

He leaned closer to look, his shoulder brushing hers.

"Gradus. Levels essentially. It's a way to rate abilities. To categorize things."

He pointed to the list labeled G-5.

"These gifts are considered the weakest abilities. Powers that affect the *user's* body only, though even within a Gradus, abilities can be weaker, or stronger, in an individual. G-5 abilities are just basic enhancements. *Et Fortitudinem* means 'and strength'. *Et Celeritatem* would be 'and speed'."

He pointed a finger at G-4.

"Gradus four and three abilities are most common within Abnormals. In G-4, they're all loosely based on elements and nature. *Ignis Dominum*, for example, translates to fire master. *Fulgur Dominum* is lightning master. And so on.... Why are you laughing?"

Shawn tipped his head, indulging her. A half smile played on his lips.

She pointed to the third group.

"Let me guess— people in this Gradus can turn into animals and fly, right?"

He stared at her strangely, mouth open and brow furrowed. "People can't fly Tess. That's a myth."

She hugged herself as more giggles bubbled up and out of her uncontrollably.

"*That's* the myth?"

He nodded matter-of-factly, looking back down at the page. "Abilities in the third tier are more powerful. This Gradus encompasses Abnormals who can affect others' bodies as well as objects. I won't bore you with more Latin terms— I think I've showed off enough of my intelligence."

He grinned at her conspiratorially.

"Basically, this includes healing, teleportation, telekinesis, and a hundred others that probably start with 'tele'."

Tess laughed again. "So we've got enhancements, nature, and bodies and objects. Is there a Gradus one and two?"

Shawn immediately fell silent. Obviously uncomfortable.

His silence stretched on until Tess felt awkward.

"Shawn?"

"Yes," he answered finally, so quiet it was almost a whisper.

She realized that if it was scaring *him*, she didn't *want* to hear his answer.

He opened his mouth to respond, and instinctively, she placed her hand over his lips. His entire body stiffened in response.

"Wait." She pulled her hand away slowly.

"Tell me the rest later, okay? I have another question."

Shawn relaxed, nodding. "I'm sure you have a *lot* of questions."

She thought back to the way he'd danced with her. His graceful style and formal bow— not the moves a typical high school boy should know. The suit he'd worn to prom. The too-nice of car that *no* eighteen-year-old should drive. And the way he talked, just a little more polished than most boys she knew.

"There are *Abnormal* people all over the world. Right?"

He gave her a stern look. "We have already established this."

She rolled her eyes, continuing. "This is going to sound dumb, but... people can't just be walking around, using abilities with no sort of government. No rules or laws. So... is there, like, a *Hogwarts* for Abnormals or something?"

A smile spread over his face, as he pondered her question.

"That's the perfect analogy for it, except I would liken it more to the Ministry of Magic. It's called the Society."

O ver the next few weeks, she and Shawn met up as often as they could. When she wasn't with Logan, that is. They had a lot more time to spend together now that track season was over.

Her senior year. Her *last* meet. Last *high school* meet, anyway.

It had been bittersweet. Since her first letter from Canisius University, she'd received *nine* offers. *Offers,* not tryout invitations, from nine different schools. Five of them were Division 1 schools.

She *truly* was excited. But she found herself growing less interested in making a final decision about college, and *more* interested in Muneras.

With every visit, she discovered more about Shawn's world. *Her* world if she wanted to accept it.

But the more she learned, the more she realized how much she had to fear.

She had received a history lesson on the Society, but more importantly, the Society's leader. The Salvator.

A man that came from a family with a legacy of destruction. A family that used their abilities to hurt people and retain political power. The prospect of coming into contact with this man, or his family made her sick.

Then Shawn had further terrified her, describing both Gradus one and two powers. And he'd informed her that one of his abilities spanned both levels.

He described G-2 as abilities used to affect an individual's mind.

A gift that can be used to manipulate people into doing almost anything.

And G-1. Abilities that directly relate to a Genesis or a life.

Several of these gifts, like Genesis mimicry, Genesis deactivation, and resurrection, were believed to have been mostly lost over time. Rarely occurring in only the most *elite* families. Others, like *Mortale Injuriam*, allowed an Abnormal to kill if they wished. Using only their mind.

After a lot of coaxing, Shawn had reluctantly explained that he was a Munera prodigy. His Genesis had activated at four years old.

A prodigy *and* a *Fulgur Dominum*, or lightning master.

Manipulating electricity came as natural to him as breathing.

A Gradus four power handled like a G-1.

He could also search your mind and retrieve your fears, then recreate that fear to stimulate visions. Visions so strong and realistic that it could induce panic attacks or cause cardiac arrest.

He could kill people.

Gradus one.

But he was adamant that he *never* wanted to use his abilities to hurt people. That gave her a little relief.

When she managed to remain completely relaxed around him, she had learned she could feel his Trace. It never lasted longer than a few moments though, because she grew anxious when she felt the beat, and then it always disappeared.

She didn't particularly like the feeling of the Trace, so she wasn't bothered by this. In fact, Shawn told her it was probably better if she focused on understanding how she could block it. And attempt to block her own from other Munera.

"I wish I could sugarcoat this information," Shawn told her, scanning the street where they walked. Looking everywhere but at her. "But you deserve the truth."

A shiver ran down her spine. "Okay..."

"The Society doesn't know you exist. You are an undocumented Munera, which is a punishable offense. That puts you in an extreme amount of danger. If the Society attains knowledge of your existence, they'll assume you're a vigilante. An Abnormal that isn't with the rebels but is against the Society. Munera births are strictly regulated. Without their knowledge, *you* shouldn't exist. They have ways of obscuring the truth. They could put you on trial, and...."

He stopped, finally meeting her eye with such intensity that it frightened her.

"Most people don't survive the trials, Tess."

I shouldn't exist.

Her heart pounded fiercely.

"But I'm *not* a vigilante!" she protested, trying to force down her panic. "I didn't even know the Society existed!"

Shawn put a reassuring hand on her shoulder.

"I know that, Tess. And if, God forbid, anyone *does* find out about you, I will be your witness. I can help to explain your case."

"But the trials..."

He reached out, lifting her chin. Watching her intently.

"There won't be a trial. I'll make sure of that. I won't let anything happen to you."

CHAPTER 21

LOGAN

Logan held Tess in his arms, her head tucked into the curve of his neck. She lay snuggled in his arms, chest to chest. He could feel her heart beating against him.

They'd been dating for exactly one month. And *everything* about it was perfect.

He remembered their first date after prom.

He had taken her to the school track. Probably not the most romantic spot, but it was built at the highest point of elevation in Joshua, and the field was completely empty and open. The school was situated on the outskirts of town, away from most city lights.

She'd told him once how much she loved the stars. It was just in passing conversation— she probably didn't even remember telling him, but he hadn't forgotten.

The moon wasn't out that night, an unforeseen detail that helped make the night even more magical. Without any lights, it seemed like *every* star was visible.

Millions of tiny pinpricks sparkled in the velvet sky.

She'd gasped, gazing up in amazement. Her hazel eyes had positively glowed.

The night had been *absolutely* perfect.

"What are you thinking about?"

Her quiet whisper brought his attention to the present. They were back at the track, content with repeating their first date. Only, tonight, her focus wasn't on the stars.

He smiled, pressing his lips against the base of her jaw, and she shivered.

"I'm thinking about how much I love holding you."

She drew back to meet his gaze.

"Is that all you love doing?"

She gave him a wicked grin, setting his face, and body, on fire.

"I might also love kissing you."

"Oh yeah?"

"Mmhm."

"Show me?"

He did. Trailing kisses along her jaw, her neck, her collarbone.

His heart *pounded*. Hard enough he was *positive* she could feel it.

God, she was beautiful.

Her arms snaked around his back, pulling him to her. Her body curved seductively against his, and he had to focus on *not* letting himself become too turned on.

God. I've wasted so much time.

She could have been his years ago, but he'd been too blind, and too scared to see what was right in front of him.

Warm hands slipped under his shirt, and all reason escaped him.

She was with him now.

Logan's stomach tightened as her fingers traced the curve of his back.

Perfect. Everything. Just... perfect.

It was over too quickly. She pulled away, breathless, and he was left panting, wanting more.

"You were wrong, you know," she said, rolling him onto his back, and staring down at him.

He grinned, enjoying her long legs straddling him. "That's not possible. I'm never wrong."

She swatted his arm, and he laughed, pressing another kiss on her lips.

She smirked, turning her face so his lips ended up on her cheek.

"I guess you'll never know what you were wrong about."

"Oh yeah?" He expertly wrapped her in a bear hug and flipped her onto her back.

Her eyes widened as she found herself pinned under his weight.

He raised an eyebrow. "Well, Tess, that's just rude. I think you need a lesson in manners."

He started to tickle her, and she immediately began thrashing her arms out, squealing and giggling wildly.

"Okay, okay! Stop! Please! I'll tell you!"

He smiled, wiggling his fingers threateningly in front of her. "I'm waiting."

She frowned at him in mock irritation.

"I was *going* to say that unfortunately, prom was not *actually* the best kiss I've ever had."

"What?" He clutched his chest dramatically, scowling. "Come on! Those were my best moves! I even used a classic line and everything!"

She giggled, shrugging and tucking her head under his chin. "Sorry, but I need to be honest with you. Prom *was* pretty spectacular, but... I think you outdo yourself *every* time."

He stared at her silently for a moment, then began tickling her again. She burst into a fit of hysterical laughter. And Logan felt *it*.

That feeling that he'd never had with anyone before her.

He felt light, and completely comfortable. Like he could be exactly himself with her. He could laugh or cry, or be the goofy awkward guy that he tried so hard to hide at school. And no matter what side he showed her, she still liked *him*. There was no way he could ever explain the joy he felt.

"Logan, stop! I think I'm going to pee!"

He stopped abruptly, laughing as he took in her panicked expression.

She scowled. "Brat."

He lowered his head to hers, gently nuzzling her neck.

"Forgive me?"

She moaned, but didn't respond to his question.

He kissed her neck, and then across her chest, pressing his body into hers.

She whimpered softly, and he felt his heart begin to race as he moved cautiously down her body.

"Logan, stop."

Shit.

He was going too fast.

She pushed against his chest, and he slid off of her, looking down apologetically.

"I'm sorry, Tess. I got carried away."

She smiled meaningfully. "I *like* when you get carried away."

He sighed in relief, pulling her back against him. "Well in *that* case..."

"But..."

Oh no.

That was her *'You aren't going to like this'* voice.

"What is it?"

She exhaled, and he knew instantly where the conversation was headed.

Munera. The Society. The fact that she really *did* have some kind of supernatural power, even though *Spidey-senses* hardly counted as 'powers' in *his* opinion.

The hormones that had been racing through his body immediately disappeared.

The whole thing was absolutely insane. But he knew she couldn't make up the things she'd told him. And if her words weren't proof enough, Shawn Mason had provided her a book, detailing the history of the Society.

He'd never been much of a reader, but they'd gone over it together, cover to cover.

And he didn't like what he'd read.

"Shawn told me something. About the Society. It's not like anything is going to happen, but—"

She stopped, clearly uncomfortable.

"Tess. Talk to me."

He didn't want to push her. He knew she didn't like talking about the Society with him. And for good reason. According to the *Society*, Logan was a *freak*. Hardly higher on the evolutionary ladder than dog shit. And quite frankly, he didn't like hearing about it.

But she was obviously worried. And that meant *he* needed to be worried.

"What did Shawn say?"

Tess sighed.

"So... Because I'm *undocumented*, if I'm ever caught by the Society, I might..."

She trailed off, unable to finish. *Terrified.*

She was shaking in his arms, her breath coming in short gasps.

Logan didn't need her to finish. He knew exactly what she was going to say.

She *might* be in danger.

The idea of anyone hurting her was too horrible to imagine. He tensed, feeling sick in his stomach.

She looked up at him with a worried expression, knowing he was upset.

"But I really think it's *fine*. Shawn said he could protect me!"

He narrowed his eyes at that, and she quickly rephrased her statement. "From a trial. He can protect me from a trial. And I really think he can. He's got, like, some kind of authority in the Society. I just don't know what it is."

Shawn Mason.

Logan hated everything about the guy. From his shiny black car to his invasive blue eyes.

And he *definitely* didn't like the idea of Tess needing *Shawn's* protection.

"He's a *nobody,* living in Podunk, USA. What kind of authority could he possibly have?"

He couldn't keep the contempt out of his voice.

Tess made a face, shrugging.

He could tell she wasn't happy about his assessment of Shawn.

"I don't know. I just get this vibe. And I can tell he's holding something back from me."

"So he's lying to you too."

She glared at him. "No. He's not."

Logan sighed, pulling her closer, nestling into her neck.

She smelled *so* sweet.

"You trust him, Tess? *Honestly?*"

Tess nodded, without hesitation.

A long moment of silence passed. Tess's quiet breathing and the crickets singing in the grass were the only sounds.

"Fine. Then I can... I can *try* to trust him too." He paused, realizing he *actually* meant the words.

Shawn cared about Tess. There was no doubt about it. And if Shawn could protect her when Logan couldn't— in a society of superhumans —then he would make an effort to get along with the guy.

She smiled in relief.

"But I don't like him. He's too *pretty*. And too *powerful*. What if you decide you don't want to be with a boring, powerless, Lusus whatever-it's-called." He threw his hands up, feigning defeat. "I'm sorry, but I can't fly, Tess!"

"That's a myth, Logan. Munera can't fly."

"Wait, really?"

"Of course not." She laughed, before raising a brow at him. "They can levitate things, though."

"Oh my God, I give up."

She snorted, turning over and snuggling against him. They fell into a comfortable silence. He breathed in the delicious scent of her. She wiggled against him, settling in, her butt pressing into his groin. He groaned inwardly, forcing his anatomy to behave, as she drifted off, her chest rising and falling.

No *way* he could sleep with her pressed up against him like this. He had no control of his body when he slept, and waking up like *that* would be extremely awkward.

Logan curled his arms around her, pulling her tighter against him as his mind continued to race.

He'd tried to hide his fears from her, playing it off as a joke.

But he was *terrified* this new world would steal her from him.

She had a Genesis and a Trace and powers and... He was just a regular guy. With a regular family and a regular life. *She* was special. Even *before* she'd discovered *what* she was, she'd been too good for him.

He was going to lose her. And if that happened, he wasn't sure he'd ever really feel alive again. Tess stiffened suddenly in his arms, gasping and struggling to breathe.

"Tess? What's wrong?" He shook her, trying to bring her fully awake.

"Tess!"

She rolled over to face him, managing to gain control of her breathing. "I saw something— I saw myself... and you. I was *leaving.* And you—"

She choked out the word again. "You. You were so sad. *Broken.*"

Great.

"It's okay, Tess," he murmured, kissing her forehead. "It was just a dream."

I hope.

She nodded, breathing slower now.

He held her close, trying to convey his feelings without saying the words.

I love you.

"Logan? Logan?"

His eyes snapped open, and he saw his little sister standing at his half-open door.

"What is it, Squirt?" he called, trying to form a coherent thought.

What time is it?

His room was still dark, no sunlight streaming through the blinds.

Kennedy pushed the door open all the way poking her head into his room.

"I- I- um..."

Only then did he register the sound of the rain splattering his windows.

Kennedy was seven, and *terrified* of storms. His parents were trying to wean her off sleeping in their room. So she came to him, knowing he couldn't say no.

Logan sat up, rubbing his eyes.

"Come on. Close the door so Daisy doesn't—"

Too late. In front of his sister, a long black shape leapt onto the bed, frantically burrowing under the comforter.

Logan sighed, blinking sleep from his eyes.

"I'm sorry..." Kennedy sniffled, burying her face in his shoulder. "I know I'm supposed to stay in my room, but it's so *loud*."

He wrapped one arm around his sister's shoulders, and dug the black and white weenie dog out of the covers with the other.

"Go to sleep, Squirt," he whispered, moving to cover her ears as the thunder grew into a house-rattling roar. "I'm right here."

Kennedy laid back on the pillows, pressing the dog to her chest.

"Are you and Tess going to look at stars tonight?" she murmured.

He breathed a quiet laugh, twining one of her blonde curls through his fingers.

"No, we went yesterday. And it's raining."

"I saw a movie where people kissed in the rain."

"Did you?"

"Yeah... I like Tess a lot."

Logan smiled. "Me too."

"You should marry her."

His eyes widened, and he stared into his sister's serious brown eyes.

Marry her?

An image of Tess, years older, in a gorgeous gown invaded his mind. Her smile, bright and radiant. Her hazel eyes shining.

Perfect.

He tweaked his sister's nose, making her giggle.

He was eighteen. He didn't need to be thinking about marriage.

He smoothed her hair out of her face.

"Only grownups get married, Squirt. Go to sleep."

She mumbled an answer, but he didn't understand a word she said, as she buried her face into his pillows.

Marriage.

He shook his head, annoyed that he'd let his little sister's words get to him.

Marriage to Tess was *years* away. If it happened at all.

Getting out of the bed, he grabbed a pillow and throw blanket, curling up on the floor.

"Goodnight, Squirt," he muttered, even though his sister was already asleep, and he fell into a dream.

A girl in a white dress, with chocolate hair and *beautiful* hazel eyes.

CHAPTER 22

TESS

She held the knob of her parents' bedroom door, muttering to herself and concentrating on not crushing the metal.

"I can do this. I— I can't do this."

She turned around, ready to head up to her room and postpone the conversation again.

Her mom opened the door just as Tess reached the stairs.

"Tess? Need something?"

"Um, no. Not really. I..."

She sighed, torn with indecision.

Shawn had explained that Basics couldn't produce Abnormal children. He'd also said that Abnormal parents usually hired a mentor once they sensed the Genesis had activated.

He had been patient, not pushing her for the last few weeks, while he waited on her to piece it together.

And now, she had.

Her parents *weren't* her parents. Not biologically, anyway. Compared with everything she'd discovered in the last few weeks, learning that she was adopted wasn't that surprising.

But it hurt.

She'd spent eighteen years completely oblivious. Never questioning why she had never heard the story of her birth. Never realizing she'd didn't know her birth weight. Never even *pondering* the difference in her family's appearances.

Two people with brown eyes and blonde hair didn't make... well, *her*.

But even though she knew, she *needed* to hear it from her parents.

"Mom, can we talk?"

Her parents began crying long before she did. She'd hardly spoken the question, "Was I adopted?" and her mom burst into tears.

"I'm sorry, baby," she sobbed, her face buried in her hands. "We wanted to tell you, and— and—"

Tess rushed forward, wrapping her mom in a hug.

"Mom, it's okay. Dad, please, stop crying. It's okay, I promise."

And it was.

Of course, it stung to learn they had hidden the truth from her, but she knew they hadn't done it to hurt her. And they'd raised her in a home *full* of love, acceptance, and beautiful experiences.

She couldn't be angry. They loved her with all their hearts.

They were her mom and dad.

Whoever her birth parents were, they had given her up. Shawn believed they must have done it to hide her. Protect her. And for that, she couldn't be angry with *them* either.

"I love you guys so much," she insisted, pressing her face

in her mom's shoulder. "You're my parents. That doesn't change because of this."

They sagged with relief, still crying.

She held her mother for a long time, whispering quiet reassurances that she wasn't mad at them, until her mom went silent, only the occasional hiccup escaping.

"I have to know, though."

She pulled away, looking into her mom's eyes, then turning to give her dad an encouraging smile.

"Do you know who my birth parents are?"

Her father shook his head regretfully. "Even the lady running the center had no idea who gave you up."

Tess sighed, rubbing the bridge of her nose.

"Which agency was I from?"

Her dad squeezed her mom's hand as she began to cry again. His eyes focused on Tess, filled with concern.

"Do you want to track them down, honey? Believe me, we tried. The woman at the agency had *no* idea who your birth parents were."

He sighed, seeing the disappointment on his daughter's face. "What about a DNA test? We could do a 23 and Me. The results would take a few weeks but—"

"No, that's okay."

Shawn's warning about doctors echoed in her mind.

Due to the stronger genes carried in the Munera DNA, they were less susceptible to sickness and injury. When they *did* need medical attention, it was imperative they only saw an Abnormal doctor. They *never* went to a Basic doctor if it could be avoided.

X-rays or MRIs could reveal the Genesis. Or more accurately, the *presence* of the Genesis. It wasn't a tangible organ, but more a darkening that displayed its existence.

Lusus Naturae doctors often mistook it for a tumor, or some other growth that needed to be removed.

Would a DNA test reveal something dangerous?

She didn't want to take a chance. She could ask Shawn about it tonight, after she got back from the movies with Logan.

"I'm okay." She tried to keep the disappointment out of her voice. "I'll be alright. I promise."

W hen she left for her date, for once, her dad didn't remind her about her curfew. He didn't even tease her about making sure Logan kept his hands to himself.

He could obviously sense that she needed time to process the news.

She desperately wanted to know why her birth parents couldn't keep her. If they'd been on the run from the Society, why hadn't they taken her with them? Hidden her among the rebels? Surely that's where they would have gone, right?

What were her parents' names? Did they look like her? And *why* did she have more than two abilities?

Even Shawn didn't have an answer to that question.

The movie theater came into view, and all thoughts of her birth family evaporated when she saw Logan standing near the ticket booth.

With Shawn.

Smiling. Like they *didn't* hate each other.

Tess stepped out of her car, and Shawn immediately turned her way. Sensing her Trace, no doubt.

Logan followed Shawn's gaze, and his grin widened as she approached.

He wrapped an arm around her waist when she reached him, putting his lips close to her ear.

"I told you I'm gonna *try* to trust him. But I'm pretty sure he's still a stalker."

She pulled away, punching him lightly in the arm.

Shawn scowled to hide his grin. "Shut up, Tucker. I was here first. If anything, you two are following *me*."

"Sure. That's *totally* believable."

"Who are you guys? And what have you done with the *real* Logan and Shawn?"

She smiled, threading her fingers through Logan's, then reaching with her other hand to squeeze Shawn's arm lightly.

"Thank you."

She couldn't think of a better way to end an exhausting and emotional day.

They glanced at each other quickly, then turned back to smile at her.

Shawn rolled his eyes. "Just don't expect me to come over for a sleepover." He crossed his arms, nodding in Logan's direction. "I don't like him *that* much."

She giggled, gazing around at the people in line, stopping when she felt the eyes of an elderly couple. Staring at her.

No. Not at *her*. At Shawn.

Tess looked at him, but he was too busy bickering with Logan to notice.

Trying to avoid looking at the couple, she forced her body to relax. To search for a new rhythm in her chest.

Shawn said that picking out an individual Trace among a group of Munera took years of practice. But she'd memorized the unique feel of his Trace, and she thought she should at least be able to identify if the couple were even Abnormals at all.

Shawn's familiar beat began in her chest and she winced, but didn't allow herself to block it out.

She exhaled slowly, reminding herself to breathe, as another rhythm joined Shawn's Trace. And then another.

She had known other Abnormals lived in Joshua, but she'd never actually thought about the possibility of people she passed on the street being... *not* normal people.

She looked up, turning nonchalantly in their direction.

They looked nervous. Anxious.

The man leaned over, whispering to his wife.

Tess tried to focus on his voice, waiting. And then, his words carried to her. A whisper that should have been too quiet for her to hear.

"You're right. That *is* Shawn Mason. His nephew. Let's go. Quickly. We can come back tomorrow."

Tess glanced at Shawn, oblivious to the hasty retreat being made behind him.

"I forgot something in my car. Shawn, will you come with me?"

Shawn glanced at Logan, curious to see if he would object.

Logan paused, then smiled at Tess. "I'll hold our spot in line."

Tess nodded, grabbing Shawn by the arm and pulling him towards the parking lot.

When they'd reached her car, she whirled around, jabbing a finger in the direction of the couple.

"Do you know them?"

He looked confused, peering in the direction she pointed. "I don't think so. Not by name, anyway."

She narrowed her eyes. "Well they know you."

He shrugged, frowning slightly, but he didn't meet her eye. "No idea."

"You're lying to me."

He looked away, but he didn't deny it.

"What are you keeping from me?" she demanded, louder now.

His blue eyes studied the ground, refusing to look at her. "What did they say?"

"They knew your name. Said you were someone's nephew. They *left* because *you* are here. Why would they do that?"

She hugged her arms around her chest, trying to stay calm.

She *needed* to be able to trust him.

"Please, Shawn. Tell me the truth."

No response.

"*Please.*"

"Tess, I *can't*," he finally said. "I just can't."

Angry tears stung her eyes, and she tried to blink them back.

"*Why?*"

He stared at her. Avoiding the question.

She turned away from him furiously, but he held his hands out to stop her.

His eyes were wide and distressed. When he spoke, desperation tinged each word.

"You'll never look at me the same way again."

She glared. For a long time, neither of them said anything, though her thoughts were racing.

When he spoke again, the words came out flat. Despondent.

"I didn't lie to you. I told you it would take time to explain, and there are things I haven't told you *yet*. But I've *never* lied to you."

She scowled, frustrated with his reluctance to open up to her.

"It's been over a month, Shawn. I don't even know the *Salvator's* name!"

His face drained of color instantly.

She froze, instinctively recognizing she'd discovered the cause of his reluctance.

"What's the Salvator's name, Shawn?"

Silence.

"*Shawn*. Say his name."

He took in a ragged breath, the confession visibly causing him pain.

"Koden," he whispered. "His name is Koden Mason. I'm the Salvator's nephew."

She blanched, trying to understand.

"You told me that he's heartless. And his family is insane. Killers."

"Yes."

Shawn looked to the ground, ashamed.

She took a step back, fear racing through her veins.

"You said you've never hurt anyone," she breathed.

"No, Tess." He shook his head, sadly, finally meeting her eye. "I said, I never *wanted* to hurt anyone."

This was a horrible joke. It *had* to be. Shawn, her *friend* Shawn, could not be a part of the Salvator's family. The family Shawn had claimed was riddled with insanity, destruction, and murder.

She felt sick. She needed him to say that it wasn't true.

Instead, he reached out, tentatively touching her face.

"I'm not like him, Tess,"

She slapped his hand away, unable to comprehend what was happening.

"Why didn't you tell me?"

She felt betrayed. Devastated to know she couldn't trust him. Couldn't trust anyone.

"I knew... I knew this is how you'd react. Please... I *can't* lose you," he whispered. His blue eyes filled with regret. "Tess—"

"What do you do, Shawn?" she demanded, stepping forward until she was inches from his face.

"You told me you don't *want* to hurt anyone, but you *do*. You *do* hurt people. Don't you?" She glared at him. Furious. "*Why?*"

Shawn didn't hesitate this time, venomous words spewing out.

"He's my *uncle,* Tess. Do you even have a clue what that means? What I've had to see? To do? Just to survive? We *are* heartless. We *are* insane killers."

His eyes flashed as he continued.

"If I don't do what they ask, if I go against their beliefs— they'll kill me, too."

He dropped to his knees, despair washing over him.

"I went against them once. I *refused* to do what they asked. And I was *punished.*"

He looked up at her, imploring her to understand.

"You have *no* idea what they did to me."

His hands shook violently.

"I won't get another chance. My parents, my uncle... they will *kill* me if I don't do my job."

His eyes were filled with tears, "I interrogate people. And it *always* comes down to my life or theirs, and...I'm sorry, Tess. I *know* it makes me a horrible person, but I *can't* go through the torture again... I won't."

He stood abruptly, taking a step away from her.

"I've done things that are unforgivable, and it will haunt me for the rest of my life. But I can't take them back. I *wanted* to be honest with you. I *wanted* to tell you. But how could I? I *couldn't* lose you."

She couldn't breathe. She couldn't think. So she moved, lunging forward, wrapping him in her arms. He went stiff in her grasp. Stunned.

She believed him. And she didn't know if it made her a despicable person, but she understood why he'd made the choices he had. Even worse, she knew she would make the same choice if she were in his position.

Finally, he wrapped his arms around her. His entire body shook.

"Please. Please tell me you don't hate me."

Shawn's voice was soft, hardly audible.

"I don't hate you," Tess murmured.

She pulled away, repeating herself. Meaning her words. "I don't hate you, Shawn Mason."

CHAPTER 23

CHLOE

Chloe dragged a red sharpie through the date on the calendar.

One day closer.

Only a month now until her birthday. Just one more month until she could leave, and Reese and Charlotte wouldn't be able to stop her. She felt ridiculously optimistic today. Happy even.

Dalton had just dropped her off after an evening at the mall. He'd stopped far enough down the street that she was *sure* her parents hadn't seen him.

He had *finally* kissed her yesterday. They'd become an 'official' couple at prom, and Chloe had taken every opportunity to escape her house to see him.

At school, he walked with her to all her classes, and used every break available as an excuse to be near her. The four of them, Logan, Tess, Dalton, and Chloe, formed a tight knit group. *And* Shawn Mason.

Before prom, Chloe wasn't sure if Tess had said more than ten words to the guy. But now, he'd apparently become a part of their circle. Tess seemed to *crave* his company. Even Logan, who had looked ready to *murder* Shawn at prom, seemed to accept his presence. And none of them seemed interested in explaining the situation.

Secrets.

Thankfully, Logan had honored his word and kept *her* secret about her father from both Tess and Dalton.

"Chloe!"

Speak of the devil.

She groaned silently, bracing herself before she stepped out of her room.

One more month Chloe. Just one.

She stepped into the hallway. Opened her mouth to ask her father what he needed.

And pain burned across her cheek as her father backhanded her.

She cried out in surprise, stumbling back into her room.

She tried to call out. To ask him what she'd done wrong, but before she could speak, his hands were on her again.

He raised his fist, slamming it into her face.

"Little *tramp*!"

Grabbing her hair, he yanked her backwards, his hands tearing at her skull. She screamed, clawing at his hands.

"Who the hell was that? Huh?"

He released her abruptly, shoving her hard into her dresser.

Tears streamed down her cheeks, and she gasped, backing away as she tried to speak. To *beg* him to stop.

Her mother's voice rang out. "Reese, she's too close—"

"Shut up, Charlotte!" Spit flew from her father's mouth as he advanced on her. "How dare you? You brought a *freak* here! Disrespecting this household, this *family*."

She'd reached the back of her room. There was nowhere to go.

He stared at her, his eyes red. Inhuman. Insane. And then he began to punch her.

Repeatedly.

Stars exploded behind her eyes, and she curled into a ball, trying to cover her head. His hands landed on her ribs and her back.

"Reese!" Her mother screamed, for once trying to protect her. An unexpected ally.

But he was too far gone. He picked her up like a rag doll, dragging her into the living room, and throwing her across the sofa.

Her head collided with the edge of the end table, leaving a gash in her forehead. Blood dripped into her eyes, turning the world around her a brilliant crimson.

She opened her mouth to cry out to her mother, but his hands were suddenly around her throat. Tight. *Too* tight.

Her vision blurred. She scratched at him, desperately trying to pry his fingers from her neck.

"Reese!"

Black tinged her vision. Spots danced behind her eyes.

He is going to kill me.

She screamed as thunder erupted in her chest. Her head *pounded.*

I can't breathe. I need to breathe.

Her father's grip released instantly, and he lurched backwards, away from her. He held his hands out in front of him. Looking at them in disbelief.

Relief raced through her, as air rushed back into her lungs. Too fast. She coughed, hacking and holding her throat.

"Shit! She— she *stopped* it!"

Whatever that meant.

She rolled over, trying to breathe.

Something was wrong.

Her vision was blurry. She couldn't see her parents clearly.

There was something *blocking* them.

A curtain of black had materialized between her and Reese. Like a solid shadow, pushing towards her parents, backing them into the kitchen.

She couldn't move. She was paralyzed with fear. And her head was *pounding*.

Then, a thought came to her. A desire she'd had for the last eighteen years, but had been too terrified to follow through on.

Run.

With the black wall advancing on her parents, she knew this would be her only opportunity. She stood, drawing every bit of strength she could muster, and she ran.

Throwing open the front door, she limped out. She had to go. *Anywhere* but here.

She tried to scream for help, but the words immediately died in her throat as she realized her parents would hear her. And find her.

Tears poured down her face, mixing with blood in a sickening mess.

She ran, forcing one foot in front of the other.

She was desperate to get as much distance from her home as possible, but agony came with each step.

The beat in her chest finally subsided as she reached the end of the block.

Oh God. Oh God.

I have to run.

She had nowhere to go, no one to—

Logan.

She began to sob again, running until her legs gave out. Terrified to stop for fear they were following her. With the last of her strength, she crawled under an old truck, laying on her side and breathing in the stench of oil and gasoline.

She had no idea where she was. She knew she needed to put more distance between her and her parents, but she had reached the limits of her strength.

Her head pounded and her hands trembled. So violently that she dropped her phone several times before successfully dialing his number.

"Hey, Chloe, what's—"

Hearing his voice caused a relieved sob to escape from her throat.

Thank God.

"Chloe! What's wrong?"

"Chloe?" Another voice joined in.

Dalton.

All this time spent trying to hide what her parents were doing to her... all of her carefully constructed walls crumbling around her.

Before today, she would have hung up.

Instead, she just cried harder.

"Babe, what's wrong?" Dalton demanded, clearly taking the phone from Logan. His voice rose in panic when she didn't answer.

"Chloe? Talk to me, what happened?"

She finally managed a broken sentence.

"My dad— he's— he's trying to kill me and— I don't know— I can't—"

"He's trying to— *what?*" Dalton paused, listening as Logan spoke urgently in the background.

"Chloe, where are you?"

She glanced around, trying to find a landmark. But her head hurt *so* bad. Blood continued to run from her forehead. Her vision grew blurry again, and her breath came too fast.

To her right, there was a bright blue Mustang parked in a driveway.

She breathed a few words into the phone, trying to focus on Dalton's voice coming from the speaker.

"What street, Chloe? Chloe, talk to me! Where do I need to go?"

His voice cracked and he screamed out, "Answer me, Chloe!"

She opened her mouth, trying to tell him. To tell him thank you. For everything.

But it hurt too much. The smell of gasoline was in her nostrils. And then she couldn't say anything at all.

"There she is!"

"Oh my God, there's so much blood!"

The voices were so faint they might have been a dream.

"Chloe? Why won't she answer me?"

Hands cupped her face, holding her gently.

"Oh my God. Her face! Look what he did to her face!"

"Dalton, I told you— her dad."

"Help me lift her up. She needs to go to the hospital or the police station or... or somewhere!"

Logan's voice stayed calm. "I don't know if we should. If her parents know she ran away, the police station would be the first place they check."

"Well what the hell do we do?"

Dalton sounded angry. She wanted to hear him laugh. She tried to tell him, but her throat hurt. The words wouldn't come out.

"My mom. She can help her."

Chloe finally found her voice, murmuring. "No. Not the hospital... Just tired..."

Dalton gripped her hand.

"Logan, help me!"

"On three. Ready?"

She screamed as they lifted her. Pain igniting all over her body.

And mercifully, her vision went dark.

C hloe woke in a room that was *definitely* not hers. It was dark, save for a lamp in the corner. She laid on a soft leather sofa that smelled like cinnamon.

Panicked, she tried to throw the covers off and find a door. To run.

But her entire body exploded in unbearable pain when she tried to stand. She collapsed back onto the sofa, sharp needles attacking every inch of her body. She looked around, trying to move slowly.

She was in a living room. On the table beside her, was a picture of Logan and a little girl with blonde pigtails.

Everything came rushing back, along with a nauseating wave of pain.

She let out an involuntary moan. Someone spoke from the next room.

"I think she's awake."

Logan's voice.

A muttered response.

Tess.

"Do you want to stay in here?"

Another whisper. She strained her ears, trying to hear.

"I *couldn't* tell you. She begged me not to. It was her choice, Tess."

Guilt pricked at Chloe as her friend's voice rose loud enough to be clearly heard.

"I should have known... I should have *done* something."

Tess broke off in a quiet sob.

"She's my best friend and I didn't see? I didn't even realize—"

"It's not your fault, Tess. And she's not gonna be mad."

Before the events of tonight, Chloe *definitely* would have been mad. It seemed like Logan had shared her secret with half of Joshua. Now, she found herself desperately relieved to have the secret finally exposed.

She started to call out, but froze at Tess's next words.

"She has a Trace, Logan. She's like me."

Trace?

Logan paused, sounding confused.

"Do you know what she can do?"

"No. But when I unblock it, her Trace is so strong. Suffocating. Like I can't breathe. That's how Shawn said *mine* feels."

Unblocking? Trace? Shawn?

What on earth were they talking about?

Logan spoke up, sounding annoyed. "Great. *Another* Munera."

"I don't know, Logan." Her words came out apologetic. "I need to talk to Shawn. He *had* to have known about her."

Chloe forced herself to sit up, tossing the blanket to the other end of the couch. Only then did she realize she was wearing a loose, sheer tank top that *absolutely* did not belong to her. It had been years since she'd worn a sleeveless shirt. She immediately felt self-conscious, grabbing the blanket, and wrapping it around her to hide the ugly scars.

Then she reminded herself how stupid that was. They knew *everything*.

Wincing, she stood up, only to collapse a second time. *Everything* hurt.

She sighed, stretching her legs, and preparing herself to stand again.

"I wonder if she's used her abilities at all..."

"I wonder what her abilities *are*."

The memory of the black wall rushing at her parents entered her thoughts.

It hadn't been some figment of her traumatized mind. It had been *real*. And it had come from *her*.

And she had a feeling that Tess knew what it was.

She staggered into the next room. The kitchen. Tess and Logan were sitting on the counter.

They looked towards her in surprise when she entered the room, leaning against the door for support.

"What's a Munera?"

CHAPTER 24

KODEN

The driver pulled into the parking lot. Koden stared out the window, watching as some of the red robed seniors began streaming towards the football field, while others milled around in the stands. Talking and laughing with friends and family.

He turned to look at his sister in law, sitting beside him. Konrad sat on her other side, a sullen scowl on his face.

Alyssa looked stunning. He let his eyes travel the length of her body, from her sky high Louboutin heels, to the low neckline of her impossibly tight Chanel blouse. He felt his body react, and he reached over, taking her hand in his.

She leaned into him, giving him a slow, seductive smile.

"Thank you for being here, Koden," she said, her sweet, melodious voice washing over him.

Konrad turned to glare at them, then returned to staring out the window.

Koden grinned. "Of course." He squeezed her hand softly. "I wouldn't miss this for the world."

Actually, he would rather be *anywhere* in the world than here.

The thought of suffering through the graduation was torturous enough. Even more unappealing than the ceremony itself, was the forced socialization with so many Lusus Naturae.

Truthfully, he had business in the area.

A Charge.

His nephew's graduation just happened to involve the Charge, a young girl, he needed to see.

When he'd gained custody of the girl as an infant, he hadn't known how he would benefit from her existence.

Only that he would.

She was nearing her eighteenth birthday, and he had an invested interest in her current well being.

That, and a visit with the esteemed Dr. Miranda Nandez was long overdue.

Hopefully, the Charge he'd placed under Reese and Charlotte Hale's care would provide the doctor with a promising new specimen.

Two birds, one stone.

He ran a finger across Alyssa's thigh, stopping just under the hem of her skirt.

Make that three birds.

"Stop," Koden ordered, and the driver did, parking the limousine next to the stadium in the area he'd had his assistant block off.

As they exited, Koden noticed one of his guards standing among the Lusus Naturae. The man blended in well enough, but a look of disgust was evident as several graduates hurried by, unintentionally brushing against him.

Lusus Naturae *freaks*, scurrying like cockroaches towards the ceremony.

Two girls in crimson raced past them, jostling against him.

"Oh my gosh! Oh my gosh! Bailey, come on! We're gonna be late!"

"Brooke, it's fine! They haven't even started."

"Sorry, sir!" one of them called over her shoulder.

Koden observed their departure, irritated.

"I do wish that you had put my nephew in a private school," he murmured. "Maybe then, we would have avoided some of the *inconveniences* we've faced.

Alyssa pursed her lips tightly when Konrad opened his mouth to respond, and immediately began to cough. Koden stifled a laugh as his brother gasped from lack of air.

"Alyssa," he admonished quietly, yet indulging her tantrum.

She released her husband, glaring at him as he moaned softly, massaging his throat.

"It was *his* decision," she hissed. "I fought to put Shawn in a *proper* school, but—"

She cried out in pain, stumbling forward as a muscle in her calf suddenly cramped. "Bastard!" Alyssa leaned against Koden's shoulder, trying to regain her balance. Konrad remained silent, though an expression of satisfaction had settled upon his face.

"That's quite enough. Both of you," Koden commanded, though he continued to allow Alyssa to lean on him, enjoying the feel of her warm skin through her silk blouse. "You're causing a scene."

He extended his hand to Alyssa, nodding for Konrad to take the lead. His brother didn't move, staring pointedly at his wife's hand. Encased firmly in the Salvator's own. In response, Koden dropped Alyssa's hand from his, placing an arm firmly around her waist.

He raised an eyebrow, waiting, and Konrad dropped his gaze, uncomfortable under Koden's scrutiny.

The stands were packed with red. Students chattering. Parents gushing.

As he entered the stadium, a multitude of new Traces erupted in his chest. Many Munera were in the audience. Most obviously belonged to parents of graduates, though a few appeared to reside in the younger students.

Shawn was nowhere in sight. Probably sulking in a corner waiting for the ceremony to start.

As if on cue, the announcer called out over the speaker.

"Graduates, please take your seat on the field. The ceremony will begin shortly."

A sea of crimson caps and gowns stood, making their way towards the field and the rows of chairs.

From this vantage point, Koden could see how several students had decorated their caps.

Red sharpie proclaimed, 'Thank God!' in all capital letters. The face of a bulldog, the school's mascot, was painted on another.

He rolled his eyes, quickly losing interest in the display of limited Lusus Naturae creativity, and began searching for his nephew.

It would be impossible to find him by appearance alone. Other than his unkempt hair, the boy had no distinguishing qualities to search for.

Nothing remarkable.

However, his Trace was easy to identify. The boy was sitting in a middle row. He was leaning forward to converse with a dark haired girl in front of him.

She rested against the back of her seat, thick brown hair thrown over one shoulder. Her cap obscured her features, leaving her identity a mystery.

As more people crowded into the stands, the number of

Traces increased, making it harder to distinguish Shawn's from the others, and it added to his annoyance.

His skin prickled.

It was hard to feel at ease being surrounded by so many *common* Munera.

He tried to remain rational.

His guard would never have allowed him to attend the ceremony if they suspected that an assassin would be present. Furthermore, this area had long since become one of the predominantly Pro-Society regions.

There hadn't been a single report of rebels in the area in years.

Paranoia still nipped at his mind.

The ceremony began, and after several mindless speeches from the valedictorian, salutatorian, and senior class president, the principal finally called the first senior to the stage.

"Eli Abrigo."

"Draven Anderson."

"Amanda Bartlett."

"Terrin Benson."

On and on and on. Until finally, the name he was waiting on.

"Chloe Hale."

There was wild applause from the brown haired girl in the front row, and a dark-skinned boy let out a whistle, yelling, "That's my *girl!*"

Most of the crowd chuckled, as the girl onstage, Chloe Hale, stepped forward to receive her diploma.

She seemed to be doing well, which pleased Koden immensely. He'd had reservations when he had placed the girl in Reese Hale's care.

The man was an alcoholic. A truly *appalling* choice to entrust with such an important Charge.

However, his advisors had encouraged the placement,

reminding him that the girl wasn't likely to activate early in the Hale's care.

As demonstrated in his nephew, a young child exposed to a high volume of strong Muneras, tended to activate earlier.

Reese Hale was *extraordinarily* ungifted, limited in even his use of Gradus four and five abilities.

It had been imperative that the girl remain inactive as long as possible. Even more so now that her importance to the Society had been revealed.

He closed his eyes, remembering the events surrounding the girl's birth. He had been young then, driven almost insane in his search for answers.

In the weeks prior to the delivery, he had interrogated her parents, pushing his powers to limits he'd previously believed *unethical*.

He had been willing to go to any lengths. Cross any lines or boundaries. Desperate to uncover the information that he sought.

To find *her*.

He opened his eyes, dismissing the sentimental nonsense.

Never again.

Now, his prudent choice in Guardians was finally paying off.

An inactive Munera would be *much* easier to transport.

He watched as the girl turned to face the photographer.

The moment he caught sight of her disfigured face, he stiffened. Rage consumed him, and he found himself moving to stand. To act.

How dare he disobey my orders?

Alyssa reached for him. Unaware of the reason for his anger, but recognizing the need for her intervention. She ran her hand across his arm lightly, then leaned in to whisper in his ear. Her breath was warm, and the promise she spoke made his entire body come alive with need.

He turned to look at her, eyes narrowed as he watched her. She bit her lip, nodding at him slowly.

He exhaled carefully, forcing himself to stay calm. He closed his eyes, allowing himself to visualize Alyssa. Following through with her promise.

That's better.

He smiled, opening his eyes, and searching for Reese in the crowd.

He could wait.

Names continued to be called, and then...

"Tess James."

The girl who had earlier captured Shawn's attention, stood from her seat, moving swiftly to the stage.

She looked familiar. Brown hair. Hazel eyes. A warm smile.

She was the girl from Shawn's memories.

A *Lusus Naturae*.

The rest of the ceremony passed in a haze of anger, as disgust and disappointment mingled to form a sickening lump in his stomach.

He'd hoped after his last visit, his nephew would have opted to socialize with more appropriate company. Clearly not.

The girl would have to be exterminated.

Once the final name had been called, the graduates cheered, then streamed off the field in a red blur.

The Masons, of course, stood away from the crowd, waiting for Shawn to come to them.

Five minutes passed. Seven. Then ten.

"What is taking him so long?" Alyssa demanded, glancing around. "He knows we're waiting."

Koden searched for the boy's Trace.

Useless.

There were too many Traces to identify Shawn's location.

Frowning, Koden gestured to his brother. "Find your son."

His brother grinned, inclining his head in a show of mock respect.

"Of course." He sneered at his wife. "Coming dear?"

She ignored him, looking away as her husband began to move through the crowd of Lusus Naturae. Once he was out of sight, Alyssa sighed, running her hand through her long wavy hair.

He glanced at her, "What is it?"

She looked up, her blue eyes sad and luminous. "Nothing."

He didn't appreciate her secrecy.

He intended to press the matter, but as more families had left, the Traces around him cleared. Leaving one separate from the others.

There.

Shawn stood with a group of children. Two boys, Tess James, and *Chloe Hale*.

And in that moment, Koden felt another Trace. And it came from *her*.

She's active and the Hales didn't report it?

Clearly, there was *much* information the Hales hadn't reported.

He searched the area, finding them hovering at the edge of the crowd.

Reese and Charlotte Hale.

Watching *him* as he watched Chloe.

Koden made his way over to them, ignoring Alyssa as he walked towards the couple.

"Reese!" he called, clapping the man on the shoulder.

The man reeked, the stench of whiskey seeping from his pores.

"Good evening, Sal— Sir."

Koden kept his smile in place.

"I couldn't help noticing that your *daughter's* face has

significant bruising. It would *appear* she's not been being given *proper* care."

His voice lowered to a dangerous whisper.

"And she's *active*."

Reese flinched and looked away.

Koden reached out, gripping the man's chin and forcing him to meet his eye.

A line of crimson blood began to run from Reese's ear, inching towards his throat.

Charlotte cried out softly, reaching for her husband.

Koden grinned at the woman. "Shhh."

Her eyes widened in terror, and she began to beg. "*Please* sir. We had no idea she would activate early."

Her voice was rising as she watched the blood slowly drip down her husband's throat.

Koden's smile disappeared as he gripped the man by his collar, pulling him forward.

"You have *failed* in your duty. *Explain*."

Reese nodded quickly, eager to oblige. "She ran, sir. She deactivated my Genesis."

Koden glared, tugging the man closer.

"And?"

Reese gulped, his Adam's apple bobbing up and down.

"A wall of shadows appeared and she escaped. Truly! That's all I know, I swear."

He released the man, shoving him into his wife. "Follow her. You are *not* to touch her. I don't need her to become aware of how her abilities work. Do you understand?"

Reese nodded again, frantically. "Yes, Salvator."

A gasp came from his wife, and Reese turned towards her in alarm.

She held her neck. Obviously in pain. Blood trickled out from underneath her fingers.

"*Don't* fail again, Reese. I don't give second chances."

CHAPTER 25

Tess

Her parents had already left, hoping to get a front row seat at the ceremony, leaving Tess to drive herself. Chloe, who was still staying at Logan's house, would be riding with the Tuckers. The Tuckers had been amazing, not forcing Chloe to talk yet. Giving her time and space.

She was relieved that Logan's family was taking care of her best friend. With Logan's father being the deputy sheriff, and his mother a Physician's Assistant, Tess was confident that Chloe was in good hands. Still, she couldn't shake the feeling that Chloe wasn't out of danger yet.

Tess grabbed McDonalds on the way to the school, trying to eat away her stress.

And her confusion.

She'd taken a break from learning about the Society, telling Shawn she was too busy with her EOC tests. But in reality, she needed a break from *him*. Time to process who he was and what he had done.

She wasn't angry with him. She had meant what she said when she'd told him she didn't hate him.

How could she?

He was... Shawn.

But it scared her to discover what he was capable of. And it *terrified* her that she could understand why he'd made the choices he had.

The collar of her red gown scratched her neck, and she pulled at it absently.

Why hadn't Shawn told her about Chloe? Obviously, he had to have known she was Munera.

He knew how much she meant to Tess, how much she cared about her— so why hadn't he told her?

Reaching the school, quarter pounder in her hand, she hopped out of her car.

Logan met her at the front gate, swinging her up in his arms.

"Ready to say your goodbyes to this place?"

He set her down, plucking the burger from her hand and taking a bite.

Tess swatted him, snatching it back.

"Definitely. I was done with this place the minute I got those division 1 offers."

Logan's eyes lit up. "So you *are* going to go? You've been so caught up in all your Munera drama, I wasn't sure anymore."

She frowned. "Some parts of the Society are a little... terrifying. But I think I can be a part of both. And I *definitely* want to go to college."

Logan bit his lip, looking uneasy. "Seriously, though, Tess. I'm worried about Chloe. If her parents are Society, I can't imagine her wanting any part of it."

"You're right."

Logan and Tess turned around, facing Chloe as she joined them.

Her makeup accented her warm gold eyes, which glowed with happiness. She looked better than she had in days, despite her injuries.

The bruises around her eye still ranged from purple to green, and a rainbow of colors was displayed from her temple to her jaw. The cut along her forehead had been butterflied, and was healing nicely, but it *hurt* Tess to look at her friend's face, knowing what had caused the damage.

"I don't want *any* part of that *Society*. Not if my parents are involved in it." Her eyes slowly scanned the crowd. She hadn't said anything, but Tess knew she was nervous her parents would show up tonight.

"But I *do* wish I could figure out how... or *what* I did, to stop Reese."

Tess wrapped her arms around Chloe, being careful not to squeeze too tightly. She had several bruised ribs, but thankfully, nothing had been broken.

"At least you have an idea what you can do," she said, offering the last of her burger to Chloe. "All I know is that I'm not *normal*. In *any* world."

"Yeah, you're definitely not normal."

Shawn had snuck up, joining their conversation without anyone noticing him.

Logan jumped at his voice. "I'm gonna put a bell around your neck, Mason," he muttered.

Shawn ignored the jab, giving Tess a stern look.

"You know, you're talking pretty openly about a subject I told you was *classified*. What if a Basic hears you?" Then he glanced at Logan, smirking. "Well, any *other* Basics."

Tess nodded, catching the warning in his bright blue eyes.

She quickly changed the subject. "Where's Dalton?"

Chloe grinned, her cheeks flushing pink. "He's on his way — he was setting up for the party."

Logan and Tess glanced at each other smiling. Dalton was good for Chloe. It was nice to see her so happy.

"You're all coming, right?"

Tess rolled her eyes, laughing. "Well, yeah."

"Obviously, Chloe," Logan teased. "Aren't I your ride?"

Only Shawn remained quiet, though he continued to smile.

Chloe glanced at him, grinning.

"You wanna go, Shawn? It's gonna be fun. Lots of single girls."

She wiggled her eyebrows comically, making him snort, but before he could answer, the announcer asked the graduates to take their seats.

Chloe grinned at Tess, adjusting her cap so that the Bulldog painted on top was clearly visible. The girls gave each other one last hug before moving to sit in alphabetical order.

Once seated, Tess forced herself to take in a deep breath, and relax.

She squeaked in surprise as she immediately felt Shawn's Trace take root in her chest.

She turned in her seat to find him sitting right behind her. He chuckled, a handsome smile spread across his face.

But it looked unnatural.

"What's wrong?" she asked.

Shawn glanced into the small stadium, where a crowd of people sat, cameras ready.

"My uncle is here."

Horrified, her eyes flew to the stands. Shawn shook his head, a smile still plastered on his face.

"No, Tess. Act natural. Nothing is going to happen. There are too many Basics here. He won't do anything."

"Somehow I find that hard to believe," she whispered.

He reached out, giving her shoulder a reassuring squeeze,

murmuring, "Focus on blocking your Trace, please. Don't let him feel it."

Tess did as he instructed. Creating a barrier that enclosed the beat in her chest. Surrounding it with a mental wall, forcing it down until Shawn muttered, "Good."

She closed her eyes, inhaling deeply, then releasing her breath.

"You knew about Chloe?" she asked quietly.

His brows furrowed. "Knew *what* about Chloe?"

She huffed, irritated. "That she's an Abnormal!"

"Of course I did. Chloe is a Charge. I explained all about Charges. The equivalent of a foster kid, remember? Though it's a situation *much* less prevalent within Munera communities."

She threw her hands up in disbelief. "And you didn't think telling me my best friend was *also* Munera might be kind of important?"

Shawn shrugged, looking away. "Why didn't *she* tell you?"

His eyes roved nervously through the crowd. He was obviously distracted by his family in the stands. She couldn't blame him.

"Tess, my family isn't interested in Charges. Typically, they are poor, inconsequential children, bred by poor, irresponsible, low Gradus families that have too many children to mentor *or* control." He paused, sounding disgusted. "There's a reason low Gradus Munera couples should limit their offspring."

Finally, he looked at her, meeting her eye and sighing apologetically. "The only reason I would ever need to interact with a Charge would be if their Guardians betrayed the Society."

Tess faltered. Confused. "But Shawn... Chloe didn't know."

At that, Shawn's eyes narrowed. "Of course she knew. Her

Guardians would have told her when she was six. It's custom. The Society believes early education helps to discourage reckless mating and over breeding, and teaches control. Allowing the Charge the opportunity to break the cycle they were born into."

She found herself shaking her head, even before he finished talking.

"They never told her anything. She only discovered she was gifted when Reese attacked her and she was somehow able to protect herself."

"You're kidding."

"*Shawn*! Why would I joke about this! You saw her face, right? He tried to kill her but she activated."

His mouth dropped open, at a loss for words. "Tried to kill her? That's illegal."

Tess rolled her eyes, answering sarcastically. "Murder is illegal? *Really?*"

He grabbed her shoulder, trying to convey how serious the offense was. "No, I'm serious. Discipline is one thing, Tess, but there are *strict* laws about Charges and how they're to be treated. They might have been given orders not to reveal her Munera heritage, but *no one* would have given them permission to abuse her."

He bit his lip, looking troubled. "There has been evidence that highly traumatic events can stimulate early activation."

As the seats around them began to fill in, he snapped his mouth closed.

Tess growled, frustrated. Wanting to ask more questions and annoyed they were out of time. Unfortunately, the ceremony didn't care.

Sighing, she attempted to focus on the speeches and the names being called to the stage. And she reminisced about the last few months of her life.

She'd finally gotten the boy of her dreams. She'd made a

friend she never expected. She'd discovered that she was special, and different in the most *amazing* way.

"Tess James."

God... I'm going to miss this place.

A fter the ceremony, she met up with her friends, laughing and smiling as she watched her classmates tracking down their thrown caps and tassels.

She felt an unexpected weight lifted off of her. Keeping everything under control and hidden during school had been exhausting.

Now, all of that worry was gone. Even if it was only a temporary relief.

Chloe snatched Tess in a hug, squealing in excitement.

"Ready to party?"

"Of course, I'm ready!"

"Same here," Logan said, grinning.

"Hey, don't forget about me!" Dalton demanded, then smirked. "Oh wait. It's *my* party. I forgot."

The group laughed, turning to Shawn for his input. Tess was glad that her friends had accepted his quiet presence. Even though he rarely added much to their conversations, he'd become an integral part of their group.

He shook his head.

"I have family here for graduation."

Tess heard the trepidation in his voice, though she seemed to be the only one who did.

An image appeared, uninvited in her mind.

A man. Dark-haired, dark-eyed, fair-skinned. A cruel smile of radiant white teeth.

Then it was gone, and she shivered, trying to discern what she'd just seen.

The man. He looked like Shawn.

The same angled jaw and black hair. The same broad shoulders and attractive features.

The differences between them were apparent, but they faded into obscurity in light of the extreme similarities.

Recognition settled like a weight in her stomach, and she felt paralyzed with horror.

This was Shawn's uncle.

The Salvator.

But how did she know?

Shawn had never shown her a picture of him. He'd never even *described* him. It was almost like the image had come from Shawn's mind. She dismissed the thought immediately.

That wasn't possible. She couldn't read minds.

"Tess?"

Shawn was looking at her, concerned. Inconspicuously, he tapped a finger to his chest. She'd momentarily released control over her Trace.

She looked around quickly. Shawn, Chloe, and Logan were all staring at her strangely. Thankfully, Dalton was distracted with finalizing details for the keg.

She stammered out an excuse. Something lame about Lauren giving her a dirty look, but it was obvious no one believed her.

Especially Shawn.

"Really, it's nothing," she insisted.

Logan gave her a skeptical stare.

She smiled at him, hoping he'd get the hint and drop it, when suddenly, Shawn's face went pale. Draining of all color as a hand clamped down on his shoulder. His blue eyes grew wide and alarmed.

A man stood behind Shawn. Not the man she'd seen. A watered down, less attractive version.

His father?

The Generalis.

The name slid into her thoughts and with it, a familiar rush of fear.

And a room. Devoid of furniture or decoration. A boy lay curled on the floor. Sobbing. Covered in blood that completely obscured his face and coated his hair. Hundreds of slits marred the boy's half-naked body, each in various stages of healing. Some freshly oozing, while others had the beginnings of scabs forming over them.

He coughed, vomiting a fountain of blood and mucus. Screaming when the cuts reopened from the impact.

The Generalis and the Salvator stood over the boy, glaring down at him.

"Please. Please!"

The boy's voice was hardly a whisper, and he struggled to crawl away from the men, leaving a wet trail of blood.

Shawn's uncle and father. The boy.

The vision cleared and Tess was faced with a motionless Shawn, his face stark white and his breathing shallow. His eyes focused on her.

Horrified.

Oh my God.

Bile rose in her throat.

The bloodied boy was Shawn.

Oh my God. Oh my God.

"Your mother and uncle are waiting," the Generalis said, giving his son's shoulder a tight squeeze.

Shawn nodded, following his father wordlessly.

Tess turned from her friends, ignoring their questions, and sprinted to the restroom. She dove into a stall just in time for her stomach to revolt, bringing up the hamburger she'd eaten.

Where the hell had those images come from?

She didn't want them in her mind. She wanted to claw it out, the memory of Shawn's bloodied body making her feel ashamed and dirty.

His blue eyes.

Terrified. *Betrayed.*

Please. Please!

Shawn's voice.

Her stomach churned, threatening another round of vomiting as tears streamed down her face.

"Tess?"

Chloe's voice at the door made her jump.

She spoke again, annoyed.

"For Christ's sake, Logan, I've got this. Go wait in the car, I'll meet you there."

"I'm not leaving her like this."

"Yes, you are."

With that, Chloe moved into the bathroom, knocking on the stall.

"Tess? What's wrong?"

Tess sucked in a breath, the taste of bile coating her tongue.

"I saw something..." she whispered, thankful for the closed stall door as she wiped tears from her cheeks and vomit from her chin. "I don't know what it was, but I saw..."

She trailed off, unable to describe the vision. She took a few shallow breaths, opened the door, and threw herself into Chloe's arms.

"Don't think about it," Chloe murmured, her mouth close to Tess's ear. "It's okay."

She stroked Tess's hair gently.

I went against them once. I refused to do what they asked. And I was punished.

That was what he'd meant wasn't it? What else could it have been? What had he done... what could *anyone* have done to deserve that?

Tess pulled away, unable to hold back a sob. She shook her head violently.

Chloe didn't know. She knew she was Abnormal, but she had no clue about Shawn's family, his past, or the Salvator.

It wasn't okay.

Things were most definitely *not* okay.

The memory of Shawn's pain replayed in her mind.

His betrayal. His desperation. His *terror*.

"Come on," Chloe whispered, brushing Tess's hair from her face. "Let's get you cleaned up. And you can tell me when you're ready. Okay?"

Tess nodded, unable to shake the image of her friend, lying on the bloodied floor.

It *hadn't* been her imagination. It had come from Shawn's mind, not hers.

He could see people's fears. Could he show her *his* fears? He hadn't told her he could do that...

"Come on," Chloe said, tugging Tess's hand.

They stepped into the parking lot, searching for Logan's Bronco. Her eyes were immediately drawn to a dark-haired family, sliding into a sleek limousine.

Shawn.

His blue eyes staring blankly. Empty.

Hopeless.

Then, the car was gone, taking her friend with them.

CHAPTER 26

Shawn

Tess had his ability.

It was the only explanation possible.

It had taken all of his strength to separate the vision from reality.

But that's what it was.

A *vision*.

A vision that represented his fear.

Timor mortale.

It had felt *so* real.

That day. The day of his punishment.

Begging his father and Koden to stop.

The scars across his chest and arms and legs and shoulders burned with the phantom pain.

Scars everywhere.

His uncle had left the marks on his body, but his father had left the scars imprinted upon his mind and memory.

His heart.

Don't think about it.

It was impossible not to. Not with his uncle seated beside him, and his parents across from him.

He could still taste the blood. He could still feel his flesh ripping and tearing, and the muscles in his body shearing from the tendons.

He could still hear his uncle laughing.

No.

His uncle *was* laughing.

Right now.

Shawn forced himself into the present, realizing that Koden was laughing at a joke Alyssa had made. The sound grated on Shawn's nerves, making him want to lash out.

To hurt his uncle.

To kill him.

He could do it.

It would be relatively easy to take down the man. He had grown complacent in Shawn's company.

And then my parents will kill me.

He froze, realizing that his hands had started to spark, bolts of lightning racing across his palms.

The reawakened evening of terror had stirred up the bitter hatred he tried so hard to force down.

He shoved them into his pockets before anyone could see, mentally reprimanding himself. He didn't have the luxury of letting his thoughts run away with his senses.

He took a deep breath, bringing his mind back to the issue at hand.

How had Tess induced a vision on him?

Timor mortale, mortal fear, was an ability traditionally exclusive to the Mason family. It was near impossible for the ability to transcend families.

He hadn't been exaggerating when he'd told Tess it would

take weeks to explain everything to her. Centuries of events and history couldn't be consolidated into a brief summary. However, there was some of the history he preferred not to tell her.

His history.

The history of the Tribus Viribus, the Three Forces.

The three ancient Munera families.

The Caines, the Masons, and the Roses.

Over the years, the families had kept their trees small, with as few branches as possible.

So small in fact, that the families were actually in danger of extinction.

He sighed, leaning back against the leather seats and flicking the AC vent closed.

It had something to do with Tess having multiple abilities. That much he was sure of.

Strength, speed, senses, healing. And now, *timor mortale*.

It isn't normal to have multiple gifts. It isn't possible.

"Shawn."

Koden's voice. Cold and calculating.

Shawn forced his mind to go blank, should Koden decide to take a look through it.

"Yes, sir?"

Koden watched him with curious interest. "Are you aware that Chloe Hale has activated?"

Shawn nodded respectfully.

"Yes sir. I believe she recently activated. No more than a few days ago."

Koden glared, suspicious. Waiting for Shawn to lie. So that he could catch him in that lie. And he could have a legal reason to kill him. Not even Alyssa would have the power to intervene if he committed another offense.

Shawn didn't bother to dwell on it. His impending death was nothing new.

What *was* news was the treatment Chloe had received at the hands of her Guardians.

And why was Koden so interested in the girl? By all logic, Koden shouldn't have even known her name.

Charges were dealt with by officials, and *occasionally*, the lower Court. But *never* the Salvator and his family.

His uncle narrowed his eyes, trying to gauge the truth in his nephew's words.

"Did you hear that she ran away from her Guardians?"

Shawn inclined his head slightly. "Yes sir. I believe they beat her."

Red flooded Koden's face at his tone. Sardonic and loathing.

Shawn sneered. "It's horrible actually. Those scars are the work of a monster."

A sharp pain burned across his face as Koden used his ability to mimic the pain of a hand, exploding against his cheek.

Unlike the phantom pain Shawn's ability could cause, this was real. A red splash began to bloom on his face.

"Don't get smart with me," Koden snarled.

Shawn winced, instinctively raising a hand to touch his tender skin.

"Apologies, Salvator. I was simply pointing out that the wounds visible on her back are *scars*. Meaning the abuse has likely been going on for years unnoticed."

While he *was* trying to get under his uncle's skin, he wasn't exaggerating. He had seen Chloe's fears. The memory of Reese Hale, a leather belt, and the welts and scars that covered his friend assaulted his mind. It hit too close to home.

"With all due respect, sir, why are you worried about Chloe Hale?" Shawn asked, maintaining eye contact with Koden. "Yes, the abuse is illegal, and *horrible,* but she's a

Charge. Hardly worthy of your time." He allowed a condescending note to enter his voice.

"Let the officials handle her Guardians. Unless there's more to the situation?" He forced his words to come out nonchalant, masking his curiosity.

Koden touched his lip. A warning, nodding almost imperceptibly at their driver.

Shawn got the message and stayed silent for the rest of the drive.

His home came into view. The appearance of the grandiose manor gave him no comfort. His home was a prison. A resting place while he waited on his death sentence to be carried out.

Koden sent the driver away, and the Masons stepped into the entryway.

Alyssa immediately began to question her lover as the door closed behind them.

"How could the abuse have gone unnoticed? Reese sends you quarterly reports, does he not?"

Her eyes flicked to her son, and she waved her hand in his direction.

"Stay. I believe you'll be needed."

Shawn nodded, keeping his hands in his pockets, as he slouched towards the stairs, slipping his silent earbuds in. To disappear.

And wait until someone, probably his own father, slipped up and revealed the classified information.

Koden would never intentionally tell him Society news, but his family tended to overlook Shawn. They considered the silent, sullen teenager to be too consumed with loud music and irrational emotions, generally, a waste of space.

They underestimated him. And Shawn preferred it that way.

"Reese needs to stand trial, Koden," Alyssa hissed. "The man was given an important role and now..."

Usually, the word *trial* filled Shawn with dread, knowing he would likely be needed. And he *hated* being needed.

The image of Chloe's battered face crossed his mind, and he gritted his teeth.

He would gladly make an exception for Reese Hale.

But why had Chloe been entrusted to such a weak man? Traditionally, Charges were given to mid rank Guardians, ensuring the Charge an opportunity to rise above the station they had been born into. Shawn had *never* heard of such a low Gradus, low class couple, being given a Charge.

And regardless, why had Koden bothered to monitor her status?

What could *possibly* make her so important?

"She wasn't supposed to activate early. That was the point of placing her in the Hale's care." Koden's voice was low. Frustrated.

Alyssa's heels created a harsh cadence as she stalked across the marble floors, pacing in front of the men. She was relentless when she was angry. For years, Shawn had witnessed her berate her husband. Now, she had turned on her leader, furious that he had allowed the Hale's to undermine him.

"Eighteen *years* we've waited for the right opportunity, and now you've allowed Reese and Charlotte to make a mockery of our patience!"

They had been keeping tabs on Chloe for eighteen years? *Why*? It made no sense.

At last, his father spoke up.

"Dr. Nandez needs another Caine to continue her research. Now that the girl is active, it will be significantly harder to gain her obedience. How do you plan to detain her?"

A loud crack echoed through the room as Koden slapped his brother hard across the face.

"*IDIOT*!" he seethed, turning and staring in Shawn's direction, where he waited on the top stair.

He forced himself not to react, keeping his features flat and unemotional. But he was stunned.

Chloe is a Caine?

It didn't make sense. Surely, at *some* point, he should have heard something. *Felt* something.

He'd spent his entire life researching the ancient family.

It seemed impossible that he would have been unaware of her existence. Her *true* existence.

For years, he'd known that she was Munera, occasionally running into the Hales at school events and around town.

While *his* family didn't associate with *her* family, the Hale's had always demonstrated the proper respect when they crossed paths.

But he'd never bothered to talk to her, or *bond* over their shared genetics.

He was different. His family status had always separated him from other Munera children.

Even if he *hadn't* been a loner, his presence was simply too intimidating. No, his well-known and widely-feared *abilities* were too intimidating.

Judging by Koden's reaction, the fact that Chloe was a Caine was one secret that should *never* have been revealed to those outside his circle.

Which didn't include Shawn.

Until now.

Koden sighed, running his fingers through his hair. "My father raised at least *one* intelligent son," he muttered.

Then he straightened, smoothing down his shirt.

"I had planned to visit the facility tonight. *With* the girl.

Reese has been instructed to find her. To follow her. He will report her location to me in the morning."

Alyssa crossed her arms. "You think he can be trusted with another assignment?"

Koden shrugged, regaining his confidence. "If he doesn't, I'll have trackers find her. Ultimately, the means I use is unimportant. She *will* be found. Without the protection of her Guardians, it's likely that she will stay with one of her classmates. And we have records on all of her contacts?" He turned his attention towards his brother.

Konrad nodded, still holding a hand to his face. "Everyone in the senior class," he confirmed.

Koden clapped his hands together with an air of finality. "It's settled, then. We will wait on Reese's information. In fact, I believe I will pay his wife a visit before I attend to Dr. Nandez."

A wicked grin snaked across his face. "Let's see if that gives him the *proper* motivation needed to handle his responsibilities."

Alyssa, assessing the smile on his face, quickly put a hand on his arm. She smiled sweetly.

Shawn gagged.

"You'll be back tonight?" she asked. Her voice was soft and seductive. A woman laying claim.

Koden's grin widened. He glanced at his brother, the glint in his dark eyes triumphant.

"Of course," he murmured, giving Shawn's mother's hand a squeeze before he made his way to the door.

As the door closed behind his uncle, Shawn's father muttered something under his breath. Quiet enough that only Alyssa heard. She whirled on her husband, furious, the air around her deadly.

"What did you say?"

Konrad glared at her.

"*Whore.*" The word carried more malice than Shawn had ever heard from his father.

The sound of screaming filled the home, and Shawn smiled.

His parents had gotten married at an age much younger than was prudent. His father, like so many men before him, had been taken in with Alyssa's soft smile, sweet voice, and wide, innocent eyes.

That had been foolish.

He stood, slipping silently up the stairs and into his room.

He had to warn Chloe, but he needed to *ensure* Koden wouldn't be able to discover his involvement.

He reached for his phone, dialing a number from memory.

He just hoped the plan he'd come up with didn't make him an even bigger fool than his parents.

CHAPTER 27

KODEN

He couldn't pinpoint exactly what he was feeling. He was furious, obviously.

Reese Hale had been given a simple task. Keep the girl safe. And he'd failed. Now, the *moment* Koden had found a use for her, Reese had let the girl escape.

He wasn't accustomed to people disobeying orders, and it greatly displeased him.

Although it *had* afforded him several hours to explore what pleasures Charlotte Hale had to offer.

But Chloe Hale should be here with him now, ready to join Sapphire in her efforts to find the cure.

And the fact that she *wasn't* infuriated him.

Yet he also felt a rush of excitement. Anticipation.

He needed to know if his suspicions about the Caines, and more precisely, Sapphire, were correct.

He tried to tell himself he was only interested in Sapphire Caine because she potentially held the DNA to create a cure, but the anxiety he felt coursing through his body told a different story.

He hadn't spoken with the girl when he'd toured the facility several months ago. She had been sedated at the time of his last visit.

Now, she was awake, though she hadn't appeared to notice him when he had entered. In fact, she hadn't moved once in the last ten minutes since he'd been in the room.

She was laying on her back, staring at the ceiling with dull blue eyes.

He studied the girl, searching her face for any physical resemblance to *her*.

She had a sallow, unhealthy appearance, but he could see that in normal circumstances, she would be a strikingly beautiful woman.

Her eyes, though devoid of emotion, were the same startling shade as the woman he sought.

But other than her eyes, and her petite size, she bore no likeness that he could see.

He fought the wave of disappointment that threatened to overwhelm him.

There is still a chance...

Heels clicked rhythmically against the tile floor, and Dr. Miranda Nandez swung the door open. Her eyes remained focused on the tablet screen in her hand.

"Alright, Sapphire, I'll need you to be on your best behavior. The Salvator is—"

She stopped abruptly, spotting Koden standing motionless in the middle of the lab. The tablet slid to the floor, shattering against the tile. Nandez choked on her next words.

"Salvator! I- I— You're early!"

She bowed formally, trying to hide the panic in her eyes.

Koden smiled. Calm. Serene.

Inside, he seethed.

Months ago, Dr. Nandez had appealed to him, asking for an increase in financial support.

She had revealed her theory, outlining the years of research supporting her belief. The belief that the Caine family held the key to providing a cure.

The possibility of the Caine Genesis *potentially* reversing the toxic effects of Lusus Naturae DNA.

Consequently, he had thrown more and more money towards her research, and redoubled his efforts to root out Caines. All in an effort meant to *save* the Munera people.

His people.

And the woman had failed.

Fury consumed him, and he had to take in a slow, calming breath before allowing himself to speak.

I have trackers after the girl. We will *find her.*

"Dr. Nandez," he said. "A pleasure as always to see the Society's money hard at work." He spread his arms to indicate the room around them.

Nandez fought to control her breathing, giving him a respectful nod.

"It's an honor to have you here, Salvator. I'm hopeful that you will be satisfied with the strides we have made towards our goal. "

He raised an eyebrow. "I'm sorry. I wasn't aware your lab had completed a successful trial."

Nandez gulped, allowing a tentative smile. "No sir. I apologize for any miscommunication. I have not *completed* a successful trial. However, I have made tremendous progress—"

He frowned, lowering his voice. "I hope, Doctor, that you are aware of how important the success of our *project is*. To the Society and all Munera as a whole."

Nandez gulped, nodding.

"And are you also aware that a positive outcome from our

project is *crucial?* Every day, the moment of extinction draws nearer, and yet, here I am. With nothing to show, despite your *strides*."

He had moved closer to the woman, until he was standing within inches of her.

"Explain."

The doctor began to babble. "I did everything correctly, sir. The mutt's body simply wasn't strong enough to handle the activation, although she *did* activate. I have a limited supply of the serum we used in our first trial, and I've made a change in the formula I *believe* will eliminate our previous problem. However, I'm hesitant to use it. We have such a small supply at this time, and our donor can't lose any more marrow yet. Not without a significant risk to her life."

He leaned in, whispering, "Then, *heal* her."

Nandez turned to glare at Sapphire, gesturing towards her angrily. "She has deactivated every healer I've brought in. She simply *refuses* medical attention."

Koden glared at her. "Am I hearing excuses?"

Dr. Nandez shook her head frantically.

"No, Salvator! My team has located several potential mutts that we believe are more compatible with the girl's strength. As we speak, they are being processed in admissions. But I'll need another Caine if I am to continue the research immediately. I- I had hoped—"

Koden concentrated on her face, studying the line of her brow, and trailing his gaze down her face.

The woman screamed as a deep gash opened from the corner of her eye to the bottom of her jaw.

More gashes opened across the backs of her knees, and she collapsed to the ground.

He knelt over her, cupping her chin tightly in his hand.

No one came to see what the commotion was about. Everyone in the facility knew the cost of failure.

And Koden was free to do whatever he wished.

Her eyes gazed at him, terrified. Begging. Her lips trembled.

"Please, Salvator," she whispered. "I just need more time. I won't fail again, I swear it!"

A slow smile spread over Koden's face, and he ran a finger slowly down her arm.

Excited.

It was a shame she wasn't more attractive.

"I know you won't."

K oden snatched a white towel from the table, wiping the blood from his hands. Nandez, no longer sobbing, lay silent now in unblinking horror. Her naked body was coated in a thick layer of crimson. Several of her extremities were broken, and she had countless ripped tendons and ligaments.

All wounds that would be taken care of by a healer.

Later.

Koden had placed a hold on the medical order. Let her wait a few hours.

Let her suffer.

Let her *learn*.

He couldn't accept failure.

Of course, the researcher *had* made tremendous progress. The news that she had successfully reactivated a mutt's Trace was impressive.

But Koden needed results. *Real* results. And if he tolerated the doctor's shortcomings, he feared he would *never* get them.

His gaze flicked to Sapphire, still staring blankly at the ceiling.

He needed more Caines.

"You." He spoke to the guard posted at the door, then waved a hand towards Nandez. "Get her out. Now."

The guard's gray eyes darted to the doctor's mutilated form, his face going pale before dropping into a low bow.

"Yes, Salvator."

The man dragged Nandez's limp form from the room, and finally, Koden was left alone with Sapphire.

The girl sat up, her once-dull eyes now sharp and watchful. A small satisfied smile rested on her face.

"You should have killed her."

Koden nodded grudgingly. "Correct. I should have. Unfortunately, she's my top researcher. I need her."

Sapphire shrugged, then moved to lay back down. "That's a shame."

The girl's impertinence annoyed him, making his eye twitch. He forced himself to remain calm, reminding himself that it was necessary to gain the girl's compliance.

Not only was a cure likely embedded in her DNA, but there were other, more *personal* reasons for questioning her. He could afford a degree of tolerance.

However, he needed to remind her who was in control, and who was in a cage. As he opened his mouth to reply—prepared to give her a subtle demonstration of his power if necessary, pain exploded in his skull. It tore through his head, searing his temples, like nails being driven into his brain.

He tried to summon his gift, searching to escape the pain.

And there was nothing.

A complete *lack* of feeling filled his chest. There was no Trace.

The girl had deactivated his Genesis, using the ability Nandez had insisted was necessary when she first revealed the Caine discovery.

The pain in his head sharpened, darkening his vision and blurring the room around him.

"I want to know what *you* know."

The voice was distant, like a whisper in a far corner of his mind.

Sapphire.

As the girl's name crossed his mind, a memory was reawakened, streaming into his thoughts like a scene from a movie.

He was with Dr. Nandez.

"I'm not interested in excuses, Doctor. We need that cure. Find Sapphire's siblings and the problem is solved. They will provide more than enough Caines for you to use."

Nandez spoke quietly, her tone deferential. "Yes, Salvator, we do need Caines. But it must be a Caine with specific abilities. They must possess either the deactivation gene or the mimicry gene. Should the siblings, or Chloe Hale for that matter, lack that gene, they would be essentially useless."

No. Not useless.

Not to him.

He had spent years hunting the most recent generation of Caines for another reason entirely.

The moment his mind strayed to that reason, the image changed.

A woman. Her vibrant blue eyes wild with excitement, and her beautiful face full of joy.

Amora Caine.

His heart raced as he displayed the antique ring in front of her, kneeling on one knee. Terrified she wouldn't accept. Leaping to his feet and swinging her in the air when she nodded. Holding her body in his arms. Her quiet moans in his ear later that night.

Then waking the next morning to find her gone.

An unexpected rush of despair washed over him, joining the excruciating pain in his head.

The girl was in his thoughts, rifling through them relentlessly.

It shouldn't be possible. She *shouldn't* have this ability— a *Mason* ability.

Unless...

He needed to stop her. He struggled desperately against her hold, but he was powerless against her gift.

Get out of my mind.

"What happened to her?" Sapphire demanded.

He was helpless.

Never having encountered another Munera possessing *Animo*, the ability to intrude upon someone's most intimate thoughts, he'd never learned to guard his mind. He had never been forced to fight against the intrusion.

And he was unable to stop the memory from entering his thoughts.

He studied Alec Peralta. Waiting. The man, who had married into the Caine family through Amora's sister, Pearl, was completely spineless.

His golden eyes flitted nervously about the cell, and his olive skin dripped with sweat. His wife fought desperately against her restraints. Screaming in outrage.

Her belly swollen with child.

Chloe Hale.

Alec looked anxiously at his wife— the woman he had recently reported to the Society. While he claimed to still love her, he had been disgusted to discover she was a Proditor. *A blood traitor to their People.*

He had reported her, knowing he was sentencing her, and potentially his daughter, to death.

Koden blinked rapidly, desperate to think of anything else. To conceal *this* thought from Sapphire. But the girl was too deep into his mind. He was unable to stop the memory from escaping.

"Amora is pregnant with a baby girl, due within a few days," Alec said.

Pearl cried out, begging her husband to stop, but Alec ignored her. "She sent a message to Pearl. She thinks... Salvator, she thinks the child is yours."

Koden turned away immediately, his convictions finally confirmed. He had to leave. To escape this room. To get away from the pain of this woman, who so closely resembled her sister. Hope soared in his veins.

He grabbed a passing guard by the shoulder, spinning her to face him.

"Yes, Salvator?" the guard lowered her eyes, her voice shaky.

"Ares Torray," Koden hissed. "Tell him that I require his skills. Now!"

T he pain in his head vanished, and the images were swept away in the light of the lab. He leaned on his knees, panting.

Now... She knew.

Sapphire was staring at him, stunned into silence.

He watched her closely, waiting on her reaction.

She burst into laughter.

Rage ignited in his chest. Every instinct begging him to slit her throat.

"You think you're going to find your bastard child by rounding up *my* family?" she asked, her grin widening. "You thought— you *hoped, I* could be yours?"

His hands trembled with fury, and he fought to regain the upper hand. He was torn between the need to kill her and the chance— the *tiny* chance that she was his.

Unfortunately, she still held control over his Genesis.

"I need to ask you a few questions about your family," he announced, trying to keep his voice steady.

She let out another hysterical laugh, though the movement clearly pained her.

"This is *great*! Oh, Jesus, this day gets better and better!"

Koden stiffened at her tone. "I'd advise you to—"

"To what, Salvator?" she hissed, finally sitting up to glare at him through hate-filled eyes. "Maybe the good *doctor* didn't fully explain the situation to you. You can't threaten me. I've already lost *everything*. I *wish* I was dead. My siblings are gone. They left *me* behind. And I don't have any other family. What information do you really think you can gain from me?" She met his eye, her lips twitching slightly. "Your Genesis is useless, *Salvator*. So tell me again what exactly you'd *advise* me to do?"

She was right.

He couldn't force her to talk. If she *was* his daughter, his *heir*, he wouldn't be able to procure that information without his ability reactivated. Additionally, she clearly had no regard for her own life.

Threats would not work.

Reasoning.

He needed to reason with her.

For that, he needed to stay calm.

"Regardless of my personal reasons for tracking the Caines," he started, taking a deep breath. Regaining his composure. "My primary concern is saving our people from *extinction*. The Caines are the only ones with the ability to—"

"To save the Society?" Sapphire interrupted.

His fingers twitched. His measured breathing wavered.

Calm. Stay calm.

He was in control here. *She* was trapped and eventually, he would discover her weakness. Just as *she* had discovered *his*.

Ultimately, she would tire, and lose her hold on him. And then, he could pry the information from her head himself. Piece by piece.

"You could save *all* Munera," he said. "Especially the

hybrids with dormant Geneses. How can you be so selfish to withhold that gift?"

Sapphire shot upwards, throwing herself into the barrier.

"*Liar!*" she screamed, beating her fists against the glass. "The rebel Munera want you *dead—* don't pretend you're willing to save them, too. Not when they're all *traitors* to you. You and your Society want to destroy the Basics. Wipe them out to *preserve* the 'people's purity'. Don't act like you're doing this with noble principles."

He stared at her incredulously.

"Really, Sapphire. Don't be ridiculous. That's absolutely absurd. I would think you're old enough to know facts from fantasy." He chuckled, feeling his confidence return.

Her blue gaze narrowed with revulsion. "That's great. You find *genocide* funny?"

He stopped laughing. His patience was growing thin.

"Child, I have *no* intention of exterminating the Lusus Naturae. They're incompetant enough to destroy themselves without my help."

The girl stared, confused, and he continued, his voice dripping with condescension.

"Admittedly, as a whole, they are low-class, ignorant creatures. Their filthy DNA has tainted Munera bloodlines for milenia. Should their end come about within the near future, I'll be the first to say 'good riddance'. However, wiping out the Lusus Naturae is not on my agenda."

Sapphire frowned at him, and for a moment, he caught a glimpse of Amora in her blue gaze.

Intense. Powerful, and yet...

Weak. She was weak. *She ran to avoid becoming Domina.*

She had run away from *him*.

And *that,* was a thought he had no desire to share with this girl.

246

He stood quickly, dipping his head slightly towards Sapphire.

Despite the girl's physical condition, she wasn't as weak as she had initially appeared. It wasn't ideal, but he always had the liberty of revisiting the facility tomorrow. Perhaps Dr. Nandez would be more inclined to provide a solution now.

"There are other ways to break your will, Sapphire Caine," he said, his voice serious.

If she were his daughter, he would have to help her see reason. To see it was to her advantage to help him.

If she is my daughter...

Sighing, he turned from the girl, starting for the door.

"Salvator!"

Koden paused at her voice, glancing over his shoulder.

"Thank you for the entertainment. But I'm not your kid. She's probably a rogue. A *traitor.* Just like her mother. Lucky for them, she escaped you."

The girl had a satisfied smirk plastered on her cracked, dry lips.

"I wonder how your Munera would feel about their *Salvator* falling in love with a *Proditor*."

He ground his teeth, growing more grateful by the second that the child was likely, *not* his. He smiled at her, allowing himself a moment to revel in his triumph. The girl had inadvertently given him much of the information he desired.

"That won't be a problem, Miss Caine. I don't think you'll be telling anyone about my past... *indiscretions*. Tampering with memories can be *very* useful."

CHAPTER 28

Chloe

Chloe chewed on her thumbnail, lost in thought. Unable to escape her memories of Reese.

His hands tight around her throat. The inhuman strength he'd held her with that had suddenly disappeared, replaced with the black wall of shadows, forcing her parents back.

She had been horrified to learn the truth. That the shadows had in fact, come from her.

While she was grateful that she had been able to protect herself from her father, she wasn't sure what to think of this world she'd been thrust into.

Last night, she had unintentionally summoned the shadows. A nightmare jolted her awake, and she had opened her eyes to see the Tucker's family room had taken on the appearance of a 2-Dimensional picture. Like a drawing with no shading.

She panicked, as all the shadows in the room began to flow around her, like an inky storm.

When Chloe had cried out, the river of black exploded, sending shadows returning to the crevices of the room.

Logan had witnessed it all. He was in the kitchen, grabbing a late-night snack, when he'd heard her startled cry from the living room. He'd sat with her for the rest of the night.

She chuckled, remembering his sweet attempt to help her calm down.

Tess was really lucky.

"Logan, would you set the table for dinner please?"

Chloe jumped, startled by Mrs. Tucker's voice calling from the kitchen.

She blinked in an effort to clear her thoughts, but her fear refused to dissolve.

What if Reese came after her?

Stop it, Chloe.

Logan shouted back, feet already hitting the first stair, "Coming!"

Chloe stood, forcing a smile as she moved into the kitchen to intercept Logan.

"Need any help?" she asked.

He frowned, taking note of her plastic grin. Too wide. Haunted.

"You're a guest, Chloe." He winked at her. "Take advantage of it."

Chloe appreciated his efforts to make her feel welcome, but she needed a distraction.

She reached out, taking the stack of plates from his hand. "I'd hate to wear out my welcome."

The scent of Mrs. Tucker's spaghetti wafted into the dining room, rich and full of seasonings. Kennedy, Logan's little sister, ran into the room, wrapping her arms around Chloe's waist.

Chloe winced as the girl's hand pressed painfully into her ribs.

"Squirt!" Logan called quickly, seeing Chloe's look of pain. "Come help me set out the silverware."

Chloe shot him a grateful look, giving Kennedy a final squeeze. Logan's sister was adorable. Bouncing blonde curls, huge brown eyes, and a precious personality. Chloe adored her, but she wasn't accustomed to physical affection, and it made her feel a little uncomfortable.

She could still feel Reese's arms around her, dragging her into the living room.

It's a seven-year-old girl. Not Reese. Relax, Chloe.

"Is Tess coming over?" Kennedy asked, reaching to take the spoons from Logan. "She comes to dinner sometimes."

Chloe turned to Logan, giving him a wicked grin. His face flushed.

She'd walked in on him and Tess at the graduation party last night. Logan was sitting on the bathroom counter, one hand under Tess's shirt. Tess's face had turned beet red, as Logan had struggled to catch his breath. Chloe had backed out of the room quickly, shouting a reminder to lock the door next time.

He was *definitely* remembering that moment. Chloe snorted as he awkwardly cleared his throat.

"Yeah, she's coming."

Kennedy didn't notice her brother's flaming face, continuing to chatter, "I *love* Tess. She lets me brush her hair. *And* she always brings a treat for Daisy."

Logan gave Chloe a dirty look, and she giggled.

Tess arrived just as Mrs. Tucker began dishing the pasta.

Kennedy hugged her tightly, while Tess fixed herself a plate and moved to sit between Logan and Chloe.

Somehow, the little girl ended up squeezing her chair next to Tess. The Tuckers had enrolled Kennedy in a summer art class, and now she was obsessed with watercolors. She spent ten minutes telling Tess about her newest painting before her mother reminded her to finish eating.

Mr. Tucker immediately picked up the conversation, telling about a man he'd pulled over that morning that had tried to get out of his ticket by offering donuts.

As Tess and Logan recounted a story about the party last night— obviously skipping over details about make-out sessions and the keg Dalton had managed to procure — Chloe's eyes drifted around the table.

She stared from Mrs. Tucker, her full cheeks lifted in a kind smile, to Mr. Tucker, laughing and clapping his son lightly on the shoulder. And Kennedy, slurping up long spaghetti noodles and slipping her green beans under the table to her puppy.

Chloe's chest felt impossibly tight.

Dinners at her house had never felt like this. There was no laughter. No smiles. Only silence and tension

No *happiness*.

Here... Here she could *feel* how much this family loved each other.

Tears welled in her eyes, and she blinked, trying to force them back. There was no reason to cry here. No reason to ruin the moment.

She reached over, grabbing Tess's hand, hooking her pinky through her friend's.

Tess glanced over, noticing the dampness of Chloe's eyes. She opened her mouth to speak, but Chloe gave her a tiny shake of her head.

I'm okay, she mouthed.

Tess gave Chloe's hand a soft squeeze, nodding slowly.

Chloe stood, offering to clear the table. If she was going to stay here until she found a place of her own, she needed to pull her own weight. Her friends joined her, and Logan's mom smiled gently, teasing Logan about what a good influence these girls were on him.

Mr. and Mrs. Tucker left to join the neighbors down the street for a domino game, reminding Kennedy she needed to let Daisy out.

Everyone's always smiling. It's perfect here.

Chloe scraped off a plate, and Tess grabbed it, running it under the faucet.

"So," she asked, nudging Chloe's shoulder. "Have you... you know... felt anything lately?"

The shadows.

Chloe shook her head. "Not on purpose. But I had a nightmare last night. I woke up, and... I don't even know. It's all so weird. I wish Shawn could help me."

Tess handed the dripping plate to Logan to dry, grimacing at the mention of Shawn.

"Shawn's... preoccupied. His home has been kind of crazy. He hasn't really had time for me lately."

Chloe glanced at Tess, suspicious of her tone.

She's lying.

About what, Chloe had no idea, and she made a mental note to demand an explanation once they were alone. Maybe Logan was uncomfortable with how much time his girlfriend was spending with another guy.

She started to scrub sauce from the last plate, when a furious knock sounded at the front door.

Logan glanced at the girls. Nervous.

The knocking came again, louder this time.

"I've got it!" Logan called over his shoulder before his sister could try to answer.

He cast an anxious glance at Chloe, then dropped his rag on the counter.

Tess and Chloe followed him to the door, standing back as he opened it.

Hunter Garcia stood there. He was a stout guy, not much taller than Chloe, but heavily muscled. His arms were crossed over his chest as he inspected the group.

Then, he pointed at Chloe.

"Shawn told me you'd be here. He said to tell you they're coming."

Apprehension settled in Chloe's stomach as she tried to make sense of his words.

Over the last month, Shawn had become Tess's shadow, but he didn't talk much to Chloe. They had nothing in common.

Other than her parents.

It was the only explanation that made sense. Reese and Charlotte were coming for her.

Logan and Tess stared at Hunter in utter confusion.

"What?" Tess was the first to break the silence, her face going pale. "What does that mean?"

Hunter shrugged, stuffing his hands in the pocket of his hoodie. "I have no clue, dude. I just owe the guy a favor, alright? No questions asked— that's the deal."

Chloe's hands began to shake violently and her breathing came out too fast.

Panicked.

She was going to throw up.

I can't go back.

"Tess? He's your friend. You're the expert here," Logan murmured, giving Hunter a suspicious glance.

Hunter let out an annoyed sigh. "Look, Shawn sounded pretty damn serious. And either way, I have somewhere to be. Figure out what you're gonna do so I can get out of here. Shawn told me to wait until you made a decision."

Tess glanced at Chloe, noticing the violent shaking of her hands, then turned back quickly to Logan.

"Okay. Let's go. If Shawn said they're coming for her, we have to leave."

She looked at Hunter. "Thank you."

He shrugged again. "Whatever. You believe me?"

She nodded, and he spun around, hurrying down the front stairs. "I'm outta here. No way I'm getting caught up in y'all's bullshit."

The door closed behind him, and Tess and Logan turned to face Chloe.

"Where can I go?" she whispered, her voice saturated with fear.

She couldn't breathe.

She couldn't go back.

She *wouldn't* go back.

"Chloe!" Tess hissed, bringing her to the present. "You have to *stop*."

The shadows around Chloe had started to shimmer, flowing towards her trembling hands.

Tess reached out, and the shadows retreated as she enclosed Chloe's hands.

"I know a place. No one will find you. I promise, I'm going to keep you safe. Trust me."

Logan nodded his agreement, reaching out to gently squeeze Chloe's shoulder.

Tess looked at him, regret in her eyes. "You'll have to come up with a story. Tell your parents something. I'll let you know once we're safe."

His eyes flared with anger as he realized she expected him to stay home. "No. You're not doing this alone!"

Tess released Chloe, turning to face him. She wrapped her arms around him, kissing him hard.

"I'll be fine. We both will."

Dalton.

Chloe put a hand on Logan's arm.

"Tell Dalton. Tell him everything."

His eyes widened.

"He won't believe me," Logan said, his voice low. "And even if he did, it's bad enough that Tess told *one* Basic about the Society. But if I tell Dalton—"

Chloe tightened her grip on him, digging her fingers into his arm.

"If something happens to me, I need him to understand."

She narrowed her eyes, hoping he understood.

"I owe him. And I don't want to leave without an explanation. If you can't tell him the whole truth, at least... let him know that none of this is his fault."

Logan finally nodded, giving Tess one last squeeze before the girls turned away.

"Stay safe."

Chloe glanced at Tess, raising an eyebrow, trying to slow her breathing.

"Where are we going?"

CHAPTER 29

SHAWN

Hunter should have made it to Chloe's by now.

His friend wasn't an exceptionally noble character, but this one act might be enough to justify his existence.

If Hunter did nothing else with his life, at least he'd helped to save Chloe's.

Shawn thanked God for his friend at that moment.

He hoped Chloe would understand his message. He'd told Hunter to relay the warning, but it had been fairly cryptic. Just enough to warn her, but not enough to provide details to his family should Koden get suspicious and decide to dig around in Shawn's mind for information.

Shawn had no idea where to find Chloe now.

Where would Logan take her? What would happen if Koden found her before Shawn did?

What if he couldn't get to her at all?

One problem at a time.

He had to believe that Hunter had succeeded. That Chloe was safe, and that he could explain everything when he got to her. *When*. Not *if*.

Right now, he had to call in a second favor.

Nervous sparks danced occasionally around his hands like fireflies as he drove. Usually, dispelling them was easy. But today, his mind was too preoccupied to focus on containing them.

Thankfully, Shawn's family was out for the night. Koden and Alyssa had left for an early dinner, and his father had been sent out of town to clear up a scandal involving a high ranking Court official. Typically, the Generalis would not be involved in something as petty as Court drama. Based upon the length of his mother's *very* tight Versace dress, Shawn suspected his uncle had an ulterior motive for wanting his brother out of town. Judging by the look he'd seen in Koden's eyes, Shawn didn't expect to see them until the morning.

Giving him an opportunity to find Ace Lane.

After what seemed an impossibly long drive, Shawn saw the familiar house. Run-down, sagging roof, with an uncut lawn and cracked sidewalk. A home representing a man, who received too little pay for too much work.

Shawn exhaled, relieved, when he spotted a small gray car parked in the driveway of the home. The man was there.

He pulled up to the curb, leaping from the car before he could back out. He didn't have a plan. He had no idea if the guard would even help him.

When he had impulsively made the decision to conceal Ace Lane's betrayal to the Society, he'd done it for multiple reasons. He didn't *want* to hurt the man, and he certainly hadn't wanted to be the cause of his death, but another desire had also motivated him. He had *hoped* that by saving the man's life, he would ultimately gain an ally.

While he couldn't be sure the decision had been enough to guarantee the guard's trust, he was hopeful.

And it was the only chance he had.

Shawn walked to the door, keeping his head down, and knocked loudly. In this neighborhood, his black Mercedes Maybach parked on the street would draw unwanted attention. If anyone saw him or recognized him, word would get back to his family. If word got back to his family...

This needed to be a quick visit.

He mentally prepared himself. He was willing to cross whatever line he had to cross to get the information he needed. The Turncoats' location.

Any line except murder.

Ace Lane opened the door. Like the first time Shawn had seen him, the man was in the process of winding down from a day of work. Shoes off, uniform unbuttoned, and his hair a mess.

A gold wedding band on his finger.

The guard stiffened when he recognized Shawn. He glanced around, searching.

"I'm alone," Shawn said. "The Generalis and Orator are attending to other matters with the Salvator."

He winced at his tone. Too formal and arrogant.

Shawn sighed, trying to sound more natural. "Please, I need your help. May I come in?"

Ace, after another moment of hesitation, stepped aside, closing the door behind Shawn, and bowed slightly.

"Forgive me, but two visits from the Salvator's nephew is quite overwhelming for someone like me. To what do I owe this honor?"

Shawn rolled his eyes, annoyed. "Ace, spare me the formalities, and don't patronize me. We both know you aren't loyal to the Salvator *or* the Society. I need your help."

Ace raised an eyebrow, skeptical, then crossed his arms in

resignation. "To be fair, you're the Salvator's nephew. How can you expect me to trust you?"

Shawn leaned forward, speaking in a low voice. "How about the fact that I know *exactly* who and what you are. And I kept your secret. I saved your life!"

He took a breath in an effort to regain composure. He didn't want to scare the man. He needed him.

Ace watched him silently, twisting his wedding band around his finger. Shawn remembered the vision of Ace's husband. Betrayed. Crying.

A wave of hopelessness washed over him.

What if Ace refused to give up the Turncoats' location? After betraying them once, he wasn't likely to do it again.

Shawn knew *he* wouldn't if the roles were reversed.

"I don't expect you to trust me," he conceded, hoping to placate the man. "But I *desperately* need your help, and I believe saving your life should at least warrant you hearing me out."

Ace nodded slowly, glancing around. Seeking out an invisible threat. As if the Generalis and Orator were somehow hidden, just waiting for Ace to give himself away.

"I promise you. I'm alone," Shawn insisted.

"Yeah, promises from a Mason aren't worth shit to me," the man muttered. Despite his words, he looked up and asked cautiously. "What do you need?"

The guard walked into the kitchen, taking down a mug, then walking to the coffee pot. Observing Shawn carefully.

Shawn bit his lip, anticipating the best way to broach the subject. He decided to be blunt.

"I need to know where the Turncoats are. Or at least, point me in the right direction to someone that knows."

Ace froze in the middle of pouring a cup of coffee. The liquid splashed over the side of the cup, but the man didn't seem to notice or care.

"Absolutely not."

"I'm not asking. I'm telling you, I *need* to know. You *owe* me."

Ace's lip curled into a snarl. "No. I don't owe you anything. You haven't earned that. Turn me in if that's what you need to do. Or try to pry it from my head yourself. You're good at that, right?"

He spat the last sentence out angrily. Full of contempt.

Shawn's fury ignited. He wanted to scream at Ace. Wanted to do exactly what the man had suggested. He could search Ace's fears more thoroughly.

While Shawn was an excellent interrogator, specifics like location and time were hard to pinpoint when reading fears. But not impossible.

An intrusive, prolonged look into the depths of Ace's fears and conscience would likely come at a high cost, though. And he had vowed *not* to cross that line.

His insides burned with hatred.

But not for the guard in front of him.

He'd given up everything for the Society. Spent years doing anything they asked, at the expense of his own soul.

And later, to save himself.

As a child, he had followed the Society's teachings without hesitation. He believed in the Salvator's cause and he adored his uncle. From early on, he had been expected to take a role in the Society command, and while Shawn had never liked participating in the interrogations, he did so willingly. To help save his people.

Until the day he realized it was all bullshit.

The years he had spent truly believing he was doing the right thing, only to discover it was all lies. To realize the awful acts he had participated in weren't to save the *people,* but to strengthen his family's political allegiances.

He squeezed his hands into tight fists, forcing down the urge to lash out as he struggled to repress the memory.

"I'm trying to save someone," he said, quietly. "Of all people, I think you can understand that."

Ace stiffened, but remained silent.

Shawn's mind spun. Should he mention Chloe? That she was a Caine, in danger of suffering the same fate as Sapphire? It might get the man to talk. To understand that Shawn *wasn't* his enemy.

He had a small advantage over Ace, having first hand knowledge of the man's fears and experiences.

The guard hated the way he'd been forced to treat Sapphire Caine. Watching, and occasionally participating in, her abuse was destroying him. He had grown to care about the girl and wanted to help her

But it wasn't possible to save Sapphire. She was under constant surveillance, and the man wouldn't do anything to risk another interrogation. To risk the life of the man he loved.

But Chloe wasn't yet under the Society's watch. Maybe he would take a chance to save her.

Ace groaned in frustration. "How can you expect me to trust that you won't give them up to the Society? I *can't*. And I think you know that."

Ace wasn't going to help him. Not if he had any lingering doubts that Shawn was loyal to the Society.

He had to prove that he wasn't.

He hesitated, taking in a deep breath, and praying it would be enough. He rolled up his sleeves, exposing the scars along his arms.

Hundreds of raised white marks trailed from his wrists, to his shoulders, then disappeared underneath his clothes.

"Koden did this to me three years ago," he said, watching Ace's impassive stare as he inspected Shawn's scars.

"He discovered my aspirations to find the Turncoats. I had hopes of abandoning my Society obligations for a more *noble* cause." He gave a sharp humorless laugh. "I tried to get the Turncoats' attention, so that I could join them. After I—"

He paused, refusing to allow the memories of that bloody night to overwhelm him.

"I made a mistake when I was younger. I was naive, and very blinded by my love for my family, but that doesn't excuse what I did. What they asked me to do."

He looked down, realizing that he'd never discussed that night. With anyone. And he *needed* to talk about it. About what he'd done. To beg for forgiveness.

But not to Ace. Shawn *needed* Ace to believe him and give up the Turncoats. Hearing the details of the night that had haunted Shawn's memory for so many years wasn't likely to earn his trust.

"It's no secret that I've done terrible things. I know what people say about me. But one night, I was asked to do something I didn't want to do. My uncle insisted it was necessary. For the good of the Society. And this night— it made me realize what the Society— what my family —really was. Since then, I've just been trying to survive."

Ace bit his lip, silent as Shawn kept talking.

"I'm no more loyal to the Society, to the Salvator, than you are. I've been a coward. I didn't want to go against him. But I need to save my friend. I'm trying to make things right. Please help me."

The guard studied him. His gray eyes somber. Conflicted.

"*Please.*" The desperation in his voice was real.

Because what he'd said was true. He *had* been a coward. He had repeatedly done terrible things to save his own life. And he *hated* himself, recognizing he was irredeemable. But he would never again be loyal to the Society. He would never again allow himself to be used to hurt another. And he would do *anything* to keep his friends safe, even if that meant the end of the Munera.

Ace finally nodded.

"Alright."

Shawn sagged with relief, letting out a breath he hadn't realized he'd been holding.

"Thank you," he murmured, giving the man a grateful nod.

Ace smiled sadly, wiping up the spilled coffee, then tossing the sopping paper towel into a trash can. He studied Shawn's face.

"We have a problem."

Shawn's immediate relief turned into suspicion. "What?"

"No matter how many scars you have, you're still the Salvator's nephew. The Turncoats won't help you." Then he paused, rethinking. "Actually, they're more likely to kill you on the spot."

Shawn sighed again. "That's not a problem."

Ace's mouth twisted in confusion. Shawn smiled, adding a sardonic laugh.

"I'm a Mason. Someone *always* wants to kill me. My own family has been threatening to do it for years."

"You're willing to die for a friend? Even knowing the Turncoats probably won't help you?"

"It's better than the alternative." Shawn nodded. "Her name is Chloe. It's imperative that the Society doesn't get their hands on her. I believe I'll be able to convince the Turncoats to take her in."

Ace gave him a dubious frown. Shawn couldn't blame him, but he didn't have time to explain.

"They either help me, or they don't." He shrugged. "I'd rather die trying to save her than to willfully hand her over."

Ace smiled gently. "You love her?"

Shawn laughed. "No. She's a *friend*. But some things are worth dying for."

He gestured to the man to continue.

Ace sighed. "Towards the edge of Mesquite Ridge, there are rows of enormous drainage tunnels."

Shawn nodded, committing every word to memory. Mesquite Ridge was a good hour and a half drive from here. He had driven past the tunnels on numerous occasions.

"They're near there?" he asked.

"They're *in* there," Ace corrected, grinning as he caught Shawn's stultified expression, before continuing.

"That area of town is largely abandoned. When you reach the tunnels, you need to know that there will be sentries posted. Even if you don't see them, trust me, they'll see you."

Shawn nodded, turning to leave, but Ace reached out, grabbing his arm.

"Tell them I sent you. It won't guarantee your safety, but it might save you from a death sentence."

He left the man's home, thanking him again. Grateful that he hadn't had to use his ability to retrieve the information.

He *was* scared. Scared of the Turncoats' rejection. Scared of his uncle. Scared of failure. Worry and fear threatened to consume him. Weighing him down.

But he had meant what he said. He would rather die than allow the Society to have Chloe. He could never make up for his choices, but he had to try. Even if he failed, he had to try.

As he began the drive back to his house, sirens sounded behind him. He pulled over, and several fire trucks raced past him.

His eyes followed them, curious to see where they were heading.

He watched, and an uncomfortable feeling of unease settled in his stomach. He turned, following the emergency vehicles.

Something was wrong. When he saw where the trucks

were headed, his stomach heaved, nearly bringing up his dinner.

He scrambled desperately for his phone, jamming his finger down on Tess's contact.

She answered, but he didn't give her time to speak.

"Where's Logan?"

CHAPTER 30

REESE

H is vision swam, and he stumbled, struggling to stay upright.

Little tramp.

He'd given eighteen years of his life to her, and *this* is how she thanked him?

Ungrateful little traitor.

When the Salvator had come to him, years earlier, and explained his assignment, Reese had been overjoyed. Hopeful.

His wife, Charlotte, wasn't able to have children, and the prospect of raising a child had thrilled him, though his wife wasn't excited about the opportunity. She had never been the 'mothering' type.

But Reese had dreamed of being a father, and he had thought that over time, Charlotte would grow to love the girl.

The house he approached was simple. Two stories, no balcony, with only two exterior doors.

266

It was made entirely of wood.

He could hear muffled voices inside.

He had followed his daughter here last night.

She'd arrived late. With a blonde boy. A different Lusus Naturae than the black boy he'd seen drop her off at their home.

Slut.

His head was pounding, and his stomach churned in rebellion. He typically preferred to start his day with a Bloody Mary. It took the edge off his morning hangover. His chosen cure to make it through the work day until the evening, when he could enjoy a night cap.

But today, he hadn't had a drop of alcohol, per the Salvator's orders, and he was starting to feel the effects from the unwelcome detox.

Fury built in his chest and sweat dripped down his face, burning as it ran into the gash the Salvator had left.

Damned Salvator. Blaming Reese for his Charge's early activation, then claiming he had the right to screw his wife.

Damn Lusus Naturae. Making a fool of him, and disgracing his family's name.

Damn Chloe. Stealing eighteen years of his life only to disappear and ruin his chance to advance within the Society.

Chloe.

She had been a beautiful baby. Luminous golden eyes, soft tufts of dark hair, and rosy cheeks.

He had immediately fallen in love. She had inspired him to become a better man. He had stopped drinking, working to be the father she deserved.

He had been determined to build a family for her.

He was only her Guardian, but he had loved her like a daughter. She *was* his daughter. And that's why he had been devastated to learn where she had come from.

On her first birthday, the Salvator and a team of officials

had made a visit to do a welfare check to inspect Chloe. Unusual in itself, as the Salvator *never* dealt with Charges and Guardians.

Reese had spent weeks preparing, knowing if he failed, they would take his daughter. Charlotte had refused to help, claiming it would be a blessing if they lost custody of the girl.

He had been terrified during the inspection, but finally, the Salvator had turned to him, beaming, announcing that the girl was officially being placed as a permanent Charge in the Hale home. As her permanent Guardian, he was given access to her file.

The Salvator had insisted on reviewing every detail with him, to ensure he understood the magnitude of the duty he was being given.

The *importance* of this Charge.

Because his beautiful little girl, Chloe Hale, was a Caine.

Born into a filthy family of traitors.

Proditors.

He had been horrified. Disgusted. And ashamed.

How could he *possibly* love a Caine?

Charlotte was livid. Furious that he hadn't demanded the Salvator remove the child from their home. Furious that Reese, even after knowing *who* the girl was, had desired to keep her.

She had almost left him. He'd begged her to stay, to *try* and accept Chloe as their daughter. And she'd agreed to stay, *if* he agreed to her conditions. She would be in charge of disciplining the girl.

He had hoped Charlotte would warm up to Chloe. With her charming laugh and curious nature, how could she not fall in love with her?

Instead, Charlotte began to point out things about the girl. Things that frightened him.

Even as a toddler, Chloe had possessed a fierce independent streak. Her tantrums lasted hours, often through the night and into the early morning. And she lied.

Countless times, Reese had come home from work to find Chloe in trouble for various offenses. And no matter how many times he asked her to explain herself, she always said she hadn't done anything wrong.

She's a liar! Charlotte had insisted. *How can you take her side?*

And she was right. How could he argue? It was in Chloe's blood.

There was only one solution. He had to rid his daughter of any trace of her treacherous heritage.

He still remembered the first time he'd taken a belt to her. It had very nearly killed him. She had been three, and the betrayal in her bright eyes had broken his heart.

But Charlotte had been proud of him. And proud of Chloe for accepting her punishment. Maybe there was hope they could become a *real* family.

The next day, when he arrived home, Charlotte informed him that Chloe had stolen a piece of candy from the store that morning. She had hidden the trash and then lied to her mother when she had discovered the evidence.

I won't have a thief in my house, Charlotte hissed.

He hadn't wanted to hit her again. Not when she had held his hand, begging.

Daddy, I didn't!

He'd had a drink that night to help numb the pain. And every night since then.

But it was for her own good.

Through a darkened window, he could see the boy. Obviously nervous as he watched the front door. Waiting.

Reese had seen Chloe and the other girl leave earlier.

Driving away in a panic. Somehow, they must've known he was coming.

Which meant she'd alerted the Lusus Naturae to his presence as well.

Yet another reason to follow through with his plan.

He'd considered intervening. Disposing of the girl and the boy, restraining Chloe, and holding her here while he waited for Koden's detention teams to arrive.

But he had orders not to touch her.

However, Koden hadn't said anything about the Lusus Naturae boy.

Burn it down.

At his mental command, his hands lit with blazing flames. Liquid fire, exploding out like magma, silent as it coated the base of the home with bright orange, gold, and red.

He heard the first crackle as it started to burn through the wood of the home, much faster than an ordinary fire should.

Faster.

He moved around to the back of the house, targeting the eaves and setting the roof ablaze.

As more fire shot from his outstretched palms, he willed the flames at the front of the house to grow. Hotter. Faster.

Faster.

Trap him.

He smiled as he heard the first scream from inside the home. Simultaneously, he heard a neighbor, screaming to call 911.

He listened closely, hoping to hear the sound of the Lusus Naturae crying out.

Don't mess with a man's daughter.

With one last command, the flames soared higher, effectively blocking any window exit.

I never touched my Charge, Salvator.

He grinned, satisfied as he watched the house become an inescapable tomb.

And then he fled.

CHAPTER 31

LOGAN

I'll be fine. We both will.

He felt an impending sense of doom as he replayed Tess's words, and his stomach turned, remembering her lips against his.

The kiss had felt wrong, leaving him with a feeling of finality.

Everything felt wrong.

He hated this. Hated the worry that was building in his chest, making him want to scream.

He shouldn't have let her go.

He should have gone with her to make sure they were safe. He didn't have Abnormal superhero powers, but he needed to do *something*.

He should at least *be* there.

And something was bothering him. Nagging at the back of his mind like a pesky fly.

Why hadn't Chloe's parents come for her the night she ran? Or even a day or two later?

She had a cell phone, so her location wasn't a secret. If they had wanted, they could have tracked her.

And according to what he understood about Munera, couldn't they sense each other? Why wouldn't they have just... searched for her until they felt her Trace? And *insisted* she come home? The Tucker's couldn't have stopped them. Chloe was still a minor.

So why now?

She wasn't a normal Charge, according to what Tess had said. Shawn hadn't been able to explain everything fully, but *something* about Chloe was different.

If they were coming now, the reason behind it was important.

And it felt wrong. Sinister.

Groaning, he dragged his hands down his face. He was just torturing himself.

His gut wrenched, and he pulled out his phone.

He wanted to talk to Tess. No, he *needed* to talk to Tess. If he could just hear her voice, it would probably settle his nerves.

A loud pop drew his attention away from his phone. Like the sound wet wood makes as it burns.

Then, the smell of smoke.

The light from flickering flames rose outside the window.

He was stunned, unable to react. He stared numbly out the window, confused as he watched the flames rising.

Why was there a fire?

The scent of smoke grew stronger, and he looked back towards the kitchen. A wisp of black smoke seeped out from under the back door.

A surge of adrenaline hit him, and his stomach lurched. "Kennedy..." he rasped.

His throat constricted in terror, his hands shaking.

He willed himself to move.

"Kennedy!"

He shot from his chair, knocking it over as he shoved away from the table. He took the stairs two at a time up to her room, barreling down the hall and slamming open her door. It crashed into the wall, knocking picture frames down.

His sister glanced up from her bed, startled by his frantic entrance. "Logan? Why are you yelling? What's that smell?"

"There's a fire," he said, trying to sound calm. But frantically slamming her door open had ruined all attempts to keep her panic at bay.

Kennedy's lip trembled, her brown eyes wide and scared. "A fire? How? Where?"

He rushed to her bed, scooping her into his arms. "Where's Daisy?"

"I want Mommy."

"Squirt, listen to me! *Where* is Daisy?" he repeated, watching as the flickering orange light downstairs grew, painting ghostly shadows across the floor.

"She's outside." A loud sob escaped his sister and she buried her face in his chest. "Are we gonna die? I don't want to die! I want Mommy!"

Logan held her tighter. Whispering that they would be fine. He kissed her head softly, heading for the stairs.

Then the gas stove exploded.

Kennedy screamed in his ear.

He dove back from the staircase as flames rocketed towards them. He fell hard on his shoulder, just managing to cradle his sister's head from the blow.

The fall had knocked the breath from him, and he let out an involuntary wheeze of pain.

Everything hurt.

The heat from the blast had blistered his skin, and the

pain registered through his shock. He allowed an agonized wail to tear from his throat. Everything was blurry. His mouth was filled with the gritty taste of ash and his thoughts were too jumbled to make sense.

What was he supposed to do?

How could they get out if he couldn't get up?

"Logan! Logan!"

Kennedy.

She was sobbing, shaking him. But her voice was far away and his ears were ringing. "Get up! Please get up! Logan, I'm scared!"

Her face was wet against his neck, tears streaming down her face.

He hated when Kennedy cried.

Coughing, he tried to sit up, but the movement sent shockwaves of pain through his back. His head exploded in agony, spinning from the impact. He couldn't breathe. The smoke was engulfing him.

It was in his lungs, his eyes, his nose.

He screamed, furious.

He couldn't do it. He couldn't move or breathe or think or *anything*! Let alone carry his sister out of here.

Her face was burned. She was coated in soot. Her blonde curls were singed and her right ear was covered in blisters.

And she was crying. Begging him.

She *needed* him to protect her. Like he'd always sworn to do.

His beautiful baby sister. Afraid of storms and thunder.

He forced himself to stand, letting the instinct to protect his sister take precedence over his pain. His legs shook from the effort. Breathing had become impossible through the thick haze of black smoke over his head, so he ducked as he moved.

There was less smoke near the ground, but there were also

flames racing across it. The carpet had caught fire, and the thick material was ablaze. He had to move faster, and he couldn't do that crouched this low to the ground. He had to stand.

Cursing, he sucked in one last breath of clean air and straightened. The smoke immediately enveloped him.

Kennedy's fingers dug into his scalded back, and he grimaced in pain as he tightened his hold on her.

He ran, diving into her bedroom. There were windows here, and the fire hadn't quite reached this space yet, but smoke filled the room.

A glance out the window crushed his hopes, filling him with despair. Kennedy's room looked over the driveway. They were too high off the ground, and a drop would end with his sister landing on the concrete pad.

She might not survive the fall.

Logan squeezed his sister tightly against his chest, running for the bathroom, stopping when he remembered that it only had a skylight.

There were no other options.

Logan glanced towards the stairs, trying to clear his head. He felt fuzzy. Unable to think over his sister's wails and the faint buzzing in his ears.

I have to get downstairs.

It was suicide.

It was his only option.

The bottom floor was engulfed in fire, but if he could get there fast enough, they might make it to the front door.

His skin burned. Blistering and peeling in the inferno, and his lungs were raw from the smoke. He blinked, trying to clear his eyes, as he darted down the steps.

Flames licked the side of the staircase, creeping across the landing, and he could feel the rubber in his shoes melting, burning the soles of his feet.

At the bottom of the stairs, he found a pocket of breathable air amid the smoke, and he gulped at it greedily, but the ash in his mouth gagged him. He coughed, choking, struggling not to double over.

Kennedy bawled, pressing her face into his shoulder, begging him to hurry.

His vision was fuzzy.

He needed to stop. To rest. The heat was too strong and he was too weak.

He watched as flames danced across the living room drapes.

He was frozen, fear planting him on the floor.

Kennedy screamed as a series of explosions erupted from the kitchen.

Logan shook his head, trying to clear his vision as he searched for an exit.

A wall of flame completely covered the room, making it impossible to reach the front door or the windows.

He turned to the kitchen, rushing to the side door. He turned the knob, but it refused to open, blocked from the outside.

The brass knob left a large burn across his palm. He braced Kennedy in his arms, then kicked the door. Hard. It didn't move. Again. Again. Harder and harder, desperation stealing his rationality.

It was useless. Every exit was blocked. Trapped.

No no no! God, don't let us die here.

He'd always been a believer, but never as devout as he should have been. Now, he found himself praying. Begging for a way out. Mercy for his sister if nothing else.

He hugged Kennedy tightly, raising his voice above the popping flames.

"You're okay, Squirt," he promised. "You're gonna be just fine."

She shuddered, hiding her face in his neck.

He was lying to her. He had no idea what to do. No idea if there *was* a way out.

An unearthly sound came from above. Horror surged through his veins, and he glanced up.

The upstairs floor.

It was going to collapse.

Tears poured from his eyes, from the smoke and the realization that they were going to be crushed

There was no way out.

"*No...*" he whispered, unable to breathe as the ceiling began to sag.

"Logan!" Kennedy shrieked. "Daisy's dog door!" She pointed frantically towards the laundry room at the back of the house.

He pictured the door. A small hole cut in the wall, covered with a thin rubber flap. The image of his sister climbing out of the house through the tiny door filled his mind. The image of her making it into the yard safely. She would fit, but just barely.

He kissed her head and sprinted down the hall, stomping out the flames nearest the dog door. Reaching down, he pushed out the flap, shouting in pain as a flurry of sparks erupted next to him. The rubber was melting, sticking to his hand. Still, he yanked at it and the flap came away so it wouldn't burn his sister.

His efforts had revealed a small space. Fresh air poured in, and he inhaled deeply, relieved.

It was big enough for Kennedy to slip out.

He set her down, urging her forward.

"Squirt, go! I'll be right behind you!"

She stared at him, her brown eyes filled with tears. "Promise?"

He smiled gently. "*Go*, Kennedy. I love you. I love you so

much. When you get out, I want you to run. Find Mom. Don't stop until you get across the street, okay?"

Finally, Kennedy nodded. She pushed her head through the dog door.

Logan watched, as her narrow shoulders vanished into the yard outside. Then her stomach. Her hips. Her feet.

And she was gone. She was safe.

Logan couldn't follow her out.

He stood slowly. Listening to his sister screaming for him outside.

"Logan? Logan, come on!"

He let out a sob, and immediately began to cough.

He had to move. To reach a window. Without Kennedy in his arms, he could break it. He could slam a chair into it or, hell, even his elbow. Anything to get outside.

He stumbled, staggering through the maze of fire that covered his home.

Every breath was laborious. Agonizing. Torture.

He wasn't just inhaling smoke, but the bits of debris flying in the air as well.

Burns marked his arms, decorated his face, and *covered* him in painful blisters.

The top floor moaned again, and he cried out, the sound bubbling out weakly from his burned, smoke damaged throat.

The window. He needed to get to the window.

Something above him cracked. Popped.

The noise grew louder.

He looked up.

The ceiling was too close. Ash and bits of glass rained down on him. Slicing his skin and floating into his face. He blinked and it felt like sandpaper, grating across his eyes. The groaning of the house grew louder, as the floor above him finally gave way, collapsing inward.

A rafter crashed through the burning top floor, the massive ceiling beam plummeting towards him.

Move. Move *damn it!*

But his feet refused. He remained rooted to the spot.

Something landed on his back, and an audible crack rocked his insides. Making his teeth grind against each other. His mouth opened, and he released an inhuman sound.

The weight of the beam brought him down, slamming his head into the burning hardwood.

A nd then, there was no pain. Just a dull ache. A feeling of numbness.

He felt heavy pressure on his back, but he couldn't move his head to turn and see what was causing it.

Actually, he couldn't do anything. He tried to move his arm. But even that seemed impossible. He felt so heavy. Sluggish and slow and hot and...

He blinked, weary. And then he closed his eyes. Flashes of light flickered behind his lids. Like a campfire.

He liked camping. He'd gone a few times with his family, out near Monroe State Park. Kennedy loved camping. She liked the s'mores. When they ran out of chocolate, she would keep roasting the marshmallows, eating them until she got sick.

He had wanted to take Tess there this summer. He wanted to show her the stars. Before they went to college and started their real lives.

A life together maybe?

He remembered the feeling of her lips on his. Soft and sweet and always smiling.

He loved that. He loved her smile.

He loved her.

I still haven't told her. I still need to do that.

There were a lot of things he still needed to do.

He needed to make sure Chloe was alright. He needed to know if his sister had gotten away and found their parents. He still needed to take the trash out and do his laundry and help Kennedy with her painting like he'd promised he would.

Suddenly, he realized he was crying. He was crying, and it was hard to breathe and he realized that he would never get to tell Tess that he loved her. To tell his parents and sister that they were everything to him.

To *live*.

He wouldn't get to live.

He was going to die.

Someone screamed.

It might have been him screaming, but he didn't know. He couldn't feel anything anymore. The roar of the flames and the pounding in his head seemed to drown out everything.

Then, it came again. From outside. Someone was screaming. Crying. He thought he should recognize the voice. It sounded familiar, but he couldn't place it.

And sirens.

Everything was too loud.

He wanted his mom. He couldn't remember if he'd hugged her today. And he really wanted to hug her.

And his dad. His dad was his best friend. He just wanted to tell him that. Had he ever told him? He couldn't remember.

He heard a loud roar above him, and he opened his eyes. He thought it might be thunder. Kennedy was so scared of thunder.

Would his parents let Kennedy sleep with them now? He hoped she wouldn't be mad that he couldn't follow her out.

His baby sister.

He wanted to see her one more time.

Just one more time.

There was so much noise, but he didn't hurt anymore.

He smiled, listening to the sound of the rumbling around him. Was it raining?

"I saw a movie where people kissed in the rain."

"Did you?"

"Yeah... I like Tess a lot."

"Me too."

"You should marry her."

He closed his eyes. And then, there was nothing at all.

CHAPTER 32

TESS

Tess drove by her house first, quickly grabbing some supplies. Blankets, a pillow, and a few essentials. They tossed everything in the back of her car, more worried now than ever.

She wished she had let Logan come with her. Pushing away the guilt, she led Chloe into the empty rental house. Where she had once killed a snake and escaped stupid arguments with her mom over something as trivial as colleges. Chloe glanced around, covering her nose against the stench.

"That smells disgusting!" she muttered under her breath.

Tess nodded her agreement. The smell had gotten worse since the last time she'd been here.

Hopefully, Chloe wouldn't have to stay for long.

"Try having enhanced senses," she muttered, covering her own nose with her shirt. "I think you'll get used to it, though. And I doubt you'll be here long anyways."

From outside came a faint high pitched whine and the gentle cadence of the summer locusts.

Chloe was spreading a couple of the blankets over the floor. "I swear to God," she declared, brushing dust away from the makeshift pallet, "if I see a roach in the middle of the night, I'm sleeping outside."

Tess laughed. It felt good to laugh, even if she was frightened.

Chloe looked up from her work, smiling. "Thank you, Tess."

Her voice was soft and her eyes started to fill with tears again.

Tess dropped down beside her best friend, wrapping her in her arms.

"You're gonna be okay," she murmured. Tears stung her eyes. "I promise."

Chloe nodded, her face buried in Tess's neck, her tears soaking Tess's shirt. "I know. It's just scary, you know? This whole situation is so crazy. A whole world I didn't know about and my parents—"

She sat back on her knees, wiping tears from her eyes and managing a weak smile. "I'm sorry I never told you about Reese. Or my mom. It wasn't that I didn't trust you. I *wanted* to tell you. It's just, they told me—"

She paused, taking a deep breath.

"I didn't want to be a burden."

A pang of guilt slammed into Tess's chest. She wrapped Chloe in another embrace, holding her tight.

"I *love* you," she murmured. "You could *never* be a burden on me. I love you so much, Chloe Hale."

"I love you too," Chloe whispered, holding onto Tess. "Logan and his family and Dalton have done so much for me, but you... you're my everything. You've always been here for me, even if you didn't know it."

Tess started to respond. She wanted to tell Chloe how much she meant to her, and that she would always be there, no matter what.

Her phone rang just as she opened her mouth.

She gave Chloe an apologetic look, reaching for her phone.

Maybe it was Logan. She *hoped* it was Logan.

It wasn't.

Her breath caught when she saw Shawn's name on the screen. Hopefully, he would explain what was going on.

She answered, putting the call on speakerphone so Chloe could listen.

She started to say 'Hi', but Shawn immediately interrupted.

His voice was frantic. Screaming into the phone.

"Where's Logan?"

She felt like she had been punched in her stomach, and her throat tightened. Chloe's golden eyes were lit with fear.

"Why? What happened?" Tess demanded.

"I can see the smoke from here. He's in trouble!"

Smoke?

The high pitched whining had grown louder, and now she recognized it for what it was.

Fire engines. She could hear them from here, the sirens raging urgently.

Shawn was still talking, but she disconnected the call, hanging up and jumping to her feet.

Chloe stood with her, but Tess stopped her.

"No. I'll be okay. You have to stay here. I'll tell Shawn where you are and he can... I don't know. He'll do something. But do *not* leave until he or I come back."

Without waiting for a response, Tess ran to her car, slamming the door behind her and racing to Logan's home. From several streets away, she could already smell the smoke and see a column rising in a heavy black plume.

She reached his street and slammed on her brakes. Her body lurched against the steering wheel, and a cry escaped from her mouth.

She had nearly plowed through a crowd of onlookers, gawking and pointing. All gathered around Logan's home.

Several police officers were blocking the road, and she couldn't get her car close enough, so she stopped, leaving the car stalled in the middle of the road.

She didn't want to look, terrified by what she would see, but she did. Scanning the crowd anxiously, her eyes searching for a sign of hope.

The Tuckers' home was engulfed in flames. The fire was spreading rapidly, crackling so loud that it drowned out the voices of the people outside. The front lawn was burning, turning from green to a crispy brown, and forcing neighbors to back into the street.

As Tess watched, a huge chunk of the patio tore away from the roof and crashed with a thunderous roar in front of the side door.

Blocking it.

If there was anyone inside...

No! No, they made it out! They're here somewhere.

Tears streaming, she threw open her car door and vaulted out, falling and scraping her palms in her rush to search for Logan and his family.

But she couldn't move. She stood, dumbfounded. Listening to the pop of flames and the violent creaking of burning wood as it started to give way.

Beads of sweat erupted along her brow and neck from the heat. It was going to collapse.

Suddenly, someone put a hand on her shoulder. She spun, hope surging in her veins.

Logan!

It wasn't him. Shawn stood there, his blue gaze intense.

Before she could get a word out, Shawn yanked her forward, holding her tight against his chest.

"Shawn! What—?"

"The Society did this," he hissed, his lips close to her ear. "Tess, it's a warning. They know something— about you or Chloe. But they know Logan is involved. It's the only reason they would have done this. You and Logan and Chloe— you need to disappear."

Tess pushed away, staring at him in confusion. Tears were blurring her vision and her hands trembled.

"What are you talking about?" she snapped. "This wasn't the Society. Why would they care about *Logan?* They don't know anything about him! This was an accident!"

Shawn frowned. "Tess, don't you understand? Logan is involved. He's in danger."

Tess shook her head violently. Her entire body was shaking now and her throat was burning from the stench of smoke.

"You're wrong. Logan's fine! He's somewhere in that crowd. I have to find him."

Shawn grabbed her arm as she moved to walk away. "I thought you already found him! Isn't he hiding Chloe?"

She glared at him. "*I* hid Chloe." She was furious with him. But it wasn't his fault.

It's mine.

If she hadn't left Logan alone. If she'd let him come with her. If she'd never told him *anything* in the first place.

Shawn dropped her arm, his eyes widening in horror as the realization that Logan wasn't safe hit him. She didn't give him a chance to respond, spinning away from him and pushing into the spectators.

The crowd was thick. People everywhere had gathered around the inferno that had become Logan's house.

She elbowed her way through them. Pushing. Shoving.

Desperate.

Blonde hair, brown eyes. Blonde hair, brown eyes.

She needed to see him. She needed to see him and make sure he was okay.

Nothing.

The people she pushed out of her way glared at her until they saw the panic in her eyes.

Then, they looked at her with pity.

Her heart raced. Her stomach twisted. Shawn called her name from somewhere behind her, but she pushed deeper into the crowd.

Blonde hair, brown eyes.

Blonde hair, brown —

There!

She raced to him, grabbing him by the arm.

He spun around, looking down on her in confusion. Then recognition as he burst into tears.

Mr. Tucker. Logan's father.

Her heart plummeted.

"Where is he?" she whispered.

She couldn't breathe.

Someone wailed, and Tess realized that it was Logan's mother. She had fallen to her knees, screaming, sobbing.

There were two officers restraining her, as she struggled to escape their hold.

She was watching the flames with a look of such despair, so intense, that Tess knew.

Logan had not gotten out. He was still inside.

Her knees buckled and her hand came up to cover her mouth as sobs began to escape.

The firemen were working to remove the debris from in front of the door. Desperately trying to unblock it.

But their efforts were interrupted by a loud explosion.

The house groaned. The flames roared, surging upward from the blast.

There was a scream from inside that only she could have picked out among the cacophony of noise.

Logan's scream.

She couldn't think. She only ran. Towards the flames. Towards Logan.

People in the crowd reached for her, trying to stop her, but she broke free of their holds, racing for the house.

Logan was inside.

Just as she crossed into the yard, arms wrapped around her waist, dragging her back. She lashed out, fighting. Screaming in outrage. "Let me *go*!"

"No! Tess, stop! There's nothing you can do! You're going to get yourself killed!"

Shawn. He was restraining her, pulling her away from the house. From Logan still trapped inside.

"I don't care!" she cried, kicking at him. "I don't care! Let me go!"

Shawn's grip was strong, refusing to relent. It only made Tess fight harder. Her sobs come faster.

"He's going to die in there!" she begged, digging her nails into Shawn's arms.

Trying to make him let go.

"Let me *go*!"

She twisted, throwing her head back, hitting him in the nose. He cursed, loosening his grip just enough for her to break free.

Over the roar of the fire, she heard something.

Kennedy!

The heat was so intense that Tess's skin began to blister,

even standing yards away from the flames. The sounds of the wood popping and burning almost drowned out Kennedy's next scream, but Tess was able to make out her words.

"Logan? Logan come on!"

Tess sprinted to the back of the house, with Shawn following close behind, and vaulted over the fence. Kennedy was knelt by the wall of the inferno, hardly recognizable through the burns covering her face.

She was screaming, trying to push her way through a small dog door. Trying to go back *into* the home.

Tess made it to her side, snatching the girl before she could make it back inside.

Kennedy sobbed pounding her tiny hands into Tess's chest.

"No! He's still in there! Logan's still in there! He promised he'd come right out!"

Tess's throat constricted, and the last of her hope that Logan had somehow made it out of the blaze vanished.

Shawn caught up to her, and she thrust Kennedy into his arms.

"Take her back to Mr. Tucker!" she shouted, trying to be heard over the flames.

Shawn shook his head, holding Kennedy with one hand and reaching for Tess's arm with the other. His hand clamped around her wrist. Tight. Tight enough that it hurt.

She tried to wrench away from him, but he spun her towards him, pinning her against him.

"I'm not going to let you die!"

There was a loud crackling, and her muscles seized. She screamed as a shock of electricity pulsed through her.

It felt like thousands of needles were stabbing into her skin. Her mouth no longer tasted like ash, but like old pennies.

And she couldn't move.

She didn't understand what Shawn had done, but she was powerless to fight him. He held her lifeless body against him, lifting her, and carried her and Kennedy away from the flames. She wanted to fight. To beg him to let her go.

Instead, she sobbed. Helpless. Watching the inferno blaze around her. Listening to Kennedy scream for her brother.

Listening to the moan as the house started to give.

Shawn kicked at the gate to the backyard and the latch snapped, letting the gate swing outward.

Gasping from the smoke, he laid Tess and Kennedy far from the flames. People immediately crowded around them.

Paramedics knelt beside Kennedy, moving her onto a stretcher. Her parents began crying in relief at the sight of her.

Mr. Tucker looked up, hope lighting up his face as he searched the area for Logan. Then dread transformed it, as it dawned on him that his children were not together.

The paramedics tried to move Tess, but she waved them away. The effects of Shawn's electric touch had worn off, and she was able to sit up.

"Tess, I... I'm sorry." Shawn knelt beside her, his blue gaze intent upon her.

She ignored him, unable to look away from the blaze.

Logan had been in the house for too long.

Someone had to help him. He had been in there too long.

No!

No. He was going to be fine! He would find a way out! He had to.

He had to.

"Shawn," she whispered. "Please—"

She couldn't finish. Her voice choked off, and she buried her face in her hands.

God, please.

A violent crack filled the air, and her head snapped up in

time to see the house begin to sway. The entire structure was going to collapse.

She heard a thunderous snap.

And she saw him. Through the haze of smoke and flame, she saw an opening had burned through the wall.

And she could see him.

Logan.

He was covered in soot and burns and ash. He was staring up. At the ceiling.

He knew what was going to happen.

And, just for a moment, he looked out. He had a way to escape.

He seemed to look at her.

It was impossible. He couldn't possibly see her through the flames, but she *saw* him. He was *there*.

She stood up, screaming. "Help him! Someone help him!"

She took a step forward. She could see him. She could reach him in time.

The beam collapsed.

Knocking him down.

And he was gone.

CHAPTER 33

SHAWN

Shawn watched Logan disappear underneath the beam.
Heard Tess scream.

He heard her, but it didn't immediately register what it was. It was an inhuman sound.

A sound he had heard a hundred times when he interrogated criminals. A sound he had cruelly ignored. For the good of the Society. And to save his own life.

But now, it reverberated through his bones and pierced his ears, tearing at his insides and forcing tears into his eyes.

She didn't deserve this.

Logan didn't deserve this.

No one did.

It wasn't fair.

Shawn ground his teeth, fury building in his chest.

For years, Shawn had loathed Logan Tucker. But he was a good guy. Good to Tess, good to his family and friends. Good to Shawn.

Logan had *known* Shawn was in love with Tess, yet he tolerated him. In fact, Shawn had felt like they were actually becoming friends, even if it was a tentative friendship for Tess's sake.

He hadn't deserved this. To burn in his home and to have his life stolen when it was only just beginning.

And the Tuckers. The little blonde girl.

They didn't deserve any of this.

And someone needed to pay.

The Society.

They had to be behind it.

The fire hadn't been a normal fire. It had spread *too* quickly. Burned *too* intensely.

His words to Tess came back, replaying over and over in his head.

It's a warning.

He'd said the words out of panic, jumping to conclusions. But they made sense.

Why else would they have attacked a Basic instead of targeting Chloe or Tess directly?

And according to Koden, Reese Hale was given orders to *find* Chloe, not harm her or detain her.

If Shawn hadn't warned her, she would have been *in* the house with Logan.

What sense did it make to monitor her for 18 years, *find* her, then burn her alive?

Chloe wasn't the target.

So that left only one option.

Tess.

Somehow, his family had discovered her. Or they at least had some idea that he was hiding *something*.

They would go after her next.

Tess was sobbing in his arms, and the fire was dying,

though the ruins were still burning hot. Several firemen worked to dislodge rubble, trying to get inside.

They would find nothing but a body.

Vomit rose in his throat, as the image of Logan's raw, burned flesh entered his mind. He forced himself to swallow it back down. He ran a hand lightly over Tess's hair, cradling her against him.

She wailed, burying her face in his chest. Clinging to him.

Her pain was tangible, twisting his insides into a tight knot.

"I'm so sorry," he murmured, over and over. "I'm so, so sorry, Tess."

Four firemen were inside, and when Shawn realized what they were doing, he looked away quickly.

As the firemen lifted something from underneath a ceiling beam. Some*one*.

He wanted to tell Tess to turn away. He would have done *anything* to spare her from this moment.

But the words stuck in his throat, and the air was abruptly pierced with the agonized wail of Mrs. Tucker as she watched her son's ravaged, lifeless body be pulled out.

Tess didn't move, staring blank and horrified.

Shawn refused to watch. He'd seen enough death in his lifetime.

His arms tightened around Tess, wishing he could take her pain away. Wishing he could replace the horror she was seeing with something better.

But his ability was meant to cause pain. He would only make it worse.

So he just held her, praying for peace for Tess. Peace for Logan's family. And peace for Logan. And even though he *knew* he didn't deserve it, he prayed for forgiveness for what he knew he was going to do.

. . .

S hawn carried a limp Tess to his car and drove her home using the address he found in her wallet.

He knocked on the door of a sweet, simple two-story home that reminded him painfully of the Tuckers' home.

Of the charred and blackened walls. Of the flames eating at the collapsed remains of the wooden frame. Of the burns and blisters that Logan had suffered.

It's my fault.

Tess's father opened the door, thankfully forcing the thoughts to the back of Shawn's mind.

Shawn opened his mouth, but discovered he couldn't speak. He couldn't make his words come out. Tess's mother joined her husband at the door, puzzled when she saw her grief-stricken daughter in the passenger seat of his black car.

Saw her face.

Blank. Tears still streaming from eyes that refused to blink.

Shawn quickly filled them in, trying desperately to keep his voice steady. A pointless effort. His voice trembled and broke on the word '*dead*'. The James's eyes filled with tears.

Mr. James had known Logan personally. As an athlete, a student, and the person who made his daughter practically glow.

Mrs. James was too stunned to speak. As she reached out a hand to her husband, Shawn turned away, walking quickly to his car.

He opened the door.

"Tess. You're home." He spoke quietly, hoping not to startle her.

She didn't move.

"Tess?"

She didn't look at him. Her eyes didn't seem to register that he was there.

He reached into the car, and gently lifted her out of the seat.

Carefully, he carried Tess to her parents, setting her feet down as softly as possible. Both of her parents engulfed her in hugs, murmuring words of pointless promises and condolences.

Tess did not hug her parents back. She didn't speak. She didn't seem to notice Shawn, even when he gripped her hand, saying he'd come back soon.

Her movements were mechanical. Lifeless. Empty and numb.

It terrified him to see her like that.

He left, hoping that her parents might possibly be of some comfort to her. But he knew from experience that nothing but time would *really* help her now. And even then, the pain would never disappear.

Tears stung his eyes, and he clenched his jaw, forcing them back.

Tears for Logan Tucker. For Tess.

And tears of guilt.

He'd already made his decision, but that didn't make it hurt any less.

The fire was a warning. A warning for *him*. And that made all of this his fault.

Logan was dead because of him.

People *always* died because of him. It was in his DNA.

He was a killer.

A sob escaped his lips, and he jerked the wheel, pulling over to the side of the road. He stared in silence as cars drove past.

Then he exploded, slamming his fist into the dashboard.

Over and over until his knuckles were a bloody mess.

It was all his fault.

He forced himself to breathe, and gradually, the tears stopped falling. He pulled back onto the road.

He had to be stronger than this. He couldn't afford to show weakness. Not now.

His home came into view, threatening to trigger another wave of fear and anxiety, but this time, he managed to drive it back down. *So* deep into his conscience that not even Koden's *Amino* could reach it.

Shawn took in a final breath, climbing from his car and walking up the path to his home.

He threw open the front door. His father had returned from his trip. The Traces of his family were *all* present in the dining room, but he didn't spare the thought to wonder why his mother and uncle had returned early.

Their voices fell silent momentarily as they felt him enter, but no one called to him.

For a moment, he wondered what it felt like to have a mother, like Mrs. Tucker. To *know* that you were loved. To have a family. To never have to be afraid.

Shawn straightened his shoulders, preparing himself. Keeping his head up, and his hands still, and he made his way to the dining room.

Koden, Alyssa, and Konrad all stood, stopped mid-conversation by his appearance.

His mother wrinkled her nose. "Why do I smell smoke?"

Koden's eyes appraised him, noting the grass stains and soot on his clothing, and the blood drying on his hands. He frowned, pointing a finger at Shawn. "Where were you?"

Amazingly, Shawn's voice came out steady.

"Salvator, if you would permit me to speak with you in private?"

His family stared at him, stunned. He held his head high, refusing to acknowledge the voice screaming in his head.

Traitor. She trusts you!

No.

He was doing this to protect her. He had *promised* to protect her.

Finally, Koden gave the Masons a dismissive nod, beckoning Shawn to enter the room. Reluctantly, they left, staring at their son with confused bewilderment.

And fear.

They knew that Shawn had information. Information that they had kept from the Salvator. Information that branded *both* of them as traitors.

Koden waved a hand towards Shawn. "Go on."

Shawn took in a breath. "Do you remember the girl you saw in my mind, Salvator? Brown hair, hazel eyes?"

"Of course I do. She's the Lusus Naturae you were speaking with at graduation, yes?" Koden snorted in disgust, quickly losing interest in the conversation.

"I was very disappointed to see that you'd stooped *so* low as to seek out *that* sort of company. Though, I suppose I shouldn't have expected anything else."

Shawn clenched his fists furiously, then forced himself to meet Koden's eyes. Watching every reaction.

"Her name is Tess James. She's an undocumented Munera."

His uncle froze, his face twisted in genuine surprise.

"I felt her Trace. Just recently— she's newly active. I know her personally, sir. She was raised by a Lusus Naturae couple. Until now, she was completely unaware of *what* she is. She truly had no idea that the Society existed."

Shawn dipped his head, trying to appear indifferent.

"Her parents also seem to be ignorant of our world. She was adopted and according to them, she was abandoned. I think she could benefit from a mentor. Proper education about the Society and Munera."

Koden continued to stare at him. Then, he smiled broadly.

"You're enamored with her, Shawn."

It wasn't a question.

He felt his cheeks redden, and he spoke quietly.

"She is— she *was* seeing someone else. A Lusus Naturae."

Calling Logan a Lusus Naturae felt wrong, the word like poison on his tongue.

"And that brings up another point," Shawn said, lifting his gaze to meet his uncle's.

"That same Lusus Naturae was killed in a house fire tonight. It was no accident. I believe someone targeted him because he spent so much time with Tess and they assumed she was a rogue. Either way, I have no doubt after seeing the fire that it was the work of a Munera."

Desperately, he searched the Salvator's expression, but the man appeared genuinely unaware of the information Shawn was revealing. And uninterested for the most part.

But Shawn saw his eyes narrow slightly, and in that moment, he knew.

Koden had *not* ordered this fire. But someone had.

He was positive the fire had been a warning. Every instinct was screaming that the Society was involved.

"They're—" He caught himself again. Talking about Logan in the present tense.

Talking about him *period*.

"*She's* not a rogue. And the Lusus Naturae didn't know anything about us."

He swallowed hard, preparing himself for what he was about to do.

He was playing a dangerous game, but he was already too deep to back out.

"I could bring Tess to meet you, if it would ease any

concerns you have. From what I've observed, her abilities appear to be low Gradus."

That was a lie. But Shawn kept his voice steady, determined not to give anything away.

Koden raised an eyebrow, skeptical. "Why would I waste my time on a low Gradus?"

Relief overwhelmed him, but he didn't allow any emotion to enter his voice.

This is what he had been counting on.

Arrogance.

If Koden had *one* trait that might eventually lead to his downfall, it was arrogance.

The leader of the Society did *not* typically associate with low Gradus Munera, undocumented or not.

"I could educate her." Shawn shrugged, feigning nonchalance. "Unfortunately, due to fault of my own, I have no political standing within the Society. If anything, Salvator, I seem to be in your way more often than not."

He frowned. "I'm aware that my company displeases you, sir. I also know that you have matters to attend to with the Caine research and tracking down Chloe Hale. Allowing me to educate the girl would kill two birds with one stone."

If Koden agreed to give Shawn clearance to train with Tess, he would continue working with her, maintaining the charade that she was of a weak Gradus.

But if Koden didn't agree, they could potentially send officials to interrogate her. To bring her in for a trial.

If that happened, Shawn would be forced to hide her, provided he was able to reach her before the Society did.

Shawn looked down, and his cheeks burned red as he appealed to his uncle's crude nature. "Salvator, I hope to one day regain my standing within the Society. However, I won't pretend I'm asking for this opportunity out of a desire to earn that honor. Truthfully, I would appreciate a chance to spend time with this girl. I recognize she is not of a Gradus befitting my station. I understand that, and I assure you I am purely interested in a *physical* relationship with her. Nothing more."

He raised his eyes, finding his uncle's amused gaze on him. A lewd smile spreading slowly across his face.

"Well, well."

He sat back in one of the dining room chairs, observing Shawn in silence.

Shawn focused on controlling his breathing. Concentrated on letting his mind go blank. Permitting only one thought to enter his mind.

Her long legs, squeezed into those tight jeans.

He felt a soft prodding, as Koden gently but *deliberately* began searching his thoughts. Shawn's face burned as he allowed thoughts of Tess to fill his mind. Thoughts he typically reserved for late nights. Thoughts he was *humiliated* to expose to anyone. Let alone his uncle.

And thoughts he was ashamed to think after what he'd witnessed today.

Finally. *Mercifully*. Koden nodded.

"Very well. I'll have that fire looked into. If your suspicions are correct, that is a breach of *several* protocols."

He stood, a vulgar leer displayed upon his handsome face.

"Teach the girl, Shawn. Screw the girl." He gave a lascivious wink. "But don't fall in love with her."

He waited until Koden had disappeared into the living room, where his parents were waiting. As soon as his uncle was gone, Shawn let out a breath of relief, then made his way up the back staircase, slipping silently into his room.

There, the relief turned into self-loathing. Shame. Disgust.

He had betrayed her.

Revealed her to Koden. Given her up to the Society.

And essentially, portrayed her as nothing more than a disposable slut.

He lay down, closing his eyes, opening them immediately when his imagination provided an image of Logan.

Burned. Blistered. Broken.

A cry escaped, and he covered his mouth to stifle it.

Tess's secret was out.

And it was his fault.

He hadn't meant to make things worse, but he had a feeling that's exactly what he had done.

CHAPTER 34

CHLOE

No one came for her that night. Not Shawn, not Tess, not Logan.

Not even Reese.

Chloe tried to stay calm. Rational.

It was late. There was a good chance no one could come until morning considering there was a fire at Logan's house.

So she waited, trying not to overreact.

Her friends were all under a lot of stress. She couldn't expect everyone to drop their problems and take care of her. It made perfect sense that no one had come to check on her.

It does not *make sense that Tess hasn't answered her phone all night.*

Or Logan. Or Dalton. And if she *had* Shawn's number, she felt certain he wouldn't have answered either.

She thought about leaving the vacant home, and searching out her friends. But Tess's warning stuck with her. If she went out in the open, she'd be risking her parents finding her. Her body tensed at the mere thought of Reese near her. Or Charlotte.

That probably made her a coward. She was being selfish. Staying holed up in a safe location while something might really be wrong with her friends.

What if someone had been hurt in the fire?

The image of Logan's sister crossed her mind. Her sweet smile and innocent questions.

She had grown to adore Kennedy. And the idea of her being hurt was horrifying.

But *she* didn't want to get hurt, either. So she stayed, waiting for a phone call.

She glanced at her phone, checking the time. Four AM.

Groaning, she rolled onto her back, covering her face with her arms.

I could try calling Tess again.

She'd already tried a dozen times with no answer.

She shook her head, turning off her phone to save the battery.

Tomorrow, she decided. If no one answered tomorrow, she'd go to Tess's home and check on her. If Tess was at Logan's, which was just as likely, she'd go there.

And if she couldn't find them, she'd go to Shawn's. She knew he lived a couple streets over from her, in that enormous mansion. She'd seen him once. Getting out of his *too-nice* car and slinking up to that *too-nice* front door. She was hesitant to be that close to her house, but she had to know what was going on.

She felt better, having a plan and she closed her eyes, finally allowing sleep to come.

She woke to a familiar sour stench. The sickening sweet smell of decay, mixed with sweat and alcohol.

It made the hair on the back of her neck rise. Her stomach clenched, and her hands began to shake.

Reese. He was here. He'd found her.

She couldn't see him, but the voice at the door was unmistakable.

"I'll kill you!"

Chloe's chest heaved, the unexpected rush of fear surging through her veins, leaving her lightheaded.

A figure stepped through the door, and then, Reese was there. Standing with his belt in hand.

Chloe tried to scramble away, but her legs were wrapped too tightly in the blankets she had used for her pallet.

She was trapped.

He would kill her this time.

"Get away from me!" she cried, and the darkness around her shifted. Shadows drifting from their crevices and materializing to form a wall in front of her.

"Chloe!"

The sound of his voice infuriated her.

Fueling her. Empowering her.

Years of torment and suppressed rage exploded, and the curtain of shadows shattered into broken glass. *Black* glass. Rocketing in all directions, earning a satisfying cry of pain from Reese.

Only it *wasn't* Reese.

Chloe's eyes refocused.

It was morning. Soft sunlight streamed into the window of the front room.

Shards of black still hovered in midair, melting as she became fully conscious and flowing back into their rightful place in the corners of the room.

Her terror slowly eased, as she realized what had happened.

Reese *wasn't* there.

He *wasn't* going to kill her.

She *hadn't* been discovered by the Society.

It was just a nightmare.

Her relief was short-lived as her eyes landed on a figure crouched against the wall of the rental home. His face contorted in pain and shock.

"Shawn?" she demanded, rising shakily to her feet. "Why the hell are you sneaking in here like a freaking stalker?"

Shawn raised his eyebrows and smiled, but it didn't quite reach his eyes. "I knocked, but you didn't answer. I suppose if you prefer, I can leave you to your nightmares."

His words had a bite to them, and she winced, feeling guilty. Only then did she notice his eyes were red, bloodshot like he had spent a night crying.

"What's wrong?" she asked, and he glanced down, not quite meeting her stare.

He touched his side tentatively, and when he pulled his hand away—

Blood.

There was blood there, running from a wide gash across his ribs.

"You stabbed me, that's what's wrong," he muttered, leaning down to inspect the wound.

Other than a slight grimace, he didn't seem fazed by the pain.

Chloe stared in horror at the blood. The fabric of his hoodie was torn, as well as the shirt under it. Ripped open to expose a bloody chunk of missing skin.

"I- No, I wouldn't...I don't even know—"

Shawn laughed, but there was no humor in it. It sounded hollow.

"You have better control over your gift than you think you do. I've never seen a Munera summon their abilities on command within weeks of activation. Impressive."

Most of what Shawn said went right over her head and she stared at him blankly.

Shawn caught her expression and sighed. "That's not important, I guess. Anyway, it's just a graze. I've had worse."

His voice had turned glum.

He straightened, making a half-hearted gesture for Chloe to follow him, but she didn't move.

"How did you know where I was?" she asked, confused. "Did Tess tell you? Or Logan?"

At the mention of Logan, Shawn looked away.

"No," he murmured quietly. "No one told me. I divided the town into quarters, then drove each block until I found a lone Trace in an unexpected area. It wasn't that complicated."

His tone was off. There was *definitely* something wrong. And it involved Logan.

Was it drama between Logan and him over Tess? Or did it have something to do with the fire? Or with the Society?

Shawn narrowed his eyes, growing noticeably edgier. "Are you coming? There's a reason I had Hunter warn you. We need to go."

"Where are we going?"

"Somewhere safe. Now, are you coming or not?"

"Not until you tell me what happened last night." Chloe crossed her arms defiantly. "Why didn't anyone come for me? Why hasn't anyone answered my calls? What happened with the fire and *who* is coming?"

Shawn sagged against the wall, burying his face in his hands, then he slowly lowered himself down to the floor.

"It's Logan. The fire," he raised his head to meet her eye. "Logan didn't make it out."

Chloe froze.

Shawn was lying. He had to be lying.

"You just didn't see him." Her voice shook, tears beginning to blur her vision. "Maybe he made it out and you just missed it. You must have missed him—"

"Chloe. The house collapsed on him."

It wasn't possible. Logan couldn't be dead. Shawn had to be wrong. She *needed* him to be wrong.

Suddenly, Shawn's hand was on her shoulder. A gentle touch. She recognized he was making an effort to comfort her, but it was pointless.

She couldn't make sense of this. How could Logan be gone? After everything he'd done for her. Had she even once told him how grateful she was?

And now... Now he was gone.

Shawn spoke to her, murmuring that they had to leave. That there was no time. That they were coming for her.

She didn't care if they came for her. What was the point of any of this?

Logan had been so good. So many people had loved him.

His family, Tess, Dalton. And Chloe. *She* had loved him.

Shawn was shaking her.

"Chloe! I understand. Believe me, I understand. But we have to go now. Think of Tess. She *needs* you. If you stay here, you're dead, too."

She looked at him in silence, then stood in resignation.

Her legs felt weak and her throat burned with sobs that refused to come.

She followed him out of the house, leaving her phone with the blankets.

He insisted it was necessary. Cell phones were traceable, and he was taking her somewhere where other refugees would be staying. They couldn't risk endangering anyone else.

She felt numb. She wanted to believe this was a dream.

Shawn spoke occasionally, but she struggled to focus on his words. Instead, she remembered Logan's smile when Tess accepted prom-posal. And how he would laugh so hard that his soda would shoot out his nose. How he had saved her. The moment he looked into her eyes and announced that she was safe. That Reese would never touch her again.

He had saved her. But she hadn't been there to save him.

She bit her lip in an effort to stop the wail that threatened to escape.

Had he thought of his family? Of Tess or Chloe?

Or had he just laid helpless, waiting and begging for someone to save him?

"Distract me," she whispered. "Please... just talk to me about anything else..."

Shawn glanced at her, his hands tight on the steering wheel. He was silent for a minute, trying to think of what to say.

At last, he asked, "Would you like to know a little about who you are? It won't be comforting. But you deserve an explanation for what's going on."

Chloe grimaced, uncertain. "Okay."

Shawn took in a breath, then began to speak.

"There are three ancient Munera families: Tribus Viribus. Traditionally, the most powerful, wealthy, and influential Munera in history. The Caines, the Roses—" He paused, glancing at her quickly, then continued.

"and the Masons. The Society encompasses all of North and South America. Technically, it's a democracy. However, the Mason family— *my* family — has remained in power for several generations. My uncle is the Salvator, our leader, and my parents hold rank immediately beneath him. It *was* expected that I, providing my uncle does not produce an heir, would eventually take the place of Salvator."

Chloe stared at him, dumbstruck. Tess had told her that the Society was corrupted, and the Salvator was a dictator and a psychopath. She had *not* explained how Shawn's family fit into everything, although she *had* said his home life was kind of crazy.

Talk about an understatement.

"It *was* expected?"

Shawn smiled, concentrating on the road. "Long story. Let's keep it simple today."

"Fine." She nodded in agreement. "Continue."

"For almost twenty years, the Salvator has been hunting down members of the Caine family. It was all political at first. The Caines are considered *Proditors*. Blood traitors. They advocated against the discrimination against Lusus Naturae. Particularly against the treatment of the hybrid children produced when a Munera and Lusus Naturae produce offspring."

He looked at her. "Tess explained the issues with Abnormal and Basic DNA mixing, didn't she?"

Chloe nodded.

"Well, just a few months ago, one of Koden's top researchers made a discovery. She believes the Caine's DNA might be able to reactivate hybrid Geneses."

"But that's a good thing, right?"

Shawn laughed.

"You would think so, but no. I said they *believe* the DNA will work. They are still in the trial phase of all of this and the statistics aren't pretty. In order to *get* this DNA, the facility needs Caines to experiment on. And hybrids. Hybrids are actually pretty rare. Hybrid children don't usually reach adulthood because they rarely— if ever —survive trials. And the Society doesn't have enough Caines to keep the research going. Seeing as my uncle declared all Caines traitors years ago, they weren't that keen to stick around the Society. For the most part, the family appears to have disappeared. The Caine they *do* have possession of has been tortured nearly to the point of death."

He fell into silence, giving her time to absorb the information.

Chloe was grateful for the information about the Society. And she was thankful he was being open about his family. It made her feel like she could trust him. Still, she was beginning to regret asking for a distraction. She was already terrified of her parents, and this definitely wasn't helping to ease her concern.

Shawn glanced at her, sensing her thoughts. Her fears. Tess had told her that sensing and discovering fears was one of Shawn's abilities. *Timor mortale*, whatever that meant. Was he searching through her fears right now?

She shuddered at the thought.

She might be starting to like Shawn, but *that* was creepy.

He blushed. "I apologize for the history lesson... I assumed you'd want to have a little background knowledge before we reach Mesquite Ridge."

"What's in Mesquite Ridge?"

Shawn's lips stretched into a tight line. He looked uncomfortable, maybe even a little scared.

Chloe pressed him. "What's in Mesquite Ridge?"

For a long moment, he didn't answer, and they sat in uncomfortable silence.

She sighed loudly, growing annoyed with his reluctance.

"There's a group in Mesquite Ridge that will protect you," he said finally. "They want to protect all Caines."

Chloe started to protest— her question had nothing to do with the Caines.

Then, she registered what he was saying.

They'll protect you. They protect *Caines*.

Shawn gave her a sad smile as she pieced it together.

He couldn't mean what she thought he did. She wasn't anything special, much less a Caine.

"I'm just a Charge," she muttered, shaking her head in protest.

Her friend looked at her, raising an eyebrow.

"If you were '*just* a Charge', I wouldn't have needed to send Hunter to warn you. You wouldn't have been tracked in the first place. Charges are supposed to be protected and prepared and given the path to a better life, but ultimately, they're the least of the Society's concerns."

Speechless, Chloe stared at him, waiting for him to laugh, to say he was joking. Trying to lighten the mood after...

Stop.

Logan had entered her thoughts again, bringing tears immediately to her eyes, and she blinked them back.

"I'm not a Caine," she insisted, wiping away the tears that had begun to track down her cheeks. "If I was important, they would have come after me the day I ran. If I was important, they wouldn't have spent eighteen years abusing me!"

"Chloe," Shawn said quietly, gentle and reassuring, despite his next words. "I overheard my uncle. You were their next target. You were purposely placed with Reese due to his weakness. They hoped by placing you with the Hale's, you wouldn't activate early. If I hadn't sent Hunter to warn you, you would have already been detained by officials and shipped off to one of Koden's facilities."

She started to respond, to tell him that he was wrong, but he stiffened, pulling over and glancing out the window.

Chloe looked around, panicked.

Were they being followed? Why were they stopping *here*?

Outside, there was nothing but scrawny trees, and hills pitted with sewer tunnels.

"What is it?" she demanded. Seeking out the threat. Searching for Traces. "Shawn, tell me what's wrong!"

His Adam's apple bobbed, nervous sparks flying from his hands.

"We're here," he whispered, his voice full of dread.

Something about this place was terrifying him. She had only seen him like this once. At graduation.

His already pale face had drained of color, and his blue eyes were wide with fear.

It made her stomach drop.

"You said these are the good guys," she reminded him, her voice shrill. "That they're going to protect us."

Shawn shook his head, finally managing a half smile, full of self loathing. "I said they'd protect *you*. They want *me* dead."

CHAPTER 35

SHAWN

That was *not* the right thing to say to get Chloe out of the car.

"What the *hell* do you mean they want you dead?" she growled. "Don't you think we've lost enough today?"

Shawn inhaled sharply, wincing at the memory of Logan disappearing beneath the rafter. The smoke.

The body.

"I said they *want* me dead," he insisted. "It's not going to happen, okay? It's more likely they'll want to use me as a hostage, considering who I am." He snorted, then gave a dark laugh.

"With my uncle in town, I could use a break from my family, so is that really such a bad thing?"

More lies. Ace had warned him that it was highly unlikely he would survive his time with the Turncoats. He was tempting fate. But he couldn't tell Chloe that.

"Trust me, Chloe," he said, squeezing her hand tightly

before letting it go. "We're going to be fine. This is the only way."

He reached out, lifting her chin so her eyes met his. He smiled gently, but his words were firm. "Listen to me, Chloe. There are sentries posted outside. I have no doubt they've already seen us and are watching us right now, so it's very important when you step out of this car, you keep your hands visible. And *don't* use your abilities, alright?"

She didn't respond. Her bright eyes were wide and frightened.

"Tell me you understand."

She nodded slowly, whispering, "I understand."

After several minutes of coaxing, he convinced her to step out of the car, and they made their way cautiously towards one of the drainage pipe entrances. Ace hadn't given any indication which way he was supposed to go to. He assumed someone would stop them before they got too far. He limped as they walked. The wound Chloe had given him ached, and every step he took burned.

Though, if what Ace Lane told him was true, the wound was *nothing* compared to what he could expect from the Turncoats.

Chloe frowned, glancing around. "I don't want to be here," she whispered.

Shawn sighed, trying to be patient. "It's either this or the labs. Believe me, if I knew another way, I would take it. But I'm not letting the Society touch y—"

He froze, his words choking off as something wrapped around his throat.

A crushing pressure, closing off his airway. He gasped, his hands flying to his throat instinctively. His vision blurred, his lungs screaming for air.

Chloe cried out, running towards him, but an invisible wall stopped her. She fell to the ground screaming.

"Shawn! Shawn, what's happening?"

Through the haze enveloping his mind, he could make out figures emerging from thin air.

Inuisibilitas. Invisibility.

They advanced on them, and his legs were swept out from beneath him. The ground raced towards him, and the impact forced all remaining air out of his lungs.

He couldn't breathe. Something pressed into his back, shoving him against the grass.

Chloe screamed, pinned to the ground several yards away from him.

"Tyler. Let go. You're going to kill him."

"Good! I hope I do. One less Mason on the Earth suits me just fine."

The voices around him were hard to make out. His ears were ringing and instinct kept his chest heaving, desperate for air that wasn't coming. Still, he refused to fight.

I didn't think I would die this *quickly*.

"Shawn!" Chloe sobbed.

"Tyler. Release him, *now*. That's an order!"

A disgusted breath. "Fine."

The pressure at his throat disappeared, and he coughed, sucking in a grateful breath of fresh air.

Tyler was right. He and his family *did* deserve to die.

But Chloe did not. The sound of her crying, alone and terrified beside him, gave him strength.

"I need your help," he said, his voice hoarse. "My friend is in danger. She's a Caine. She is the target of the Salvator's newest experiment. Do whatever you want with me, but please! I'm begging you to keep her safe."

Chloe made a strangled sound in her throat. "Shawn! Please! I can't do this without you!"

The people above him began to talk at once in hushed voices.

"She's a Caine?"

"Brandon, you can't *seriously* believe him?"

"How did Shawn Mason get *here*?"

"We should just kill them!"

Another voice rang out louder than the rest. "Enough!"

The man's voice rang with authority, and in that one word, Shawn recognized he was the leader. The crowd quieted, though there was still disgruntled muttering from Tyler.

"Let the girl stand," he ordered.

Chloe cried out as she was yanked roughly from the ground.

Shawn wished he could see everyone around him. If he was going to die, he at least wanted the opportunity to see who he had been obsessed over for *years*. Who he'd idolized and researched and sacrificed everything to find.

Someone kicked at his injured side, and he did his best not to flinch.

"Yo Brandon. His Majesty is hurt."

"Get him up."

Hands grabbed his arms and hauled him unceremoniously to his feet.

The dark man in front of him was several inches taller than Shawn, his eyes piercing. His umber skin was scarred—though nothing like Shawn's —and pulled tight over bulging muscles.

His mouth seemed to be set in a permanent scowl.

"Shawn Mason... damn it really *is* you."

Shawn's eyes widened in recognition.

"You're Brandon Proctor... you... You *killed* two of the Salvator's Senators! You were reported dead... How...?"

Despite the fear running through his veins, Shawn couldn't keep the childlike wonder from entering his voice.

Brandon's scowl didn't lessen, but his eyebrows lifted.

"I guess the Society doesn't know everything." He moved

towards Shawn. Close enough Shawn could see the golden flecks in his eyes.

"But you, Shawn Mason. *You've* sentenced *countless* Turncoats to death. *You* are the Salvator's nephew. And that's what *I* want to know about."

Chloe turned to stare at Shawn in confusion. "What is he talking about?"

Shawn ground his teeth, lowering his head as he was filled with shame.

Brandon spoke before Chloe could continue. "Take them both into the Post. But I want the Mason brought in for questioning. As for the girl, I want a *memoria lectorem* on her. Alex would be best. Find out if she's really a Caine."

A memory reader? What good would that do?

One of the Turncoats started to argue, but Brandon snapped at her. "That's *enough*. Go."

The same force that had been at his throat was suddenly pressing his hands behind his back. Telekinesis. He realized that it was the girl who'd been arguing with Brandon. Tyler. She was blonde with bright colored stripes dyed into her hair and a thick scar across her throat. Her green eyes were sharp as she glared at him, and an invisible force shoved him forward.

"Move," she snarled.

Shawn complied, ignoring Chloe as she assaulted him with questions. "What is he talking about? Who are these people? What did you do? Shawn? Shawn, talk to me!"

They entered one of the drainage pipes, and despite his expectations, there was no stench of sewage or stale water. In fact, the tunnels were clean and dry. Wide spaces that seemed to go on forever, branching off in different directions. The air was crisp and cool. And it was light. Sunlight seemed to travel all the way through the tunnels, even though they had seemed dark and endless from the outside. It was incredible.

People emerged from openings cut into the sides of the tunnels. *Rebels.*

The Traces were overwhelming as they pounded in his chest.

Shawn was accustomed to large groups of Munera, but the sheer amount of power he felt in this space was exhilarating.

There must be thousands of Abnormals in these tunnels.

He was so distracted by the Traces and the cavernous space in the tunnels that their words didn't immediately register.

When they did, he felt his heart sink.

Screams and accusations came from all around him.

A woman ran to him, slapping him hard across the face before his captors could stop her. *If* they would have stopped her anyway.

"I lost my husband and daughter because of you!"

Brandon touched the woman on the shoulder, gently moving her to the side.

Shawn's breath was coming in short pants, and he looked down. He could feel their hatred. Overpowering. Painful as they screamed insults and hurled small objects at him.

The Turncoat leader walked beside him, not bothering to quicken his pace or stop the abuse. He was purposely humiliating him, and Shawn couldn't even feel angry.

He deserved this. He deserved every furious insult thrown his way.

I deserve to die.

Suddenly, Brandon held up a hand. Not to stop the angry shouts, but to direct Shawn down one tunnel and Chloe down another. Chloe, who had been walking in silence, began yelling and trying to pull away from those restraining her. Shawn saw a hazy wall of black beginning to form in front of her, and he screamed.

"Chloe, no! Don't!"

She stared at him desperately.

"Don't," he whispered again.

The few shadows she had begun to gather immediately dispersed.

He shook his head sadly, giving her a small smile. "They're going to take care of you. Everything is going to be okay."

She stared at him a moment longer, then allowed them to lead her down the tunnel. Away from him. He sighed in relief. He had done it. She was safe.

The rest of the walk passed in a blur. He had accomplished what he had come to do. He resigned himself to whatever fate awaited him.

They entered a dark room, and he was shoved into a chair as they bound his wrists and ankles. Brandon stood in front of him, scowling. He meant to bow his head respectfully, reminding himself he truly deserved anything they did to him. He had *earned* their hatred.

But old habits die hard.

He smiled, sparks flickering across his fingers. "Lovely welcoming committee."

Brandon didn't acknowledge the comment, bending down to meet Shawn's eye.

"This is your one warning," he growled. "Every entrance, exit, and the acres surrounding us are *heavily* guarded. You don't have a chance in Hell of escaping. I don't give a damn what Gradus you are. The only reason you've made it this far is by *my* grace, because I believe you might have some valuable information. But don't think for one minute that I give a damn about your life or that I won't hesitate to end it. In fact, I look forward to it."

Shawn frowned, feeling slightly let down. He had expected something *different* from the legendary Turncoats. Something *more*. Shawn met the man's stare, nodding in an attempt to appear respectful. "I do have information. What do you want to know?"

Brandon's eyes narrowed, shining in the dim light. "*Everything.*"

S o he told him.
    Everything.

Every detail of every horrific Society trial he had participated in.

He told him about the night he had tortured Jonas Vandenburg, and then stood by as his mother ended the man's life. Willingly gave him the specifics of every legal, and *illegal* interrogation he had been called to oversee. Described the countless tragedies he had allowed to happen as he blindly followed his family's instructions.

He went into detail about the Masons, explaining how their abilities worked, and how far they could go. How far they *had* gone. In trials. In the massacres. In the '*disappearances*' of Basic families they suspected were involved with the rebels. About his role in disposing of the bodies.

The Turncoats had expected him to resist, and Brandon had obviously anticipated needing to use force to get the information out of Shawn. Even bringing in extra Abnormals as reinforcements.

Instead, as Shawn spoke, Brandon and the others in the room began to look ill.

But he couldn't stop. It was like his words were water pouring from a dam.

Every abominable thing he'd ever done was exposed. The unstoppable wave of violence and terror he had brought into people's lives. He was *truly* a monster.

And then, he only had one thing left. A night of unspeakable horror that had left him broken beyond repair.

Irredeemable.

The night that he'd kept buried for the last six years of his life. Refusing to discuss or think about. The night he had finally realized what he was, and fully understood the sins he had allowed to be committed.

He had been twelve. He'd attended a trial. It wasn't by any means his first judgment or sentencing. He had been called to serve the Society at nine years old, so he had seen enough blood and death in just those three years that he had already begun to grow numb to the horror of it.

But he had never sentenced someone he knew. Someone he loved.

Cary Scott, one of Koden's most valued Senators.

The man had always offered to take care of Shawn when his parents were away for business. His wife, Phyllis, loved Shawn like her own, and Calan, their son, had been Shawn's best friend. The only person he could open up to. He had loved Calan like a brother.

Senator Scott had been accused of plotting to overthrow Koden. He had grown to believe the Salvator's methods were too harsh. Brutal. He was using his position in the Senate to sway the other members into staging a coup against the Masons. He swore his wife and son had been completely unaware of his indiscretions.

Koden had questioned the man relentlessly, but to no avail. Cary had remained stoic, refusing to name any co-conspirators. He had refused to talk, even after hours of torture. He had managed to hide his thoughts from Koden, but the Salvator couldn't afford to kill him. If Cary died, the Salvator would lose all hope of unraveling the network of dissenters.

So he'd called on Shawn, in hopes that he could *'motivate'* him in other ways.

To torture Phyllis.

Knowing that Shawn hadn't fully learned to control his abilities. *Knowing* he could accidentally kill the woman. But also knowing that it was likely that Cary would break after watching his lover suffer.

Shawn had refused, not wanting to hurt her.

"They are trying to destroy our family. Your family! You want these Proditors *to hurt us? To tear down the Society?"*

No, Shawn didn't want that. He *loved* his family. The Society was good. Koden was doing everything he could to protect the Munera people.

So he did as he was told. Inducing horrific vision after vision, sobbing as he listened to Phyllis's screams.

But there had also been a rush. Excitement. Sick and twisted as it was, he had been amazed at his strength. At how much power he held over the woman.

By the time he'd been ordered to stop, Phyllis was still. Her eyes empty of all emotion. Her warm smile and bright copper eyes had been replaced with a blank nothingness. Not dead, but not entirely alive anymore.

The rush had disappeared instantly. He'd broken down in front of everyone, trying to speak. To tell Koden that she was innocent, that she didn't deserve this. Begging for an Elite healer to fix her shattered mind.

No one had listened. No healer had come. Cary Scott still refused to speak, even as he stared at the hollow shell of his wife. Koden snapped and a guard began to drag someone forward.

Calan.

"No! No, he didn't do anything! Calan didn't—"

Koden had slapped him. It was the first time he'd ever hit Shawn. It shocked him into silence.

"I need you to protect our people, Shawn. You will *do as I say."*

His uncle's dark eyes had been lit with a dangerous fervor Shawn had never seen before.

He was scared. Scared to do what the Salvator was asking, but terrified to refuse. Horrified, Shawn followed his uncle's orders. Listening to the agonized screams of his only true friend. Calan begged Shawn to stop. Begged him for help. Shawn had allowed his mind to go blank, so that he had no longer heard his friend's cries.

In the end, neither Phyllis, nor Calan could withstand the strain Shawn had forced onto their minds. As he watched his son scream in agony, Cary finally broke.

And so did Shawn.

For months afterward, he was haunted with nightmares and waking dreams. His grades in school dropped. He'd become angry and temperamental, snapping at his teachers, his mentors, his family. Nearly exposing himself at school on multiple occasions. Depression had taken root in him. He'd refused to eat, refused training with his mentors, refused spending time with anyone in or outside of the Society.

He didn't deserve to be happy. To eat. To have friends.

To live.

After hours of talking, he finally fell silent. Brandon stood, his face pale and grim as he released the restraints holding Shawn in place. He gestured to the others in the room, cocking an eyebrow.

"Make sure he didn't leave anything out. Enjoy yourself, but don't kill him."

Shawn let out a breath. *This* was what he'd been expecting.

The people in the room began to smile. Anticipating. This is what they'd been waiting for too.

A chance to get revenge.

Shawn welcomed the pain. But he knew nothing they did would ever be enough.

Before he could ready himself, a fist slammed into the side

of his face, rocking him sideways. Blood filled his mouth and he bit his cheek to keep from crying out.

A blow landed on his injured side, and this time, he did scream. There was a crunch as some of his ribs cracked, and his side was instantly soaked with blood.

An invisible force slammed him against the wall, then began to choke him. He almost blacked out. It released him at the last moment. He fell to the ground, instinct begging him to crawl towards the door. To escape. He heard laughter. Someone spit on him, then kicked his side.

He found himself coughing up blood, pain racking his body as his broken ribs moved. Waves of heat began in his toes, moving slowly through his body. It felt like they were boiling his blood.

It went on for hours, but his story never changed.

Brandon finally sent the others away, kneeling by his side.

Shawn couldn't breathe. He was slick with blood, his muscles moving in involuntary spasms. His throat was raw, his ears rang, and he could feel his bones grating against each other every time he took a breath.

He turned his head, seeing Brandon watching him.

Shawn drew a rattling breath. "Thank... you."

The man watched him wordlessly, then shook his head.

"I'll be sending in several healers in an hour. In the meantime, I'm going to have my *memoria lectorem* look at you. You're leaving something out."

He wasn't. He had told them everything. Brandon started to stand, but Shawn spoke. He struggled to make the words make sense.

"What?" Brandon asked, and Shawn tried again.

"Two... hours. Talk with Chloe... P- Please."

Brandon stared at him. Then, finally, nodded. "I'll bring her in."

CHAPTER 36

CHLOE

As they walked, Chloe stared around the tunnels in fascination. How was this possible? She'd heard of homeless populations in huge cities living in communities like this. Underground in sewer tunnels or drainage pipes. Always having to be fearful of flooding. But the images of those communes had been filled with shopping carts, trash, and filth. People with matted hair, gaunt and withered faces, and blackened teeth.

This was nothing like that.

Here, the tunnels were clean and filled with light. It almost appeared to be a military bunker. The people she passed looked like normal people. Though many had scars or bruises, the vast majority of them could have been people she passed on the street or in the grocery store.

They were just ordinary people.

Ordinary people that had separated her from Shawn.

Her hands trembled, and her breathing sounded too labored. Loud and echoing throughout the wide chamber. She slowed her breathing, making an effort to take several deep breaths. She needed to focus.

When they had first entered the tunnels, her chest had filled with Traces, making her feel like she might explode. And then the screaming began. Vulgarities being hurled at Shawn. It had made her heart pound and her fury rise, but he'd only lowered his head, accepting the hatred with no protest.

Why?

The question nagged her. She hadn't known Shawn for long, but in the time she had, he had saved her. Not once, but twice.

Then they had separated them, marching Shawn to the left and Chloe to the right. She had fought to reach him, struggling to summon her ability. She had no idea what her plan was. Only that she had to stay with him.

He had stopped her. His bright blue eyes intent. And sad.

Don't.

She fought against the despair threatening to consume her.

What if they tried to hurt him? She couldn't stand to lose another friend.

They had walked for miles it seemed, and her fear grew with every step. She had no idea who these people were. No idea where they were taking her. Finally, she couldn't stand the suspense.

She stopped, turning to speak to her two captors.

"Where am I going?" Despite her trembling hands, her voice remained steady.

One of them was a man, with red hair and eyes so dark they appeared nearly black. He glared at her.

"You think I'm telling you anything? You showed up with a Mason— I'm not telling you nothing."

The dark-haired woman walking beside her gave the man a scathing look. "The Mason said she's a Caine, Nathan! And she's a child! You shouldn't—"

"Mari," Nathan snapped, "you're gonna tell me you really believe Shawn Mason? They're probably both spies!"

The woman, Mari, turned to Chloe, giving her an apologetic smile.

"I'm sorry, hun. Nathan isn't usually so unfriendly. But you have to understand his concerns. It's not like our whereabouts are common knowledge. Then you showing up with a Mason? The Salvator's very own nephew?"

She frowned, studying Chloe carefully. "That boy knowing where we are is a terrifying thought."

"He didn't do anything wrong!" Chloe demanded, finding courage in defense of her friend. "He doesn't deserve this."

Nathan snorted, crossing his arms. "I hope he gets everything he deserves. And then some."

Chloe turned towards the woman. "I want to know where I'm going! And what is a *memoria lectorem*?"

When both hesitated to answer, Chloe planted her feet firmly, refusing to move.

Nathan shoved an elbow into her back, grunting in annoyance.

"Move, kid! Or I'll *make* you move."

Mari sighed. "Nathan, stop."

"Tell me where I'm going, *now*," Chloe snapped back.

Mari placed a calming hand on Chloe's arm. "I promise, no one is going to hurt you here. A *memoria lectorem* is a memory reader. Sometimes, people refer to them as Elites."

Nathan spluttered out a protest, but Mari ignored him, pressing a gentle hand into Chloe's back. With no more argument, she moved, listening to Mari.

"All they want to do is find out if you truly are a Caine, and if so, who your parents might be."

The thought of someone digging around in her head made her squirm. Mari seemed to understand her thoughts, and patted her arm gently.

"I know it sounds strange, but it's actually... almost therapeutic. Nostalgic. Like seeing an old friend after years apart."

Reese's belt flashed through her mind, and she suppressed a shudder. Nothing about those memories would be nostalgic or therapeutic.

They fell into silence as they neared the end of the tunnel, then entered a tiny room. Mari gave her a small smile, saying the Elite would be there soon, then she and Nathan left, standing just outside the door in case she tried to escape. There was a small cot, like one would find in a school nurse's office, and she threw herself across it.

The Elite would be here soon. But not yet.

In the silence of the room, she finally allowed herself to cry. To think about Logan and how good he was. To think about Tess. She must be so lost right now, and Chloe couldn't even be there to help her. And Dalton. He had lost his best friend and girlfriend, and she had no way to tell him where or why she'd gone. And Shawn. Was he even alive? Where had they taken him?

She cried until she had no more tears. And then she lay there. Waiting.

Her head snapped up when the door finally opened. She sat up, her eyes red and puffy from crying.

"Sorry," she mumbled, wiping furiously at the tears to see who was there. "It's been a rough day."

In the doorway, there was a boy about her age. The first thing she noticed were his eyes. His dark irises were cloudy. He was blind.

Despite the way he stared sightlessly at her, he appeared alert and intelligent. He brushed his dark hair out of his face, then gave her a kind smile.

"Don't apologize," he said, his voice soft and calming. "I know this is a difficult experience. It definitely was for me."

Chloe nodded, slowly. Then remembered that he couldn't see her, so she spoke. "You're the memory guy?"

At that, he laughed. It was a bright and musical sound. His blank eyes seemed to sparkle with amusement.

"'*The memory guy*'?" he repeated. "That's a new one. Yeah, I guess I am. My name's Alex."

Alex held out a hand. When Chloe didn't take it, he furrowed his brows, tilting his head.

"Is my aim off or something?"

Reluctantly, she took his hand, shaking it.

"I'm sorry," she said as she let it go. "I lost one of my best friends today... And now, I'm here and they took Shawn and I have no idea what's gonna happen and I—"

Her voice had started to rise as she spoke, and Alex's eyes narrowed in concern. He stepped closer to her, tentatively reaching for her hand again. He missed at first, then brushed her fingers and gripped them softly.

"I'm sorry for your loss," he murmured, giving her hand a squeeze. "But I can promise you that Brandon won't have the Mason killed. He needs him for information."

That did *not* give Chloe much relief. "Why do they hate Shawn?" she whispered, her voice low. "The people out there were screaming at him. Saying that he was the reason they lost their families and yelling *horrible* things. I know his family is crazy. But what did *he* do? Why do they hate him?"

Alex frowned, looking away, then let go of her hand. "The Mason—"

"*Shawn*."

He sighed. "Alright. *Shawn* is one of the Society's lead interrogators. He uses his abilities to not only *discover 'Proditors'...*" Alex made air quotes around the word. "But to *torture* them. He's the reason so many of our undercover have been caught over the last several years."

Chloe began shaking her head adamantly. "That can't be right. Shawn hates the Society. He saved my life. He would never intentionally hurt *anyone*."

Alex shrugged. "For someone who hates the Society, he sure does a lot of work for them."

Before Chloe could protest again, to say he was mistaken, someone called in. "Alex, hurry up! Brandon will be back soon to check on her."

Alex rolled his eyes, scowling at the door. "My brother can wait, Nathan. This girl is new and scared. Kinda like *you* were when you first showed up."

He smiled mischievously in Chloe's direction as he added the last words, and she heard Mari laugh appreciatively.

Alex grinned, satisfied, then turned back to Chloe.

I don't want to do this.

"I'm sorry," Alex said, oblivious to her thoughts. "He's right, though. As much as I'm enjoying your company, I'm here to be the 'memory guy'."

Chloe recoiled. She didn't care how nice he was. She didn't feel comfortable with anyone poking around her mind.

He seemed to sense her fear, and he slowly backed away from her.

"You're scared," he noted, his tone gentle. "I won't hurt you. I don't have to look at everything if you don't want me too. It's difficult, but I can pinpoint certain memories with the right triggers. Would you rather me do that?"

Chloe glared at him. "I'd rather you didn't see my memories at all. Why do you need to know if I'm a Caine, anyway? I thought only the Society hunted Caines."

At that, Alex sighed, leaning back on his heels. "We need to know because taking you into our community is a risk. If you aren't trustworthy, we need to know. But Caines...they're worth *protecting* from the Society. We haven't seen a Caine in years."

He paused, then tightened his lips into a thin line. "You know what? I'll make you a deal. Let me find out the truth so I can report to Brandon. I won't look any further than I have to. And if Brandon says you can stay, I'll personally give you a tour of our home. And I'll answer any questions you have."

Don't do it.

She had spent *years* hiding her life. Fearing exposure. She was still reluctant to share her home situation with anyone.

But she needed to know her own story. So she reached out, grabbing Alex's hand and shaking it. "Deal."

He smiled. "Thank you."

Then, he was gone.

The room around her vanished, plunging her into darkness. She screamed in panic, and tried to reach out in search of Alex, but her arms didn't respond. She felt a heavy fog envelope her, dulling her senses.

She looked around, and slowly, the darkness began to recede, bringing a white room into focus. A hospital room?

Someone was crying nearby, and there was an unpleasant astringent smell. Someone was holding her and a man stood before her. He looked at her, scowling. He had dark eyes and black hair, and something about him seemed familiar. "I want a plan for her Guardian placement by tomorrow. Someone we can trust with her identity."

He grimaced in disgust. "Finding a Guardian willing to take in a Proditor's spawn will be challenging. Ensure whoever takes it is compensated well."

Another voice. "Yes, Salvator. Right away. Anything else, sir?"

"I want Alec Peralta standing trial before the Senate. The coward is still hiding something."

"Yes, Salvator."

"That will be all."

Then, another voice. Weak. Hardly louder than a whisper. "Koden..."

Chloe's throat tightened at that voice. Something about it was desperate and *familiar*. Home.

It ignited a bittersweet longing in her chest that she couldn't place, and her fear was overridden by curiosity. By a need to know who it was.

"Koden... Please... If you're going to take my daughter from me... If you're going to have me executed for treason... At least let me hold her. Once. Just once."

The dark haired man glanced away from her, narrowing his eyes slightly. The arms holding her shifted, and now a woman was visible, her face covered in sweat and strands of damp curly hair sticking to her forehead. She had deep circles under her blue eyes, but the expression in them was determined.

"Please," she repeated. "You have nothing to gain from denying me that. Just let me hold my daughter."

Daughter.

The word echoed in Chloe's mind, blossoming there, and filling her with a desperate desire to be near the woman.

Her mother.

This was impossible. This memory, if it was truly Chloe's, should not exist in her mind. Her brain wouldn't have been developed enough to form memories. And yet, these were *undoubtedly* memories.

The man sighed, nodding his permission, and she was carried towards the woman, then placed gently into her arms.

"Thank you," the woman whispered, holding her reverently against her chest.

Koden looked away. "Consider it a last request, Pearl Caine."

The woman— Chloe's mother —gave him a wry stare, and raised her eyebrows.

She looked nothing like Chloe. Her eyes were pale blue instead of gold, her skin milky white rather than olive. But the expression she wore was the twin to one Chloe wore often.

"I don't know what happened to you. There is good in you, Koden Mason. I saw it. My brother saw it. My sister fell in love with it."

Koden's lip curled into a snarl, but Pearl turned away from him, ignoring whatever else he had to say.

Her eyes stared down at Chloe. Loving. The expression of a woman looking at her whole world. She smiled, running a finger down Chloe's face.

"I love you, Chloe," she whispered.

Tears fell down her cheeks, but her voice was strong.

"You're going to do amazing things, baby girl. I won't be around, but I believe it. I can see it. Who knows? Maybe you'll find your cousin. Maybe you will grow up happy in the Society. I don't know. I just... be happy... love..."

Her mother's face began to blur, and her voice became soft. Too soft to hear.

No. No, stay!

Alex was releasing his hold on her memories. She didn't want to leave her mother. Her *real* mother.

Stay! Please!

But Pearl Caine's voice faded, and her face disappeared behind darkness.

Chloe's eyes snapped open.

Alex was standing in front of her, his milky eyes wide. Behind him, Mari and Nathan had come into the room, joined by Brandon and the girl named Tyler.

"It's true," Alex whispered, dropping Chloe's hand. "She's a Caine."

Chloe's eyes stung with tears. "Take me back," she pleaded. "Take me back to her. I want to see her again!"

Alex started to speak, but Brandon cut him off. "Not now.

I need my brother to see to the Mason. And then, he wants to speak with *you*."

He pointed a finger at Chloe.

She started to shake her head. She wanted to fall back into the memory that was already growing hazy.

But Brandon's words meant that Shawn was okay. She'd get to talk to him, and he would explain where they'd go from here.

"Okay," she murmured.

The Turncoats started to file out of the room. Only Alex remained, staring at her in awe.

"Your mother... she was beautiful. Is that what you look like?"

Chloe looked at him, surprised. "You could see her? But I thought you—"

She cut off, embarrassment coloring her face.

Alex didn't look offended. He let out another musical laugh. "I can see when I'm reading people, because the memories are through *their* eyes, not mine."

That made sense. She reached out, taking his hand again. He startled at her touch, but didn't pull away.

"What if *I* think of a memory? Can you see just that one?"

Alex nodded slowly, understanding dawning on his face.

The room disappeared again as she fell into another memory. Something simple, but it brought a small smile to her face.

She was staring at herself in the prom picture she had just bought. Her golden dress flowing to the floor. Her scars covered by its decorative back. Her eyes outlined in blacks and golds and her hair pulled into an elegant half-updo.

Dalton was on her arm, grinning brightly at the camera.

Now, he stood beside her, looking over her shoulder at the picture. He placed a kiss on her cheek.

"You're beautiful, Chloe."

The image disappeared. Alex was smiling, though it didn't appear as bright as before.

"He's right. You are stunning, Chloe Caine."

CHAPTER 37

SHAWN

Everything hurt.

Especially his head after that *memoria lectorem* had spent the last hour digging through his memories. For the second time that day, he'd had to relive every horrible experience.

Everything.

He'd managed to move himself into a sitting position against the wall. He was beginning to regret prolonging the arrival of a healer. He stripped off his hoodie, using it to clean away the blood so he could assess the damage. The *memoria lectorem* had just left, dry heaving after taking a trip through Shawn's nightmares.

You and me both.

As the blind Turncoat disappeared through the door, another voice sounded in the tunnel outside. Brandon Proctor.

"You have one hour. Alex— what did you see?"

He tuned out Alex's response as Chloe stepped through the door.

He sighed in relief.

She was okay.

Chloe gasped in horror, gaping at him.

He smiled through bloody lips.

"Thank you for the encouragement— I was worried it was bad," he muttered dryly, wincing as he cleaned blood from his chest. "If you had screamed, I would have been concerned."

Chloe continued to stare, and Shawn realized she wasn't just startled by the blood.

She was transfixed by his scars.

He glanced down at his bare chest, fighting the wave of anger and embarrassment he felt as her gaze ran over the thousands of raised, white scars crossing his skin.

"I need to talk with you," he said before she could ask any questions. "It's about Tess."

Chloe hesitated, her eyes lingering on his torso. Finally, she looked away, meeting his eye. She nodded, moving cautiously and sliding down to sit next to him.

"I did something. Something horrible. Actually, I've done a *lot* of horrible things. But this is—"

Shawn took in a breath, searching Chloe's features.

"I revealed Tess to Koden. He and my parents know about her."

Chloe's mouth twisted in confusion. "But you said—"

"*I'm aware* of what I said," he interrupted, more furious with himself than irritated by her. "And it's true. The Salvator is a psychopath and my parents are just as bad."

He sighed, looking away. "I'm no better. But I am sure—I *was* sure that the fire was a warning. The Society wouldn't have targeted you in a lethal attack. They *need* you. And they wouldn't go after a Basic unless they were suspected of assisting rogues. At the time, all the signs pointed to Tess. I thought I was being given a warning. I wasn't in the correct state of mind. I assumed that—"

He stopped, realizing that the tangent he was starting would be a waste of time. What he *should* have done didn't matter. It was too late. He had already turned Tess in and there was no going back. He only had one hour. There was no point in spending it trying to change the past.

Chloe was staring at him in disbelief. "What's going to happen to her? Will she have a trial? Is she— Is she gonna be attacked?"

Her voice rose as she spoke, shrill and terrified for her best friend. Shawn shook his head, struggling to appear confident.

"I passed her off as a very low Gradus. Koden isn't too concerned with a weak undocumented. I assured him she has *no* knowledge about the Abnormal world or the Society, nor do her parents. After a little convincing, my uncle gave me permission to train her. I am operating under the idea that she was abandoned and then adopted into Basic society."

He left out exactly *how* he had managed to convince Koden, knowing the details would likely make Chloe eager to kill him, stealing the privilege from the Turncoats.

"For the time being, Tess is safe."

Chloe nodded slowly, sagging in relief.

"The Salvator is also looking into who caused the fire. The idea of someone breaking protocol regarding Basics, aggravates him. He assured me there will be a consequence."

And I might just accompany him to make sure he follows through with it.

That, he kept to himself. No doubt, the Turncoats had already painted him as a murderer, and Chloe would be understandably wary of him. Mentioning his overwhelming desire to take revenge on whoever had killed Logan would only solidify that title.

Chloe pursed her lips, her golden eyes narrowed and alive with fury. "Good," she hissed.

Despite his pain, Shawn smiled, impressed with her courage. When they'd first arrived, she'd been overwhelmed and terrified. He hadn't been sure how she would handle all of this. Now, she exuded strength. Determined with her chin held high.

"What are we going to do then?"

Shawn blinked, shaking his head. "*We* aren't doing anything. I'll need to talk to Brandon once I can move. Then, if he doesn't decide to kill me, I'm going back home."

The pieces clicked into place as he spoke. Her eyes widened.

Living in Joshua was too dangerous. And even if it *was* safe, her Guardian's home clearly wasn't an option and Logan's home was gone.

She had no choice but to stay here.

"I'm not *staying* with these people!" she demanded.

"Where else do you think you can go?" Shawn snapped back. "You can't stay in that shack, if *that* was your plan. It's illegal by Basic *and* Society laws to stay in a home you don't rent or own. And Tess? You clearly can't stay with her. I just *told* you she's on the Salvator's radar. The Society will be tracking her now. And that will lead them right back to *you*. Are you that eager to be a specimen for their experiments? *Think*, Chloe."

He stretched an arm out feebly, pointing beyond the room.

"If a group like the Turncoats is willing to take you in and protect you, you *take* that chance! They can teach you how to use your abilities. You'll be provided trainers and shelter and safety. What *isn't* appealing about that?"

He glared at her, but she met his stare evenly, glaring daggers back.

"What '*isn't appealing*' is leaving Tess out there alone knowing that *you* just threw her to the wolves!"

She threw her hands up, exasperated, before continuing.

"And what about Dalton? He just lost his best friend. And now what? His girlfriend just disappears? He's probably so confused and hurt. Hell, *I'm* confused. I want to be out there helping, not stuck here living my life in a glorified sewer!"

She was angry, but Shawn could see the fight was leaving her.

She knew he was right. She didn't have another option. For a long time, they sat in silence.

Both wishing that there was a different answer.

Finally, Chloe spoke.

"Shawn, I'm scared," she whispered. "What if I never get to leave? What if I'm stuck here forever because the second I step outside, I'm going to be whisked off to some Society lab? Or what if these people won't *let* me leave?"

Shawn opened his mouth, prepared to tell her the Turncoats wouldn't hold her against her will. That she would be better off here.

But did he really *know* that? How could he be sure? This was the first— and probably the *last* —time he'd ever been here. So far, he'd been attacked by a random lady, forcibly separated from his friend, tortured, and then had his mind manipulated. Witnessing all of that had probably been terrifying to Chloe, who unlike Shawn, hadn't spent her life immersed in Society violence.

But Shawn was a Mason. As far as the Turncoats were concerned, that alone was reason to torture and kill him.

On the other hand, Chloe was a Caine. A descendant of one of the *reputable* Tribus Viribus families. A family with roots in *creation*. Not *destruction*, like Shawn's own. She would be protected here. She could have a life here.

He wanted to reassure her. To express how important it

was that she stay. She would be better off here. And maybe, Brandon would even allow her to check on her friends when it became a little safer.

But his tongue felt immeasurably heavy and the words stuck in his throat. His eyes desperately needed to close.

Chloe noticed his silence, and she let out a cry of surprise. "You're still bleeding!"

He followed her gaze down to the concrete floor where a pool of crimson blood had been growing as they talked. Just the movement of looking down made him nauseous.

"Healer," he murmured, trying to determine exactly where he was bleeding. "Ask Brandon to bring in the healer."

By the time Chloe's Trace had disappeared into the tunnels, his vision was swimming. He shouldn't have waited this long. He hoped the healer they sent would be ruled by ethics and not intentionally work slowly, in the hope that he would die.

Shawn couldn't blame the Turncoats for wanting him dead, but he needed to stay alive.

He had to get back to Tess.

Chloe was right.

He had placed Tess in an extremely precarious position, and he couldn't leave her to deal with the repercussions alone.

He closed his eyes, and when he reopened them, a healer was sitting next to him. Even through the haze, Shawn recognized him.

It was Morgan. Ace's husband.

He was still alive.

Shawn tried to smile. Ace's sacrifice hadn't been in vain.

"Alex said you saved my husband."

The man's voice was quiet. Kind.

His hand rested on Shawn's side, and Shawn watched as a small gash stitched itself back together. New, white skin

343

covered the wound, leaving no trace that an injury had ever been there. Not even a scar.

The man looked at him quizzically.

"Why would you do that? You *knew* he was a *Proditor*."

It was beginning to dawn on Shawn why Brandon had sent the memory reader.

He'd needed to know *everything* Shawn had done in his interrogations.

Including the good things. The times Shawn *hadn't* killed. The times he'd been brave enough to defy his family.

He needed to know if there was any good in him.

If there was a *chance* he could rely on him.

Not to trust him, but to use him.

What better ally than a Mason who wanted to depose the Salvator?

A flicker of hope began to grow in his chest. He offered Morgan a small smile.

"I know I'm not worthy of forgiveness," he muttered. "But I couldn't sentence him to death. Ace isn't a *Proditor*. The only traitors to the Munera people I know are the ones leading the Society..."

He sighed in relief as Morgan turned away, moving on to a larger wound.

"What my family does is horrific. It's sickening. And I believe one day, they will have to pay for it. I *want* them— us —to pay for it. But keeping Ace safe seemed a good place to start working towards a path of redemption."

He frowned, wanting to be honest. "It wasn't completely without a motive. I never would have found the Turncoats otherwise."

Morgan studied his wedding ring, no doubt thinking about its twin on Ace's finger.

"I'll do what I can to influence Brandon's decision. I will vouch for you." he said.

Shawn dipped his head. "Thank you."

The healing process took less than an hour, then Morgan took him to a wash alcove where he could clean the blood from his newly-healed skin. Hot water ran in rivulets through his hair, washing blood down his back and leaving the room full of steam. He wasn't offered different clothes, so he rinsed out his ruined hoodie and threw it on.

Brandon met him outside, arms crossed over his chest.

"Making friends?"

Shawn shrugged, running a hand through his dripping hair. Glad that the movement no longer made him cry out in pain.

The leader scowled and demanded, "What is so important that my healer insisted I come talk to you?"

"I need your help."

Brandon snorted. "I let you live. I agreed to take your friend in. And now you want *another* favor?"

Shawn nodded. "Believe me. You'll enjoy this favor."

CHAPTER 38

TESS

She wrapped her arms tightly around herself as she walked out of the church.

Logan's friends and family began pouring out behind her. Many were crying or telling stories about him. Some were silent in grief.

Tess fell into a fourth category.

Numb.

She sat on a stone bench next to a statue of the Virgin Mary, staring blankly at the ground.

How could this be real? How could Logan really be gone? How was it possible that she wouldn't ever see him again?

She held her phone in one hand. Wasn't he just one call away? If she dialed his number, he would just pick up and say that of *course* she could come over. Of course, he wanted to go to the mall. Of course, they could go look at the stars tonight.

Of course he was still here.

A shadow fell over her, but she didn't look up. Someone

sat down beside her, saying nothing. Instead, reaching for her hand.

When gentle fingers wrapped around hers, she finally stirred. She glanced up to see soft blue eyes and dark hair that had started to grow out.

An unexpected pang slammed into her chest, tightening her throat, and filling her eyes with tears. The world blurred, as she leaned against Shawn's shoulder and finally allowed herself to cry.

He said nothing, letting her tears fall. He didn't judge her or try to move her somewhere more private. And he didn't offer condolences.

She appreciated that. She'd been hearing the words, 'I'm sorry for your loss' for the last five days.

Five days since the fire.

Five days since he kissed her goodbye.

She let out a gasp as a wave of fury washed over her. All of those condolences were pointless. Infuriating.

She was *angry*.

Angry at the people trying to comfort her. Angry with herself because she had made Logan stay behind. He wouldn't have been in that fire if she'd let him come with her.

Angry with whoever had set the fire. She *hated* whoever had done it.

Shawn squeezed her hand, drawing her attention to him. She realized she was digging her nails into his hand and she quickly let him go.

"Sorry," she whispered, her voice hoarse.

Shawn shook his head. "Don't apologize."

They fell back into silence.

Tess suddenly wanted him to talk. Needed him to say anything that would distract her. She had to think of something else. *Anything* else.

But what could he really say? Shawn had been strangely

aloof since the fire. He hadn't explained where Chloe had gone. He hadn't explained exactly *why* she had to go. He hadn't said where *he'd* disappeared to for an entire day. And he couldn't explain what the note he'd handed her yesterday meant.

"*I can't look at it,*" he'd said, wearing the slightly bewildered expression he'd had since he returned. "*I just know I'm supposed to deliver it.*"

The note was short, and reading it left her more confused than ever.

I'm safe. I'll find you when I can. I love you Tess.

Three brief sentences. Nothing more. Yet she knew that it was from Chloe.

And while her heart was broken, leaving her mind dull and grief-stricken, she was desperate for answers.

Answers Shawn *had* to have.

Before she could speak, Shawn pulled his hand away, stiffening beside her.

His face went pale, and his lips tightened into a thin line.

Tess glanced up, seeking the cause of his behavior change.

Bile rose in her throat as she saw the Salvator striding towards them. A beautiful dark-haired woman was at his side.

He resembled his nephew, but he was lacking the sincerity that defined Shawn's appearance.

He looked exactly the way she remembered him from Shawn's vision. The memory of Shawn invaded her mind. Bloodied and broken. Sobbing as he begged his uncle and father to have mercy on him. Or kill him.

She tried to dissolve the image before it could continue into something worse, but her brain had its own agenda.

She gasped as the bloody image of Shawn transformed into the fire.

The falling rafter. The audible shattering of Logan's spine

that only she could hear. His scream of agony cut short. The burns covering his face and arms and—

Stop it! Stop it!

She had to make the memories go away. To stop the flow of thoughts that would force her to spiral into a dark place of agony.

Shawn stood abruptly, facing the Salvator and the woman Tess could only assume was his mother.

"What are you doing here?" he demanded, moving to stand in front of Tess.

Protecting her.

The Salvator furrowed a brow, his handsome features drawn in concern. *Mock* concern.

"Shawn," he murmured, reaching out to grasp his nephew's shoulders sympathetically. "I'm here for you. To make sure you're alright." His eyes flickered towards Tess, and he gave her a gentle smile. "Tess. Shawn has told me *all* about you. My condolences, Miss James. Such a tragedy. The loss of someone who meant so much to you. Shawn has expressed great concern for your well being during this time."

Koden Mason's dark gaze studied her curiously.

This man is a murderer.

"Did he?" She looked down, hoping he couldn't hear the tremble in her voice. The lie.

"I'm sorry. Have we met? Everything feels a little fuzzy right now."

She grimaced, trying to withhold the scream threatening to escape. This man had *tortured* Shawn.

Koden's curious gaze had turned scrutinizing. He didn't offer a hand to shake or make any move to touch her.

"I'm Koden Mason. Shawn is my nephew. He speaks *very* highly of you. Though your abilities leave something to be desired, I am hopeful you will be able to integrate into the

Munera Society. I imagine being raised by *Lusus Naturae* might make this transition difficult."

He frowned, his voice tinged with condescension.

How? How did Koden know about her abilities? He wasn't supposed to know she *existed*, much less that she was Munera.

Had Shawn told him? And if he had, why? Why would he betray her?

He wouldn't. It wasn't possible.

He would *never* have told his uncle about her.

"I hope you will be patient with my nephew," the Salvator continued, casting a small insincere smile at Shawn. "Shawn has never been assigned to mentor before, but he was *adamant* that he was capable of taking on the responsibility."

The words Koden spoke proved his betrayal.

Shawn *had* revealed her to the Salvator.

She turned to stare at him, fighting a wave of panic and confusion.

Mentor? Only Society children and Charges were assigned mentors.

Not a nobody who according to the Society, shouldn't even exist.

Shawn was nodding slowly at his uncle, but the tension in his shoulders told Tess that she needed to remain quiet. She could not afford to appear too knowledgeable in front of this man.

She shouldn't understand what Koden was saying.

The smile faded from Koden's lips, replaced again with feigned sadness.

"What was I thinking?" He frowned deeply. "My *deepest* apologies, Miss James. This is hardly the time or place for a discussion such as this. Again, my condolences for your loss. I assure you, I am currently looking into the situation. I *will* find out who did this, and once I do, the culprit will be punished accordingly."

He nodded slightly, then turned away, heading across the green lawn towards a black limousine. Hatred churned in Tess's stomach. For all of the Masons. She fought the feeling. Trying to control it before it exploded.

Shawn's mother stayed behind. She narrowed her eyes, an unreadable expression on her face as she held Tess in her icy gaze. She frowned, studying her carefully.

Then she turned to her son, her lip curled in disgust that she made no effort to hide.

"I expect you home in half an hour, do you understand?"

Shawn didn't disguise his disgust either. "Of course, *Orator*."

He raised his eyebrows, giving her a tight smile.

Tess stared, trying to read the unspoken exchange happening between them. Shawn's mother sniffed, then turned to follow Koden.

Shawn looked after her for a moment, his expression a mixture of hatred and despair, then he turned back to Tess.

"Tess, I can explain—" he started.

She didn't hear him. She shoved past him, trying to process what he'd done.

Why?

And why today? Why do this moments after Logan's *funeral?* Why do this *ever?*

"Tess!"

He was following her, and she sped up, hurrying to her car. She fumbled with the buttons on her key fob.

What the hell had he done?

After *everything* he'd told her about the Society. After he had promised that he would protect her from them.

He had betrayed her. He had willingly *told* them. Worse, he had told the *Salvator* about her!

Shawn caught up to her easily, taking her hand in his. He opened his mouth to speak.

She slapped him. She didn't even know she was going to do it until her hand connected with his cheek in a loud *slap*.

"You asshole!" she screamed, trying desperately to ignore the guilt she felt as an angry red handprint blossomed on his cheek.

She shoved him.

"You said you would *never* let that happen!"

Her fists pounded into his chest, but he didn't move to stop her.

"You said they'd *kill* me if they found me!"

Thump.

"You're going to *mentor me*?"

Thump.

Shawn just stood there. Silent. Accepting her anger. Her accusations.

Her voice broke as she yelled, tears choking her. Hitting him. Beating her fists against his chest even as he pulled her close. Still, he didn't stop her. Instead, he whispered apologies into her hair and let her cry.

"They *killed him*." Her words interrupted her broken, angry sobs. "They killed him, Shawn! Why would I want *anything* to do with the Society after this?"

Shawn pulled away, at last catching her hands in his and holding her fists still.

His blue eyes silently begged her to understand. To listen to him.

She stilled, her shaky breathing finally steadying.

"What the hell did you do?" she whispered.

"Tess, I had no choice." He carefully released her hands. "I believe the fire was a warning. I thought Koden, or maybe my parents, had somehow found out about you."

His voice dipped lower. So soft she had to strain to hear

each word. "I told Koden because I wanted to protect you. I had to intervene before someone else did." He sighed, running a hand through his dark hair. "I passed you off as an Abnormal that slipped through the system. I didn't want him to uncover the truth. I was *protecting* you."

Tess stared at him. Dumbfounded. The fire had been a warning? What did that even mean? A warning for *what*? For Logan?

Why would they target him? A Basic?

Unless...

Unless they weren't going after *him*.

Unless the Society was targeting *her*? And Logan had just been caught in the middle?

Agony ignited in her chest.

It's my fault.

He would still be alive if not for me.

I killed him.

Her breathing quickened.

I told him about the Society.

I stood by and watched him die.

I could have saved him.

"Oh my God." She covered her mouth in horror.

Shawn gripped her shoulders, assessing what she was thinking. "Tess, it is *not* your fault. The only person to blame is the one who did this."

"Because of *me*," she whispered. "Whoever did this, did it because of me. No one would have even known about Logan if I'd never told him anything in the first place."

It's my fault.

Shawn reached out, tentatively brushing the tears from her cheek. "Koden will find who did this, Tess. And if he doesn't, *I* will."

Tess found herself leaning into his touch, desperate for comfort.

"I'm so sorry, Tess."

She shook her head. Still furious. Still confused and hurt that he'd lied to her *again*.

But just like before, she understood why he'd done it.

Her anger surged, and she clenched her fists. Her jaw ached from grinding her teeth.

"Promise me that when he finds them, he's going to kill them."

She expected a pang of instant regret.

She expected herself to take the words back.

How could she want that for someone? For another human being?

How could she ask Shawn to promise that? Especially after everything his family had put him through?

But she didn't take it back.

She felt no regret or guilt.

And Shawn nodded, his expression darkening.

"Believe me, he *will* kill them."

As soon as she got home, she headed up the stairs to her room. Her parents were probably still at the church. They'd expected her to leave early, unable to handle it, so they'd driven two cars. There would be no graveside. Logan had been cremated. But her parents wanted to stay and help to clean up from the meal.

Why was it that people seemed to think food could help soften the pain? Tess hadn't been able to eat a bite.

Neither had Mrs. Tucker.

She collapsed on her bed, expecting another round of tears, but none came.

Shawn has never been assigned to mentor before.

She allowed the Salvator's voice to fill her head, driving away the painful memories.

Why would Koden agree to assign Shawn to help her?

Shawn had told her before she had driven away that he'd led Koden to believe she was a low Gradus. He said it was imperative that if she was near his family, she pick two of her weaker abilities to work on.

She snatched the book Shawn had given her off her nightstand. In it was a list of the English and Latin translations of each Gradus.

She searched through the G-5 list, spotting the highlighted ones she had demonstrated.

Strength. Speed. Senses. Self-healing.

Tess carefully avoided the Gradus one list, knowing she would find *timor mortale* highlighted. After the graduation ceremony— after seeing that vision that could have only come from Shawn's mind —she'd put two and two together.

Somehow, she had Shawn's ability. She had yet to talk to him about it.

But she and Logan had laid back on his bed for hours piecing it all together.

Reading the book aloud. Drifting off as they struggled through the biology portion. Worrying as they moved through the history section. Laughing as they pointed out the strange Latin words.

Stop it, Tess.

She could almost feel Logan beside her. His fingers entwined through hers. His eyes bright with curiosity.

"*This is insane. All of this has been around... What? Forever? And no one knew?*"

"*None of the Basics know,*" she'd corrected.

"*Some must have. Like me.*"

"*Well you aren't supposed to know either.*"

He'd grinned at her, leaning forward to pull the book out of her hands and kissing her.

"I'm glad I know. Thank you for telling me. I want to be a part of this with you, Tess."

She cried out, snapping the book closed and flinging it across the room.

It slammed against the wall, rattling the picture frames and knocking over a cup of pencils on her desk.

She pulled her knees to her chest, fighting the waves of guilt and anguish that threatened to overwhelm her.

Oh my God... Oh my God, this hurts.

Her chest felt like it was caving in. Her breath was coming too fast.

She wanted to call Chloe.

Chloe would know what to say. She'd know what to do.

But she was gone. Disappeared. Leaving only the briefest of notes that Shawn couldn't explain.

Shawn....

Tess believed he was telling her the truth. She believed he had betrayed her in order to protect her. She *believed* he wanted to help, but she was *terrified* at the idea of having anything to do with the Society or the Salvator.

And yet, despite her fear, she knew that she didn't have a choice.

CHAPTER 39

KODEN

Alyssa was the one to piece the mystery of the house fire together.

Due to the nature of her political position in the Society, she often met with Senators, Ambassadors, officials, and Guardians. It was prudent to study and know every detail of the Munera she frequently came into contact with.

Including their abilities.

Reese Hale.

The man was gifted with *ignis dominum*. The ability to manipulate fire.

He had also been assigned to find and track his charge. Chloe Hale— *Caine*.

Koden remembered seeing the girl at the graduation. Laughing and smiling with Tess James, and three boys: Shawn, a black boy with an obnoxious laugh, and a blonde boy. The third matched the photos he had seen in candlelit frames at the funeral.

Logan Tucker.

Chloe had been hiding out with the dead Lusus Naturae boy.

Reese Hale *had* followed Koden's orders. He had not touched his former Charge.

Instead, he had risked exposing himself, the Society, and the entire Munera world.

If one of the Lusus Naturae neighbors had seen a man with flames pouring from his palms, it would have gone *beyond* raising suspicions.

"What are you going to do, *Salvator*?" Alyssa whispered, her lips brushing his ear.

Her voice was alluring and seductive. A shiver of pleasure snaked its way up his spine and his skin prickled where her hands had run over him just the night before.

He turned, grabbing Alyssa by the waist and pushing her back onto the desk. His hands on either side of her, brushing her thighs. His lips against her neck.

Alyssa moaned softly, her hands circling around to draw him closer.

He leaned into her, moving from her collar to the base of her jaw.

"Shawn and I are going to pay Reese Hale a visit."

Alyssa drew back with a smile. Her icy gaze was cold and ruthless. Her grin widened.

"And afterwards?" she murmured.

Koden shifted his hands. One tight on her leg. The other trailing the curve of her neck and down her decolletage.

"Patience."

With that he roughly squeezed her thigh, and drew away.

His nephew was lurking on the stairs, leaning against the banister. Smirking at him.

Koden frowned, not bothering to hide his irritation at the arrogant boy's presence.

If Shawn wasn't so gifted in his interrogations, Koden would have long ago come up with an unfortunate accident for *him*.

"My apologies, Salvator. Orator," Shawn bowed in mock respect. "I didn't realize you were, ah... *occupied*."

He was blatantly disrespectful, and had been even more so since the funeral. No doubt the boy was furious with him for speaking to his little tramp.

Koden smiled at the memory of the girl's grief.

He waved a hand towards Shawn, gesturing for him to follow.

Shawn's eyes narrowed in suspicion, but beneath it, there was something more.

Eagerness.

"You know? You know who caused the fire?"

Koden grinned in surprise.

Over the last few years, Shawn had repeatedly rejected his family's values. Somehow believing he was better than the Masons. He thought the trials and Koden's methods for enforcing his mandates were inhumane. Cruel.

But there had always been a darkness in Shawn. A craving for power.

He *was* a Mason, after all.

Koden didn't have to look into the boy's thoughts to know that he was eager for an invitation. Anxious to execute Reese Hale.

To *torture* him.

"Yes. You are coming with me," Koden announced, raising an eyebrow. "I believe your *fulgur dominum* may be of use after our business is finished."

Shawn paused, but only for a brief second. Then, a burst of electricity ignited in his palm, and he dipped his head respectfully in the Salvator's direction.

"Of course."

. . .

The sun had just started to set when they arrived, casting the street in a fading purple glow. The lights in the Hale household were on.

Shawn sat silently beside him, staring out the windshield of the Aston Martin. Blue sparks erupted sporadically from his fingertips.

"Getting cold feet, Shawn?" Koden asked, a grin spreading across his face as he nodded towards Shawn's nervous hands. "You seemed more enthusiastic at the house."

Shawn looked up, glaring at him. "Of course not, Salvator. I assure you I am prepared to follow through with this."

He frowned, lowering his voice. "But this visit is nothing more to you than a simple breach of protocol. An annoyance."

He opened the car door, stepping out onto the sidewalk and cocking his head at Koden as he continued.

"But for me? It's *justice*. This man has earned his fate. Even the Lusus Naturae believe in the death penalty."

Koden's grin curled into a sneer, but he didn't answer, instead leading the way to the Hales' front door.

Charlotte Hale answered, her cold eyes going wide when she recognized him. As she understood the intention in his gaze.

She didn't bother with formalities.

Tears welled in her eyes and she shook her head, trembling.

"Please," she whispered.

Koden pushed past her, Shawn close behind.

The stench of alcohol, sweat, and vomit tainted the room, making Koden wrinkle his nose. Reese was slouched over the dining room table, his face buried in his hands. He looked up as they entered the room.

"What the hell did I do...?" The man was mumbling, drunk and incoherent. "What the hell did I do? I'm sorry. I'm so sorry."

Koden slammed his palms down on the table, making Reese jump.

"You nearly exposed yourself to the Lusus Naturae," Koden hissed. "You could have been *seen*, Reese."

The man's red eyes were tear-filled. He was shaking, a visible tremor passing through his entire body.

"Salvator, I didn't mean to—"

A gash opened across the man's cheek, and he screamed. Crimson poured from the wound as Koden ran his eyes over the cut. Deepening it until it scraped bone.

He moved on to the man's limbs. Watching with satisfaction as Reese's body convulsed and twitched. Jerking in spastic motions.

Koden listened to the screams as though they were music. He smiled, his mind buzzing from the exhilaration.

Suddenly, Reese's scream morphed into an inhuman wail. He reached up, clawing at his eyes with his nails.

"No! *No!* Get them off of me! Get them off!"

Koden glanced back to see Shawn leaning against the wall. His arms were crossed and his jaw was tight. Bright blue eyes were focused on Reese Hale. They were devoid of humanity as he lost himself in a vision. The corner of his mouth lifted as Reese let out an agonized cry.

Charlotte began to scream. She huddled in the corner, weeping as she wrapped her arms around herself.

Koden ignored her, focusing his abilities on Reese Hale alone. Shawn did not.

He turned away from Reese, staring intently at the woman. His eyes blazed with fury as he moved slowly towards Charlotte Hale.

Charlotte's eyes darted around the room, staring in horror

at the vision Shawn was conjuring in her mind. She gasped, clutching at her throat. Blood began to trickle from her nose. Whatever he was creating to torture the woman would certainly strain her mind beyond repair.

"Please! No! Help me! Reese!"

Koden looked back to Reese. His screams were still ringing through the home, and his face was coated in blood running from the gashes covering his skin. His eyes shined a vibrant red as the capillaries began to burst in his eyes.

Slowly, Koden clenched his fists, focusing on the bones throughout the man's body. He began crushing them. Severing ligaments one by one and letting muscles shear from tendons.

Just as he'd done to his nephew three years ago.

He traced gashes along the man's flesh. Pressing deeper until he'd carved a hole through Reese Hale's side. His thigh. His shoulder.

Charlotte screamed, and Koden watched as she collapsed on her side. Shawn looked away from the scene.

Weak.

Koden *thrived* from these moments. He took pleasure in the way blood spattered the curtains from spurting arteries. The crimson pools growing from Reese's severed veins. The small chunks of shattered bone peeking through the man's torn flesh.

It seemed like hours of bliss had gone by, though it couldn't have lasted more than one. A headache had begun to form at the base of Koden's skull, and he was growing weary from the exertion. From pushing his abilities more intensely than necessary for the sheer pleasure of listening to the man's dying screams.

Reese lay on the ground. His ruined chest was still. His breathing and drunken mutterings silenced.

His wife still huddled in the corner, and Koden began to move to her.

Shawn made it there first.

His nephew stood in front of Charlotte, towering over her hunched figure. His blue gaze hard and burning with hatred. With the intent to kill.

Koden hesitated, curiosity keeping *his* hunger to kill at bay. He wanted to see how Shawn would handle the woman.

"You were the reason for Chloe's abuse, weren't you? It was you that demanded she be punished. Not your husband," Shawn murmured.

Charlotte stared up at him, her eyes confused and terrified.

Shawn's eyes narrowed and he hissed. "Answer me."

The woman snapped out of her stupor as his voice dipped into a deadly whisper, and she nodded her head violently.

"I- I hated her! That child ruined my life!" The woman's usually steely voice faltered, stammering. "M- My husband was weak! Falling for her conniving smile and innocent face. He shouldn't have— He *never* should have taken her in! It was humiliating. A *Proditor* in *my* home!"

Shawn stared at her for another moment. Searching her fears.

Finally, he rose to his feet, his expression blank. No trace of emotion crossed his face, even as he glanced at Reese's broken body. Koden had never seen him like this.

When the boy was a small child, he had seen him take pride in his role in the trials. Excited to know what an honorable thing he'd done for the Society. He'd seen the boy scream and cry and beg for mercy for his own life. He'd seen the boy vomit after particularly gruesome trials.

But this was different.

The expression on his face reminded Koden of himself.

After *she* left.

When he couldn't decide what to feel. Whether to be angry with Amora, or with himself. Whether or not to put orders out to detain her for trial like the rest of the Caines.

When he'd allowed himself to go numb in order to survive.

Koden expected Shawn to let the woman go. To turn away and give Koden the freedom to do as he wished. Waiting for instructions to clean up once Koden finished the deed.

Instead, Charlotte Hale let out a sudden strangled cry. A sound that was impossibly fearful. Desperate. The sound of a woman who was experiencing a fate worse than death. Who was witnessing something so horrific that *if* she survived, her mind would forever be scarred from the experience. Would never heal. Never allow her to be fully sane.

By the time the woman's screams had silenced, her ragged breathing nonexistent, Shawn's forehead was covered in a sheen of sweat. His pupils were dilated with excitement.

Koden stared at his nephew, intrigued.

He appeared intoxicated from the torture.

The rush of *power*.

Even when Shawn was younger, he'd participated in trials strictly out of duty. Out of the knowledge that he had to protect his people and his family from the *Proditors* who threatened them. He had never enjoyed the *process* of getting those answers needed to protect the Society.

In the driveway, he'd claimed that his participation in this ordeal was justice.

But Shawn had the opportunity to walk away from Charlotte Hale. She wasn't the cause of the fire.

And yet he'd killed her. Not only killed her, but he'd been *eager* to accompany Koden. To participate in what he surely knew would be a bloodbath.

Was there a chance that his nephew *was* starting to accept

— maybe *embrace* —his role— his obligation— to the Society? His likely position as the future *Salvator*?

Doubtful. But maybe.

Koden nodded his approval as his nephew fought to catch his breath.

"That was..." he paused. Debating how to respond to the boy's performance. "Impressive."

Koden smiled, watching the boy stare down at the body of Charlotte Hale.

Her vacant, lifeless eyes. Her motionless body. The look of terror still frozen on her face.

Shawn nodded, tearing his gaze away from Charlotte. "Thank you, Salvator."

Koden noticed a shadow passing over his nephew's face, just a small twist of his mouth. A wisp of regret in his eyes. Then it was gone, disappearing into steely resolve.

Koden turned from his nephew. An emotion was bubbling close to the surface of his mind. Not fully formed.

But it was undoubtedly there. Something he hadn't felt for his nephew in years.

Pride.

"I'll clean up," Shawn offered, his voice quiet.

Koden nodded. He himself had no useful abilities to dispose of the bodies.

As he left the room, loud crackling from Shawn's electricity followed him, making the lights flicker and the hair along Koden's arms stand and tingle.

Within seconds, the sulfurous coppery stench of burning flesh had filled the room.

That night, Koden lay awake. Alyssa was beside him, her bare skin milky in the dim moonlight that filtered through the curtains. Her chest rose and fell with even breaths, and strands of her hair stuck to her face and neck from their earlier endeavors.

Like Amora's had.

The night he proposed.

He tried to force away the thoughts before they could develop further. But it was impossible. Amora filled his mind, and the questions began attacking him in droves.

Where was she? Why had she left? What had he done wrong?

Where was his daughter?

Amora's blue eyes. Her soft, dark hair. The splash of freckles across her nose. The way her mouth was always slightly turned up.

Now, after nearly twenty years, she was probably dead.

Dead...

His mind flashed to the funeral.

The low-Gradus girl.

An undocumented Munera girl. Eighteen years old. Abandoned by her birth parents then adopted by Lusus Naturae who had *no* idea about the world around her.

About the Society.

About *him*.

Could the girl be Amora's?

No. He knew it wasn't possible. The Amora Caine he had fallen in love with would never abandon a child. Especially not *her* child.

Years ago, they had discussed having children. Knowing that he was going to ascend to the position of Salvator as his father's illness worsened, and being *very* aware of their feelings for one another, an heir seemed inevitable.

She had always fawned over the idea of raising a child, though she'd specifically wanted a son.

She could on for hours about baby names, and dreaming about what he would look like. What his abilities would be. She'd fallen in love with the idea of someone that didn't even exist.

And admittedly, Koden had too. That was why he had loved Shawn so fiercely when the boy was younger. The son he never had. The future of the Society and the Mason legacy. Until the little shit decided he was morally superior to that legacy.

No.

He repeated the word in his mind, convincing himself that it was true.

Amora would *not* have abandoned her child. She would not have left her under the care of Lusus Naturae knowing the girl would reach activation and suffer through the confusion of an adolescent Munera *without* the help of a mentor.

Tess James, the *low-Gradus* girl, raised by *freaks*, could not be his daughter. His *heir*.

It was impossible.

It was *impossible*.

EPILOGUE

Dr. Miranda Nandez woke to the sound of beeping. Someone was using the entrance scanner outside the door. She glanced around the lab, confused at the mess of notebooks, pens, and empty coffee cups scattered about her at her metal desk. Coffee had seeped into the papers at her elbow. She must have fallen asleep and knocked over her drink.

Sapphire had been sleeping in her cell in the rear of the room, but she woke instantly as the door to the lab slid open.

Ace Lane strode through the door, followed closely by the Salvator, two more guards, and her newest assistant.

She rose, getting shakily to her feet. Her hands trembled at the sight of the Salvator. His cruel smile widened when he saw her reaction, and his eyes slowly ran the length of her body, lingering on her breasts. She shuddered, remembering his last visit.

Dear God, no. Please no.

She tried to bow, but her swollen belly— while not as large as it should have been at seven months —made it awkward.

"Salvator," she acknowledged, looking warily at the guards. "To what do I owe the honor of this visit?"

Koden's lewd smile made her skin crawl. Nausea settled in her stomach.

"Dr. Nandez," he murmured, inclining his head towards Sapphire. "You still have the marrow solution from your most recent trial?"

Sapphire glared at the Salvator, and Nandez nodded slowly, trying to make sense of the question.

"I do. It's in the vault right now. However, I have yet to test it. I'd like to find a compatible mutt that's strong enough to—"

Koden shrugged, nodding at the guards.

"It's really no loss if it dies."

His tone was bored. Flippant and unconcerned.

The guards were on her before she had time to process his words. They grabbed her by the arms. Restraining her with an iron grip.

If it dies...

Her baby.

Her stomach dropped. "Salvator, please! She's premature! She might not survive the delivery, much less the serum!"

Koden didn't answer. He watched with a bored expression as the guards led her out of the room.

He was crazy. A complete psychopath. She wanted to struggle. She wanted to restrict the airflow in their lungs. To force them to let her go.

He was going to induce her labor. Her daughter would be delivered two months early. *If* she survived the delivery, he would inject her with the untested drug. A drug whose predecessor had killed the last subject!

She ignored the twinge of guilt she felt as she remembered the death of the mutt.

Elizabeth.

There was no point in fighting. She wasn't strong enough to affect this many people at once. Especially not the Salvator.

So, she cried. She pleaded and begged, listing off every reason that this was a waste of a specimen. That even if by some miracle the serum worked and reactivated the child's Genesis, the marrow solution couldn't be reproduced until Sapphire's body healed.

No one listened to her. They dragged her into the neighboring room with a medical bed and silver instruments laid out on trays.

Forced her onto it.

The Salvator gave her a small smile. Snakelike. Vicious. His dark eyes danced with a crazed insanity.

"Doctor, I need results. I've reiterated this for months, and you have *still* failed to produce them. So, if I must do everything myself, then so be it. You have both a specimen and a stimulant. We can simply hope we'll have better luck with this candidate, yes? If nothing else, this makes for an interesting last day in Joshua."

S he didn't know how long the labor lasted. She only remembered the pain.

Koden would not allow her to have an epidural or a local anesthetic. He said he didn't want to risk damaging the specimen.

Her child.

Lies. He simply *enjoyed* hearing her screams of agony.

The baby cried.

A wonderful sound that made her feel alive, extinguishing her exhaustion.

Her daughter had survived.

The image of a stillborn baby vanished, giving her a brief moment of relief.

Dr. Nandez opened her eyes, gazing across the room. A nurse held the crying baby out, away from her chest. Disgusted by the child.

Nandez should have felt the same. The baby was a mutt. A freak and an abomination that should not exist.

And yet, she couldn't look away. She stared at the tiny girl in absolute awe. Her dark eyes squeezed shut as she whimpered and squealed, her tiny hands flailing. Reaching out. Reaching for her mother.

Mine. She's my child.

Abomination or not, the baby was just that. A *child*. Helpless and innocent.

"Prepare the solution," someone instructed. "The Salvator wants the child injected as soon as possible."

"On it."

"No..." Nandez croaked. She hardly recognized her own voice. "N- No... I'll find another candidate. I'll find a way to heal Sapphire faster. I'll do anythi—"

She tried to sit up, but her wrists were bound to the bed. The residual pain and exhaustion from childbirth seemed to render her immoble and her gift useless.

The nurse holding her child gave her a condescending stare. "Miranda, you brought this on yourself. There were others willing to take on the project, but you insisted that you had to be the one."

She tried to answer, but the nurse turned away, setting the child on a towel on the medical table. Her partner held a syringe, sloshing with dark, thick liquid.

The image of her daughter screaming in pain invaded her mind.

Elizabeth Bell.

She remembered the elation she initially felt when the serum worked, and she felt the girl's Trace. And then watching her go still as her body shut down. Too weak to handle the Genesis.

"No!" She began sobbing. "Lydia! Mei! Don't do this!"

The needle sank into the child's arm.

The baby wailed, and Nandez found herself screaming with her. The air around the nurses went still, trapping them in an oxygen-less vacuum. They gasped, their eyes flying wide. The empty syringe clattered to the floor, shattering.

Lydia collapsed, clutching her throat, gasping in an effort to call for help.

Mei leaned on the counter, searching desperately through her pockets.

She pulled out a small remote, her thumb landing on the large, red panic button.

Alarms sounded, and the door to the medical room burst open. Four guards streamed in, destroying Nandez's focus. Air rushed back into the room, and they coughed, hacking as the air reentered their lungs

Two of the guards moved to help the women to their feet, leading them out of the room. The other two rushed to Nandez's side, pinning her struggling body to the bed.

As if she could get up.

One of the guards' hands was hot. *Too* hot. Painful to the touch.

A warning.

She stilled, gasping from the exertion. She began to cry weakly.

There was nothing to do but wait.

Her daughter was still screaming.

Dread filled Nandez's chest along with another sensation.

A tiny beat.

Like a pulse. A second heartbeat.

Her daughter's reactivated Trace.

The guards stared at the child wailing on the medical table. Their hands flying to their chests. The Salvator came into the room then, stopping short as he registered the tiny Trace.

It was incredible. It was unheard of. A miracle among Munea.

There was only one Munera to have *ever* activated nearly this early, and that was the Salvator's prodigy nephew.

While this was artificial and chemically induced, it was unmistakable and it was *real*.

The newborn mutt had a Trace.

And Nandez's tears fell harder.

"No..." she moaned, leaning her head back. Trying not to look. Not knowing if the results of this serum would be the same as the last. "*Perdóname*... Forgive me, God. *Don't* take my daughter..."

Tears were making her throat tight. It was hard to breathe, hard to think. She continued to pray. Begging for mercy for her baby as hushed murmurs filled the room.

"Impossible."

"But... it's a mutt."

The Salvator's whisper joined the guards'.

"Incredible."

Nandez could barely hear him. She watched. Waiting for her baby's Trace to stop. Waiting for her daughter to cough and begin to bleed.

Waiting to watch her die.

Nothing. Five stunned minutes passed before anyone approached the child.

Her Trace was still beating steadily.

Lydia gently picked up the child, looking at the Salvator for permission.

Koden glanced between the baby and Nandez, a smile turning up his lips.

A smile of victory. Not relief.

Six minutes with a constant Trace.

Nandez finally allowed herself to look up. To see her daughter. Still alive and breathing, though no longer crying.

Elizabeth Bell had only survived three minutes after activation.

"Congratulations, Doctor," Koden said. He nodded, and Lydia made her way over to Nandez, placing the child in her arms. "You've made quite the breakthrough, yet again."

Her daughter cooed softly.

Seven minutes.

Nandez stared up at the Salvator. The man who willingly risked her child's life. The man who had sadistically tortured her.

She couldn't even summon the hatred that boiled through her, begging to be released.

Instead, she smiled down at her daughter.

Still a mutt. Still a disgrace in the Society's eyes.

But likely the most important person in the world.

Eliza Hope Nandez.

The future of the Society.

H ours later, Nandez leaned against the wall of the cell that Elizabeth Bell had once occupied. She stared through the glass into the lab. At the desk she'd been sitting at several hours ago.

Koden had given the order for Nandez to be healed. Then he'd immediately had her and her daughter detained.

She held Eliza against her chest, rocking her gently. Savoring the continuous tiny Trace beating beside Sapphire's in her chest.

"The tables have sure turned, Doc," muttered a voice from the other cell.

Nandez bit her lip, glancing behind her. Through the reinforced glass, she could see Sapphire curled in the corner of her cage. Her blue eyes sharp. Her smile venomous.

"Top researcher for the Society's efforts to 'save our kind'. Well renowned, respected, even *spared* when you failed the Salvator."

The girl tipped her head, nodding at Eliza.

"Naming your kid after a girl you murdered. That's sick."

Nandez instinctively curled her daughter closer to her chest. The air wavered in front of her, seeming to shimmer as she erected a shield around both of them.

As if Sapphire could actually do anything.

"Elizabeth Bell was never supposed to die, Sapphire," Nandez murmured. "Surely, you can understand my desperation to find a cure."

Sapphire's cerulean gaze landed on Eliza. Her expression softened slightly.

"I understand that you're just as twisted as the Salvator. Having a child doesn't change that."

Nandez sighed.

She couldn't expect anything different from this girl.

What Nandez had done, the sacrifices she'd made— she had done in the name of research. In an effort to *save* their people from extinction. They could purify the Munera people! Reactivate Geneses and give the mutts the abilities they had been deprived of for generation upon generation.

Sapphire was from the rogues. She did not see the reason behind everything that had happened. Even now, with the reward of her suffering cradled in Nandez's arms, the girl was blind.

"Hey Doc," Sapphire muttered, pulling her knees to her chest. Still staring at Eliza.

Nandez raised an eyebrow, giving the girl an answering nod.

Sapphire bit her lip. "I want you dead."

Nandez rolled her eyes, prepared to look away from the girl. To ignore her. But Sapphire continued.

"And I hope it happens soon. But until it does, I'll let them heal me. I'll let you take more marrow."

Nandez whipped her head around, startling Eliza. Her eyes were wide, her mouth fell open.

Was the girl serious?

Sapphire didn't blink, staring Nandez in the eye as she spoke, then jabbing a finger towards the doctor.

"Under the condition that I won't be locked in a cage. Keep a guard on me at all times or whatever. But I want to be able to walk around. And I want decent food. If you make that happen, I'll be a willing donor."

The girl raised an arrogant eyebrow. Daring Nandez to refuse the deal.

She didn't.

When Dr. Nandez got out of this cell— and she was confident Koden needed her enough that she *would* get out of this cell —Sapphire Caine would be given certain freedoms.

If she kept her word, and would allow healers to keep her healthy while she donated bone marrow to create more of the serum, Nandez would make sure she got whatever she wanted.

A spark of hope ignited in her chest.

I've done it.

She had created a serum that had just changed the world.

A serum that would provide the Munera people hope for survival.

They *would* rise again.

. . .

G lossary

A ctivation- Awakening of the Genesis and Trace. It reveals a Munera's abilities with painful side effects including headaches, powers going out of control, severe mood swings, and it makes Traces feel stronger than they truly are.

A mbassadors- People who reside in the lower Court, just below the Senate. They deal with minor convictions that are not worthy of the Salvator's attention, but often involve the Generalis, Orator, and lead interrogators

C harge- A foster child/orphaned or detained Munera child raised by Society Guardians

C ourt- The lower Court is made up of the Ambassadors and often the Generalis, Orator, and lead interrogators. They act as a sort of jury for minor convictions.

E lite- Typically a *memoria lectorem*, or memory reader, but can be used to describe any Munera of Gradus two or higher.

G eneralis- Second in command of the Society, similar to a vice president. He/She carries out the Salvator's mandates and would take over the position of Salvator should the standing Salvator be removed from the position by any means

Generalis- General

Current Generalis- Konrad Mason

Genesis- A seed-like presence that gives Munera their abilities. The Genesis typically activates around 18, but they are unpredictable. They can activate earlier when young Munera are around large groups of more powerful Munera and later when surrounded by less powerful Munera.

Gradus- A system to categorize Munera abilities into five levels. Enhancements, Nature, Body/Objects, Mind, and Life/Genesis

Guardians- Similar to foster parents for abandoned Munera children

Hybrid- Mixed, powerless offspring of Munera and Lusus Naturae. They still possess a Genesis, though it's inactive and dormant. (Slang word— Mutt)

Lusus Naturae- Ungifted people with no abilities. They are suspected to have devolved from too much inbreeding within Munera families. (Slang word— Basic)

Lusus Naturae- Freak

. . .

Mentors- Mid-ranked Munera hired to teach newly-active Munera about the Society and help them learn to control their abilities

Munera- Gifted people with two supernatural abilities — one from each side of their families. It's believed their ancestors possessed *Omnem Potestatum*, all power, the ability to create more abilities. It's believed that this ability was lost over time, diluted into the hundreds of different powers in the modern day. (Slang word— Abnormal)

Munera- Gift

Officials- Similar to police. They enforce mandates, deal with legal interrogations, deliver the accused to trials before the Senate/ lower Court. They also report larger accusations to the Orator

Orator- Third in command of the Society. He/She is similar to a speaker of the House and helps the Generalis in carrying out mandates. He/She also acts as a lead advisor and often speaks on behalf of the Salvator or Generalis at Senate meetings if neither is available

Current Orator- Alyssa Mason

Proditor- A traitor to the Society

Proditor- Traitor

. . .

S alvator- Leader of the Society of the American Munera. He/She creates laws and employs people to carry out the mandates. Traditionally, the Salvator and other high-ranked positions are elected by the Munera people

Salvator- Savior

Current Salvator- Koden Mason

S enators- Typically acts as advisors to the high-ranked positions and make up the Senate. They deal with trials involving serious convictions worthy of the Salvator's attention as well as the Generalis, Orator, and lead interrogators

S ociety- The Society is the government of all North and South American Munera. It's led by the Salvator, and has for the last three generations been ruled by the Mason family.

T race- 6th sense that all Munera have that's produced by the Genesis. It's described like another heartbeat and it indicates when other Munera are nearby. Each Munera has a unique Trace, which can be used to identify where Munera are, *who* they are, and how recent the Genesis activation was

T ribus Viribus- The three most ancient, influential, and powerful Munera families: The Caines, the Masons, and the Roses.

Tribus Viribus- Three Forces.

Caines— Oldest of the three families, and are currently estranged from the Society. Most Caines currently reside in hiding. This family has roots in creation and abilities that typically affect an individual's Genesis, such as *imitationis*, mimicry, or *vita furem*, life thief, but commonly referred to as deactivation.

Masons— Currently the most influential of the three families, and are currently ruling the Society. Most Masons hold positions of power and status. This family has roots in destruction and abilities used to manipulate or harm others such as *mortale injuriam* or *timor mortale*, mortal injury or mortal fear.

Roses— The most peaceful of the three families, and are currently uninvolved with Society business. They tend to be seen as neutral and/or nonthreatening as a whole. This family has roots in preservation and abilities used to protect and preserve life, such as *vivifica*, revival/resurrection and *sanitatem*, healing.

ABOUT THE AUTHOR

Chaselyn Roderick was born and raised in the great state of Texas.

Her love for books developed early on, starting with Good-night Moon, and growing as she discovered series like the Magic Tree House, Harry Potter, and Gone. She was particularly inspired by the writing of Rick Riordan.

She aspired to become an author in elementary school after being influenced by several teachers, and started writing her debut novel at 11 years old.

When Chaselyn is not writing, she can be found shell hunting at the beach, welding in shop class, and leading her high school cheerleading squad. She also enjoys cooking and drawing, and loves doing special effects makeup.

She currently lives in South Texas with her family and three dogs, along with a herd of cats.

After graduation, she hopes to attend college and continue working towards her dreams to spend her life doing what she loves...writing.

Made in the USA
Middletown, DE
19 March 2021

35234747R00231